THE BIG BRIDGE

BY RICHARD MARTIN STERN

THE BRIGHT ROAD TO FEAR
SUSPENSE
THE SEARCH FOR TAHATHA CARR
THESE UNLUCKY DEEDS
HIGH HAZARD
CRY HAVOC
RIGHT HAND OPPOSITE
I HIDE, WE SEEK
THE KESSLER LEGACY
MERRY GO ROUND
BROOD OF EAGLES
MANUSCRIPT FOR MURDER
MURDER IN THE WALLS
YOU DON'T NEED AN ENEMY
STANFIELD HARVEST
DEATH IN THE SNOW
THE TOWER
POWER
THE WILL
SNOWBOUND SIX
FLOOD
THE BIG BRIDGE

Richard Martin Stern

THE BIG BRIDGE

1982
Doubleday & Company, Inc., Garden City, New York

This is purely a work of fiction, and as such it does not portray, nor is it intended to portray, any real persons, living or dead.

There *is* a river gorge in New Mexico which resembles the one I describe near Tano. And there *is* a bridge across that gorge. But the actual bridge bears no resemblance, other than its setting, to the bridge I describe in the book, and as far as I know, none of the events and incidents I have related in the story ever took place during the bridge's actual construction.

The fiction writer's task is to create the *illusion* of reality. If he succeeds, there are bound to be those who cry, "Aha! This is John Doakes, thinly disguised! So now we see what really happened behind the scenes!"

Believe me, it isn't so.

Library of Congress Cataloging in Publication Data

Stern, Richard Martin, 1915–
The big bridge.

I. Title.
PS3569.T394B5 813'.54
AACR2
ISBN: 0-385-18018-7
Library of Congress Catalog Card Number 82–45149

Printed in the United States of America
First Edition

For D.A.S.
with love always

THE BIG BRIDGE

In later years, as old men, they would talk about it, and remember with pride and even pleasure what at the time they cursed and fought against, bloodying themselves—some even dying. All for the bridge, a construction of steel girders and concrete foundations, of cables and rivets, at dizzying heights above a gorge so steep that it seemed to mock them.

And they would remember the men who had worked with them, some no longer alive—Bob Anderson, Pete Harmon, big Zabrinski, MacAndrew, Hard Nose Jud Wilder . . . And, of course, Sam Taylor.

This is their story.

PROLOGUE

Such a simple thing, unnecessary and inexplicable, and yet when he came to look back on it, Jud Wilder could see that in a way it had set the tone for the entire project. At the time, he only stood and watched helplessly.

There was a big semi-trailer hydraulic-lift dump rig loaded with twenty-five tons of sand to be piled near, not over, the edge of the gorge that the bridge would span. Simple enough. And the driver backed the rig square and straight, with the kind of precision that looks easy and isn't—unless you know your business.

But, Jud told himself, he had learned a long time ago that a fool determined to get into trouble can usually manage it, and that was about as close to an explanation as they were ever going to get.

The driver backed too far. That was all there was to it. And as Jud watched, incredulous, the rear axle wheels slipped over the edge. What followed was inevitable.

Cliff edges tend to crumble, and beneath all that weight on the next axle, this one did just that. The rock gave way, and the rear of the trailer, suddenly unsupported, dropped maybe five feet to point down into the void.

In what was slow motion at first, then quickly gathering

momentum, twenty-five tons of sand began to shift to the rear of the trailer bed, adding more weight to the imbalance.

It was ridiculous, insane. It could not be happening. But it was.

There was a sudden, almost hysterical hiss of air as the driver hit the brakes. Pure futility. He floored the accelerator then, and the big diesel engine howled as the tractor drive wheels spun in the dirt. But the power did not even slow the rig's backward slide.

"Jump, you fool!" Jud shouted, but against the engine sound he might as well have been mute.

The big rig continued its inexorable slide over the edge.

The driver's frightened face turned to look out the window at Jud standing on the ground, waving his arms like a man trying to fly, mouthing inaudible pleas into the engine's roar.

The truck was moving backward faster now, and the driver jerked desperately at the door handle. The door opened and, too late, the driver lunged out toward safety. Under the pressure of the underbody of the trailer—heavy stiffening beams that could support twenty-five tons and more without sagging—another piece of the cliff edge suddenly gave way, and the rig's quickening slide became almost a free fall.

"That," as Jud said later, "was the ball game. Over it went, and the poor damn fool with it." He paused reflectively. "Hell, I didn't even know his name."

This was the first entry on the casualty list.

And there were other matters in the early days of job preparation that followed more or less the same pattern:

A carload of steel shipped out of Chicago inexplicably found its way by slow stages to Florida instead of north central New Mexico, an error of about two thousand miles.

An eighteen-wheeler trailer truck loaded with cement sacks, also headed for the bridge site, ran into heavy weather, a flash flood in an *arroyo* that submerged the rig to its cab window almost drowned the driver, and turned the cement sacks into solid, pillow-shaped rocks good only for shoring up levee walls.

A strike in Pittsburgh delayed shipment of cable, and the custom-tailored baseplates for the great bridge towers, when X-rayed, were found to be substandard and had to be replaced.

A computer error in the home office in San Francisco screwed up the ordering of rivets and eyebolts, and what eventually arrived would, in Jud's words, "be about enough to put together a footbridge across a goldfish pond. Tell the goddamn computer to think again."

And so it went. Why? Nobody could explain. Nobody ever can. As every construction stiff knows, some jobs go together easily, and some are pure snafu right from the start. And with this second kind, after a bit you find yourself constantly looking over your shoulder in case something might be sneaking up on you. It is not a pleasant feeling, and it tends to make folks edgy.

But with all these problems, they had yet to come face to face with the real, and devastating, threat.

You must understand the setting, and the circumstances.

PART I

1.

It was called the Tano Gorge, seventy-five miles north of Santa Fe, New Mexico, a north-south slit in the high mesa, fifteen hundred feet wide at the point where the bridge was to be built and the better part of one thousand feet deep. To Jud, the precise depth was unimportant—and it took only one look down into emptiness to understand that.

But it was not the Gorge's measurements that tended to grip your guts. It was the feeling of mystery with which it overwhelmed you. Even when you looked down from the top of something as high as one of the World Trade Center buildings in New York or the Sears Tower in Chicago—higher by far than the Gorge was deep—you didn't get the same feeling. It was the hell of a long way down, sure, far enough to make cars on the street look like kiddie-karts, but to an ironworker, mere height had no importance.

When you looked down into the Tano Gorge, the bottom was in perpetual deep shadow, another world. It didn't take much imagination to think of a fall into that as a fall into the Pit itself, out of the bright sunlight of this world into the perpetual darkness of who knew what. Particularly in the light of the tales the local folks—Spanish, Indian, and anglo alike—told about the

Gorge and its evil spirits. That was the screwy part that somehow got to you. And there was more.

From above, the river at the bottom of the Gorge, the Rio Largo, didn't look like much, but its reputation as a killer was something you heard everywhere you turned in the town of Tano—talk of white-water rafting trips wiped out, fishermen caught and drowned, other deaths merely hinted at, bodies sometimes recovered and sometimes not. Like that driver who had gone over the cliff with the sand truck; his body had simply disappeared.

"That river has muscle," a gabby state cop said to Jud one night at Josie's Place. "Take a look at the depth of rock it's cut through, or go down and look at some of the white-water rapids these damn fools ride through in rubber boats. It's five hundred miles to where the river empties into the Gulf. A body makes only part of that trip through rapids and around rocky bends, and there's not much left to fish out. If you ever find it, that is."

These were not things to brood about, of course, not and keep your sanity, too. But the knowledge would be there, more or less bottled up, and no matter how you tried, it would color some of your thinking. There were jobs and there were jobs, as any man who worked on steel knew full well, and it was evident right from the start that this was not going to be one of the easier ones.

And then there was the wind, whose force out over the Gorge had stunned them all by its erratic violence. Their first encounter with the wind came about in this way.

The drawings called for a single cable to be stretched across the Gorge between the east and west tower sites, to carry a tramcar which would haul back and forth light supplies and supervisory personnel for the eyeball oversight and face-to-face interchange needed on any construction job.

As usual, the first problem was getting the messenger line across—the light line to which would be attached a heavier line which, in turn, would carry a still heavier line, and so on, until, at last, they had stretched across the chasm a line of sufficient strength to haul across the required steel cable, which would then be stretched taut by means of a power winch.

"On some bridge jobs," Jud Wilder said, "you can throw a line across." Jud was superintendent of construction, a man in his fifties, big, solid, weathered, and now in one of his rare talkative moods. "On one job, I remember, we borrowed a cannon from the Coast Guard and shot a line across." He smiled suddenly. "But I guess the best idea I know of was back in the eighteen hundreds when they were starting to build the first bridge across the gorge below Niagara Falls. Eight hundred feet from side to side, it was, and a fellow named Ellet, chief engineer, solved it for five dollars."

Daryl Chambers was chief engineer and overall boss on this Tano Gorge job, and very much aware of his position. He hated having to ask, but couldn't pass it up. "How?"

"He offered the five bucks as a prize," Jud said, "for the first kid who could fly his kite across the gorge. Then they used the kite string as their messenger line. How about that?"

As with all ingenious ideas, Chambers thought, the simplicity of it stunned you. He wondered if he would ever come up with anything as good. He doubted it. "Clever," he said, "but all we have to do is carry a light line down that cliff road, across the wooden bridge at the bottom, and up the other side. Then we haul it taut, and there's our messenger line."

Jud pursed his lips in a silent whistle. "You're the boss."

"You have a better way?" Chambers had the sudden feeling that this was going to be another of those embarrassing times when the working man was already way ahead of him. It was.

"There's a chopper at the Tano airport," Jud said. "I asked, and it does do charter work."

The helicopter pilot was willing, and saw nothing difficult in the job. He had flown helicopter gunships in Viet Nam, dusted crops in Texas and California, flown hunting and skiing parties into the ruggedness of the Brooks Range in Alaska. He considered this job a few minutes' work for a full day's pay.

On the belly of the helicopter, between the skids, they rigged a loose reel carrying eighteen hundred feet of light nylon line. The end of the line they made fast on the east side of the Gorge, and as the chopper took off—the wind from its blades throwing up rock dust that set Jud and everybody else nearby to coughing—the reel paid out the line without a hitch.

The helicopter swung up and sideways, as from the ground choppers always seem to do, and roared out over the Gorge at an elevation of about fifty feet, trailing the line behind it. It was almost halfway across when the trouble began.

Without warning, a sudden wind gust flipped the helicopter up on its side with the axis of its rotor blades pointing straight down into the Gorge, in that attitude no longer providing lift. The aircraft began to fall. Fast.

The pilot maneuvered stick and throttle with desperate haste, and muttered under his breath. Nothing happened except that the fall continued. The sides of the Gorge were now above the helicopter's level, and the east wall was suddenly too close, and coming closer.

"Move it, you bitch!" the pilot said, shouting now. Instantly, the chopper flipped back into normal flight attitude, and without warning bounced a hundred feet straight up. The pilot felt as if he'd had a hard kick in the ass.

He could see the paid-out nylon line sending waves back to its anchorage, in its oscillations coming dangerously close to fouling the helicopter's tail rotor, which would have been disastrous.

The aircraft was still rising fast. Too fast. With eighteen hundred feet of line on the reel, the pilot had leeway, but it was not unlimited, and if he reached the end of the line that was secured to the reel, he and the chopper would be jerked right out of the sky in a hurry.

He tried to take the helicopter down, but the updraft was irresistible, and against all his efforts he continued to rise. Then, all at once, he was going down again like a heavy stone dropped from a height. The sensation was not unlike that of going down in a New York express elevator. His belly felt suddenly empty.

"Jesus Christ, cut it out!" the pilot shouted. "You hear me? Cut it the hell out!"

His left side flipped up again without warning, and *again* he was looking down into the Gorge. The nylon line already paid out was acting like a long snake, sending waves right back to the east side anchorage. The pilot could feel the vibrations from those waves shuddering right through the fabric of the chopper's body.

He dropped again, and again shot upward. He bounced on invisible columns of air. He was hurtled off course, headed downstream instead of straight across, and he clawed his way back with difficulty. At one moment he thought he was going to vomit, something that had never happened to him in the air.

And then, all at once, like a ship passing from stormy seas into the shelter of a breakwater, the helicopter was again on an even keel, riding steadily and without bumps. And the spot selected for the western terminus of the line was directly beneath it.

Stretched back across the Gorge, still oscillating but no longer as violently, was the nylon line. Mission accomplished.

The pilot set the chopper down as if he were landing on eggs. He switched off the engine, and as the rotor blades whirled slowly to a stop, got out cigarettes and Zippo. He found it a trifle difficult to bring flame and cigarette into proper juxtaposition.

The walking boss of the ground crew opened the chopper's door. "What the hell were you trying to do out there?" he said. "Think this is a circus and we want thrills for our money?"

"We aim to entertain," the pilot said, and that was all.

One thing for damned sure, he told himself. On the way back, he was going up three, four hundred feet—maybe even more—before he tackled those wind currents again.

Using the light nylon line as a leader, Jud's people hauled across heavier line with a power winch, and finally the steel cable itself, which they carried up and over sturdy tripods anchored securely in concrete on each side of the Gorge. From the cable they suspended the open tramcar.

Jud rode alone on the first trip of the tramcar. The trip east to west was, as he reported to the headquarters trailer command group, okay. "It was coming back that I found out that chopper pilot wasn't just showing off."

Understatement. The vicious updrafting wind gave no warning. One moment the tramcar was traveling right side up, out over the Gorge, and the next moment, Jud was hanging on for his life, looking down from an almost upside-down tramcar at the river far below.

"Hold it!" His response was automatic. "Goddamn it, hold it!" But he was shouting into space, unheard and unheeded.

Buffeted by the wind gusts, the tramcar flung its weight this way and that, setting the taut cable to vibrating at its natural pitch like a gigantic bass viol string, each oscillation adding to the wildness of the tramcar's gyrations.

Bracing himself against the tramcar's sides as best he could, Jud felt as if he were being shaken inside a steel box by some gigantic monster intent on his destruction.

There was the howling sound of the wind gusts against the cable and into the tramcar's interior, a banshee wail of elements in fury. One moment there was bright blue sky to be seen, and in the next moment he was gaping again into the depths of the Gorge. There were the shrieking, protesting sounds of metal, both tramcar and cable, under tension and stress, and at one moment, with a sense of shocked fatality he would never forget, Jud was sure that the cable had parted and he and the tramcar were on their way to the bottom of the Gorge.

How long the torment lasted, Jud could never know. Time alternately sped by and stood still until at last, incredibly, all motion seemed to cease, and here was the sturdy tripod on the east rim of the Gorge. The tramcar, suspended from the still intact cable, swayed in mere gentle docility as if its wild bouncing, bucking gyrations had never been.

Jud clambered out, and stood quite still for a little time while his legs regained some of their strength, and his mind some of its normal equanimity.

"We could sell tickets," he said now to the group in the headquarters trailer. "The girls would scream and hang onto their skirts, and the guys would have just the hell of a time."

Huge, shaggy Carl Zabrinski, the stress engineer, said, "Interesting. You were bouncing around like a cork float in a high sea."

Chief Engineer Daryl Chambers swallowed hard, and tried to keep from imagining how it would feel to be buffeted around like that, almost a thousand feet above the river and at the mercy of a single cable—no matter what its test rating.

Zabrinski said, "We'll work out some kind of fix. Then I'll give it the next try." His tone was thoughtful. "I wonder why there's that much wind out there. Maybe it's a complicated aerodynamic stew of convection currents, thermals generated by the heated bare ground, and the Gorge acting like a funnel . . . or maybe even a Venturi tube. You know about them?"

Jud shook his head.

"A thing shaped like an hourglass. Wind rushes into one large end, then is compressed as it passes through the wasp waist before it flows out the other large end. When the air is compressed, it has to flow faster to maintain the same flow. See what I mean?"

It made sense. The wind pushing from behind would keep the air moving, and in order for the same amount of air to keep passing through the narrow opening as it came in through the large end, it would have to speed up. "Got it," Jud said.

"That could be just what we have here at this narrow part of the Gorge," Zabrinski said. "Because it's a narrow point, it's a fine place to locate a bridge. But it may also be the worst place because of the Venturi tube effect on the wind currents." He was silent, thoughtful. "Something to ponder," he said.

One of Jud's walking bosses, his second-in-command, put it a little differently. "You stand out on the edge of that goddamned gorge," he said, "and it's always blowing. But sometimes you catch a sudden gust strong enough to snatch a man bald. I don't like that."

And so, Jud thought without enthusiasm, when the two towers of the bridge began to rise, the connecting gangs and the riveting gangs working on top of the steel were going to have their problems. As were all those who would be working out on the roadway stubs, when they began to cantilever themselves out over the Gorge depths.

A twelve-inch I-beam is plenty wide enough for a man to stand on while he does his work. If he doesn't think so, he has no business working on steel in the first place; he belongs on the ground. But with this kind of wind, gusting and unpredictable, a three-foot sidewalk might not be enough.

If you are going to work at height for some time on one specific job, like a telephone lineman making hookups, or an electrician setting a transformer atop a pole, then you can, and damn well should, wear a safety belt.

But when you work on steel, maneuvering a ton of I-beam into position as it swings from the crane hook, subduing it, connecting it, riveting it, moving here, moving there, then safety belts are just not possible. They have been tried, and they don't work, even if you can get an ironworker to wear one.

That leaves safety nets, and they have been proved. Way back in the thirties when they were building the Golden Gate Bridge out in San Francisco, Strauss, the chief engineer, insisted on a safety net to stretch beneath the growing roadway. The thing cost $300,000, which was considered a scandal and a waste of bondholders' money. But it saved the lives of nineteen men who promptly thumbed their noses at the devil and formed what they called the Halfway-to-Hell Club.

But the mere *possibility* of saving lives is one thing, as Jud was well aware, and budgets are something else. Budgets, like schedules, he often reflected, are made by men with no calluses on their hands—only on their asses. And their decisions have nothing to do with people; they are strictly the products of computers which, as all the world knows, do not listen well.

Jud had a *Penthouse* centerfold nude thumbtacked to the wall of his construction shack just above the bridge drawings. He could talk to her without restraint, because she never asked questions, never talked when she shouldn't, and never argued.

"You and me, honey," he told her on this day, "could have just one hell of a time out in that open tramcar swinging and swaying and bouncing around. It would be like standing up in a hammock." He turned somber then. "But my guys, when they see what they're up against, aren't going to find it quite so funny. We got problems."

Daryl Chambers, chief engineer on the project, was thirty-three years old, and this was his first independent overall command. He was, and had always been, the bright boy, the leader, the take-charge guy, with a 3.8 grade-point average through Cal Tech, and a Class One Humm-Wadsworth rating for steadiness and dependability.

Wilt Ross himself, the founder, owner, and in his late seventies still very much the boss of Ross Associates, had tapped Chambers for the job during lunch at San Francisco's Bohemian Club.

For a little time, Ross had been nostalgic, as if the occasion, and perhaps even the circumstances, started a train of thought that would not be denied. "Right here," he said, "maybe even at this same table, I got the promise of the construction loan for my first big job, and I was in business." He looked around the dining room as if he saw clearly into the past. "Long time ago," he said.

It was indeed, Chambers thought. Ross Associates, like Bechtel and Kaiser, was already a large and growing engineering and construction firm when World War II exploded and there was work to be done, unlimited work, worldwide.

"You whip this job," Ross said, coming back to the present, "and there'll be others. And you'd better whip it because I've got a score to settle with that Tano Gorge. There are those who say it can't be done. The hell it can't."

Chambers listened and did not remember eating. Prove yourself to this fierce old man, and there was no limit to your future. Look at Sam Taylor, for example, already Ross Associates' crown prince and heir apparent, and not even ten years older than Chambers. Who needed food, even if it did come from the Bohemian Club kitchen, when your mind held shining visions of success?

Now, in the small cubicle that served him as an office in the large headquarters trailer, Chambers looked up as Jud Wilder walked in and dropped two pieces of paper on his desk.

Chambers was never exactly sure how to take Jud. Other construction superintendents he had known tended to run true to form. They were sturdy middle-aged workingmen with little educational background, outside knowledge, or even outside interests. A knack of leadership and a broad practical knowledge of construction work, but no theoretics and/or imagination. But Jud was different, and sometimes full of surprises.

"Beam bridges," Chambers had overhead Jud saying in Josie's Place one night, "post and girder, cantilever, arch, suspension—the Chinese were building all of them two thousand three hundred years before Christ. That's over four thousand years ago. And they had pontoon bridges, too, what they call sampans anchored and connected by planks. And mountain people, like Indians down in the Andes, have been building suspension bridges across gorges for thousands of years too."

Somebody said, "Using what?"

"Sometimes vines. Somctimes handwoven ropes. Two main ropes for the strength. Then hung by smaller lines from them, either a single rope or planks as a walkway. Same principle we use today."

And later, as the discussion ebbed and flowed, "You think of concrete as something pretty new," Jud said. "Late seventeen hundreds. That's crap. The Romans had it, a volcanic clay they called *pozzuolana*. The Romans were damn fine engineers. The bridge they built with *pozzuolana* at Amalfi is still standing. Sixth century. Then everybody forgot all about the idea of concrete for twelve hundred years. I've seen the Amalfi bridge. Walked across it."

Chambers looked it up, and Jud had it right, which was a little unnerving. Now, "Trouble?" Chambers said.

"Not yet." Jud sat down without being asked, large and solid, wearing his hard hat as if it had grown on him. "But I have an idea it's coming when we start raising steel." He gestured at the two pieces of paper.

Chambers glanced at them, and then bent forward to study them carefully. He looked up. "Safety net designs?"

"We need them."

"Tell me why."

"That wind."

Chambers settled back in his chair. In time, he thought, he would get to know this construction superintendent of his much better, and then be able to judge with some precision just how much weight to give his suggestions. But now he was flying more or less blind, so he temporized. "There's always wind."

"Strauss's net in the Golden Gate saved nineteen lives."

"I'm aware of it. This isn't that big a job. And the cost—" No, in honesty, it wasn't just the cost; it was the impression he, Daryl Chambers, was going to make on Wilt Ross, that demanding old man back in San Francisco, on this, his first big command. "Was this the men's idea?"

"They haven't thought about it yet. They will, but we have some time."

"I'll have to think about it too."

Jud nodded then as if he had expected no more. "Do that," he said, and stood up. "It's a long way down into that gorge. Take a look some time." He walked out.

There was that workingman's arrogance you ran into every so often, Chambers had long ago found, and there wasn't a damn thing you could do about it. But it never ceased to annoy him.

Damn it, he *had* looked down into that gorge, not only once, but a number of times. And each time, particularly when he looked at what remained of the sand truck, it had almost sickened him. He had never had a head for heights. It was all very well for characters like Jud and his ironworkers to behave as nonchalantly as mountain goats when they were perched on next to nothing over empty space. Monkeys didn't mind treetops, either. But it wasn't for Daryl Chambers, and Jud seemed to be implying that he knew it and scorned the weakness.

The light through the doorway was suddenly blocked out by enormous Carl Zabrinski, one-time defensive tackle for the San Francisco Forty-Niners, all two hundred and eighty pounds of him, bearded and shaggy, and, except when rarely riled, as easy to get along with as a puppy. Chambers put Jud out of his mind. "Come in, Carl. Sit down. What's on your mind?"

The visitor's chair that had borne Jud's solid one hundred and ninety pounds without complaint creaked now as Zabrinski lowered himself to it. "In a word," he said, teeth showing white through the black beard, "wind. It's still a little hairy out there in that tramcar. Got me thinking. And doing some checking."

Out of a clear sky, Chambers was thinking, somebody mentions a new subject, and all of a sudden it's Topic A with everybody else. "What about it? You've calculated wind loads right from the start."

"Sure. Routine."

"Then?"

"Things change." Zabrinski waved one huge hand to illustrate the vagaries of change. "You know what I mean? Sometimes they change so slowly, or imperceptibly, you don't even notice. Or sometimes something happens and you just . . . overlook it."

"Like what?"

"Like last year up in Cheyenne, Wyoming, they had a tornado. It damn near totaled part of the town."

"So?"

"And later, down in Silver City, New Mexico, another one touched down."

"I don't see the point. There are tornadoes every year."

"Not in this kind of high, mountain country. Those were the first. *We're* not supposed to have tornadoes. They're for Texas, Oklahoma, Kansas—flatland, not rugged country like Wyoming or New Mexico. But some weather people think maybe the climate is changing, the jet stream may be on a new track."

First Jud, now this one. There were always doomsayers, Chambers thought, and tried not to show his impatience.

"The highest recorded windspeed in this area," Zabrinski said, "is in the seventy-mile-an-hour range. So the bridge is designed to stand up to hundred-and-twenty-mile-an-hour gusts. That's a margin of a safety of—"

"Hell's fire, man," Chambers said, "that's ample!"

Zabrinski, large, solid, unflappable, almost seemed to intone like an ancient, bearded prophet delivering a judgment. "The winds in one recorded tornado," he said, "were measured at two hundred and fifty miles an hour—before the windspeed measuring equipment blew away."

At last they were face to face with the enemy.

2.

SAM TAYLOR

"You're getting too goddamned big for your britches," Wilt Ross said. "And in case you've forgotten, *I* still run Ross Associates."

The old man's voice had lost none of its youthful volume, Sam Taylor thought, and those big hands, that in other days had at need curled into fists or grappling hooks and settled disputes on the spot, showed no aging signs of tremor. But changes there were, subtle but unmistakable. Try as he would to silence it, the word *senility* kept sounding in Sam's mind.

"I wasn't here when the Tano Gorge job was bid," Sam said.

"I know where you were. I sent you there."

"And for what it's worth," Sam went on as if there had been no interruption, "I'd have voted against even bidding it."

"Would you now? Well, you weren't asked. And why the hell do you think you would be asked? Do you think every god-damned thing we do has to have your approval? Is that the way you see it?"

Sam sat motionless in one of the leather visitor's chairs. Faint sounds of traffic drifted up from San Francisco's Montgomery Street far below. A ship's whistle sounded three blasts as she backed out of her slip on the Embarcadero, probably heading out the Golden Gate to the open sea.

"I've been over the drawings and the specs and the geology reports and cost estimates and schedule," Sam said, "and I've seen other engineering studies—" He shook his head. "I don't like it. It's got a bad feel to it."

"Now you listen to me," Ross said. "I found you, and I brought you along, and I'll have to admit you've turned out pretty well. But I still know a thing or two myself. You don't like the Tano job. Well, I do. So you keep your goddamned hands off it, you hear?"

They were probably hearing down on Montgomery Street, Sam thought, but no matter. "I hear."

"Well, keep it in mind. You hear that too?"

There was no more to be said here and now. "Same answer." Sam started to rise.

"Wait a minute, goddamn it. I'm not through."

Ross heaved himself out of the big desk chair, walked around the desk, and sat down again. He put both hands on the leather chair arms and squeezed hard as if to test their solidity. He looked at Sam then as if he had seen him before, but couldn't quite remember where. Slowly his face cleared as he remembered what he had in mind. "I've thought for a long time," he said in a new, softer voice, "that one day you would sit in this chair." He raised one hand to forestall comment. "I know what you're thinking. You wouldn't want to be tied to a desk facing all the nit-picking decisions that have to be made. I know how you feel. I've been there myself."

Sam watched, and listened, and hoped that the thoughts would come out straight, anyway, not garbled. It was painful.

"But when the time comes," Ross said, "you'll do it. You know why? Because if you walk away from it, you'll spend the rest of your life wondering if you were big enough for the job. I was playing poker, and winning, and making tricky deals with tricky men before you were even thought of. But I'm not conning you now. I'm telling it to you straight. You walk away, and you'll remember to the day you die that there was one time when you backed down, refused to stand up and be counted." Ross shook his head. "And you'll never be the same man again."

"I'll bear it in mind."

"You do that. Now, what were we talking about?"

It was difficult not to show surprise. The old man's mind seemed to lose contact with reality, then snap back. Sam kept his voice expressionless. "The Tano Gorge bridge job. I don't—"

"You know," Ross said in a normal, conversational tone of recollection having nothing to do with the present, "I knew the Tano Gorge fifty years ago. I fished it. Caught some damn fine trout in the Tano Box. Cutthroats they were, what the locals call 'natives.' And I almost got caught myself like a mouse in a trap when a cloudburst, a real gully-washer, flooded the Box and sent me scrambling up the cliff wall like a damn spider." He smiled wickedly, remembering, and then all at once returned to the here and now. "So I owe it one. And, by God, no matter what anybody says, I'm going to square the account. I'm going to put that goddamn suspension bridge across it." His voice had been swelling in volume again. "You hear?"

"I hear."

"You've got enough else to do. Plenty. You leave that job alone." Ross raised one hand in a gesture of dismissal. "All right," he said. "Now, beat it. And don't step out of line again."

Laura was waiting in the outer office when Sam came out. Laura had grown gray at Ross Associates and in the process accumulated both company stock and perquisites far in excess of any title she might have carried. She was Ross's executive secretary, right hand, at times surrogate, constantly loyal watchdog, and unobtrusive adviser. Her smile that Sam remembered from his first sight of her lacked its usual brilliance. "The usual shouting match?" Laura said.

"Pretty much."

Laura said, "Sam," in a different, almost pleading voice, and then caught her lower lip between her teeth and was silent.

"I know," Sam said. "It's all right."

"If anything happened to you—"

"It won't."

"He leans on you. You know that."

Sam started for the outer door.

"You'll be in your office?" Laura said, and there was that in her voice that made Sam stop, and turn.

"I will. Why?"

"Miss Lewis called. They switched the call here. I told her I would give you the message." Laura hesitated. "She has heard that you are back. And she hasn't heard from you. That's all the message was."

"Given in an imperious tone?" Sam let sudden amusement show.

"*Very* imperious." Laura shook her head again. "Sam, she, Miss Lewis—" She produced the smile then, full, brilliant, if not entirely happy. "Strike that. I ought to know by now that neither you, nor he"—she nodded her head toward the door to Ross's inner office—"can be pushed an inch. Sometimes led, but never pushed."

"That sounds like an epitaph," Sam said, and walked out wearing a smile he did not feel.

Liz Lewis herself answered Sam's call on the third ring. Her voice was cool. "Should I say that it's about time?"

"You could. It wouldn't surprise me."

"You left that morning like a thief in the night."

"I told you the night before. Work."

"When most men talk about work," Liz said, "they mean civilized hours—"

"In offices, behind desks. I know. I mean something else."

Liz looked out across her balcony at San Francisco Bay, spread bright and blue and clear, small sailboats heeling to the breeze, brightly colored spinnakers filled and drawing. "Dinner at Jack's that night," she said. "Very civilized. Then Franck's D Minor Symphony, Daniel Barenboim guest-conducting. Then here, fun and games. And in the morning, with the sun not even up, off you go to perform some kind of engineering miracle in some outlandish place. You are too much, Sam."

"Drop me."

"The trouble is, you even look like a hero, damn you."

"How about dinner? The evening?"

"And the night too, you mean? Dinner, yes. I want to talk to you. About the rest, we'll see."

Sam hung up, and sat quiet, letting his thoughts wander as they would, but their direction was already set, and Liz, for all her undeniable charms, was not their focus. After a time he roused himself, reached for the pile of papers and drawings on his desk, and began to study the Tano Gorge proposal.

Two hours later, Sam left his office and walked back out, past the open typing pool door, and down the corridor to the reception office and Laura, executive secretary extraordinary. The old man's door was still closed. Sam perched on Laura's desk. "I'm just back," he said, "so I doubt if there'll be any calls I have to take. And I don't want any. I'll be busy."

"You need your own secretary, Sam. You have for a long time."

"You're my girl. You know that." It was rare that he attempted lightness, and the smile that accompanied the words was quickly gone. "If he"—he nodded toward Ross's door—"wants me, I'll be in engineering, or maybe estimating, or possibly in accounting."

"What are you up to?"

"Nothing he"—again the head gesture—"needs to worry about now." He got down from the desk and walked back toward engineering.

The drafting room had drafting tables in neat rows, and at one end the office cubicles. Sam walked into the one at the end and straddled the visitor's chair.

Benny Brock said, "Hey, you're back. How was Alaska?"

"I think we got it straightened around."

"Did you leave any corpses?" Benny watched Sam's faint, brief smile, mere acknowledgment that a joke had been made. Only it wasn't funny, Benny thought, not really. He had heard the tale from an eyewitness:

"That Sam Taylor got out of the truck he'd hitched a ride in, walked into camp without so much as a by-your-leave from anybody, spent about fifteen minutes looking around, and then came into the trailer," the eyewitness, an engineer named Epstein, said. "Billingsley was sitting with his feet up on his desk the way he usually was.

" 'I'm Sam Taylor,' Sam had said.

" 'I know who you are,' Billingsley said. 'I've heard all about you.'

"Along about then," Epstein added, "Billingsley decided he'd better get on his feet. You know him? Big fellow. Handles himself well. Lazy and sloppy, and he'd let the job slide bad, but he's cocky, and tough, and doesn't listen very well. 'Nothing good though,' he said.

" 'I'm taking over,' Sam said.

" 'Are you now? What about me? I run this show.'

" 'You used to, and you blew it. You're fired.'

"Well, Billingsley thought about it," Epstein said, "and then he made a mistake. A thousand miles from the San Francisco head office, and old Wilt Ross apparently losing his grip according to the scuttlebutt, Billingsley was thinking he was pretty much his own boss, if you see what I mean."

Benny had nodded, seeing exactly what Epstein meant.

"So," Epstein said, "like I said, he made a boo-boo.

" 'No son of a bitch from the city's going to walk in here and fire me just like that, mister,' Billingsley said. 'Now haul your ass out of here before I kick it all the way back down to Anchorage.'

"Well, Sam just sort of smiled. 'We'll forget you said that,' he said. 'Now clear out your desk, and—'

"Billingsley made his second mistake then," Epstein said. "The big one. He threw a punch." He was silent for a few moments, remembering how it was.

"It didn't land," Epstein said at last. "Sam moved his head out of the way pretty as you please, and then moved in himself. No hesitation. No argument. Talk time was over."

He paused for emphasis. "I drove Billingsley all the way to Anchorage. They've got a good hospital there. Sam was already in charge by the time I got back."

Remembering the tale now, Benny thought again, as he had so many times, how happy he was here, as chief design engineer, rather than out on a project that might go sour and bring Sam Taylor in to straighten things out. "All quiet here," he said.

Sam said, "I've been looking over the Tano bridge job."

Benny shook his head then. "You'll have to talk that one over with the old man, Sam. His baby."

"You don't like it? Tell me why."

"Damn it, Sam, don't put me on that spot. When the old man talks, I listen. And on this one, he talked."

"Your name's on the drawings."

"Are you trying to crucify me?"

Expressionless, Sam thought that over, then stood up. "Okay, Benny," he said. "I think I understand."

Benny watched him walk out, and let out his breath in a sigh of relief. The palms of his hands were damp.

Sam went to estimating next, the quiet desks, each with its computer terminal, and in the next large room the computers themselves, spinning their endless tapes and calculations. Sam perched on the corner of Mike Marlowe's uncluttered desk.

"I heard you were back," Mike said. He peered out at the world through heavy lenses which gave his eyes an almost owl-like size and fixed expression. "A couple of things I'll want to check out with you."

"They can wait, for now," Sam said. "What about the Tano bridge job?"

Mike leaned back in his chair, lifted his hands and let them fall. "The computer is a goddamned ass," he said. "I'm quoting you-know-who." He was silent for a few moments, thoughtful. "I'm sorry you were in Alaska, Sam. We could have used you."

Sam stood up from the desk and nodded. "That's all I wanted to know. Thanks, Mike."

Accounting next, and Charley Webster, timid Charley, like Kipling's muskrat, Sam always thought, afraid to venture out to the center of the room.

"Welcome back," Charley said. "Is there something I can help with?"

"The Tano bridge job."

"Oh, dear." Charley picked up a sharpened pencil as if to reassure himself by its familiarity. "I can't really tell you much about that, Sam. Not yet."

An adroit evasion, Sam thought, worthy of Charley Webster, but still merely a hopeful, opening ploy. Sam sat quiet, and waited, his eyes on Charley's face.

Charley swallowed. He took a deep breath. He said at last, "Please, Sam."

As with Benny in engineering, Sam thought about it briefly, and again stood up. "Okay, Charley. I won't twist your arm."

As he walked out, he told himself that there were other directions within the vast organization he could go, and, being who he was, get answers; but these three, engineering, estimating and accounting, had already told the entire story. The Tano bridge job was a foul ball off the first pitch. He walked slowly, thoughtfully, back to his own office. To be, or not to be, he thought; call me Hamlet.

Liz herself answered Sam's ring in a simple dark dress that probably cost, Sam guessed, what he once would have considered an out-of-reach monthly wage. It clung to her breasts with fidelity, showing off just so much of their splendid creamy separation. It demonstrated, but did not overemphasize, the slimness of her waist and the swell of her hips above rounded thighs. Its length was carefully calculated to show off her legs to stunning advantage.

In her beauty, her grace, and above all in her poise, she was,

Sam had always thought, a breathtaking example of the ultimate achievement of modern civilization. No expense, no care, no polish had been spared in shaping the finished product.

"Are you undressing me already?" Liz said.

"The dress does that for me. Maybe that's why you wore it?"

Always and without hesitation he was ready to fight back, Liz thought, and experienced again the familiar feeling of excitement.

"You said you wanted to talk to me," Sam said.

And that, too, was typical of the man, that he stepped right up and faced directly whatever the problem might be. Well, she, Liz, could be direct too. "I've been warned off you," she said, and watched the first real anger she had ever seen in him begin to take shape.

"By whom?" His voice was soft, but the two words held a quality of menace that was unmistakable.

"Wilt Ross."

The large room became still, poised, as a theater becomes still when the lights are dimmed and the curtain slowly rises. Sam walked over to the open doors leading out to the balcony. He stood there motionless and silent for a little time, looking down at the Bay, blue and sparkling against the green of the rising Berkeley hills. One more sign, he thought, that the old man was losing his grip on reality, because he would never, never have interfered with Sam's private life otherwise.

He turned back into the room. Liz had not moved. She waited, her eyes steady and questioning on his face. "Tell me about it," Sam said, and dropped into a chair.

The tale was short. Laura had telephoned an invitation to lunch. The St. Francis Hotel grill. Public. And a car had been sent, driven by an elderly chauffeur.

"His name is Homer," Sam said. It was all he said during the entire recitation; but his eyes did not leave Liz's face.

"Mr. Ross didn't beat around the bush," Liz said, "and he didn't hammer on the table, either. But the message came through loud and clear: Don't mess with my boy. You're not good for him. You take his mind off his work." She waited then, eager to see what would happen next.

Sam sat quiet for only a moment. Then he heaved himself out of his chair. "I booked a table at Jack's," he said. "Shall we go?"

Liz opened her mouth, and closed it again with great care. "You," she said, "are out of sight. No reaction? No resentment? No . . . nothing?"

"Hunger," Sam said, and produced a crooked smile. "I've been living on primitive cooking, so I'm hungry for good food. Shall I add that I'm also hungry for you? All of you that's under that dress?"

"Am I supposed to be flattered?"

Sam, watching her still, was silent.

"All right," Liz said, and smiled, finding at last the ease that had eluded her. "I am."

It was not yet sunrise when Sam, showered, shaved, and dressed, sat down at the phone in Liz's library and dialed Laura's apartment. Laura, instantly awake, answered at once.

"I'm taking the jet," Sam said. "The Tano Gorge bridge job. I want to see how deep we're in and how bad it is."

"You've been warned off."

There was no need to ask how Laura knew. Laura knew everything that went on at Ross Associates. Sam said nothing.

"This isn't like you, Sam."

More silence.

Resignation sounded in Laura's voice. "What do you want me to tell him?"

"I'll leave that up to you."

"Thank you very much. He'll be furious, Sam. You know that. He won't stand insubordination."

"I know. But it has to be. I tried to talk to him yesterday. No dice."

There was a long pause. "I think I understand," Laura said at last. "Take care. And good luck."

Sam walked quietly back into the bedroom. Liz was lying on her back, hands behind her head, coverlet drawn up, eyes wide open. "This thief in the night act is getting to be a habit," she said.

"Can't be helped. Sorry."

Liz's eyes widened. "Apology? From you? I don't believe it." She sat up suddenly, ignoring the coverlet which fell away, baring her remarkable breasts. "Kiss me, and then beat it."

Sam showed one of his rare smiles.

"Kiss me, I said."

"What's the hurry? I enjoy the view."

3.

"Well, now," Floyd Babcock, the governor, said into the phone, "that's real fine news, Henry, that the bridge construction is going right along." Was it, really, fine news? That answer would come later.

"There is bad news too," Henry Evans said in the eastern prep school and Ivy League college accent that had never left him, despite all the years in the oil fields and on his vast ranch. Accent or not, when Henry Evans spoke, people listened—oil field roughnecks and state governors alike. "The bad news is that they are not hiring either Spanish or Indians, only anglos." He made no further comment. None was needed.

"Why, hell's bells," the governor said, "that's Tano County! Everybody up there is either Spanish or Indian! You take as many anglos as you can round up, ranchers, businessmen, those artists and writers and the like, and even the *turistas* just passing through, and you still wouldn't have enough to invite to a fair-sized barbecue!"

"I am merely stating a fact, Floyd." Evans's voice had not altered. It sometimes seemed to Floyd that nothing, not even that crippling auto accident, could disturb Henry Evans's cool. "I believe they are called 'boomers,' " Evans went on, "and when a bridge job turns up, they appear out of nowhere. From beneath rocks, perhaps. Skilled men, largely."

"They still need hewers of wood and drawers of water." The governor's biblical knowledge was sketchy, but what there was of it he used to advantage.

"Those are turning up too, anglos all. On bridge construction, I am told they are called 'punks.' "

The governor's eyes went automatically to the framed photograph on the far office wall while he digested this information. The picture was of Big Luke, the governor's top quarter horse, posed in front of the sprawling, homey ranch house down in the corner of the state which the governor considered God's country. The horse and the house symbolized what was most precious in the governor's life.

Big Luke had recently won the Futurity at Ruidoso Downs and a purse of two hundred and fifty thousand dollars which, even by his own high financial standards, the governor considered a pleasant amount of walking-around money.

The house and the vast ranch around it had sheltered five generations of Babcocks, the governor's own brood included. It represented roots.

"You know, Henry," the governor said at last, "I'd do well to ponder on this. There are, you might say, wheels within wheels, if you see what I mean."

Evans had already seen what was meant. "Joe Trujillo, for one."

"Joe," the governor agreed, "is not a man to let things, like who gets hired for jobs, go unnoticed."

"You are not doing the hiring yourself, of course," Evans said. "On the other hand, the bridge was your idea from the beginning, so you'll get whatever blame there is, along with whatever credit. I will leave you to your dilemma, Floyd."

As usual, the governor thought as he hung up, his eyes still on Big Luke and the ranch house, Henry Evans saw the situation clearly, along with all of its implications.

The governor recalled a conversation, a monologue really, that had taken place two years back when he was still Speaker of the State House. Silver-haired George Upton, state senator of the opposition party, was talking:

"A bridge to nowhere," the senator had said in his best courtroom voice, thereby creating the tag that would endure. "That's all it is, and you're using the idea as a political ploy, Floyd, nothing else. All you want to do is get elected governor of this state, to further your own political ambitions. You don't really give a good goddamn about the bridge, but you figure it will bring you votes in Tano County, so you picked the idea up and you're pushing it hard. Well, it won't work. Mark my words: it won't work."

The senator had only been saying what had been fed to him, of course. The senator always did. But he had also been expressing a view that was not uncommon.

Even Henry Evans, sitting on the shaded *portal* of the main house of his big ranch up in Tano County, had said the same. This was long before Henry's crippling automobile accident. "If I give you full benefit of the doubt, Floyd," Henry had said, "I will have to admit that the bridge proposal has great merit. Because of the river gorge, east-west movement has never been easy up here, and the bridge, plus the highway across it, will open this northern area as surely as the transcontinental railroad opened the entire west."

"Well, now," the governor remembered saying, "isn't that what you might call beneficial? Seems to me it is."

"Perhaps. Personally, I could do without it, but that's beside the point. And your motives for backing the project are probably selfish rather than public-spirited, but that doesn't really enter, either."

"I've always thought," the governor said, "that if a man could do good *and* take in a few winnings for himself at the same time, he'd be a fool if he didn't reach right out and take hold of the opportunity."

"I won't argue. But is the project feasible? The idea has come up before, and there have been strong arguments advanced against it, arguments of geology, of weather, of working conditions out over the Tano Gorge." Evans shook his head gently; the movement, like all of his actions, was carefully controlled.

"They say it can be done," the governor said.

"And you are willing to stake what amounts to your political future that *they* are right." Evans added, nodding gently this time, but in understanding rather than approval. "You are, you know, Floyd. If you tie yourself to this bridge idea, and if anything happens to screw it up, you will be remembered forever for the failure, and probably nothing else."

"You fish, or cut bait," the governor said then. "Nobody knows that better than you. You put up, or you shut up. And if you win"—he shrugged and spread his hands—"then you rake in the pot. Isn't that the way it is?"

Evans showed his faint smile. "Nobody ever went far by being timid. Is that what you're saying? By the way, how far are you aiming, Floyd? To that big white house on Pennsylvania Avenue?"

"Far as I know," the governor said, "there's never been a cowboy in it. L.B.J. don't count. He was really a schoolteacher."

Well, that was two years back now, two years in which a lot had happened: a successful election, a bunch of legislative maneuvering, a bond issue against highway taxes, bridge designs long since approved, contracts let, now the work actually begun.

Usually, the governor enjoyed the feeling that the cards were dealt and the chips were down. But this time, he had an uneasy hunch that matters were not going entirely to his liking. Clearly, something would have to be done. But not in haste. The governor believed in sleeping on his decisions.

Seventy miles away, Henry Evans hung up the telephone and stared, not at a picture, but at the towering mountains nearby. Even now, well into summer, there was snow lingering in their hanging valleys. And on their bare slopes above the eleven thousand-foot timberline, alpine tundra country, tiny, hardy plants would be flowering, blue forget-me-nots, dwarf shrub potentillas gleaming yellow, mats of gray-green pussytoes, clinging to what soil there was and defying wind and weather.

He would never see the flowers again, Evans thought, probing the ache that was never absent, just as he would never see and do a lot of things he once had savored. Because of the accident, he was no longer a participant, merely a spectator.

He was aware that across the ranch office-library, Ellie was watching, and he forced aside the bitter thoughts and made himself smile. "Floyd will ponder it in his careful way," he said.

Ellie shook her head. She was a tall, generously proportioned girl, twenty-nine this year, dressed as usual in working ranch clothes of faded Levi's; a tooled leather belt with silver-and-turquoise buckle, tip, and keepers; a short-sleeved shirt; and dusty, handmade boots from Sam Lucchese in San Antonio.

"I don't think of him as careful," Ellie said.

Evans sat quiet in his wheelchair, a light throw covering his now useless legs. He wore a short-sleeved shirt, and his bare forearms, under firm motionless control in his lap, showed the results of the weights he worked out with daily. If, since the accident, only half of his body remained functional, then that half would be maintained in sound condition. It was a vow he had made himself.

"Most people don't," he said. "It's a sometimes bad mistake they make. Floyd gallivants around. Everybody knows that. And he loves a frolic. Or a fight. Or a good horse race. And the bigger the stakes, the better. But all that comes *after* he has sized up the situation. He doesn't blunder into trouble, although sometimes he does add up his facts the wrong way."

Ellie was never quite sure she understood this father of hers, whose thinking did not always, or even often, follow ordinary paths. "You think this is one of those times? The entire bridge idea, I mean?"

"I'm not sure he sees the full implications." Evans held up his hand, fingers spread, to tick off his points. "Consider: Money, a great deal of money, is going to be won and lost as the bridge and the highway open up Tano County. Political fortunes, maybe Floyd's included, are going to be advanced, or ruined. Land that will no longer be almost worthless is going to be fought over. And water. Always water. Damn it, the entire way of life here around Tano, which in some respects is still in the eighteenth, or maybe even the seventeenth century, is going to be dragged, kicking and screaming into the present. That's what Floyd has started, a high-rolling game with bigger stakes than he's ever played for."

"You're exaggerating, of course."

"Maybe a little. But not as much as you may think."

Ellie thought about it. "How about us?"

"We will continue to be what we have always been, an island of privilege in a sea of poverty." He shook his head. "I don't know why I'm being so flowery this morning, but there it is." He raised his head suddenly and seemed to sniff the air like a hunting dog as a distant, heavy sound reached them. "Alarums and excursions offstage," he said. "On cue."

Ellie said, "Blasting?"

"What else? Bridges are built from the bottom up. As drilling rigs are. Or used to be. I'd guess they're blasting down into bedrock to set the tower foundations. It's a sound you used to hear in midtown Manhattan and down near the Battery where the tall buildings are."

"I don't like it."

Evans showed his faint smile. "Before it's finished, there'll be a lot more you won't like. Nor will I."

4.

The blast set the windows to shaking in Jud's construction shack, and by an odd trick of the light, set the *Penthouse* nude's breasts to shaking too in a brisk burlesque rhythm. "Honey," Jud said, watching appreciatively, "you maybe missed your calling. You ought to be in moving pictures." He pushed back his chair and stood up, pulled his hard hat down securely, and blew the nude a kiss as he walked out to see the blast results.

It had torn a twenty-foot hole in the rock. The rock fragments filling the hole were almost, but not quite, uniform chunks, proof that the powder monkey had known what he was about, as he had damn well better. A massive loader was already shoveling the fragments out a cubic yard or so at a time, and dropping them into the bed of the waiting dump truck. The truck shuddered beneath the impact of each new load.

Jud walked over to the watching walking boss, whose name was MacAndrew, and nodded in silent approval.

"I don't know about that rock," MacAndrew said in the tone of a man whose thoughts were frequently gloomy. "It's got cracks going every goddamn which way."

"All of a sudden you're a geologist?"

"No, but no matter what their borings and cores and reports show, I don't like it."

Jud wasn't sure he liked it, either, but at the moment that was neither here nor there. He let silence express his opinion.

"You taken a good look down into that goddamned gorge?" MacAndrew said. "Well, down at the bottom, in some places damn near blocking the river, there are big piles of this rock."

"So?"

"Those piles broke off the cliff face. Where else did they come from? And if the cliff is falling apart, then where are we going to find solid bedrock to anchor this goddamned bridge? Answer me that."

There was no answer except the age-old one known to every man who had ever worked on a construction job. "We go by the drawings and the specs," Jud said.

"And hope the geologists and engineers and computer geniuses know what the hell they're doing."

There was that, Jud thought. But, then, there always was. You went by the drawings and the specs because that was all you had. They were your scriptures. Again he said nothing.

"And I've been thinking about those winds too," MacAndrew said.

"You already told me."

"They call them 'devil winds.' Did you know that? And there's another thing, though I don't really believe it, but they say the goddamned Gorge is haunted too."

"Who says?"

"The Indians. And they've been here a long time. They say spirits live down in the Gorge, and I guess they get hungry or something every so often, because they snatch some poor bastard right off the cliff and that's an end to that."

"They talk about the bogeyman too, and the tooth fairy?"

"Goddamn it, I'm only telling you what I heard."

"Why don't you try not listening?"

Grown men, Jud thought in sudden exasperation, were sometimes the damndest. They mostly behaved like you'd expect grown-up men to behave, and then all of a sudden it was as if they were still kids, worrying about the things kids worry about, getting ideas kids would be expected to have, listening to every story or rumor that came along—and believing all of them.

They stood in silence, watching as the first dump truck, full and lurching under its load, trundled off with the howling engine driving the wheels in compound-low. A second truck moved into place, and the loader continued its work without missing a beat.

"How many yards we got to move?" MacAndrew said.

"Plenty. And the other tower leg will be worse."

"You know, that's one more thing I don't like," MacAndrew said. "Who in hell ever heard of a bridge tower with legs of two different lengths? What I mean is, you see a guy with one short leg, you watch him walk, he hasn't got any balance, isn't that how it is?"

"I don't remember," Jud said, "when I last saw a bridge tower walking. When did you?"

"Goddamn it, I'm just saying maybe it isn't right."

"Anything else?"

MacAndrew hesitated. This Jud Wilder was a hard-nosed son of a bitch. As a matter of fact, that was his nickname, Hard Nose Jud Wilder, and he lived up to it. If you had something to say, he'd listen, but when he decided you'd said enough, it was damn well time to stop. Like now, the message coming through loud and clear. MacAndrew raised his voice above the engine sounds of loader and dump truck. "Okay! Let's keep it moving! We've got a long way to go!"

Jud walked off. A little of MacAndrew went a long way. But he was a good, conscientious, knowledgeable walking boss, and for all his old-maid tendencies to see the gloomy side of everything, the men worked well for him and that was what counted.

The legs of this east tower did look funny in the drawings, Jud admitted, one almost twenty feet longer than the other. The rock formation was the cause, of course, and Zabrinski, the stress engineer, with an almost feminine sensitivity, had anticipated Jud's unspoken questions when they were first going over the drawings.

"As long as the loads are distributed evenly, and the stresses are properly calculated," Zabrinski had said, "the lengths of the legs don't matter a bit. And this way we avoid having to blast down twenty feet more on the short side. Okay?"

"You design them," Jud said. "We build them."

Zabrinski held a can of Coke in his big right hand. He waved it gently for emphasis. "There's always the gap, isn't there?" His voice was easy, friendly, merely stating facts. "Between construction and engineering, I mean? Same thing in manufacturing, between engineering and the shop. You think we deliberately make things complicated. We think you just don't understand the problems we have to solve."

"We don't."

"Sometimes I wonder. Sometimes I think you understand the hell of a lot more than you let on." Zabrinski waved the Coke can again. "You know, I envy you guys. I really do. I watch you make the hell of a tough job look easy, and I wish I could do it, and I know I couldn't. Oh, I'm physical enough, coordinated, and God knows I'm big enough, but what it takes to handle steel is finesse. Strength isn't enough. Nobody's strong enough to go to the mat with a ton of I-beam."

True enough, and Jud had thought about that many times since. A crane could swing an I-beam aloft without effort, but when the beam reached its destination, the men of the connecting gang took over and with balance, dexterity, and judgment that, as Zabrinski had said, made the job look easy, maneuvered and coaxed the pre-drilled steel into position, a ton or so of rogue metal that could crush a man's hand into pulp or nudge him off his narrow perch into eternity.

They would then make the steel fast and step aside for the riveting gang to move in with air hammer, bucking bar, and heated rivets to fix the connection permanently. When properly done, the entire operation was as precise as a ballet.

The precision did not come all at once. Even skilled men needed time to adjust to one another's rhythms. You had to learn to anticipate your partner's every move, to know without looking that he was standing here, there, or behind you, ready to take his share of the load, and you had to feel without signal the precise instant when your strength and his should be applied in exactly which direction, in order to coerce the sometimes recalcitrant steel into its proper place.

Once, when he worked in the area, Jud had been fascinated by the docking operations of the great ocean liners on the Hudson River in New York. There, too, mere power was not enough. It took skill, judgment, and exquisite timing to bring the great ships alongside their piers, to come to rest in precise position at the exact moment when their momentum ceased. A miscalculation, and the moving mass of the ship could carry the pier away. Proper judgment, and the monster was subdued and tethered almost without effort.

And so it was with steel. Beam by beam, maneuvered, captured, secured for all time by man's ingenuity. Braced cross-member by braced cross-member, level by level the towers would rise, the tempo of the work settling into its steady, seemingly effortless pace, as the triangles which made up the structure took shape.

"Why triangles?" someone had asked once. "Why the hell is all steel construction nothing but triangles?"

"Because they're stiff," Jud remembered saying. "You take anything with four sides, and it can move, change shape. Put a brace across to opposite corners and you've got two triangles and nothing can move, it's solid. That's why triangles." Where had he learned that? He was damned if he knew, but there it was.

But even the beginning of the towers was yet to come. What they were doing now with the blasting was merely setting the foundations, first things first, as politicians were fond of saying. Construction was a logical business, and that part of it, in that it tended to satisfy Jud's innate craving for order, was a definite plus.

With a house you went down maybe eighteen inches in dirt for your footings, maybe in cold country a little deeper. But for bridge tower foundations, as for the foundations of a skyscraper, you blasted right down to bedrock, maybe five feet, maybe fifty, whatever it took, and then into the rock itself, in order to pour your concrete and set your massive baseplates true, plumb, and level, solid as the big mountains all around looking down upon you. Then you could start to build, not before, and the towers would rise, tall and proud and strong.

But well before the towers were complete, more blasting would begin, into bedrock again, this time to provide anchorages for the wires which would be spun into two huge bundles to form the main cables of the suspension bridge.

Each wire—rising from its anchorage to the top of the near tower, descending and then rising again in a graceful catenary curve to pass over the far tower, and down once more to the far anchorage—would be secured at each end to an eyebolt set deep in massive concrete and bedrock.

Each bundle when completed would consist of 11,564 individual wires, and these would be hydraulically compressed and then wrapped, as a fishing rod is wrapped, with another wire to form two almost solid individual cables capable of supporting the roadway and its anticipated loads.

Meanwhile, the roadway would already have begun to project from the two towers, first merely a catwalk, then two solid growing structures cantilevered out over the Gorge.

With the completion of the main cables, the load of the growing roadway stubs could be supported from above. To Jud, that was the point at which the job would turn into a downhill run.

Day by day and yard by yard, the two halves of the roadway would describe their flat arcs farther out over space; and the distance between them would close, slowly at first, and then, as the gap narrowed perceptibly, with seemingly increased speed.

They would meet almost one thousand feet above the center of the Gorge, the last piece of steel would be maneuvered into place, and the last rivet bucked to make permanent the final connection.

There would be no bands playing, no cutting of ribbons, no speeches for posterity. But that night in Josie's Place in town, the bar cash register would play a lively tune, and in more than one group the same sentiment would be expressed: "We whipped the bitch, didn't we? We threw that steel right across that goddamned gorge. And they said it couldn't be done." And there would be affection expressed in the words.

The roadway would still have to be strengthened by the addition of the open truss stiffening, and the depth of that stiffening would be a function of the roadway's width and the length of the span.

And there would be still more work to be done before the bridge was complete, of course, the electrical work, the roadway surface, painting, and so on, but as far as Jud was concerned, the bridge job would be wrapped up when the last rivet was bucked, and the last cable secured. Jud was an ironworker.

Across the Gorge now, a cloud of dust rose suddenly, followed a count and a half later by the heavy, solid sound of the explosion that had caused it. Jud nodded faintly in acknowledgment and approval. The west tower foundations were being blasted out too. On schedule. In some ways it was good that the two parallel jobs proceeded simultaneously. For one thing, you could promote competition between them, and because not many would be riding the open tramcar from side to side, who was to say if you maybe exaggerated a little on the progress of one crew in order to speed up the other?

He walked into his shack, nodded pleasantly and approvingly

to the nude on the wall, and then stopped short to stare at the big man straddling the straight visitor's chair, his arms crossed comfortably on the chair's back. "What the hell brings you here?" Jud said.

"Hi, Jud," Sam Taylor said. "Come in. Sit down. I'll tell you about it."

5.

José María Trujillo Sanchez paid a rare visit to Henry Evans on the vast Evans ranch. He admired Evans as a man, and also resented him, maybe resented him all the more because of the admiration. Hard to tell. Trujillo was not given to introspection.

He drove the eight miles to the ranch house from the highway through rolling high mesa land, where grama grass, an occasional writhing *cholla,* and small clumps of idly curious cattle were about all there was to see. These, and the towering mountains nearby to the northeast, looking down in their changeless, and yet ever-changing, brooding way.

Trujillo hoped he would see Ellie, and also hoped that he would not. In her high-breasted, slim-waisted, solid-hipped, anglo way, she always managed to make Trujillo feel very much the poor *chicano* boy who had hauled himself up from nothing by the ear-pulls of his boots and had no idea what to do with his hands.

Trujillo had seen Ellie once in a bikini by the ranch pool, and decided then and there that he would cheerfully trade his fading hopes of salvation for a night in bed with her.

Ellie was there, with Evans, out on the west *portal,* where the air was still cool and the view of the distant, purple mountains of the Divide unobstructed.

"Joe," Evans said, and held out his hand. "Sit down. Maybe some iced coffee, Ellie?"

It was a measure of this anglo, Trujillo thought, that, crippled as he was from that deer-running-across-the-highway auto crash, and despite his basic dislike of Trujillo, he nevertheless remained gracious in manner, without bitterness, and apparently fully at ease. Trujillo wondered how he would behave in the same circumstances, and doubted that he would do as well.

"Are you going to do anything about this bridge, Henry?" Trujillo said. "That's why I came." His English was fluent, grammatical and without accent, and nobody would ever know how much painful effort that had cost a country *chicano* boy who had dropped out of school after the tenth grade. "Because if you are—"

"You would join me?" Evans nodded. "Yes, I see that. We'd make a strange team, wouldn't we? But I'm afraid it won't happen. I don't fight battles that can't be won."

"Floyd Babcock is a friend of yours, and this is his project. He's got his reputation riding on it."

"But that isn't my reason."

"And no matter what happens out there"—Trujillo gestured broadly—"beyond your fences, you won't be affected. Or very little."

"That isn't the reason, either." Evans wondered why he bothered to explain. Normally, he did not believe in explanations. Leaning over backward because basically he disliked the man, maybe. "I couldn't influence Floyd if I tried. So I won't try. I couldn't persuade the legislature to do an about-face without a compelling reason, and I don't have a compelling reason. The bond issue has been passed, the money is available, the contracts have been let, and the work has begun. The process is irreversible. That's why I won't do battle."

Ellie appeared again, followed by a maid with a tray of glasses. Ellie looked from man to man. "No blood yet?" She smiled at Trujillo, and he almost dropped the glass the maid offered him.

"Amicable," Evans said, "so far. But what about you, Joe? You don't usually enter fights you can't win, either. Why this time?"

"I have my reasons."

Evans nodded. "I can guess what they are."

"This is my county, and I know what's best for it. The bridge and the highway will bring a lot of anglo sharpies to steal land, cheat people—"

"Your people," Evans said, and nodded. "Your subjects. You're an anachronism, Joe. I wonder if you realize that. You're a benevolent despot, and they're out of style these days."

Trujillo shook his head emphatically. "If that means what I think it means, I'm not. I have an insurance business and sometimes I try to help people. That's all."

"By, for example," Evans said, "finding a janitorial job on the county payroll for Juan. So Juan, his wife, his nine brothers and sisters, and eleven *primos*, cousins, all vote the way José María Trujillo Sanchez thinks is best. That makes you more than an insurance broker, Joe. It makes you boss man in these parts. Now, how much of your dislike of the bridge and the highway is based on your dislike of Floyd Babcock?"

Trujillo tasted his coffee while he considered the question. Ellie was, for the moment, forgotten. "For an anglo, you're a pretty smart fellow, Henry," he said at last.

"Thank you."

"I guess maybe I'd forgotten how smart. I haven't seen you since your accident."

"I don't get around much any more."

"I'm sorry about your wife."

"Thank you."

"I'm sorry it happened to you."

"Thank you for that, too. And reserve some sympathy for the deer."

Ellie said sharply, "Henry!" It was as if neither man heard.

"Okay," Trujillo said, "so I don't like Floyd Babcock. At heart he's a *Tejano*, a Texan, and to him I'm nothing, less than dirt, because I'm *chicano*. He doesn't say so. He doesn't have to. It's just . . . there. And the bridge people think the same way."

"Because they hire only anglos?"

"What would you think?"

"I think," Evans said slowly, "that there's another reason too. I think you don't like the idea of the bridge and the highway because they'll open this county to the air and the sunlight, and your kind of one-man rule may cease to be possible. There are many things about you, Joe, that I find admirable. But you're still a despot, even if you are sometimes benevolent."

"Have I ever lied to you, Henry?"

"A number of times I imagine. But I've never caught you at it. Are you trying to tell me that this time your heart is pure? That your sole concern is for the people of Tano County, your people, who need protection from the sharpies?" Evans shook his head gently. "Because I'm afraid I won't buy it, Joe. You're a subtle man, and you tend to have reasons behind reasons." He raised his hand to forestall comment. "That is not meant as criticism. I am merely stating a fact."

Trujillo sat silent for a few moments, his dark eyes fixed on Evans's face. He said at last, "I hoped you'd see it differently."

"I'm sure you did, and I'm sorry you're disappointed. But it would have made no difference. I said the process was irreversible. It is, and my views are unimportant."

"Things could happen."

Evans set his glass down gently. "Do you want to explain that?"

He waited, but there was no explanation. "I thought not," Evans said then, and nodded in his controlled way. "Yes, things could happen. The Gorge and the river are notorious. We lose cattle to them. Men have been known to disappear into them. For years it's been said that a bridge across the Gorge is not possible. I understand all that. But would you go that far, Joe, whatever your reasons?"

"All I said was that things *could* happen."

"And in the normal course of things," Evans said slowly, "will happen." Again that faint nod of affirmation. "There will be accidents. There always are. That truck, for example. On a project this size they have quite probably already figured for a few more deaths as well. Men do slip. They do fall. And a fall into the Gorge is an end in itself. I see all that. What you are saying, or actually not saying, is that with a little help here, and a little help there, only a little, really, the accident and/or death rate might become unacceptable, and the project might be stopped." He looked at Trujillo in silent question.

"You're writing the script, Henry."

Evans picked up his glass again and tasted the coffee thoughtfully. His eyes watched Trujillo over the rim of the glass. "I told Ellie only a little time ago," he said, setting the glass down, "that Tano County lives in the eighteenth or perhaps even the seventeenth century. I was exaggerating to make a point. But you remind me, Joe, that I wasn't exaggerating very much."

"We're backward people, if that's what you mean."

The bitter irony was not unnoticed. "The chip on your shoulder is showing," Evans said. He allowed none of his own feelings to show. "Not that I can blame you for wearing it. But you ought to know by now that I'm not interested in knocking it off." There was subtle challenge in his tone.

Silence grew, and stretched between them. At last, Trujillo nodded abruptly. "I'll give you that."

"What I am saying," Evans said as if there had been no interruption, "is that what you are carefully not saying is a dangerous business, Joe. Very dangerous."

Trujillo stood up. He let his eyes drift slowly over the light throw that covered Evans's useless legs. He was unsmiling, but contemptuous amusement was plain. "*Living* is dangerous, Henry," he said, spacing the words for emphasis. "You, of all people, should know that."

Evans sat unmoving, expressionless and silent, his eyes steady on Trujillo's face.

"Thanks for the coffee," Trujillo said.

"Any time." Still nothing had changed in Evans's face, and his tone was normal. "Ellie, you'll show our guest to his car?"

He watched them until they disappeared around the corner of the *portal*, and then let his breath out in a long, slow sigh. Too much, he thought, entirely too much. To be looked upon with contempt by a Joe Trujillo was more than a man could, or should, be asked to bear.

Never one to shout away his frustrations or dissipate them with small acts of violence, he sat quiet now while the helpless rage within him mounted.

He, Henry Evans, was intelligent, educated, wealthy almost beyond belief—and a *cripple*. A Joe Trujillo, up from nothing and still scrambling hard, *but a whole man*, could look down and laugh even if the laugh did not show. That, in the current jargon, was the bottom line. How many others than Trujillo felt the same when they looked down at a man, himself, now helpless in a wheelchair?

All his life he had ridden high. To paraphrase Kipling, he had taken his fun where he found it; rogued and ranged in his time. Other men had watched in envy, and he had known it and cared not. Henry Evans had been a name, and a man, to conjure with. And now?

He closed his eyes only briefly, feeling a psychological pain such as he had never before experienced. Then, without change of expression, and without haste, he backed the wheelchair out of its position, turned it, and with rhythmic thrusts of his strong arms propelled it into the house, through the office-library and down the hallway to his own suite.

There, as he always did as a matter of personal pride and privacy, he closed the outer door before he wheeled himself across the sitting room to the telephone table where he opened the drawer, and looked thoughtfully at the loaded .380 semi-automatic pistol which lay there.

He picked up the weapon and sat holding it balanced in his hand, feeling its weight and its cold, deadly solidity. It was not a target weapon; beyond a few yards, for any task that required accuracy, it was useless. Its sole function was to kill at close range, say a matter of inches from one's head, or with its muzzle thrust into one's mouth.

That was a way out, as other men had discovered, some of them good men, too. Only a moment, no doubt a shatteringly painful moment, and then there would be no more contempt to be experienced, no more hidden laughter to endure. There would be—nothing.

Without warning, Ellie's voice through the outer door said loudly, "Henry! Henry! The governor's on the phone! Can you hear me?"

The script was uneven in quality, Evans thought, but the timing was good. Inwardly he was suddenly, bitterly amused by the melodrama. He raised his own voice. "I'll take the call here." And with the gun still in his hand, he picked up the telephone. "Yes, Floyd?" He kept his eyes on the gun as he listened.

6.

Sam Taylor, straddling the visitor's chair in Jud's shack, nodded toward the nude. "You've changed your tastes, Jud. The last one was a redhead." And, with no change of tone, "Suppose I said this was just a routine visit to a big, new project?"

"I'd tell you to cut the crap."

They were similar, these two: big, hard, direct men both, Jud the older by ten or twelve years, the construction man, master workman. Sam the educated man, the engineer. Between them there had long been admiration, and, inevitably, clashes of will.

"I know how it's going to come out every time I get into a hassle with you, Sam," Jud had said once. "You've got the front office behind you, so I'm going to end with my ass in a sling, or out of a job. But, goddamn it, I'm not going to roll over and play dead for anybody when I think I'm right."

And Sam had given that small, enigmatic nod of his, and said, "I wouldn't want you to. Neither would Ross. And you're wrong about always coming out second best, you know. I can think of a few you've won."

"Damn few." But there had been some. Jud had to admit that.

"So I won't say it," Sam said now. "Instead, I'll ask you how the job shapes up?"

Jud tilted his chair back. "Last I heard, fellow named Chambers was the honcho on this job. How about asking him?"

"I'm asking you."

The front legs of Jud's chair came down with an angry thump. "Now, goddamn it, what kind of business is that? There's one thing you and Ross always say, it's that there's got to be lines of authority. My men go to their pushers. Their pushers go to their walking bosses. The walking bosses come to me. Then I carry it on up to Chambers if I can't handle it. Isn't that how it is?"

"That's right."

"Then give me reasons otherwise. You've always got reasons. I never knew a man with more reasons."

"Let's just say there's a lot riding on this job."

"There always is."

"Not this much. Ross figured this one himself, and maybe he figured it a little tight."

Jud tilted his chair back again and stared through the doorway in silence. " 'The difficult we do immediately,' " he said presently without looking around. " 'The impossible takes a little longer.' " He did look at Sam then. "That kind of thing?"

Sam nodded. "Time was when he'd come out and drive a crew himself, if he thought they needed it."

"I've heard stories." Jud was studying Sam closely now. "There's a lot you aren't saying. You probably got reasons for that too."

"You build something out of nothing," Sam said, "a great, big, damn something—"

"Like Ross Associates?"

Sam nodded again. "This," he said, "doesn't go beyond here."

Jud glanced up at the nude. "We don't talk, do we, honey?" He looked again at Sam. "Serious?"

"I guess," Sam said, "the hard part is deciding when the time's come to sit back and let others do the job, make the decisions the way you're used to doing all this time. So you try to do it both ways, sit in the stands and still call the plays." He shook his head. "It doesn't work." He looked hard at Jud. "That's why I want to know how you think the job shapes up. I'll get Chambers's assessment too. But I want yours first. You've worked more jobs than he's even read about." He lifted his shoulders gently, and let them fall in a vague gesture of apology. "I'm asking."

Outside the sounds continued in loud cacophony, the bellow of the loader engine and the grinding gearbox of a dump truck laboring away from the site, voices raised, the sudden clatter of a pneumatic drill backed all at once by the roar of its compressor engine cutting in.

"Well, I'll tell you," Jud said at last, "it isn't going to be the easiest job I've ever seen. On the other hand—"

"Damn it, say what you're thinking and quit pussyfooting around!"

Jud glanced again at the nude. "Man's upset, honey." He looked back to Sam, solemn now. "Okay," he said, "I'll give it to you straight. It's shaping up to be a ring-tailed bitch. With horns. I could be wrong, but I've got a feeling I'm not. Satisfied?"

Sam sat silent for a few moments. Slowly, he nodded. "Thanks. I had a hunch from reading the reports and the specs, and asking a few questions. That's why I came." He stood up. "I'll see Chambers now. I'll be back. Be ready to tell me what you need. All of it."

Daryl Chambers had not met Sam Taylor, but he had heard a great deal about him. The comments had ranged from, "You need answers, he's the one to go to," to, "Nobody's as good as they say he is, but I'll admit, he doesn't miss often," to, "You'll know the son of a bitch when you see him. He'll hold out his right hand, and keep the knife in his left." A mixed bag, Chambers thought now, and sat quiet while he waited to see what this visit was all about. Just sitting, straddling the chair in the tiny office, Taylor was impressive, Chambers told himself; he would give him that.

"We like to get a firsthand report on big new jobs," Sam said, and left it there.

Chambers went out to meet the implied question halfway. "We've already lost one man," he said. "But I suppose that isn't news?"

"The dump truck driver." Sam nodded. "Too bad, but it happens."

"And materiel delivery leaves something to be desired."

"Seems to me I've heard of that happening before," Sam said, and produced one of his rare smiles.

In it Chambers could find no hint of menace, and began to relax. "So what else is new, you mean?"

"Something like that. Funny thing, but off and on I've heard about this Tano Gorge for years. I guess you know it has quite a local reputation. And there've been several feasibility studies for bridges across it. They've all given up on the idea."

Chambers opened his mouth to comment, thought better of it, and sat silent.

"Obviously," Sam said, "that doesn't mean it can't be done. They said the Golden Gate Bridge couldn't be built too."

"Sure."

"You've got a tight schedule," Sam said.

"Don't they always look that way?"

"And you've got Jud," Sam said. "If it can be done, Jud will do it." Again he smiled. "He doesn't actually break rocks with his bare hands, but some of the men who've worked for him think he does." He stood up then. "Nothing you need, then?"

Chambers rose too. His eyes were about on a level with Sam's chin. He was no dwarf himself, and normally a man's mere size did not faze him, but there was something about this one, his reputation, maybe, that made him seem larger than lifesize, somehow overpowering. It took an effort of will to say, "Nothing I can't handle. If I find I do need anything—"

"Holler." Sam held out his hand. As nearly as Chambers could tell, he held no knife in the other. "Luck," Sam said, and turned away to duck through the doorway.

The nude on the wall seemed to watch with interest as Sam came into the shack again, and again straddled the visitor's chair. "Chambers seems to think there's no sweat."

Jud said nothing. His expression did not change.

"I walked over for a look down into the Gorge," Sam said. "Quite a little ditch." His voice was matter of fact, unconcerned. "There were half a dozen ravens riding the updrafts, and having just the hell of a time stunting the way they do. It occurred to me that wind might be a factor." He studied Jud's face, and nodded, satisfied. "You think so too." A statement, no question. "So now suppose you tell me about it. Is it only the wind that makes you think it's going to be a ring-tailed bitch?"

Jud stared contemplatively through the open doorway. "That's part. Another part's design. I go by the drawings." He looked at Sam then, and nodded his head at the bridge blueprints on the wall. "She's a beautiful bitch, isn't she? The structure, I mean, not the girl. No fancywork, no waste, she's fined right down like a racehorse in condition. What they call modern design."

Sam thought he understood the direction Jud was taking, but he wanted to be sure. "So?"

"Remember that building in Boston, modern, functional, no waste, beautiful tight design? The one that kept throwing big glass windows out over the street? Or that big, clean-domed auditorium in Kansas City, the prizewinner that collapsed? And the Hyatt Hotel that came apart and killed how many people?" Jud was silent then, watching Sam steadily.

"You think it's designed too tight? Too little margin of safety?"

"I'm not an engineer, Sam. I'm just an ironworker."

"Do you want to drop the project?"

"You ought to know better. I signed on. And I've never walked off a job in my life."

Big Zabrinski walked into Jud's shack after Sam had left, and lowered his bulk gently to the visitor's chair. He glanced appreciatively at the nude. "Nice," he said, "but I'm a married man myself. On the other hand"—his teeth showed startlingly white through the bramble of his black beard—"just looking can't hurt. Cathy says it's when I stop looking, she'll start to worry." The smile disappeared, and Zabrinski nodded his big head toward the open doorway. "That was the fabled Sam Taylor? In person? He looks pretty good from a distance."

"Sam's a good man." It was Jud Wilder's highest form of praise.

"I thought he spent his time in the home office, except when he went out trouble-shooting."

Jud let that one go.

"You and I," Zabrinski said, "have never landed on a job at the same time before. Maybe it might be a good idea if we got together, maybe hoisted a few, got to know one another a little better. Like I said a while back, there's always that gap between engineering and construction, you know what I mean?"

The big man believed in saying right out what he thought in simple, direct terms, Jud told himself, and he liked that. Some engineers Jud had known had always tried to make things so complicated that only they could understand them, probably because they were unsure of themselves and had to hide behind their learning. Zabrinski was like a grizzly bear, fearing nothing and having nothing he felt he had to prove.

"Suits me," Jud said. "Where? And when?"

Zabrinski was showing the white teeth in a smile again as he stood up. "No sense in wasting time," he said. "How about Josie's Place? Tonight?"

Sam drove away from the bridge site in his rented car, and headed for the town of Tano. The air conditioning in the car did not work, and the sun in a cloudless sky through the high, thin air, kept the interior, even with the windows down, at about the temperature of a slow cooker on simmer. Sam, long since inured to heat or cold, sweated profusely, and ignored it.

Nice country, he thought, although some, perhaps even most, would look upon it as pure wasteland—brown dirt, *cholla*, occasional prickly pear, the ubiquitous grama grass, here and there *piñon* and juniper in near-symbiosis; lizard, coyote, jackrabbit, and horny toad country, dry, dry, dry.

But no more than a thousand feet up the slopes of the great mountains, the ponderosa pines would begin, and the scrub oak, and a little above that line, the aspens, their leaves quivering to the faintest stirring of the air. In fall, the aspens would turn brilliant gold against the green of the conifers, heralding the approach of winter.

Among the trees, deer would browse, and elk. There would be bear, marten, foxes, bobcats, and on the high slopes above timberline, mountain goats and probably Dall sheep. There would be countless streams, some of them intermittent, some constant and filled with fish for the taking. In mountain meadows, beavers would have built their dams, and otters would pause in their fishing to romp, while they watched the solemn beavers endlessly toiling at dam improvement, or repair.

The undisturbed forests would be filled with Steller's jays, Clark's nutcrackers, whisky-jacks, chickadees, juncoes beyond counting. And the predators, the hawks, the falcons, the buteos, and the monarch of them all, the golden eagle. Yes, and the great horned owls, silent death in darkness.

To knowledgeable eyes it was glorious country, huge and almost empty, and relatively little changed from Coronado's time, or before. The bridge and the highway, of course, would alter all that, and Sam felt a measure of regret that it would be so.

They might be opening barren land to a way of life no one here really wanted, a flood of tourism, wheeling-dealing, trashy restaurants and fast food shops, gaudy motels with swimming pools in this arid land, empty beer cans cluttering the landscape.

But there was, of course, the other possibility. The bridge and its highway could bring much change that could be good, opening up what was now and had been for hundreds of years an almost isolated area where, with few exceptions like the vast Evans ranch of which Sam had heard much, there existed only subsistence dirt farming, scarce laboring jobs in towns like Tano, a few tiny herds of scrawny cattle or sheep—and welfare checks.

It was the eternal argument between those who wanted the land left as it was and had always been, and those who wanted to shape its destiny. Who was right, if either, Sam did not pretend to know. His own beginnings had been in country similar to this, and he had been known to point out that while the simple life had much to recommend it, there was also quite a bit to be said in favor of indoor plumbing. He had said that once in Liz Lewis's presence, and she had looked at him as if he were a visitor from outer space.

The office of the Tano *Bugle* didn't amount to much. Sam had not expected that it would. But small-town editors were usually good sources of information, and this one was no exception.

His name was Ed Peters, and he was in his comfortable and somewhat paunchy fifties, in no hurry at all, and over a leisurely beer at Josie's Place was more than willing to talk.

"I've often wondered," Peters said, "whether big engineering and construction outfits like yours bother to look into local situations before they bid a job just from the drawings and the specs and maybe the terrain."

"Sometimes yes, sometimes no," Sam said. "It all depends."

It didn't take very long, Peters had already decided, to see that this Sam Taylor played his cards close to his vest. He liked getting information, but he sure gave damn little. Well, no matter. Peters was a newspaperman, and he enjoyed giving.

"There's been talk of a bridge across the Gorge for years," Peters said. "Some say it can't be done." He watched Sam's faint nod. "You already know all that." He altered direction. "And some don't want it. Joe Trujillo, for one. You know about him? His square name is José María Trujillo Sanchez, and if you want anything done, or undone, or fixed in Tano County, he's the one you see."

Sam made a mental note of the name.

"Joe's influence," Peters went on, "doesn't stop at the county line, either. Just for example, there's a state senator down at the capital, chairman of three, four committees, name of George Upton. Silver-haired George carries a lot of weight. They say he can't be bought. Not for any price. Know why? Joe Trujillo won't sell him." He studied Sam's face to see if the implications were understood. He decided they were. "And Joe doesn't like Floyd Babcock, that's our governor, worth a damn. Now since your bridge is Floyd's pet project, you can see the possibilities for kneeing in the clinches there." He had a long pull at his beer.

Sam said, "What about the ranchers in the area?"

"You're talking about Henry Evans. All the others follow his lead. Henry was damn near killed hitting a deer on the highway at night a few months back. Crippled himself and did kill his wife. So he's not as active now as he was, but he still calls the tune." Peters was silent for a few moments. He said at last, "Oh, hell, you really want to know just where your bridge project stands locally, there's no point talking to me. Get it from the horses' mouths, Joe Trujillo and Henry Evans and even Floyd Babcock. They're all easy to see."

Liz Lewis thought often of her first meeting with Sam, probably because it seemed to have set the tone for their relationship of confrontation ever since. The entire episode was so typical of the man.

It was not quite two years ago now, but she didn't even remember, or perhaps had deliberately forgotten, who her escort was that night. It didn't really matter. He would have been someone socially acceptable, amusing, and undistinguished—and on that occasion, unforgiveably drunk, suddenly loudly argumentative in the middle of the downtown sidewalk.

"Trouble, lady?" There was mild amusement underlying the question, as if the man who had stopped, attracted by the shouting, understood full well that he sounded like something out of a John Wayne film.

"No trouble at all, thank you," Liz said promptly, and with asperity.

Her acceptable, amusing, undistinguished and now drunk escort thought otherwise. He pushed Liz roughly aside. "I'll handle this," he said. "Fellow needs to be taught a lesson, butting in. Put a stop to it right now." He surged forward.

"Simmer down," Sam said. The underlying amusement remained. "It was just a thought." He turned away.

The wild swing intended for Sam's face landed on his shoulder blade. Sam spun around with a speed astonishing in so big a man. He caught the arm that threw the second punch, and in a motion Liz could scarcely follow, jerked the drunk forward, spun him around, and wrapped him up, helpless, his fist levered up behind his back in a painful hammerlock.

"He doesn't seem to be much of a bargain, lady," Sam said then, with no change of expression, "but there's no accounting for some tastes. Where would you like me to put him?"

Liz searched angrily for scathing words, and in the end said only, "Let him go."

Sam gave the man a stronger than gentle shove, and simultaneously released him. The man staggered a few steps, regained his balance, turned to glare at both Sam and Liz, and then, turning again on sudden drunken impulse, lurched off down the sidewalk with what dignity he could muster.

Sam looked at Liz. "Sorry about that."

"Are you always the hero type? Rushing in. Unwanted?"

Sam studied her angry face. "Independent, aren't you?" His voice was still vaguely amused. He took Liz's arm with gentle firmness. "My car's right over here. The least I can do is drive you wherever you want to go."

"Will you please let my arm go?"

Sam obeyed. "Now what? Taxis aren't all that plentiful." He studied all of her, this time with a slow thoroughness. Beauty and elegance. Obviously money. "At a guess," he said, "Telegraph Hill?"

Liz wanted to stamp her foot. With effort, she refrained. His remark about taxis was all too true. "All right," she said imperiously. "You may drive me."

His car was a Mercedes sports coupe, shiny, opulent, but in quiet good taste, which somehow made the entire situation worse. Liz would by far have preferred that he drove something egregious, perhaps with fins, a showy chariot she could look upon with scorn.

He held the door politely, and closed it with care only after she was well seated. As he slid into his own seat beneath the wheel, "Our destination?" he said.

"I suppose you make a habit of being right," Liz said. "You would. It *is* Telegraph Hill."

At the apartment house door, while the doorman remained politely out of earshot, "My name is Taylor," Sam said. "Sam Taylor. And I apologize for spoiling your evening."

Oh, damn! Liz thought. Why can't he give me a good excuse for being really angry? "It was already spoiled," she said. And she added, without really knowing why, "My name is Elizabeth Lewis. Goodnight."

There were flowers the next day. And then a telephone call . . .

But the first meeting remained firmly in memory.

Liz was not accustomed to men who could take her, or leave her alone, as apparently Sam could.

"That is a very fetching outfit," he told her in her apartment one afternoon early in their acquaintance, "guaranteed to raise more than a man's hackles. But, as I said, I have a plane to catch, and one quick drink is all I have time for. I have a job—"

Liz refused to reveal disappointment. "Where to? Some exotic land?"

"Chilean mountains. Sleeping bags and tents. How would you like a sleeping bag?"

"Drink your drink and be on your way. Find an Indian sleeping bag mate, if you must."

"While you pine away here." Sam let his amusement show. "I'll try to find a shrunken head to bring back as a gift."

He did, too, and Liz, opening the gift box tied with shiny ribbon, parting the inside tissue paper wrappings, and seeing the monstrosity leering up at her, gave a small scream of mixed shock and anger, and threw the gift, box and all, straight at Sam.

"I thought it would be something to remember me by," Sam said, and caught it neatly in midair.

Then there were the other sides to him, in Liz's view just as startling. His apartment, although spacious and comfortable, nevertheless gave the impression that it belonged to a man who cared little about his surroundings and had probably paid the bill and moved without comment into an atmosphere someone had arranged for him.

But there was one exception, the superb high-fidelity music system, and the astonishingly extensive collection of recordings, both classical and jazz.

"Call it my vice," Sam said, almost apologetically. "I didn't grow up with music, so when I discovered it, I jumped into it with both feet."

Liz did not know, and never asked, where it was that Sam had grown up. From his talk, it would appear that life for him had begun as a freshman in the University of California engineering department. He never mentioned family, and apparently his only friends were those he knew now and had met during his years with Ross Associates.

He and Liz became intimate in the accepted sense early in their acquaintance, but intimacies other than physical never seemed to develop.

"You are *mucha mujer*, much woman," Sam said once as they lay naked, comfortably spent, in Liz's large bedroom.

"Why, thank you, sir. I am flattered that you noticed."

"I'm going back to Chile next week. I'll be there two, three weeks. Care to come along?" He spoke the words with careful lack of emphasis.

Liz turned her head to look at him. His face was expressionless. Liz smiled. "Thank you, but no. I'm not a sleeping bag girl."

"Chile is not entirely mountains. I'll be carrying on negotiations in civilized surroundings."

"No, Sam. I know my . . . milieu. I haven't yet figured out what yours is."

So now he was off again, Liz thought, leaving her bed once more in the pre-dawn hours. And he was just back, too, from wherever it was last time. An annoying, if fascinating, man, Sam Taylor.

7.

The governor's eyes were again on that picture of Big Luke, but his thoughts were elsewhere as he spoke to Henry Evans on the telephone.

"I gave that bridge hiring thing a lot of thought last night," the governor said, which was only partly true because most of his thoughts, as they were now, had been on Alice Perkins, that bright, pretty, young, brushed-up sociology Ph.D., who was advising the state Department of Corrections on modern penal practice and was more than willing to show the governor her appreciation for the opportunity to do the job. "I want that policy of hiring only anglos changed," the governor went on. "Question is, what's the best way to do it?"

"Simply ask, Floyd." Evans looked down at the gun still in his hand. As fatuous a question as this had been the interruption? Again the analogy of bad script and good timing came to mind, producing bitter laughter from the wings. "You don't want to be in the position of supplicant, is that it? I suppose you want me to see what I can do?"

"I surely would appreciate it, Henry."

"Just get on my horse, ride over to the bridge site, and tell them how the governor of the state feels?" Instantly, Evans regretted the words. "Strike that. I am crippled, but I'm not helpless, Floyd. I will see what I can do. I may have to ask you for a letter—"

"You'll have it. You surely will. I'm much obliged, Henry."

The governor hung up, leaned back in his chair and smiled at Big Luke. Now he could relax, conscience clear. He flipped open the switch on the intercom. To Betty Jo in the outer office he said, "Send Dr. Perkins in, honey. And we don't want to be disturbed, hear?" He heaved himself out of his chair and walked around his desk to wait.

Alice Perkins came in, solemn, businesslike, allowing a happy, eager smile to show only after she had closed the door behind her. "Do I need to lock it?"

"No need at all, honey. Betty Jo copes real good."

The governor savored the sight of the girl as she walked slowly toward him. Long, gracefully curved legs, undulating hips, slim waist, no brassiere today, he noticed pleasurably, and remembered those high, firm, pointed breasts he had fondled and kissed so avidly last night, thereby driving Dr. Perkins to distraction, if the noises deep in her throat were any indication. "Just stop right there," the governor said, "and let me admire you, honey. You are something to look at."

Dr. Perkins had a slim leather briefcase in her hand. She let it fall to the carpet. With both hands she reached behind herself. There was the soft hiss of a zipper, and then her dress too fell to the floor. She wore bikini briefs, and nothing else. She was smiling. "Better?" she said.

"Better and better," the governor said. "Let's go over on that nice, roomy sofa-couch, and make ourselves cozy."

Sam Taylor drove the rented car in over the cattleguard that marked the beginning of the Evans ranch property. Henry Evans's immediate response to Sam's unannounced phone call had surprised him by its cordiality. In its way, the Evans ranch was just about as famous as the King ranch down in Texas, and while Sam had not expected any kind of antipathy, neither had he expected the instant invitation he received.

"I'll be delighted to see you," Evans had said. "As you may know, my mobility is limited these days, so if you have transport, perhaps you'd care to come out here where we can talk."

Now, driving through the open range, Sam studied the terrain and the occasional clumps of cattle which were, he decided, not simple range stock, lean and long-legged and bony. There had been crossbreeding, probably with registered beef stock, Herefords, Charolais, others he could not identify, and, although it took some puzzling to work this out, indications from the shaggy bangs on some animals that Evans had even tried introducing hardy Scottish Highland cattle.

Obviously Evans believed in experimenting. Well, from all Sam had heard of the man, he could well afford it.

Bandy-legged Inocencio appeared when Sam reached the main ranch house, stopped the car in the parking area and got out.

"*Señor* Taylor?"

"*Sí. Eso es.*"

Inocencio's eyebrows rose. "*Habla usted español, señor?*"

"*Sí, un poco.*"

Inocencio's face showed delight. "I will take you to the Señor Evans." He led the way, limping up the steps and around the broad gallery.

"Welcome, Mr. Taylor," Evans said and held out his hand. It was strong and firm, and after the brief handshake it returned immediately to its immobile position in Evans's lap. "Sit down." No gesture. "I think maybe a little refreshment? A beer, perhaps?" Evans's hand touched a button mounted on the nearby lamp table. Somewhere in the house a bell sounded faintly. The hand had already returned to its immobile position. "I had understood that the bridge project head was a man named Chambers, Daryl Chambers?"

"He still is. I work out of San Francisco."

"On matters of policy?"

"You might say that."

A maid appeared, and Evans ordered beer. He did not appear to be studying Sam, but Sam had the impression that he was being sized up carefully. For what reason? No way to tell.

"I am delighted with this visit," Evans said when the maid had turned away. "There is a matter of some importance. Maybe we can settle it right away." He was silent for a few moments. "Is it Ross Associates policy to hire only anglos on this job?"

So that was it. Jud's doing? Chambers's? "No," Sam said. "And if that's what's happening, it'll be changed."

Evans sighed, and seemed to relax a trifle. "I was afraid I was going to have to give a speech about the demography and ethnic makeup of these parts."

"Not necessary."

Evans seemed about to speak, and then remained silent as the maid returned with chilled beer bottles and frosted mugs. Evans poured his beer with care and efficiency, giving all his attention to the task. He looked up then, produced his faint smile, and raised his mug. "*Salud.*"

"*Salud.*" Sam tasted his beer, and set it down. "You were going to say something, I think."

"Maybe it is unnecessary too, but I like to make the point that we anglos are interlopers here. We came in and took the land, sometimes honestly, sometimes by force, sometimes by downright fraud." It was easy enough to remember that sudden flash of resentment in Trujillo's manner when it had seemed that he and his people were being denigrated. "It doesn't take much to arouse reaction."

"There's a man named Trujillo—" Sam began.

"You've heard about him? Good."

"I want to see him."

Evans nodded approval. "You and he will have quite a bit to talk about."

"It's also been suggested," Sam said, "that I see the governor." He made of the statement a question, and sat quiet, awaiting comment.

"Another splendid idea. The bridge was Floyd's idea from the start. It's his pet project." Evans showed that faint smile again. "You've done your homework. I've been wondering when someone would. I dislike using personal examples, but when I was still active in the oil and gas business, I made it a point to acquaint myself with the area and the people in the area before I exercised my drilling options. And all I was doing was poking holes in the ground, not changing an entire way of life."

Sam sipped his beer in silence.

"I had the pleasure of meeting Wilt Ross some years back," Evans said. "He didn't strike me then as a man who tended to go off half-cocked."

"No."

"But you are here now."

"I'm here now."

Evans nodded. "If we are going to have a bridge and an east-west highway, so be it. We'll accommodate to it and probably in time find benefits we didn't expect, which may even outweigh the disadvantages."

Sam listened, silent and immobile. He wondered what the point was going to be, although he already had a suspicion. This Henry Evans, he thought, laid it on the line. Sam liked that.

"But," Evans said, "what we don't want is, I'll be blunt, a botched job. I've seen enough of those. Too many. I can cite chapter and verse concerning oil and gas fields that were opened in too much of a hurry, everybody scrambling, endless opportunities for chicanery and worse, and the net result a ruined field with only a fraction of its potential realized, and the balance beyond reach, possibly for good."

Sam nodded then. "I've heard of such things."

"The analogy is not exact," Evans said. "Analogies rarely are. But if on this project of yours mistakes continue to be made, bad mistakes, such as refusing to hire Spanish or Indians, that can set the entire local population against you, then your problems are going to multiply exponentially. And unless you have a single, strong hand in control, someone able and willing to make hard decisions, then the entire project could grind to a halt, and we would have experienced only the dislocations and the annoyances, and would reap none of the benefits."

Sam tasted his beer and said nothing. The man was not through, and he wanted to hear all of it.

"Are you going to be here, in charge?" Evans said.

"No."

"Why not? Because you have too many other projects that also have to be ramrodded?"

"Maybe something like that."

"Is Wilt Ross still active?"

"Very much so."

"Maybe too much? Even the best reach a point when they'd do well to step down."

"He's still the boss," Sam said.

"And I'm asking questions I have no business asking?" Evans smiled faintly, mocking himself. "Being a cripple has its prerogatives. It's easy to take advantage of them." He looked up as Ellie appeared in the doorway. "Come in. My daughter Ellie, Mr. Taylor. Mr. Taylor represents management on the bridge project."

"And Henry has been telling you how to run it?" Ellie said. "He does, you know."

There was an obvious ease between father and daughter, Sam thought, that robbed the words of their critical meaning. Interesting. There was also a similarity between the two, not of appearance, although there was a faint family resemblance, but, rather, of calm confidence that expressed itself in both speech and manner.

"We're always open to suggestions," Sam said.

Ellie sat down, and was instantly relaxed. "Then I have one," she said. Her eyes smiled at Sam. "Stop that blasting. There are nesting eagles on the cliff face, and the noise upsets them."

"There are ravens out there too."

"Aerial acrobats," Ellie said, "stunt flyers. They are impervious." The smile had reached her lips. "The blasting has to go on, I suppose, but for how long?"

"Until we reach solid bedrock."

"And then?"

"We set our baseplates, pour our foundations, and start to build the towers."

Evans, watching quietly, wondered what was going on in the girl's mind. Thoughts and feelings no man could ever know or understand, he supposed, except in broad and general terms. Ellie was young and healthy, and Sam Taylor was a considerable figure of a man, so the sometimes not so delicate chemistry that affected relations between the sexes was probably already at work. He wondered if in time he could learn to enjoy his role of spectator.

"Men," Ellie said, "will be working right at the edge of the Gorge?"

"And later, out over it, yes."

"I read once," Ellie said, "that accidents, and even deaths, are calculated right into the plans and schedules for large construction jobs. True?"

"More or less." Sam glanced at the girl's jeans and dusty boots. "Rodeo riders figure their odds, too. And downhill ski racers."

"Not to mention race drivers," Evans said, "and stunt men, and when I was roughnecking years ago, the men who drove the nitro trucks. They collected their pay every day. And usually spent it that night."

Ellie looked from one to the other. Her smile broadened. "I am now supposed to say, 'Men!' in a tone of disgust. Well, I won't. It would just make you feel all the more *macho*."

"Ellie's favorite saddle horse is a gelding," Evans said. "That may be significant."

Despite the banter, there was deep affection between them, Sam thought, and was strangely pleased that it was so. They were two strong persons, each probably used to having his own way, and yet as adults they seemed to have adjusted amicably. Maybe Evans's accident had made a difference. Sam wondered how the commanding father and grown daughter might have gotten along before.

"Mr. Taylor—" Evans began.

"Sam is easier."

Evans merely nodded acknowledgment. "Sam is not going to remain on the bridge project," he said to Ellie. Then, to Sam, "Presumably Daryl Chambers will be in charge?"

"For the present, anyway."

"Oh?" Evans's eyebrows rose. "Does that imply some doubts about his capabilities?"

Sam considered the question, and weighed his answer. Evans, he thought, could be helpful to the bridge. The newspaperman had been positive about Evans's position as leader among the ranchers of the area, and now that he had met him, Sam had no doubt about it. And local public opinion was always important. But Evans had already made it plain that he liked information, and Sam had an idea that being less than frank with the man was a bad way to keep him happy. Perhaps a little more candor than Sam was used to was in order. But reluctance remained. "He's a competent engineer," Sam said, choosing evasion. "We know that. And he has the best construction superintendent I know to back him up."

"Wilder," Evans said, "Jud Wilder."

Evans had done his homework too, Sam thought, and merely nodded. "But nobody ever said the job was going to be easy, so I have—not doubts, but questions."

"A neat distinction." Evans wore his smile. He looked at Ellie. Silent communication seemed to flow between them. Evans looked again at Sam. "You will stay for dinner? We can talk further about the problems your man Chambers is going to face." He nodded then. "Good. Ellie, perhaps you'll tell María?"

8.

Massive Zabrinski drank bourbon shots with beer chasers that night in Josie's Place. They appeared to have little effect. Jud went along for a time, and then, deciding that he was competing out of his weight class, switched to bourbon-and-water highballs.

"Born out of my time," Zabrinski said unexpectedly. He held up the shot glass enveloped and almost hidden in his huge hand. "See this? Fellow told me once that it used to be in the Palace bar in San Francisco that they'd pour your shot right up to the top, and if your hand was big enough to go all the way around, you'd get a finger's width of booze above the top of the glass."

Jud could think of no appropriate comment. He said nothing.

"You ever been to Scotland?" Zabrinski said, switching the subject without warning.

Jud nodded.

"You see the Firth of Tay?"

The connection was immediately plain because wherever experienced bridgemen gathered, sooner or later this episode, and others, would come into the conversation as surely as Babe Ruth's batting average or the number of bases stolen by Maury Wills would be discussed whenever baseball buffs got together. Jud nodded again. He could have framed the question himself, but it was Zabrinski's show.

"December, eighteen seventy-nine," Zabrinski said. "You know what happened there then?"

"The railroad bridge collapsed," Jud said, "with the night mail train to Dundee. Drowned seventy-five people in the Firth." He gathered himself and studied Zabrinski's face carefully. "So?"

"Then up in Quebec," Zabrinski said, ignoring the question; "back in nineteen seven it was, nineteen thousand tons of steelwork collapsed while they were building the bridge. Eighty-two men were killed. You knew about that one?"

For the third time Jud nodded in silence. More was coming, that was for sure. Zabrinski had the bit in his teeth.

"Galloping Gertie up Tacoma way," Zabrinski said. "Beautiful suspension bridge only four months old. Nineteen forty that was. She began to oscillate in wind of far less force than she was designed to withstand. The roadway was thirty-nine feet wide." He held his hands apart to indicate width. "And at the height of the oscillations, one side of the roadway was twenty-eight feet above the other side." He rotated one massive palm to demonstrate. "The thing was damn near standing on edge when it finally collapsed."

"I've seen pictures."

"Then one night in December, nineteen fifty-one," Zabrinski said as if he had heard nothing, his own thoughts paramount, "in winds of only sixty-nine miles an hour, sixty-goddamn-nine miles per hour, no more than that, that great, big, marvelous Golden Gate Bridge out in San Francisco began to oscillate too. They had to close it to traffic. I've seen calculations, extrapolations. Another twenty five minutes of that wind, which was far, far less than she was designed for, and that bridge would have collapsed, too. Fact."

"You tend to look at the bright side of things, don't you?" Jud said. "That's what I like, an optimist."

Zabrinski grinned. He snapped his fingers with a sound like a whip crack. A waiter hurried over. "Drinks," Zabrinski said, waving his hand at the table and the empty glasses. The waiter hurried off. "Now," Zabrinski said, looking hard at Jud, "how many you figure to kill on this job? Even if you do get your safety nets?"

"Ask me six, eight months from now."

"How many? One? No, you'll kill more than that. Ten?"

"I don't make book."

Zabrinski leaned back in his chair and nodded solemnly. "You have a point. However many it is, it's too damned many, isn't it? So why do we do it? Do you ever wonder? Because on every project there's a big problem of some kind. Out in the Golden Gate, it was the tidal currents when they were trying to set their foundations. Up in Tacoma it was the design. Some places it's the depth of water; others it's the configuration of the land. Here we've got wind."

Jud sat silent, staring across the barroom at nothing. At the upright piano, Ewen McLean, peripatetic pianist and perpetual drunk, swung into "Ain't Misbehavin'" with a strong left hand that would have pleased Fats Waller. Smoke hung blue against the lights, and talk swirled, punctuated by laughter. The waiter arrived with the fresh drinks.

"We'll whip it," Jud said slowly. "You make sure the design is right, and we'll build it, wind or no wind, so it won't come apart. That I'll guarantee."

There was a compound of connected and semiconnected one-story adobe apartments behind Josie's Bar and Grill. Jud, accustomed to living in whatever surroundings he found himself, had taken one. He had some difficulty finding the lock with his key that night.

By his standards, he was not drunk. Drunk was when things went out of focus, when the floor tilted, when chairs deliberately stepped in front of you, and tabletops were not where they ought to be. Drunk was falling down, forgetting exactly where you were, disremembering the next morning just what it was in the first place that had started the fight that cleaned out the bar. Drunk was a lot of things, but it was not seeing matters with sudden, almost blinding clarity, as now.

Zabrinski was a good man. That was incontrovertible. Over the years, Jud had worked with, argued with, fought with, lived with hundreds, no, probably thousands of men. He had hired them and fired them and patted them on the head; kicked their asses, and on occasion busted a nose or two, listened to their troubles and their fears and their hopes, and even advised them like a goddamned head-shrinker or a holy man. And he had listened to bullshit too, from men who ought to have known better, engineers, architects, computer nursemaids, and he had not infrequently gone the way he thought was right, regardless.

In short, he knew men, and in his book, Zabrinski was a good man, a man to go along with; and you couldn't say higher than that.

And Zabrinski was—not scared; it would be hard to imagine Zabrinski scared. But Zabrinski was worried. That was the revelation tonight's drinks had disclosed.

Well, as far as that was concerned, he, himself, Jud Wilder, right from the beginning had felt about this job the way a dog sometimes seems to feel about something he can't see, or hear, or smell, but that nevertheless raises the short hairs on his shoulders and sets him to looking in all directions at once.

Sam Taylor had asked right out what Jud thought about the job, and when he heard the answer went on to ask if Jud wanted to quit. Why, hell, no! If man has pride in his work, then, by God, he goes on to finish what he's set his hand to.

Zabrinski would feel the same even though he too was worried, about exactly what, Jud could only guess.

And Sam Taylor was worried, or he wouldn't have bothered to come all this way out to the project. Maybe later, if trouble developed, but not right at the beginning. And, like Zabrinski, Sam was an educated man, trained in engineering mysteries, far-out mathematics, that kind of thing. Jud, for all his pride in his considerable abilities and accomplishments, still retained the respect tinged with awe of the working man on the job for those with the theoretical knowledge.

Well, hell, there was no point worrying about it further tonight. Tomorrow was another day, and he'd see what he thought about the whole thing come morning.

The moonlight was so bright that Sam could have done without headlights as he drove back out to the highway from the ranch house that night. Clumps of *piñon* and juniper cast black shadows on the uneven terrain, and contorted *cholla* seemed to writhe in a macabre dance to inaudible music. The scene was unreal, matching the sense of near-unreality Sam carried with him from the entire evening.

First, there had been that sunset episode.

"I like to watch the sunsets," Evans said. "Even when I was still a whole man, I tried to arrange it so I could sit on the west *portal* of an evening and see what the weather had concocted for our viewing pleasure. With our long, dusty vistas, we sometimes get coloring at sunset that would have delighted Maxfield Parrish. I never tire of it."

And so they sat on the west *portal* and watched lightning flash in a distant thunderhead, too far away to hear the thunder. And they talked. Ellie had disappeared.

"The temptation when you become crippled," Evans said, "is to become tyrannical as well. A sad commentary, but a fact. Your world has suddenly shrunk to the dimensions of your immediate surroundings, and you want to fit everything and everybody into that confined space, whether they want to be there or not." That faint, self-deprecating smile appeared almost in apology. "I don't want Ellie in San Francisco or Los Angeles or Houston or New York or even in Denver. I want her right here."

Was he being warned off, Sam wondered? If so, Evans was taking a lot for granted, whether he realized it or not. Sam's thoughts were on the bridge and its attendant problems, not on a girl he had just met. And besides, there was Liz. He said nothing.

Evans's mind jumped nimbly. "That thunderhead," he said. "This time of year they are common here. You will have winds from them. I assume you calculate wind loads?"

"We do."

"Just how exact is your science? Or is it still an art?"

"Why," Sam said, "up to a certain point we can predict what will, or will not, happen. We know the strength of our materials and the strength of the design. We have run exhaustive stress analyses by computer. We've taken into consideration certain factors having to do with aerodynamics and designed in safeguards to take care of them." He spread his hands and showed one of his rare smiles. "But when I've said that, I have to say too that beyond a certain point there are things we can't predict. Our knowledge doesn't cover the infinite."

"Bridges do collapse," Evans said.

"They have. They do. And they will." Sam's smile was gone. "But I don't intend that this bridge will be one of the casualties."

"How can you be sure?" This was Ellie, speaking suddenly, standing behind Sam's chair.

"I can't," Sam said over his shoulder, and stood up, turning.

She had changed to a dress. It was, Sam thought, nothing extra-special, but the mere fact of the switch from jeans and dusty boots seemed also to cause a switch of projected personality. All at once, there was an awareness between them which had not been so before, and it occurred to Sam to wonder if Evans had foreseen this.

"I've grown up," Ellie said, coming around and taking a chair between them, "between the mountains and the Tano Gorge. I know the mountains, and while I respect them, they don't frighten me. The Gorge is something else."

"We have lost cattle to it," Evans said. "A thunderstorm, a lightning strike, the beasts panic, four strands of barbed wire won't always stop them. You know, of course, that locally the Gorge is considered in a supernatural light? The dwelling place of hostile spirits?"

"I've heard the stories."

"It's widely believed too that from time to time malefactors who have unquestionably disappeared have actually been disposed of in the Gorge. Maybe they have. And their spirits join the others." Evans glanced at his wristwatch. "Another ten–twelve minutes." He looked at Sam. "Are you familiar with the 'green flash' phenomenon? No? Then perhaps Ellie will fix us another drink while I explain."

Ellie rose to collect the glasses. She seemed to avoid Sam's eyes. As she walked toward the bar tray, her rounded buttocks beneath the thin dress fabric moved with unconscious, or perhaps conscious, provocativeness, Sam thought, reminding him amusingly of a friend long ago watching the girls walking ahead of them, and saying, "Nice, but I'm a tit man myself." Expressionless, he looked at Evans and waited.

"The 'green flash,'" Evans said, "has other names too, 'living flash,' 'blue flash,' 'blue green flame,' 'green segment' and so on. It is only seen on a flat horizon at the precise moment of sunset, and it is a sudden brilliant green coloration of the upper limb of the sun. It's caused by abnormal conditions of refraction, and it lasts only a microsecond or so. I've spent a number of sunsets watching for it, and I've only seen it twice." He smiled suddenly. "Seeing it is supposed to bring good luck, specifically good fortune in love." His smile was suddenly saddened. "In my case, the good fortune came true, so I believe the legend."

"That's nonsense," Ellie said, "and you know it."

Evans shook his head, and the smile lost its sadness. "Leave me my harmless illusions."

Ellie passed the fresh drinks and sat down. She looked at Sam. "I meant that the legend is nonsense, not the flash. It, apparently, is real enough."

"You've seen it?"

"No."

Sam looked as if he were about to say something, changed his mind, and tasted his drink instead.

Evans, smiling still, said, "I believe, my dear, that you were about to be asked how you can know the legend is nonsense, since never having seen the flash, you haven't had a chance to test it." He waited for no answer. To Sam, he said, "I think of Ellie as a romantic realist. And if that sounds like a contradiction in terms, why, so is she." He went on as if Ellie were not present. "From time to time since she was a child, she has made me think of Teddy Roosevelt's remark about his daughter Alice. 'I can be President of the United States,' he said, 'or I can try to control Alice. But I cannot do both at once.' I have learned precisely how he felt." He glanced again at his watch and then at the sun already partially set. "Momentarily," he said. "And the conditions could be just right. Let's watch."

The sinking sun was cardinal red. In the foreground the mesa had taken on a uniform purple tinge dotted here and there with darker spots of vegetation. Above the sun, the sky remained clear, near the horizon faintly pink, then limitless light blue ranging upward to a deeper shade in which a single, tiny glint of moving light located a high-flying jet still in full sunlight. The sun disappeared slowly, and its brilliance appeared to contract like the fading image on a television screen. All three watched it carefully.

There seemed to be a pause as the upper limb of the sun disappeared, and then all at once the light contracted into a flaring spot of intense emerald green, gone in a moment, leaving only a sense of illusion. There was silence.

Ellie let her breath out slowly. Her smile and her voice were not quite steady as she looked from one man to the other. "Did I really see it?"

"I think we did," Sam said. He too seemed subdued.

Evans was smiling happily. "That makes three times for me," he said. "And now, honey, you'll have a chance to find out for yourself whether the legend is nonsense." He looked up as a maid appeared in the doorway. "Dinner?" Evans said. "Five minutes or so, María, while we finish our drinks." He watched the girl smile, nod, and turn away. "And compose ourselves," Evans added, and looked again at Ellie, smiling.

That episode of the green flash was the initial step into unreality. The balance of the evening followed the pattern it had set.

For one thing, the setting of the ranch itself was a feudal holding not only in size, but also in self-sufficiency. "We generate most of what we need in the way of electricity," Evans said, "some of it by wind, the rest by diesel power. We have wells spotted here and there, with windmills and stock tanks filled even in times of drought. We have irrigated fields where we grow our own fodder. And around the ranch buildings here, we have our gardens where we grow our own vegetables."

"Beans," Ellie said, "peas, chiles, corn, squashes, tomatoes, lettuce, broccoli, onions, garlic, potatoes—" She smiled across the table. "All we need. Plus beef from our own herd, hogs we raise, poultry and eggs, milk. We even have some sheep and a few goats. Henry is by way of being a gadget man, an experimenter, and I will admit that most of his experiments turn out pretty well."

They each spoke uninhibitedly, Sam thought, as if the other were not present. Odd.

"Most, perhaps," Evans said, "but not all." He showed that faint, wry smile. "The eucalyptus saplings I had brought in from California, for example. They lasted until the first winter storm." The smile turned to a frown. "Strange, too, because I had been led to believe that species of eucalyptus grow in the *altiplano* of Bolivia and southern Peru."

From horticulture to animal husbandry to meteorology, the table conversation zigged and zagged.

"We keep charts, of course," Evans explained at one point. "There are ranchers who crossbreed by introducing a blooded bull and letting nature take its course out on the range. We have selected stock which we control carefully, and with them we have turned almost entirely to artificial insemination."

Ellie said, "I doubt if the animals prefer it. The old-fashioned way is more fun."

"My daughter," Evans said, "has a somewhat bawdy sense of humor."

"Which I come by honestly." Ellie looked across the table at Sam. "If you were a bull—"

"I know where my preference would lie," Sam said, and felt again that sense of awareness between them, subtle, but unmistakable. He switched the subject. "You mentioned weather," he said to Evans, "that first winter storm. I'm interested in that."

Ellie watched him with a strange new intensity. "You are an attractive man," her attitude seemed to say. "I am a not unattractive woman, and I expect to be noticed carefully. I want you to watch me and listen when I speak, to study me when you think I don't realize it, and to understand that I will stoop to none of the cheap and obvious tricks women sometimes use to make themselves felt. I don't need them."

Perfectly true; she did not need tricks. She exuded health and animal attractiveness, and, merely by *being*, projected into Sam's mind thoughts he trusted did not show too plainly. Or maybe they did, because from time to time he caught Ellie looking at him with a secret smile touching her lips.

Evans, Sam was sure, was quite aware of the subtle by-play, but his only reaction seemed to be mild and quiet amusement, and this increased the sense of make-believe. Evans also talked about himself, something Sam would not have expected.

"I quit college after my junior year," Evans said. "I would probably just have gone on scholastic probation one more time if I'd returned for my senior year. Certainly I would not have graduated. A number of my friends were headed for Europe that summer on bicycle or walking tours. I went the other way, out to the oil fields. Why?" He shrugged. "Maybe because it was something nobody else was doing. I roughnecked that summer, and in the fall just didn't go back. Keats and Shelley were all very well, but they couldn't hold a candle to watching a gusher blow in, and knowing that what was raining down on you was liquid gold, and that a few thousand barrels of it were yours."

And Sam compounded the sense of unreality by talking about himself, something he never did. Even as he talked, he wondered why, and found no answer.

"I chose construction," he said. "I liked to build things. I still do." He smiled at himself. "They're there. You can see them and touch them and they'll be around after you're gone. I don't mean as monuments or anything like that. But they're real, tangible, and most things aren't."

"I think I like that," Ellie said, and drew an amused smile from her father. "Well, isn't that what the whole thing is about? We pass ourselves along in things, or in children, or in knowledge and political systems that work?" She had turned and now spoke directly to Sam.

"I suppose. I hadn't thought of it that way."

"At a guess," Evans said, "you're from somewhere in California? Originally, I mean?"

"Close enough." Astonishingly, details came out with no effort. "California-Nevada country, east of the big mountains. A postage stamp ranch, a few horses and a few head of scrub cattle, some pigs, a vegetable garden and a well, a school bus that took me twenty miles when it didn't break down, some books. Quite a few books."

Ellie was watching him with that new intensity, her expression open, not yet yielding judgment. But that secret smile was there. She said nothing.

Evans said, "A number of people came west for their health. Back then, for example, there were various ideas about how to cure tuberculosis. Most of them had to do with sunlight and clean air."

"Sunlight and clean air we had," Sam said, and then, to his surprise, found words he had never spoken aloud before clamorously demanding release. Well, why the hell not? He had come a long way from that raggedy-assed homestead ranch, far enough for people to have to judge him by what he was, rather than what lay behind him. No? Yes. "But tuberculosis had nothing to do with us. Our problem was quite a bit different."

Nothing showed in Evans's face, but Sam had an idea that he had hoped, even expected, that his apparently innocuous statement would flush an answer.

Ellie watched Sam in silence.

"My father was a drunk," Sam said. "Back East, wherever it was he came from, they probably called him an alcoholic. At any rate, they sent him regularly enough money for us to live on, to stay out of sight, and out of mind." He even found that he could produce one of his rare smiles. "Not even sunlight and clean air could fix him up. But I will say that his liver put up a good, long fight."

Ellie said, "Your mother?"

"I never knew her. She stayed wherever we came from when I was just a pup."

Evans said, "How old were you when your father died?"

"Sixteen, and I could pass for eighteen or maybe twenty. I was never refused a drink in a bar. And nobody cared anyway."

A wrong reaction from Ellie right then could have ended all interest he might have had in her. Expressed compassion for the sixteen-year-old boy would have finished it. Even the faintest air of you-did-have-it-rough-didn't-you? would have been enough.

Instead, the secret smile still hovering, "I have an idea," Ellie said gently, "that that was exactly the way you liked it, too."

Evans glanced from one to the other, and he too was smiling. "Sixteen is a good age for some men," he said. "For others it is all prep school and girls and team sports." He shrugged. "Who is to choose?"

That was all there was to it, Sam told himself now driving in the moonlight, and yet a turning point had been reached, and his relations with both Evanses, father and daughter, would never be quite the same again.

9.

Sam came into the headquarters trailer early the next morning. He nodded to Zabrinski, Yorke the architect, and Miller the computer specialist, all of whom he had met the day before, and walked into Daryl Chambers's small office.

As he turned the straight visitor's chair around to straddle it, he came straight to the point. "We're not hiring *chicanos* or Indians. Why?"

Chambers felt under attack, and resented it. "Anglos—that's what they call them here—are more dependable."

"Jud tell you that?"

"I didn't ask him. No reason I should. It was my decision. There are underlying ethnic hostilities here, and the last thing we want is that kind of friction on the job. We—"

"You let Jud worry about that. He'll knock heads together if he has to, and he'll toss troublemakers off the job faster than you can blink." Sam watched resistance forming in Chambers's face. "Go ahead, say it." He sat relaxed, waiting, his arms folded on the chair back.

"I'm in charge here," Chambers said. He was trying to keep his anger under control.

"True."

"I make the decisions."

"Also true—to a point." Sam did not raise his voice. "But when policy is involved, you can, and sometimes will, be overruled. We hire local labor, period, and we don't discriminate."

Chambers took a deep breath. "It was my judgment—"

"And now," Sam said, "you've just changed your mind, haven't you? After thinking about it, and realizing that ninety percent of the local population is either *chicano* or Indian, and knowing too that you don't build as important a thing as a bridge in a vacuum, and that getting along with the local people is very important—after thinking about all that, you've decided to change your mind. Isn't that how it is?"

The man, Chambers realized suddenly, hadn't even bothered to raise his voice. It might have been easier to take if he had. Instead, sitting there calmly, as sure of himself as a judge on his bench, he had simply laid down the law, and that was that. Well, maybe it wasn't quite that . . .

"I asked a question," Sam said in the same, quiet tone. "I'd like an answer. You have changed your mind, haven't you?" The message was plain: we decide this one here and now.

Resistance faded. Maybe, Chambers thought desperately, at some other time he would make his stand. Maybe. He let his breath out slowly. "I guess so," he said.

"Fine." Sam stood up. "I'll tell Jud. And then I'll see the local boss man, name of Trujillo, and tell him it was all just a misunderstanding." He stood for a moment looking down at Chambers, realizing exactly what the man felt. Well, it couldn't be helped. "Okay?"

"Why ask—?" Chambers began angrily, and then stopped as resistance faded once more. Slowly he nodded. "Okay," he said, and watched Sam duck through the doorway.

Jud was in his shack, on the telephone, when Sam walked in and sat down. The nude on the wall made him think again of last night. The model was a large girl, and shapely, with full, high breasts, a curving waist, and solid hips. She stood with her hands on her hips, and one knee slightly bent to show the smooth, graceful curves of thigh and calf.

It could have been Ellie Evans, Sam thought with pleasurable, mild lasciviousness, wearing her faint, secret smile that here, in naked intimacy, seemed to say, "Hey! Look me over!"

"For about a buck-fifty," Jud said as he hung up the phone, "you can buy a magazine full of pictures like that."

Sam smiled and lowered his eyes from the picture. "I prefer the real thing. Of course, at your age—"

"Screw my age," Jud said, leaned back in his chair, took off his hard hat, glared at it, and jammed it back on his head again. He scowled across the desk. "What've we got ourselves into, anyway?"

"Spell that one out."

Jud sat up straight. "Last night, Zabrinski, he's the big one, the stress engineer—" He watched Sam nod. "Okay. We hoisted a few together, and . . ." He went through the conversation as best he could remember it.

Sam thought about it. "Did he give reasons?"

"He talked about wind. But, goddamn it, there's always wind. And he's a good man, Sam."

Outside there was the sudden *whuuump!* of another dynamite blast. The walls of the shack rattled in protest. The heavy sound died slowly, and the lighter sounds of truck engines and compressors and pneumatic drills resumed. "All right," Sam said, "I'll have a talk with him, see if I can find out what's on his mind. Now, about hiring. You're going to get some *chicanos* and Indians. Chambers changed his mind . . ."

Jud listened, shrugged, and waited until Sam was finished with his explanation. "All one to me." Then he tilted back in his chair again and studied Sam as he would study a man across a poker table. "Are you taking over?"

It was the same question Evans had asked. "No."

"I've never seen you move in like this before, and then walk away."

Sam shrugged.

Jud was not through. "You mentioned Ross. Does he know you're here, shaping things up?" He raised one hand, palm out, to forestall protest. The last two joints of the middle finger were missing. The deformity lent force to the gesture. "Now don't climb on your high horse with me, goddamn it," Jud said. "We didn't meet yesterday. Or the day before. Ross doesn't know, does he? And that means that when he finds out, you and he are going to lock horns, and paw the ground . . ." He shook his head and sighed. "You've always been a good soldier, Sam, so you'll have your reasons." His voice was resigned.

Sam stood up, expressionless. "I'll see about your safety nets. I agree you need them."

Evans, alone in the office-library, was again on the phone to the governor. "So we've settled the hiring policy, Floyd. Sam Taylor will follow through. He's that kind."

"I do appreciate this, Henry."

"I'll put it on your account. Now, there is another matter, and its name is Joe Trujillo. He very carefully did not say that he was thinking about sabotage, but he was at pains to make me understand that he is. And I think you know that they do play rough up here sometimes."

The governor with an effort put all thoughts of shapely Alice Perkins and her astonishing proclivities out of his mind, at least for the moment. "Well, now, just what do you suggest? State Police?"

"With a brass band?"

"We don't run much to cloak-and-dagger, Henry. Mostly we just ride fence, sometimes carrying a .30-30. They have guards on the bridge property?"

"It is my understanding, yes."

"Local folks?"

"I would assume so. Anglos, certainly, as of now."

"How about suggesting to your friend Taylor that they see can they get one or two from the pueblo?"

There were those, Evans thought, who, looking at Floyd Babcock, saw only the folksy cowboy, devoid of either subtlety or guile. And there were spots in the state that were strewn with the political bones of those who had held that view. Although he rarely exposed them, the governor had his depths. "A sound idea, Floyd," Evans said. "I'll broach it."

"*In*-surance, *and* protection, you might say," the governor said. "Far as I know, Joe lacks the kind of influence in the pueblo he's got in Tano County generally, so I doubt Indian guards would just do what he said. And if I walked around in Joe's shoes, I'd surely think, not twice, but five or six times before I'd let anybody else do anything that might get the Indians skinned up, either. You say Taylor is coming down here?"

"That's what he told me."

"I'll look forward to making his acquaintance."

It was a small adobe building down an alley from the Plaza, facing a dusty parking lot. The flaked gold lettering on the window read: J. M. Trujillo, Real Estate, Insurance, Notary Public. Parked in front was a huge, dusty, late model Cadillac. Its rear license plate read JOE T.

A neat blend, Sam thought, of deliberate unostentation and demonstrated affluence. His opinion of Trujillo rose.

The girl at the desk inside was *chicana*, with teased black hair piled high, vivid red fingernails and a large, soft bosom. She was chewing gum. "I'll see if he's in, okay?" Her voice was Spanish-lilted. She waggled her bottom as she flounced into the rear office. In a moment, she was back. "He'll be right out, okay?" Her interest in Sam was ended.

Trujillo himself, Sam thought, was no more prepossessing than his office. He was middle height, gone slightly to fat, with sleek black hair gray at the temples and overlong sideburns, and brown, sleepy-looking eyes. "Joe Trujillo," he said. "What can I do for you?"

"Talk a little."

"Sure. Come on in." He led the way into a smaller office, sat down behind the desk, put his foot up on the opened bottom drawer, and waited in silence.

Sam took one of the straight chairs. "I'm from Ross Associates, the bridge people."

"I know. Sam Taylor. You flew here in what they call an executive jet. It's still sitting at the airport. Somebody told you to see me?"

"It seemed like a good idea."

"Why?"

"A little misunderstanding." Sam said it easily. "We plan to hire some local people. After all, it is a community project."

"That's crap, of course. Who twisted your arm?"

"My arm," Sam said, "doesn't twist very well."

A big, hard anglo, Trujillo thought, and showed white teeth in a broad smile. "You know, I think I believe you."

"Our policy has always been to hire local people for the jobs they can handle."

"You call them punks." There was open resentment in the last word.

"That's right. On some kinds of construction jobs they're called grunts. And bridgemen in general are called boomers. So?"

There was silence. "So, okay," Trujillo said at last, and showed again the broad smile. "You want me to hire men for you?"

"We'll do the hiring. But maybe you'd like to send ten–fifteen men you can recommend? Anglos, Indians, *chicanos*, blacks, *es igual*, as long as they're good men."

"You really think you can build that bridge?"

"If we weren't sure of it, we'd never have bid the job." Sam stood up. From the advantage of his height he looked down at Trujillo, who did not move. "You'll send men?"

Trujillo thought about it. His eyes never left Sam's face, and at last he nodded. "Okay. Tomorrow morning."

Sam walked out to the rented car, glancing at Trujillo's Cadillac with the special license plate as he passed. The status symbol to impress, he thought; and the shabby office that would intimidate nobody, the door that was always open, the man always willing to listen. It was no wonder that probably without even asking or trying to find out, Trujillo already knew about Sam, and the Ross Associates jet, and probably exactly where Sam fitted into the picture. Information would flow to him from all local directions as tributary water flows into a lake. Something to remember.

There was a telephone booth at one corner of the plaza. Sam placed a credit card call, person-to-person, "To the governor," he told the operator. "I imagine he's in his office." He gave his name, and added that he represented Ross Associates. It was not a long wait.

"This is Floyd Babcock," the voice said in a southwestern twang, "and I been looking forward to hearing from you. Where are you?"

"In Tano."

"You fixing to come down this way? Maybe driving?"

"If I can see you."

"I tell you what," the governor said. "There's a little town called Chimayo. You'll find it on the map about twenty-five miles north of here, north and east a bit. There's a restaurant, a good one—you like chile cooking?"

"Absolutely."

"I'll meet you there," the governor said. "We can sample a margarita, eat maybe the best enchiladas in these parts or any other, and talk. You've already helped me out whether you know it or not, so I figure I owe you a lunch."

Sam was smiling as he walked back to the rented car. A variant, he thought, on the western tradition of " 'Light and set a spell, stranger. We're just fixing to eat." He was still smiling inwardly when he reached the bridge site, parked the car, and went in to see Zabrinski.

If, as Jud said, they had hoisted a few last night, there were no signs of it visible in Zabrinski. The big man's bright, blue eyes were clear, and his huge hands, gesturing or pointing, moved smoothly with the controlled, steady caution you sometimes saw in men afraid of their own strength. "A little thinking," Zabrinski said in answer to Sam's question, "a few phone calls to guys I know, and a little more thinking—" He shrugged his massive shoulders.

Quincy Yorke, the architect; small, dapper, immaculately dressed in a Paisley sport shirt, tailored chino trousers and Clark desert boots, made a small, deprecating gesture with one hand. "A clear and present case of the fantods," he said. "Our large colleague is seeing shadows."

Frank Miller, the computer specialist, watched, listened, and said nothing.

Zabrinski seemed merely amused by Yorke. He said, "You haven't ridden that tramcar yet, small one. It sets you to thinking about quite a few things." He looked at Sam. "We're rigging a third cable to keep it from oscillating quite so badly."

"Oscillations," Sam said, and was silent, wondering if any of them would make the connection. Zabrinski did immediately.

"Exactly," he said. "Galloping Gertie up in Tacoma came right to mind."

"There is no parallel," Quincy Yorke said flatly. "The Tacoma bridge roadway was far too narrow for the length of span, and the roadway stiffening was far too shallow. In addition, what roadway stiffening they had was continuous plate girder, a solid steel wall which simply invited bad wind current eddies. We have made none of those mistakes."

Zabrinski patted Yorke very gently on the shoulder as one might pat a mascot. "He's right, you know," he said to Sam. "We're using an openwork truss support so wind can blow right through it, instead of the solid steel wall of a continuous plate which, as the little man says, almost guarantees bad wind current eddies. And we've divided the east-and-west highway roadways to relieve vertical wind pressures. Our roadway-to-span ratio is well inside the ballpark, and the depth of our stiffening is just what the standards call for." He shrugged massively.

"Still you're worried," Sam said. An uneasy feeling was building in his mind. "As Steinmann was, after he heard about Tacoma. So he altered the designs of both the Mackinac Straits bridge and the Bronx-Whitestone."

"He increased the depth of the roadway stiffening," Quincy Yorke said, "more than doubled it. But we already have ample stiffening, more than ample."

"He did something else too," Zabrinski said. "He ran cable-stays from the towers to the roadway for added stiffening." He was looking at Sam. "You're thinking about that?"

The big man was bright, and sharp, Sam thought. A good man, as Jud had said, a man to have around. "It might bear looking into," he said. "By how much would cable-stays increase resistance to wind-caused oscillations?"

From the doorway to his small office Daryl Chambers said, "And by how much would they increase the cost?"

It was a sound question, and Sam acknowledged it with a nod. "Probably by quite a bit," he said. "But that's my problem." He was getting deeper and deeper, he thought, into a job they ought not to have taken on in the first place. There was already going to be hell to pay when he got back to San Francisco simply because he had disobeyed the old man's orders. In Ross Associates you didn't do that with impunity. Now, when he proposed expensive safety nets and even possible design changes on a job he had been told to stay away from, there was no telling what Ross would do. Well, that was how it was. You called them as you saw them. There was no other way. He looked at his watch. "I've got a lunch date with the governor. Down the road at a place called Chimayo." He looked around at them all. "Anybody know where it is?"

There was a long black limousine with State license Number One already in front of the restaurant when Sam arrived. The bearded proprietor with old world courtliness showed Sam out to the terrace where the governor stood up to welcome him, a man as big as Sam, with a broad, friendly face, wearing a dark suit, white shirt, narrow tie and polished black boots. A Fort Worth Stetson rested on one of the extra chairs. The governor's grip was firm, and his hand was hard.

"Sorry if I'm late," Sam said.

"I just got here myself," the governor said. "A phone call caught me as I was walking out the door. Lady named Laura. Anxious to talk to you. You go right ahead and call her. I'll order up those margaritas."

The telephone connection was not good, but the message was clear. Laura said, "My orders are to get you back here, Sam, if I have to swear out a complaint and have you arrested for stealing a company aircraft."

In a way it was almost amusing, in another it was anything but. "That bad?" Sam said.

"He is almost apoplectic, Sam. I mean it. And at his age—"

"That's the trouble."

"I know. Believe me, I know, I understand. But that doesn't alter things."

"He's still the boss." Sam nodded. And Ross would continue to be, right up to the end. "All right, Laura. I'm having lunch with the governor—"

"Daryl Chambers told me."

"Tell Ross I'm heading back right after lunch. I'll be in the office first thing in the morning. With a full report."

The governor had the two drinks poured and waiting. He raised his own, sniffed it, and nodded to Sam over the rim before he sipped. He set the glass down. "Trouble?"

"A little mix-up," Sam said. "I'll see about it tomorrow." His tone dismissed the matter. "I've seen Trujillo."

"Joe? Good. Henry said you would be."

"He's sending men out tomorrow. That was a foolish mistake."

"Well, now," the governor said, "they happen. Lucky you were here right on the spot to set it right." His eyes watched Sam steadily. "Matter of fact," he said, "I've been kind of wondering just what did bring you here. Way I hear it, you only go where you're needed bad, like Red Adair goes wherever there's a fire. Or trouble."

"Exaggeration."

"Is it?" The governor concentrated on twirling his glass by its stem for a few moments in silence. He looked up at last. "Well,

I'll tell you. I've got a big bet out on the board. That bridge you're going to build means quite a bit to me, and I would surely hate to think that anything was going to get in the way of building it, and building it right." He was silent, his eyes again steady on Sam's face.

"All construction jobs have problems," Sam said.

"But some have more problems than others?"

"Of course."

"Well, now," the governor said, "I do believe that you and I could spend the rest of the afternoon walking around this bridge matter like two strange dogs around a bone neither one of them dares to reach out and grab. That's maybe good poker tactics, but it sure don't tell me the hell of a lot. You've got problems up there at the Tano Gorge?"

"We've got problems. As I said—"

"Big problems?"

"We don't know yet. That's the best I can do."

The governor was silent for a little time, still watching Sam's face as if probing for the thoughts behind it. He nodded at last. "That's good enough for now," he said, and waved his hand at the waiter. "My friend and I will have two more of these," he said, "and then we'll order."

They walked together out to the parking area, and a large, solid man appeared immediately to open the car door for the governor. "This here's Pepe," the governor said, "sergeant State Police. He wet nurses me. Sam Taylor."

They shook hands. Pepe's grip was that of a heavyweight wrestler. He said nothing.

"While we been eating and talking," the governor said, "I been thinking." He smiled, suddenly. "Some folks think faster than I do. I like to take my time. I figure you and I can get along pretty good. You need help, you let me know, hear?"

"I hear," Sam too was smiling. "But as I told you, I won't be on the job."

"No matter. Your man here runs into trouble, you'll hear about it."

I hope so, Sam thought, and merely nodded acknowledgment.

"And there are telephones," the governor said. He seemed then to come to a sudden decision. "You might check with Henry Evans again. Tell him I said to. He'll know what it's about." He bent to get into the rear seat of the car, and when he was settled looked out at Sam again. "Makes me feel like an ambassador to the UN," he said. "I'd much rather be on a horse. All right, Pepe, let's head on back to the jute mill."

10.

In places, severe turbulence to an altitude of fifty-two thousand feet, the Weather Service report said, and Sam, sitting in the copilot's seat and looking around at scattered thunderheads, could believe it. Each one was a potential factory of destruction. "We'll give them all a wide berth," he told the company pilot. "I have a lot of respect for them."

"Me, too." They were the only words the pilot had spoken since takeoff. He had never had any hassle with this Sam Taylor, and that was just the way he liked it. He made it a policy to tread warily when they were together.

Sam studied a single thunderhead, its anvil high above them. From this distance, it looked innocuous enough, even fluffy and clean as if freshly laundered. But within it, he knew, updrafts and downdrafts were building, ice particles were forming, torrents of heat were being released as rising air cooled, and electrical charges of unbelievable power were accumulating toward the moments when lightning would flicker and flash and rolling peals of thunder would fill the air.

Within that complicated atmospheric structure too, conflicting winds of gale force and more were being generated, winds which could tear apart unwary light aircraft, or even, given the exact concatenation of circumstances, throw their power groundward, spawning tornadoes which, freed from the parent cell, would feed upon their own fury.

"If we catch a big one head-on," Zabrinski had said, speaking again of tornadoes, "I'd say that all bets are off. And I'll admit too that I'd feel the hell of a lot better if we beefed up our design as much as we can, just in case."

Daryl Chambers watched Sam and said nothing.

Quincy Yorke said, "Those shadows again."

Frank Miller, as usual, was silent.

"All right," Sam said, "I'll be in touch."

Whether he would or not was perhaps a question. He had talked again on the phone with Laura, unwilling accomplice, and her news had been far from encouraging. "Unless he changes his mind, Sam," she said in a tone Sam had not heard her use before, a mixture of sadness and near-incredulity, "I don't think he is even going to see you. He told me to send you back to the Alaska job and tell you to stay there. He takes your—what he calls interference—as a personal affront."

"We're in trouble, Laura. I have to see him. You'll have to arrange it."

"Sam. Sam."

"It's important. I think we may have walked into a minefield."

"You might have handled it a little more tactfully."

"Tact isn't exactly my strong point."

"Agreed." This was the Laura Sam had always known, smiling, gentle, but firm, and always willing to speak out. "But it wouldn't do a bit of harm to try to cultivate it. I'll try, Sam. That's all I can do."

"I'll call you as soon as we land."

Nor had Sam's phone conversation with Henry Evans helped. "The governor suggested I call you," Sam said. "He said you would know what it was about."

"Floyd is cryptic sometimes," Evans said, "but I can guess that he has Joe Trujillo in mind." He explained.

"I told him it was a misunderstanding," Sam said, "and he's sending men out in the morning."

"That may help to defuse the situation, but I think the causes run deeper."

"Damn it," Sam said, "if he wants trouble—"

"If Joe really wants trouble," Evans said in that calm, controlled way, "then you are an isolated outpost deep in enemy territory, and your situation is not enviable."

Sam looked at the massive thunderhead. It had changed in shape and taken on a grayish cast but it still looked innocuous. Apparently, to the pilot it seemed the same. "I've never flown through one of those," the pilot said unexpectedly, "but I used to think I'd give it a try one day." He shook his head. "No more. No way."

Sam looked at the pilot and waited in silence.

"I saw a film," the pilot said, "time-lapse frames of a thunderhead taken from inside. You know what I mean? Inside, that thing is boiling, churning, like heavy surf hitting undertow. It may look harmless enough on the outside, but, brother, I don't want anything to do with what's going on inside."

Like our bridge project, Sam thought. It was a rough analogy, but somehow apt. And uncomfortable to contemplate.

They swung in for their approach over the bright splendor of San Francisco Bay, with a clear view of the city rising white and clear on its storied hills: Nob, Telegraph, Russian; beyond, the immense red structure of the Golden Gate Bridge sharp against the green of the Marin shore; and in the foreground, the Bay bridge which was not a single bridge at all, but a whole series—truss, cantilever, two suspensions, post-and-beam causeway—all tied together by a tunnel, eight miles and a bit in all, across the blue water. Ships crept here and there, leaving behind white streaks, like the tracks of snails, to mark their passage.

Since leaving the thunderhead area, Sam and the pilot had not spoken. To Sam, the silence was normal, natural and unforced, producing no feeling of awkwardness. His thoughts were on Ross and the problems of the bridge now twelve hundred miles behind them, and although he was conscious of the pilot's presence in the seat next to his, and aware of the pilot's occasional adjustments of throttle, boost, or trim tabs, he felt no compulsion to search for something to say merely in order to appear companionable.

"You are locked into yourself, Sam," Laura had said once, "and some day you are going to have to break out and meet people on terms that are not just your own."

Sam had been vaguely amused. "A popularity contest?"

"No. You'll never win that. What I am talking about is acknowledgment that other people exist."

The pilot would have known what Laura meant. It was damned uncomfortable to share a cockpit for a matter of hours with someone who wasn't there. The pilot was normally a gregarious man, at ease in conversation. But over the last eight hundred miles of sometimes spectacular country, towering mountains still bearing snow, awesome canyons carved into solid rock, a mighty river, and a vast man-made lake, desert, now mountains again and a view of the sea, the pilot had searched for, found, and instantly discarded a dozen conversational gambits that shriveled in the somehow desiccated silence.

The pilot raised the tower on the radio and spoke the few ritual words with the controller. He looked again at Sam, and at last found something to say. "We're cleared for landing," he said. "Want to take her in yourself?"

Sam came out of his thoughts briefly. "No. Take her up close to the hangar. I need a phone." He went back into silence.

They had three choices, he had decided, none of them attractive. But the question was whether Ross would even listen to the logic that underlay them.

They could carry on the project as planned—in Sam's view, badly planned. With Jud driving hard, or as hard as Jud would drive with an eye to safety, they might even come close to meeting schedule. *If* everything went well, that was, which was a very large *if*. *If* accidents, wind-caused or otherwise, were not abnormally high; *if* there was no trouble with deliveries of steel, forgings, wire, cable, cement, and all of the other thousand and one things that would go into the making of the finished product; *if* there was no trouble from Joe Trujillo or anyone else; and *if* nothing serious turned up in the inevitable snafus of design that only came to light during actual construction.

And so they would have a bridge, as ordered, as beautiful in reality as it now was on paper. As the Tacoma bridge was beautiful for the four months it lasted. And, if Zabrinski was to be believed, and Sam agreed with Jud that he was a man to believe, it could be every bit as vulnerable as the Tacoma bridge had been.

That was the first choice.

The second choice was to beef up the design, probably by adding cable-stays to the roadway, thereby adding extra work and materiel which would cause schedule delays and inevitably increase cost. Even without considering other factors, such as safety nets, this second choice would quite possibly end showing a big, fat loss, rather than the profit projected from present plans.

The third choice was to renege on the job, pay contract penalties, and admit that Ross Associates had, as he had suggested to Laura, blundered into a minefield and wanted above all else to get out with as little damage as possible.

In other words, that third choice was to admit defeat, failure. And, logical, prudent, sensible or not, Sam could just imagine how Wilt Ross would feel about that.

In the gathering silence after the pilot switched off the engines, Sam unbuckled his seat harness and stood up, bending to clear the overhead. "Thanks for the ride." He made his way aft, plucked travel bag and briefcase from the locker, and went down the cabin steps, merely nodding to the ground attendant as he passed. Now for Laura, and whatever her message might be.

She was waiting for the call. That was obvious from her immediate response to the operator's ring. Sam could picture her, poised and efficient at her desk, prepared to pass along whatever dictum Ross had issued, loyal to the core as she had been for all these years. "Sam?" Her voice was almost a plea. "Is it Sam?"

"Sam. Right here, Laura." There was no time even for a question to form in his mind.

"Oh, thank God!" Then, in a different tone. "Give me a moment, Sam."

He waited, silent, suspending thought. Out on the field, a propellor aircraft revved up its engine to rated power for takeoff. The sound seemed to come from a different world.

"All right, Sam. I'm under control again. He's—in the hospital. Intensive care. It was a stroke." The voice fell silent again.

Sam waited.

"You heard me, Sam?"

"I heard."

"I found him. At his desk. I thought he was—dead!"

"Easy," Sam said. "Easy, Laura."

"Yes. Sorry. I called an ambulance. They came quickly. They lifted him out of his chair and put him on a stretcher. There was a note on the desk. It had been under him. His writing, but barely legible." Again the voice stopped.

"Go on, Laura. The note."

"To you."

It would be, and Sam thought he could guess what it said. He waited in silence.

"All it said was, 'Sam. You're fired.'" The deep, unsteady breath Laura drew was clearly audible on the phone. "I . . . tore it up, Sam!"

PART II

11.

Bowlegged Inocencio, half centaur, already had the big buckskin curried, brushed, and wearing horsehair pad, Indian blanket and Ellie's roping saddle, with her .30-30 carbine in its scabbard beneath the off stirrup leather and her coiled rope lashed in place on the near side. He slipped on the bridle as he saw Ellie coming down from the house, freed the halter and led the big horse to the corral gate.

Ellie spoke in Spanish. "There is no need for you to wait on me, Inocencio."

"A pleasure, señorita."

It was hard not to smile. "I can remember when you called me *chica,* and slapped my rump because I brought my horse in lathered up and did not rub him down immediately."

A shrug. "That was then." He handed Ellie the reins. "He needs exercise." He glanced down with approval at the spurs Ellie had strapped on, and watched, also with approval, as she gathered the reins, hopped for the stirrup as he had taught her long ago, and, using the horn as lever, swung herself into the saddle in a single easy motion.

His hand resting lightly on the horse's withers, "You ride where?" Inocencio said.

Always destination stated, Ellie thought, for the same reason that one filed a flight plan, so they would know where to start looking if you failed to return when expected. Well, in this limitless country it made sense. "The bridge." She was conscious of the rifle beneath her thigh. Another precaution. She smiled down at Inocencio, and took the buckskin out through the corral gate at his easy trot that ate up the miles.

She could not remember when she was first on a horse, with Inocencio as her guide and teacher. But even after all these years, the feeling of *freedom* still remained, along with that other sensation she supposed was vaguely and darkly sexual, that of being astride a male beast more powerful than herself, controlling it to her will. As, she had read somewhere, ancient priestesses had been wont to do with male followers of their choice. Ancient hanky-panky.

The buckskin leaned against the bit, anxious for a run. "All right," Ellie said, "let's do it." She loosened the reins, leaned forward in the saddle and touched the big horse lightly on the flanks with her spurred heels. Cutting horse trained, in two long strides he was at full pace, and, range-wise, picking his own way through clumps of sage, around writhing *cholla*, up a small rise and over a narrow dry wash in a single leap.

They flushed a jackrabbit from a clump of brush, and Ellie smiled as she watched the animal transform itself magically from an angular, awkward, ungainly caricature with enormous ears, into smooth, flowing poetry in motion, ears laid back, belly to the ground, shifting, dodging, maintaining a speed few animals could match, as much at home in this harsh environment as a trout in a stream. He blended into the landscape and disappeared.

The buckskin was still running easily when Ellie reined him down to a walk. Leaning forward in the saddle, she patted the strong neck. The horse tossed his head against the bit, but she held him firm. "Enough," she said. "We've a ways to go." She relaxed the reins a little, and the gelding lifted immediately into his easy trot. She turned her thoughts to the bridge.

It was how long now since the day of that first dynamite blast that marked the actual beginning of construction? Two months? Three? Life on the ranch was not marked by large events, and time seemed to flow past almost unnoticed.

So far, the construction had not impinged on her life or even her consciousness to anywhere near the extent Henry had predicted. The blasting had stopped, and only yesterday, over on the rim of the Gorge, she had noticed that the golden eagles were back in their eyrie, and that two almost naked, shapeless chicks had already hatched.

From time to time, when the wind was right, they could hear the clatter of rivet guns even at the ranch house, but the sounds were faint, almost illusory, and since nothing could be seen of the rising towers, it was easy enough to dismiss the entire matter with a shrug.

Henry, with access to information sources available to the very rich, something Ellie took for granted, had told her that Wilt Ross had suffered a stroke, was incapacitated, for how long nobody knew or would even predict, and that Sam Taylor in San Francisco was in command.

From her own information sources, not available to Henry, Ellie knew that on two occasions these last weeks Sam had visited the bridge project, flying in to the Tano airport in the shiny Ross Associates executive jet, and staying on the scene only a matter of hours.

According to María, Ellie's favorite among the ranch maids, who had it from Angelita the midwife in town, whose younger brother Juanito worked on the bridge (thanks to José María Trujillo Sanchez), these visits of Sam Taylor were anticipated with interest by the rank and file of the crew, with mere acceptance by Hard Nose Jud Wilder, and with near-despair by three of the four members of the hierarchy in the headquarters trailer. Only *el oso pardo*, the grizzly bear, as the Spanish-speaking members of the crew had named Zabrinski, went his own large, placid, unperturbed way, totally unaffected.

And just this morning, even before breakfast, María, the romantic, had made a point of telling Ellie that Señor Taylor was flying in again today. "In case you might like to see him, señorita," María had added with a shy smile.

"Now, María . . ."

"You could fly with him back to San Francisco. I have heard that it is a great city, and *muy simpática*." It was María's understanding that anglo women were without restraint.

"It is a great city," Ellie agreed. "And its *ambiente* is *muy simpática*. But I am not a schoolgirl to be chasing a man."

María was disappointed. But she had another approach, too. "Juanito tells Angelita that the towers of the bridge rise like magic."

And I haven't been over to look at them, Ellie thought. True.

"Soon there will be snow," María said, apparent *non sequitur*, but the hidden meaning here, too, was perfectly clear.

With snow on the ground riding will not be as easy, or as pleasant as now, Ellie thought. Also true. "You have a naughty mind, María."

Again that shy smile. "Thank you, señorita."

And so at breakfast, "I think I'll go riding this morning," Ellie said.

Evans nodded approval. "To the bridge?" He bore Ellie's instant, sharp, questioning glance without expression.

"As a matter of fact, yes." Her voice was carefully unconcerned.

"Good. I would like a firsthand report."

She was remembering this now, when without warning, the sonic boom hit and with its double sound hammered the ground and the ambient air with a violent one-two punch. The big gelding buck-jumped half a dozen feet sideways, and Ellie almost came out of the saddle.

"Ho!" Her voice was automatic, and her hand reflexively tightened on the saddle horn, gave her purchase back to her balanced seat. "Easy, boy!" She leaned forward to pat the proud, tensed neck. "It's only the Air Force showing off again, damn them."

She touched the horse's flanks lightly with her spurs and lifted him once more into his jog-trot. Daydreaming, she told herself accusingly. Inocencio would say it served her right if she had been thrown.

Juanito had not exaggerated. On top of a small rise still a mile or so distant from the site, Ellie reined the buckskin in for her first glimpse of the unfinished bridge towers.

They rose in geometrical precision, incongruous in this ancient, weathered land; all angles and sharp, straight lines against the naturally eroded curves of the landscape. They are, she thought, structures from an alien culture, a civilization far more advanced than ours, and, remembering what Henry had said about the eighteenth or possibly even the seventeenth century way of life in Tano County, she had no doubt that there were many who saw the towers in just that way. One thing was undeniable: the sight drew from her an emotional reaction.

She bent to pat the horse's neck again. "I don't know whether to laugh or cry," she told him, "because Henry was right. We're looking at either an end or a beginning, but certainly a change."

Sam was already on the site. Driven by he knew not what compulsion, he and the pilot had left the airport near San Francisco in a predawn black sky. Sam, at the controls of the jet, climbed quickly to sixteen thousand feet to clear the towering mountains, and headed east at high cruise. The pilot promptly dozed off in the copilot's seat.

He had no real reason to visit the bridge job, Sam told himself, any more than he had reason to visit the Alaska job, or the refinery job in Saudi Arabia, or any of the other far-flung projects in Ross Associates' current work load. Reports flowed in to the San Francisco office, as they always had, bringing to the man who sat at Wilt Ross's desk more, and better, information than he could possibly have gathered flying here and there himself with the frenzy of a worker bee. Still . . .

The truth, of course, was that the Tano Gorge bridge was inextricably tied up with Wilt Ross; a stricken giant, according to Laura, lying pitifully shrunken in his hospital bed, almost unable to speak, his entire right side paralyzed, his mind maybe focusing, maybe not, but certainly not comprehending what amounted to Sam's complete takeover.

"Somebody has to do it," Laura said. This was that first evening of Ross's stroke, and by then Laura had herself under tight control. Grief, if that was the word, could come later. In private. They sat in Ross's big inner office. "And you're the one, Sam."

"The sensible thing would be to scrub the whole bridge job, take our licking, and get out from under. The other jobs can handle themselves."

"We can't."

"Tell me why. It's been done before." But Laura's face told him that he wasn't thinking straight yet, and he made himself back up to have another look. After a moment, "You're right," he said. "Ross has a stroke. Immediately we cancel out on a job already started. The obvious inference is that without Ross, we're helpless." Sam nodded. "End of Ross Associates as a going concern."

The big office was still. Laura watched Sam steadily.

"I owe him," Sam said. "There's no argument there. But what

about the note firing me? Are you going to pretend you never saw it?"

"I'll manage."

"You're sticking your neck out. What happens if and when he recovers?"

"We'll worry about that when it happens. I owe him too, Sam."

"Ross Associates," Sam said, "is no neighborhood mom and pop operation. I just step in and pretend I'm Wilt Ross?"

"No," Laura's voice was decisive. "You are Sam Taylor, known from Alaska to Indonesia to Bahrein as heir apparent. Now you have inherited. It was bound to come."

"Except that his last act was to fire me, and his first act when he's able may very well be to repudiate me. He sticks by his decisions."

"Do you know any other way?"

In all honesty, the answer was no. So be it. You learned to accept the inevitable. "You drive a hard bargain, Laura."

"I learned in a hard school. So did you."

So now, as twice before, three times if you counted the original act of insubordination, he was on the Tano Gorge bridge site again, with that feeling that sometimes came on a tricky job of trying to look in all directions at once—for what, you didn't know.

He faced Daryl Chambers in the headquarters trailer. "I'll prowl around a little," Sam said. "You don't need to come." Was there resentment in Chambers's eyes? "Unless you want to," Sam said.

Chambers sat silent and unmoving. Sam walked out. In the large outer room, he nodded to Quincy Yorke and Frank Miller. Zabrinski came in through the outside doorway with the silent, ponderous grace of a bear and watched as Sam took folded papers from his inside pocket. "The computer models you and Miller wanted," Sam said. "Let me know when you've studied them." He walked down the trailer steps.

Quincy Yorke said, "Snotty bastard, isn't he? Lord Sam."

Zabrinski shook his head. "Up-tight, I'd say," he said, and wondered why it was so.

Sam paused outside the trailer to absorb the familiar sounds and sights of construction. As often as he had heard and seen them, the fascination remained, and it was no wonder, he thought, that spectators gathered at building sites, sidewalk superintendents of all ages and both sexes, to gape at the process of fitting together massive and varying shapes of steel into structures stronger than any or all of their parts.

There was the partially completed tower and the crane swinging a ton or so of steel in the form of a single pre-drilled I-beam to the men waiting on top.

As you watched, you could admire the cunningly contrived framework of the structure; the uprights, the girders, the braces, the supporting cross-members, the precise triangles row after row. You could feel a measure of awe at the sight of hard-hatted men on their precarious perches, moving unconcernedly as they handled the ponderous steel sections, and maneuvered them into position.

You could imagine yourself in the cab of the crane, with all that power at your fingertips, as you swung tons of metal at your bidding. An organ recital, with bodily injury to any of the men waiting on the structure—or even death—as the penalty for a single false note from your moving hands.

And, as he was doing now, you could watch with satisfaction and even a sense of personal accomplishment as, under the connecting gang's seemingly effortless guidance, the huge beam came to rest in its proper position to be made fast to its adjacent members while the riveting gang moved in with chattering airgun to make the connection permanent and secure. One more strengthening piece in the Tinkertoy-like structure.

The empty crane hook was dropping swiftly for another load, and to Sam the invitation was irresistible. He whistled, two piercing notes through curled tongue and pursed lips, and, raising his arm for the crane operator's attention, swung it with unmistakable authority in a summoning gesture. Instantly the crane began to swing.

It stopped, and the end of its cable dropped within easy reach. Sam put one foot into the hook, grasped the cable, and with his free hand gestured upward. He rose swiftly beside the tower and stepped off to the narrow platform on the tower's top.

There was heavy, buffeting wind; that was his first thought, and he braced himself against it automatically. To the nearest man of the connecting gang, who watched him, expressionless, "It always blows like this?" Sam said.

"No." The man spat downwind. "Sometimes it blows hard."

"I know you," Sam said then, and produced one of his rare smiles. "From somewhere."

"Yeah. I've been there."

"Anderson. Bob Anderson."

"That's right."

Sam glanced around. The bottomless gorge on one side, the vast empty plain on the other, rising to the mountains. The constant, buffeting wind. He looked again at Anderson.

"It's all work," Anderson said, answering unspoken questions. "Sometimes it's hot and sometimes it's cold and sometimes the wind blows, but it's all work."

It was an attitude Sam understood. A workingman could bitch about his job, and, God knew, enough did. But if what you were complaining about was the natural environment, something neither you nor anyone else could change, then all you were doing was making yourself unhappy. The sensible ones, like Anderson, decided early just to take it as it came. "It's all work," summed it up.

The crane hook was rising again, carrying in a sling another pre-drilled I-beam. Sam walked along the narrow platform well out of the way, and turned to watch Anderson and his crewmates maneuver the beam into position with almost scornful ease. With bulls' pricks, tapered, high tensile strength steel rods, they lined up drilled hole with drilled hole, then cast loose the sling and moved aside for the riveting gang. The staccato clamor of air hammer filled the air, and the smell of heated rivets was plain.

Sam walked to the end of the platform and looked into the Gorge. Halfway down the opposite cliff face, the sunlight disappeared, and the shadows turned deeper against the reddish-brown of the rock. At the bottom the river was barely visible; he could make out faint patches of white water rushing through the rocks and around the bends.

In his mind's eye, an engineer's eye, he could visualize the completed bridge; the lofty towers, the great suspended cables, the roadway rising and falling in a shallow arc that would be almost imperceptible as you drove across, and the new highway stretching east and west, opening the vast country—for better or for worse.

"She's a bitch, isn't she?" Anderson's voice at his side. There was obvious affection in the tone. "She isn't going to be the biggest goddamn bridge in the world, but sitting here where she is, and reaching out over that ditch, she's going to be something to take notice of."

"She is that."

Anderson spat again, carefully downwind. "What color when she's finished?"

"Red."

"Like the Golden Gate Bridge." Anderson nodded emphatic approval. "Good." He turned away as another I-beam swung up to be fitted into place.

Not everyone shared Anderson's approval, of course, and there were those who still opposed the entire idea. Trujillo, for example, resenting the bridge, and yet sending men out to join the crew, thereby giving himself a foot in each camp.

And that was something to check with Jud about—had there been any trouble on the mixed crew? Not that Jud couldn't, and wouldn't handle it if trouble arose, but Sam wanted to keep his finger on the pulse, as it were, stay on top of this job all the way.

Another man approached. Since he seemed to have no duties either with the connecting gang or the riveting gang, he had to be the pusher. "Anything you want?" he said. His tone seemed to imply that if there wasn't, then they could do without an idle man up here on the platform, whoever he was. In Sam's view, a proper attitude.

"I've had my look," Sam said, and watched the man nod shortly and turn away. An unnecessary look, of course. The actual construction was Jud's responsibility, and in the final analysis, Chambers's; not his. But the temptation to see for himself had been too great.

He turned to face the crane, whistled again and swung his arm in that authoritative gesture. We took this job, he thought, when maybe we shouldn't have taken it, but we can't drop it now, and no matter what grief there may be in it, we accept that—as Anderson accepts the wind and the weather. There is no other way.

The crane hook arrived, coming to a precise stop where he could step into it with ease. He grasped the cable, gave his down signal, and waved at Bob Anderson. "Hang in there," he called across the narrow platform.

Anderson flipped one gloved hand in acknowledgment.

12.

Walking from the spot where the crane had deposited him toward Jud's shack, Sam looked around, concentrating this time on the men rather than the structure. Here and there a darker-skinned face beneath a hard hat showed *chicano* or Indian blood, which was exactly as it ought to be, and Sam hoped that Trujillo was, if not happy, at least, for the present, content.

Construction men, ironworkers, came in all shapes and sizes, and what mattered was not the color of your skin or the shape of your eyes or what accent was in your speech, but simply, whether you could hack it. And that meant whether you could be depended on to carry your share of the load.

Sam had no worry about Jud's ability to get rid of incompetents or goof-offs, even if it meant picking them up by neck and crupper and tossing them the hell off the job so hard they bounced. But there were other, more subtle threats and dangers in the sometimes high-hazard work of putting together anything as vast and as complicated as a bridge, and these could lie hidden for weeks, months, and then surface unexpectedly.

Sometimes feuds built up for the smallest of reasons or no reason at all, and on a construction job the opportunities for mischief were limitless. A heavy wrench or a connecting plate dropped from a tower could kill a man, hard hat or no. Piles of stacked pipe had been known to collapse and bury men beneath their tons of unyielding steel. Air hoses could rupture, and unshackled jackhammer bits could be shot from their guns like harpoons . . . And who was to say that an accident had been, or had not been, planned?

No doubt, Chambers had had this kind of possibility in mind when he had opted for an all-anglo crew, fearing that ethnic friction could increase the chances of trouble. But the dangers and the benefits had to be weighed in the balance, and as Evans had pointed out, and Sam had instantly understood, non-discrimination was a must.

Jud was at his desk when Sam walked in. "I saw you up top," Jud said. "Checking us out?" There was vague challenge in his tone.

"Just looking things over. They look pretty good."

Jud's faint nod was mere acceptance. "When do I get my safety nets?"

"You'll have them when you start pushing out the roadway."

"Hung from sky hooks?"

"That," Sam said, "is for Yorke and Zabrinski and you to work out."

Jud thought about it. "Yorke's a little smart-ass, but he's a pretty good architect." His tone had relaxed a trifle. "And Zabrinski's a good man."

Sam straddled the straight visitor's chair. "How about your crew?"

"What about them?" Jud's guard was up again.

"The men Trujillo sent are working out?"

"They'd be long gone otherwise."

"No trouble?"

Jud scowled. "You been hearing things? Couple fights, nothing serious, is all. Happens on every job. You know that."

"Sure."

"Those nets now," Jud said.

It was Sam's turn. "What about them?"

"They're going to cost a bundle, aren't they?"

"Only an arm and a leg." Maybe *my* arm and *my* leg, Sam thought, or, rather, my neck. Never mind. He had felt that wind, and safety nets were the way to go.

Jud was off on a new tack. "How's Ross?"

Sam held one hand out, fingers spread, palm down. He rocked

it to indicate delicate balance. "Improvement. They say. But it can still go either way."

Jud nodded. "Hell of a thing." He looked hard at Sam. "Anything else you want?"

"Chambers—" Sam said, and stopped it there, wondering how to phrase the question.

"He'll do," Jud said. "There are times he's a pain in the ass. But we work it out. And Zabrinski—" Jud shook his head. "I told you he's a good man. He helps."

"And Miller, the computer man?"

"Someday," Jud said, "he's going to say something, and we'll all drop dead from shock. He—"

Suddenly through the cacophony of engine sounds—compressor, rivet guns, and jackhammers—they heard a shout. And another, and then voices raised in clamor, in each clear and distinct a note of near-panic, of disaster at hand.

Jud was out of his chair and through the doorway on the instant. Sam followed on his heels.

The unfinished east tower rose against the bright, almost blinding high-country sky. Looking upward, both men had to squint, and even then objects appeared more in silhouette than in detail. But the situation was unmistakable.

Of the men on the tower's top, the riveting gang, heater, catcher, bucker-up and riveter, plus the connecting gang, only two were, at the moment, important.

One lay on his belly at the end of an I-beam girder, reaching with one hand down as far as he could stretch into space. The other man hung suspended with desperate strength from the bottom I-beam flange, holding on by only one hand, his legs flailing in space for nonexistent support, his other hand reaching frantically for the offered aid from above.

Sam whistled his two piercing notes and swung his arm above his head as beside him Jud's voice rose in a great shout, "Get that crane hook to him!" Two minds reacting instantly.

Like an obedient antediluvian monster, the crane began to swing, its hook rising quickly to tower top height.

The shouting stopped. In the sudden hush the only sounds were the clatter of the crane's engine, and the constant faint keening of the wind through the upper tower structure.

What they were watching, Sam thought suddenly, was an instant replay, slow motion, sound turned off, time almost standing still.

"Get him, goddamn it!" Jud whispered. "Get him!"

The man lying on the I-beam, in danger of falling himself, was stretched as far as he could down to the man hanging over space. Their fingertips brushed, separated, brushed again, and here on the ground there was a sighing sound as if each man watching suddenly found his breath too much to contain.

"Come on!" Jud whispered. "Goddamn it, come on!"

The fingertips no longer touched, and still the man hanging from the beam flange clung to his precarious support with impossible strength.

The crane hook was swinging as the crane pivoted on its base. A good man at the controls, Sam told himself, remembering his own rides and his observations. The crane operator had lifted Sam and deposited him in place, as he had deposited those tons of steel beams, as neatly and as gently as if he were using tongs. Get the hook to him, he thought, that's all there is to it. All?

Over the Gorge three ravens rode the updrafts unconcerned, swooping, soaring, banking in their aerial acrobatics as if gravity did not exist. One gave out his harsh squawk of excitement or joy. No man on the tower site heard.

"Easy with that hook!" Jud whispered, totally unaware that the words were audible. "Too goddamn fast, and you'll cold cock him! Sweet and gentle, that's the way! He'll hang on! You better believe it!" Ten feet, five feet more—"Oh, Jesus!" His breath came out in a long rush.

The man hanging from the beam flange made a final, convulsive effort, and his free hand, reaching for and missing the crane hook, almost made contact again with the fingers stretched from above. His body flopped in spasm, reminding Sam of the sight of a trout flopping helplessly on the bank of a stream.

And then, all at once, unbelievably, there was brilliant, clear sky between the man and the tower structure, and wind and gravity were in full command.

He cartwheeled, arms and legs flailing wildly. His hard hat came off to begin its own descent, and his shirttails came out of his jeans and billowed like a miniature sail.

He screamed, strange falsetto for a big, grown man, a rising shriek of pure terror which, as he gathered speed in his fall, and disappeared beyond the cliff brink, trailed off to a lower pitch in a Doppler effect, a sound to be remembered in nightmares.

There was silence.

Sam wanted to run to the cliff edge and look down, but he made himself stand still. There would be nothing to see. It would be as if the Gorge, that fabled, goddamned gorge, had swallowed up the body, and the man, whoever he was, had never existed.

Jud said in a low, angry voice. "A good man. A goddamned good man."

Sam said, "You know who it was?"

"You were talking with him up top, goddamn it! Bob Anderson."

Sam closed his eyes. How long ago? Ten minutes? Fifteen? What difference? He opened his eyes, turned away, and then stopped.

No more than twenty feet from him Ellie Evans stood motionless beside the big buckskin, the reins in her hand, her eyes fixed on Sam's face. They seemed to search his mind. She said slowly, "I don't believe it! I can't!"

Sam searched for words, and found none.

"Say something!" Ellie's voice was on the edge of hysteria.

Sam took a deep breath. He raised his hands and let them fall. "What is there to say?"

Sam and Jud sat again in Jud's shack, both aware of and affected by the eerie stillness outside. The job site was deserted, shut down for the day, the familiar racket of construction sounds silenced by death. Tradition? Or just common decency? Neither man could have answered, but the rule was plain: you killed a man, you stopped work for the day.

"I'll file a report in person," Jud said. "State Police." He shook his head. "San Francisco will handle details, notifying next of kin, insurance, that kind of thing." His voice betrayed his anger. "State cops say they may, or may not, recover the body. With that river, you can't tell. It could hang up on a snag and some fisherman find it, or it could end up in a pothole covered with silt. And if they do find it—" He shook his head again, remembering what the state cop had said in Josie's bar about the condition of a body after it had been through the rapids.

Sam nodded, and said nothing. His face was expressionless.

"All right, goddamn it," Jud said, "you're wondering what happened? Well, so am I, and you know what? We'll never know. It happened. That's all." He held up his hand, fingers spread to emphasize the missing two joints of his middle finger. "There wasn't any reason for this, either. I watched it happen. Goddamn it, I stood there and watched that block take my finger off, glove and all. Now does that make any sense?"

Both men looked up as Ellie Evans appeared in the doorway. She looked down in silence, calmer now.

Sam stood up.

"Come in, lady," Jud said. "Have a chair. We're having a post-mortem."

"I heard." Ellie lowered herself slowly to the chair, her eyes drawn to Jud's mutilated hand. "Is that how it is?" Her voice was filled with wonder. "It just . . . happens?"

Jud shrugged. "That's about the size of it. And you don't believe what you've seen."

Huge Carl Zabrinski filled the doorway as he came through, ducking his head for clearance. He looked around at them all. "A private wake?" There was no answer. "Phone in the trailer is ringing already," he said. "Wire service man wanting the poop. TV guy wanting to know if he fell, or was he pushed?" He lifted his massive shoulders and let them fall. "Better have something to say before they work it up into some kind of race feud. In these parts, apparently, that's always in somebody's mind."

Right, of course, Sam thought, and I should have thought of it. "Chambers—" he began, but what he saw in Zabrinski's face told him that he would do well to think again. He nodded with slow reluctance and stood up. "I'll do it."

"The front office," Zabrinski said in agreement. "The horse's mouth. Better that way."

Jud said, "At least it was an anglo, not one of the locals."

There was that, Sam thought, remembering Henry Evans's warning. "The locals," he said, "stay on the ground." He was speaking to Jud. "See that they do."

"I'm way ahead of you."

We are in deeper and deeper, Sam thought as he walked toward the headquarters trailer. And again Ross was very much in his mind, because the old man disliked publicity, and always had.

"We can't help being visible on a job," Ross had told him

once. "That's something we have to accept. But we don't attract any more attention than we can help. Get in, do the job, and get out with as little disturbance as possible. That's the way we operate."

Nice idea, but it wasn't going to work here.

At his side, matching him stride for stride, Ellie Evans said, "Henry may be able to help. Had you thought of that?"

Sam stopped and turned to face her. In her heeled boots, she was not much shorter than he. A big woman. Again the nude on Jud's wall came briefly to mind. "How?" he said.

"He knows the publishers of the papers. And the men who own the TV stations. And he knows quite a bit about public relations."

"As I obviously don't?"

Ellie shook her head. It was difficult to keep her voice steady. "You don't have much tact. I will say that." She turned away then and walked off toward the tethered horse.

Sam watched until she had mounted, turned the horse away and lifted him into his easy, mile-consuming trot. She rode, he thought, as if she and the horse were one.

The UPI man said, "What I don't see is why an experienced ironworker, as you call him, should fall."

"I'll be happy to take you up top," Sam said, "and let you see for yourself what it's like."

"What he's getting at," AP said, "is that you bring in a crew from outside, and then you hire locals as well, and, you know, there can be trouble."

"You're looking for a story," Sam said, "but it isn't there."

"As we get it," TV8 said, "you're mostly out in Frisco. Maybe you're not in touch here."

"But I am." Zabrinski walked into the room, dwarfing them all. "We've got all kinds on the job. And no trouble." He looked at them one by one. "Okay?"

TV6 said, "There's that other thing. You know, all those stories about the Tano Gorge. They scare kids with them. How about that?"

"That's what they are," Sam said, "stories to scare kids. We're building a bridge. We use concrete and steel. No ghosts." He had the feeling that he was talking to himself.

When they were gone to write their various versions of a man's death, Sam and Zabrinski remained alone. "You get across to them better than I do," Sam said. He felt no pain, only wonder, at the admission.

Zabrinski grinned. "It's called the common touch. You get it by having your nose in the dirt often enough so you suffer other fools like yourself gladly." Zabrinski hesitated as if he were about to say more, and then shook his head in sudden decision. "See you," he said, and, bending for clearance, left the trailer.

In the corral, Ellie unsaddled the big buckskin, and, carrying horsehair pad, Indian blanket, heavy saddle, bridle and rifle, was heading for the tack room when Inocencio appeared and almost angrily relieved her of her burden.

He glanced at the haltered horse. There were sweat marks where the saddle had been. "You hurried, señorita."

"*Claro*." The single, curt word was all she could manage.

Inocencio studied her face. He nodded. "I will take care of him." He watched her for a moment longer. "Do you hear me, señorita?"

"*Gracias*." Her knees felt weak.

"*De nada*." Refuge in formal ritual; Inocencio turned away from what he had seen in the girl's eyes.

Through the familiar patio entrance, across the corner of the big living room, down thc hall to her own quarters, Ellie carried still the sight of the cartwheeling body and the sounds of Anderson's screams etched deeply in memory, impossible to shake.

She closed the door to her sitting room, and plumped herself down in a chair, the question she had brooded upon all during the ride home still very much in her mind.

What did the men feel, Sam and Jud and the big one, Zabrinski? Were they really as callous as they had seemed, unconcerned, paying no heed to what had been, concentrating only on what was to be now? And the other men, those of the crew who had walked off the job silently at Jud's dismissal, gone to their cars and driven away. Were they too unaffected? If so, she thought suddenly, men were not simply another gender; they were another species—of monsters.

She was still brooding over the question when María knocked on the door with the message from Ellie's father.

Henry Evans waited in his wheelchair in the library-office. He watched Ellie come in, her face as expressionless as she could make it. "You sent for me?"

"Sit down. I saw you ride in." And when she was seated uncomfortably in one of the leather club chairs, "I heard," Evans said. "On the local radio. You were there?"

Ellie nodded stiffly. "I was there. I saw it. All of it." Suddenly the words came out in a rush, grateful release. "They tried to get the crane hook to him! One man was trying to reach him! The hook was close, oh, so close! And then—he just couldn't hold on any longer, and he fell, screaming! Into the Gorge! He just . . . disappeared! He was still . . . screaming!" She sat silent.

"I am sorry. Scant comfort, I know, but it is all I have to offer."

"They don't even know why." The words were outrage, protest.

"They rarely do. Carelessness, error, misjudgment, these are vague, blank words that explain nothing. I repeat, I am sorry."

Ellie nodded then, and said nothing.

"Sam Taylor was there? The radio report seemed to indicate that he was."

Ellie nodded again.

"You knew he would be," Evans said in the same, quiet, uninflected voice, "and you wanted to see him." He nodded and quickly raised one hand, palm out, to forestall protest. "Believe me, I am not trying to monitor your comings and goings." One of his rare, faint smiles appeared. "Nor am I trying to arrange matters. I flatter myself that I know better than that. The truth is that I am concerned, deeply concerned."

"About what?"

Evans sighed, smiling still. "A little difficult to explain."

"Try."

The smile held steady. Evans nodded slowly. "Very well. You have the right to ask. What I am concerned about is a mixture of friendship, pride, I suppose neighborly feelings whatever they are, and the kind of premonition I learned a long time ago to heed."

Ellie sat quiet, what had happened at the bridge site for the moment pushed aside in her mind. It was sometimes hard to tell with this father of hers how much of what he said was real, and how much was evasion. She had never known him to tell an outright untruth, but like magicians she had watched perform, he was, or often seemed to be, incredibly adept at the use of misdirection. But he seemed both open and sincere here, and she listened carefully.

"I told Taylor when we first met," Evans said, "that if there was going to be a bridge, so be it, but that the one thing we did not want was a botched job. For reasons. Floyd Babcock is one. A botched job could ruin him politically. And he has his heart set on bigger and bigger things."

"That," Ellie said, "is the friendship part."

"Correct. The pride I mentioned is of course a personal matter. I chose some time ago to accept the fact that there would be a bridge, opening this part of the country to the rest of the world. I don't want to be proved wrong."

"And the neighborly feelings?"

"You heard Joe Trujillo say that he knew what was best for the county, his people. What he meant was what was best for him. This is my home, your mother's and mine. And I think I know what is best for the people who live here and who have always looked to me, us, for—shall we call it leadership? I don't want them disappointed. Or hurt. And hopes raised and then dashed are far worse than no hopes at all. The bridge is taking shape, a tangible thing. It must not stop now."

Ellie said, "And your premonition is that it will stop? Or fail? Something?"

Evans rubbed his forehead lightly with his fingertips as if to stir memory. "I drilled a well once," he said. "I drilled many wells, but this one I drilled against my better judgment. I could not have said why. I had partners, and they demanded to know why I dragged my feet. I had no answer. The geology was favorable. The area was known to be productive. Our lease was without flaw." He spread his hands. "So we went ahead. And we brought in a gusher. Happy ending to the story, to my premonition? But it wasn't."

"What happened?"

"There was an explosion. We never knew why. It killed the only three men who might have explained it. And the well was afire. It defied efforts to put it out. In the end, we brought in Red Adair and his people, got the fire out, and capped off the hole permanently. It was a matter of months before it was all over. A matter of months, and a great deal of money, which not all of my partners, friends, could afford."

Ellie sat silent. She began to shake her head.

"You are thinking," Evans said, "that there is no exact parallel. You are correct. But the feeling I have now about this bridge is the same. And word I have from San Francisco is disquieting. Before his stroke, there appears to have been a sudden break between Ross and Sam Taylor." Again he spread his hands. "What it means, I have no idea. But dissension in the front office can produce nothing but trouble. That is axiomatic."

There was a brawl in Josie's Place that night. Its origins were unclear, but its results were tangible. Jud Wilder, calling Sam in San Francisco the next day at Daryl Chambers's insistence, said, "All I know is I was sitting with Zabrinski having a drink, minding our own business. We'd just agreed that the butcher's bill was mounting, with Bob Anderson number two on the list. How many more, who the hell knows?"

"Go on," Sam said.

"Somebody threw a bottle," Jud said, "and somebody else threw a chair, don't ask me why. Things more or less went on from there. You know how it is. One thing leads to another."

Daryl Chambers, listening on the extension phone, wondered if Sam Taylor did know how it was.

"There was a night in Caracas—" Jud went on as if to explain.

"I remember," Sam said, thereby answering Chambers's unspoken question. "All right. Anybody hurt bad?"

"No."

"And it was mostly our crew?"

"That's about the size of it."

"Is Chambers on the phone?"

Chambers had been no part of the brawl, and had hoped to stay entirely out of it, but Jud was looking at him, and all he could do was speak up. "I'm here."

"Settle for the damage," Sam said. "Send the bill here."

He hung up and leaned back in the big chair. He knew the feeling, and he had not needed a reminder of that bar brawl in Caracas to bring it to mind, but now that Jud had mentioned it, the details came back with clarity.

Michaels, wasn't that his name? A cat skinner, tractor driver, a big, tough, jolly Irishman with muscular, sunburned, freckled forearms covered with reddish fur. Lightning in the forest, the storm coming up without warning, and that giant tree crashing down across Michaels's Caterpillar tractor, pinning him, crushing him in his seat, two branches piercing him like spears.

They worked like madmen, Sam, chief engineer, right alongside local punks of the ground crew, to cut the tree, the impaling branches, and free the man. And above the sounds of the storm and the hammering of the torrential rain, they could hear Michaels screaming, bubbling screams that grew weaker and weaker and finally, mercifully, ceased.

The bar brawl in Caracas that night was release, pure and simple. Sam now could not even remember how it began. He doubted if Jud could either. What difference? There had been a need.

And he had felt a need last night, too, after flying back from Tano, but a need of a different kind. "It's too late for dinner," he had told Liz on the phone from the airport. "But maybe you'll give me a drink?"

"Funny," Liz said, "I was wondering if you were off on another of your sudden jaunts."

"Is that a yes? Or no?"

"Oh, I'll give you a drink. Since you ask so nicely."

A need of a different kind, but also release.

13.

As early as Sam was down at Ross Associates headquarters high above Montgomery Street on this morning, Laura was already at her desk, on the telephone. She nodded to Sam, said in a decisive voice into the phone, "This afternoon, no later," hung up and rose to follow Sam to the big office inside. She closed the door.

"I saw him last night," she said. There was no need to explain that she meant Wilt Ross. "He is able to talk a little."

Sam stood quietly, waiting.

Laura's voice now was toneless. "He wanted to know who's minding the store. I said we were limping along, waiting for him to come back to work. It seems I'm a very good liar, Sam. A—talent I didn't really know I had."

"Necessity, maybe, and invention."

"He hasn't mentioned you. Not once."

"Maybe he's forgotten my name." Sam tried to make it light, but the words didn't come out that way.

Laura's toneless voice went on. "He wanted me to get in touch with Rufe Wilson in Mexico, and tell him how things were up here."

Nothing changed in Sam's face. "Go on," he said, although now he knew full well what was coming.

"Rufe Wilson," Laura said, "has been dead for ten years, and so has that job in Mexico, wrapped up, finished. You finished it after Rufe died."

Sam turned to stare out the windows at the Bay, blue and shining in the early sun. Over his shoulder he said, "So what are you suggesting?"

"I . . . don't know. If he's that far out of touch with reality—except he isn't all the time. Not now. He . . . comes and goes, if you see what I mean. I've talked over the legal aspects with John Haskins." Haskins was Ross Associates general counsel. "There are . . . steps. I'm not clear about them. Restraining orders, that kind of thing. Even, if he loses complete touch, there could be . . . commitment."

Still facing the Bay, Sam said, "You call them as you see them, don't you, Laura?" And in the silence he turned to face her.

She stood straight and poised as he would always think of her, gray-haired, slim, still attractive, and now deeply troubled. Two tears rolled down the sides of her nose. She ignored them. "What is the right thing, Sam?" Her voice was a plea.

Only whatever gods might be could know the answer to that, Sam thought, and shook his head in silence.

"I pushed you into this."

"Nobody pushed me, Laura."

"If he recovers—"

"You said it yourself. We'll face that if and when it happens."

"He doesn't change his mind easily, Sam."

"I'm aware of it."

"If he doesn't recover—"

"We'll find an answer to that, too."

"You're a great deal like him, Sam. Maybe too much like him. This job, building and running Ross Associates was his life. And it may very well have killed him. You might think about that." She gestured at the neat pile of opened mail already waiting on the desk. "You want to be out at the Tano Gorge, running the job instead of here, dealing with—that."

"And who would, if I didn't?"

"You're worried about that job, aren't you? Because of, let's face it, an old man." There was sudden sadness in her voice, in her eyes.

He had not seen it this clearly before. "You're in love with him, aren't you, Laura?"

Her head lifted proudly. "I have been since I came to work

here as a girl just out of college. He was married then. Did you know that?"

"I heard. Somewhere."

"It was finished thirty years ago. She went East and I think remarried. He never spoke of it." Laura made an abrupt, determined gesture, and pointed again to the pile of mail. "Leave that to me, Sam. Spend your energies on Tano Gorge. What I can't handle, I'll pass along to you. It won't be too much. I owe him that."

"It would seem to me," Sam said, "that it's the other way around. He owes you."

"Don't even think that." There was surprising vehemence in her tone. "Not ever. You hear?"

Daryl Chambers rode the tramcar across the Gorge to the west site. The ride terrified him, but not for the world would he have admitted it. He was chief engineer on the job. It was his project. Periodically, it was his duty to check out the work, see for himself that no corners were being cut, no rules by-passed or ignored. There was no other way. But, oh God, this tramcar ride across and back!

The tramcar was supported now by three cables instead of the original one, and by this arrangement its stability was increased. But that was, in effect, condemning the setup by comparing it to almost nothing.

Chambers sat stiff and tense, hanging tight with both hands, staring at his feet. Even without looking over the side of the tramcar he knew how the depths of the Gorge threatened, how the deep shadows at the bottom beckoned almost beyond his power to resist.

Acrophobia, this morbid dread of heights was called, and it was as if by merely giving it a name, the whole problem was solved. But did the savants know about the nausea that came and went? About the muscle rigidity sometimes so intense that it resembled nothing so much as the rictus of death? Did they know about the sense of panic that urged one to jump, have it over with and forever after be at peace?

He was near the center of the Gorge now. He had to be halfway across, that much closer to the far side and the safety of solid ground. He had been going already for a long time, an eternity. He kept his eyes fixed on his feet.

There was no warning. He remembered Zabrinski asking Jud after that first tramcar trip if he had had any inkling of trouble, and Jud's reply: that you couldn't see wind coming, but you could sure as hell feel it when it arrived.

Despite the stabilizing force of the three cables, suddenly the tramcar lurched violently, twisted like a mad thing in torment, bucked ten feet upward, and then slammed down against the restraint of the cables as if hitting a solid wall.

Chambers knew that his mouth was open, and that he was screaming in protest, but he was powerless to stop. His arms and hands, rigid and straining, felt as if they would pull out of their sockets, and there was the sudden, sour taste of vomit in his throat.

Another wind gust buffeted the tramcar, swinging it sideways until the stretched cables snapped it back with a jerk.

Zabrinski had said he sensed a Venturi tube effect here at this narrow neck of the Gorge, and Chambers's engineering mind, ticking over like some unfeeling goddamned computer, had agreed with the analysis. It had to be something like that, because winds of this force were simply not to be expected. Or endured.

"Stop this goddamn thing and let me off!" He was never sure if he had indeed shouted the insane words aloud. "Please! Stop it!"

And then, all at once, it was over, and he was clambering out of the tramcar at the other side.

The walking boss, whose name was Gus Oliver, was waiting. "Hi," Gus said. "I've been expecting you. How was the roller-coaster ride? A rough one this time? You never can tell."

Chambers made himself smile. "Just so-so," he said, and swallowed hard to keep from vomiting. And there was still the trip back! God! "Show me around."

On the telephone again to Evans, the governor said, "Keeping your ear to the ground, Henry, like you generally do?"

"I hear an occasional rumble."

"No sounds of a stampede?"

"Nothing audible."

"That dead man, now. And the fracas in town. They're connected?"

"I would say yes."

"So would I. You watch a man you've worked with get himself

killed, and you want to kick something. Or somebody. I know the feeling. You think that's all there is to it?"

"I have no reason to think otherwise."

The governor dropped the subject and went off in a new direction. "I get word out of San Francisco through Denver," he said. "You know how that goes. Well, sir, what I hear is that old Wilt Ross isn't exactly cutting out paper dolls, although he does live a lot in the past, but that when he is in the present he doesn't seem to be exactly sure what's going on. You know anything about that?"

"I have heard more or less the same."

"And this Sam Taylor, a top hand, no doubt about it, but he may be way out on a limb. You heard that too?"

"There are rumors."

"I don't like the sound of that, Henry. There are different ways of looking at things, and if a man puts his mind to it, he can usually find disaster lurking in just about any situation."

Again Evans was reminded that behind the governor's folksy cowboy façade, there was a far shrewder man than most people realized. "True," he said.

"And there are some around who would purely love to find disaster in that bridge project I been pushing, just because I been pushing it. I'll go further. There are some who would purely love to see my hide nailed to the barn door. I can't think why, because I'm a real nice feller, but as the man said, in a poker game that's how it goes. The color of a man's eyes don't mean a thing."

Evans wore his faint, amused smile. "And just what do you think I can do, Floyd? You called for a reason."

"Well, now, that's the stickler, Henry. I don't have any ideas at all. I hoped you would."

Evans wheeled himself out of the office-library to the west *portal* to sit and stare at the far horizon. From the direction of the Gorge he could hear the faint chatter of a rivet gun, like an echo of distant battle. Well, in a sense the bridge *was* a battle, a skirmish in man's eternal war against his environment, shaping it to patterns and usages of his own devising. A pretty flowery concept, he thought, however apt. But it suited a man confined for the rest of his life to a wheelchair, didn't it? And now, he told himself, you're just feeling sorry for yourself again. He turned his thoughts back to the governor.

He could, he supposed, make a case for resenting the governor's airy confidence that all he had to do was pick up the telephone and push his problems off on his old friend Henry Evans. On the other hand, wasn't it just possible that the governor realized that Evans *needed* problems to occupy him these endless, sedentary days? Well, whatever the reason, he had not told the governor to take his troubles elsewhere, so he had, tacitly, cut himself in. And now what?

Ellie walked out on the *portal*, wearing jeans, with spurs on her dusty boots, and carrying a battered sweat-stained hat that had whacked countless horses on the rump when they hesitated at open gates. She perched on the low *portal* railing, the pressure of the position forcing the fabric of her jeans tight against firm young flesh. Her breasts were clearly evident beneath the thin blouse. "Brooding?" she said.

Ever since the bridge accident, Evans thought, and especially these last few days, Ellie had seemed more attentive to him, more frequently at or near his side, as if the sight and the sound of the man falling screaming into the abyss had sharpened her awareness that life was fragile and that death was irreversible. "Just idle thoughts. Nothing serious."

"Was that the governor?"

She knew it was, Evans thought. He had long understood, and accepted, Ellie's intimate relationship with the ranch staff; she had grown up knowing a closeness to them that Evans would never be able to approach. María, who had answered the telephone, would have said who was calling. "Nothing much on his mind," Evans said. But already an idea was beginning to stir. Was it ignoble? He pushed the question aside. "When were you last in the city?"

"San Francisco?" Ellie shrugged. "Two, three months ago, I suppose. Yes, Vicki Wilson's wedding. Why?"

"We still have the flat."

"You were going to give it up."

"I probably should." Evans shrugged. "It was our pied-à-terre, your mother's and mine." He smiled fondly. "There are memories." The smile faded. "The point is, you have no business being tied down here in the boondocks. Why don't you go out to the city, see some people, take in a concert or two, do some shopping—?"

"And do what with, or about, Sam Taylor? Your guile is showing, Henry." She smiled gently. "You are losing your fine, subtle touch."

"If I haven't already lost it entirely." Despite himself, a trace of bitterness crept into his voice.

Ellie swung one booted leg idly as she thought about it. "He's an attractive man. I won't deny it."

"I am not suggesting carnal relations."

Ellie's smile spread. "Are you not? Or at least the possibility?"

Evans sighed. "I have always considered myself enlightened," he said. "Self-flattery, perhaps, but I did consider it justified. But your generation—" He shook his head. "Some of your values I do not comprehend. The well-dressed young woman, for example, who stepped out of the taxi in front of the Waldorf, looked down, and then said in the plain hearing of both the cabby and the doorman, 'Oh, shit! I stepped in some do-do.' "

Ellie's smile was very fond. "But you bear up under it."

"Barely." Evans flexed his hands to relieve the tension that was in his mind. The solid muscles of his forearms rippled. "In the city," he said, "Sam Taylor pays particular attention to a young woman named Lewis, Liz Lewis."

Ellie shook her head admiringly. "You, and your information network."

"Do you know her, by any chance?"

"As a matter of fact, I do. Does that surprise you?"

"No. I lost that particular capacity for surprise a long time ago. A man I knew once told me that there were really only five thousand people in the world, and wherever you went, you kept running into them. I've found it so."

"She's a stunner, Henry."

"So are you when you choose to be."

"And very rich."

Evans was silent.

Ellie smiled again. When she smiled, she was almost beautiful. "You're thinking that we're not exactly paupers, either, but it would be bad taste to say so, isn't that it? I love you, Henry. There are many reasons, but one of them is that you are really an old-fashioned, old-school gentleman. Up to a point, that is. Beyond that point—" She shook her head. "I think there is a ruthless quality that as a woman I can sense, even if I can't understand it."

"You flatter me." Evans's voice was light, amused.

"Sam Taylor has it too."

"Yes." The lightness and the amusement were gone. "He plays for keeps. You might remember that."

Ellie stood up from the railing and slapped her thigh with the battered hat. Dust flew. "I'll go out to the city, Henry," she said. "I'll be social, and sociable. I'll listen to everything I can hear about Ross Associates and Sam Taylor, and I'll get most of it right from the source. That's what you want, isn't it?"

"You make it sound Machiavellian."

"Scheming father sending innocent maiden daughter into deep peril? Is that what you mean?"

Evans flexed his fingers again, and the forearm muscles rippled strongly. "You call things by their names, don't you, Ellie?"

"I grew up understanding that was the way." Her voice softened. "I'm not being resentful, Henry. I understand what you want, and why. I understand how deeply you feel about it." She was smiling again. "And I'm going to enjoy my—assignment." The smile faded. "But I'm asking a price, too, a guarantee."

The *portal* was suddenly still. Evans sat silent, motionless, unsmiling.

"A promise," Ellie said. "Shall I spell it out?"

Evans's head inclined a mere fraction of an inch in a gesture of assent. "Please do."

"María came to me the other morning," Ellie said. "She showed me something, a handgun, the .380 automatic that used to live in the glove compartment of your car. She found it, she said, in the drawer of the lamp table in your sitting room when she was cleaning."

Nothing had changed in Evans's face. He made neither movement, nor sound.

"I've known you to keep a loaded gun in the house before," Ellie said, "a rifle or a shotgun. I know that in the old days you had one or two occasions to use them." She shook her head. "But a nasty .380 that has only one function, to kill? Whom? Yourself?"

"You take a great deal on yourself."

"I have the right."

"I am your father."

"And I am your daughter. It's a two-way street. You said you can't understand my generation. I think you do. Maybe it is just that we say what you only thought. Because I think we feel the same. You don't belong only to yourself, any more than I do. A part of you belongs to me, as another part belonged to Mother. Do I have your promise that while I'm in San Francisco, you won't destroy my part?"

14.

In the shade of the great mountains, full daylight comes gradually to dissipate the gloom and the chill of the night. The sun touches the mountains of the Divide to the west and moves gradually down their slopes to the high mesa. First the unfinished top of the western bridge tower shows plain. Then the eastern tower top . . .

"For Christ sake will you look there!" MacAndrew, the walking boss, on the ground said to no one in particular, pointing upward. "I'll be a son of a bitch!" He headed at a trot for Jud's con struction shack, and moments later emerged, trotting again, this time on Jud's heels.

Jud squinted up against the lightening sky to make out the boy clinging to the tower top, one hundred feet above the ground, backlighted, little more than a silhouette. As near as Jud could tell, the boy was hanging tight to the structure, probably in panic, but as he watched, one arm came loose and waved in a derisive gesture that ended suddenly with an obvious panic-stricken clutch for support.

Kids would be kids. Anybody with a lick of sense knew that. But these local *chicano* kids were something else, and the scenario was not hard to understand. *Machismo* was a way of life, and a half-completed bridge tower would be irresistible. Climb it, man, and you've got it made, you're flying, you are the absolute most! The cat with the wildest low-rider car or the loudest trail bike in town will *fry* with jealousy. The chicks will flip, and roll over by the numbers. You'll be Mr. Big, man, the *jefe!*

"See him?" MacAndrew said, arriving panting. Then, his voice changing to command, "You, Pete, and you, Jerry, up after him! Chase him the hell down!"

"Hold it," Jud said. He had not raised his voice, but his tone brought silence.

How had it happened? That could wait for investigation, but Jud thought he knew already. The job site was surrounded by a chain link fence which was not unclimbable, but with its top three strands of barbed wire slanting outward, it would discourage most attempts.

But the Gorge was open, and there were trails along the cliff face, some natural, some probably made by generations of these *macho* kids, exploring, playing, trying to outdo one another in rock-face daring. The site was open to anyone who wanted to work along the cliff face at night, climb up, avoid the Indian watchmen and do whatever he damn well pleased to thumb his nose at the world and all the authority, particularly anglo authority, there was in it.

"He got up there during the night, right?" Jud said. He spoke to MacAndrew.

"He had to. He sure as hell hasn't gone up while I've been here."

"Then he's cold. And stiff. And scared."

MacAndrew looked as if he wanted to spit. "Okay. So what do we do? Send him up an electric blanket?"

Jud ignored him. He spoke to Pete and Jerry, the two men MacAndrew had chosen. "Go on up after him, but take along a line. First thing you do when you get to him, you get that line around him so he can't get loose. And you bring him down the way you'd bring somebody hurt. Bad. Somebody who can't hang on for himself and is going to fall if you aren't careful as hell. Got that?"

MacAndrew said, "What about the crane?"

"You can't chase him around the tower with a crane hook. All you'd do is kill him quick." And, to Pete and Jerry again, "Okay, that's it." He looked around at the rest of the crew. "If you've got work to do on the ground, get to it. But I don't want anybody but these two on that tower. You hear me?" This was Hard Nose Jud speaking, and he was listened to. Men began to disperse.

Daryl Chambers standing nearby said quietly, "Will they get him down safely?"

"We'll see." Chambers was the boss. Chambers ought to have been directing the operation. If Sam Taylor had been here—screw that; Sam wasn't here.

Zabrinski came up. He squinted at the tower top, and at the climbing men. "Little problem, no? We might have figured it." His massive calm was unshakeable.

Chambers said, "Just how could we guess that somebody would be damned fool enough to do that?"

"You build a house," Zabrinski said, "you expect kids to climb around in it soon as it's framed. A tower like this is just so much better." He looked at Jud. "I wonder who the hell he is."

His name was Eloy Padilla, and he was seventeen years old, a Tano school dropout, five feet six inches tall, weighing one hundred and twenty-five pounds in his heaviest clothes. For the last hour he had been wishing that he had worn those heaviest clothes, his big sweater, the army surplus parka and the lined gloves, because it was cold up here on this goddamn tower, cold, cold, cold.

But he had done it. That was the fact that dwarfed all else. He, Eloy Padilla, never before a hero, had done what the others had merely talked about, flapping their mouths, strutting—and doing nothing.

Take Pepe Rodriguez, big man, unaccountably in a northern mountain town of small people grown to six feet eight inches in height, laboriously kept in high school because of his basketball ability and now airily considering scholarship offers from a dozen colleges. Pepe had talked about the bridge towers just like everybody else. And done nothing.

But there they were, those towers, growing daily and just daring somebody to conquer them. Anglo towers, symbols to be defied. Okay, he, Eloy Padilla, had defied them, and now that the sun was up and he was seen, all the world would know that it was he who had dared where no others would.

He had told no one what he had in mind. Secretly, he was afraid that he might back away from the adventure at the last moment, unable to face the cliff in the dark, or the tower itself, and so it was best that his intention was not known. Thus he could not be ridiculed if he changed his mind.

It had been a near thing on the cliff face. Once he had slipped, and for a moment thought that all was lost, but his searching foot found support, and he clung desperately to the rock, motionless for a little time, while his breathing returned almost to normal and he could no longer feel his heart beating in the back of his throat.

That had been the moment of truth. Forward, or back? Prudence and desire said back. Pride said forward. Pride prevailed.

Climbing the tower was tiring but not difficult. The riveted openwork steel of the structure was cold on his hands, turning them numb, but handholds were there in plenty, as he had anticipated, and actually the ascent was easier than he had dared hope.

When he reached the temporary top, gasping for breath, his arms and shoulders aching and little strength left in his legs, he did what he had planned, tying the crude, homemade banner by feel in the darkness. Then he found as secure a position as he could among the riveted members, and settled himself to wait for daylight.

Daylight had come, and with it near nausea as the ground far beneath began to show in detail—tractors, trucks, cranes, piles of materiel, even scattered buildings, and then men, all foreshortened by his height. The entire scene somehow seemed to revolve slowly until the dizziness he felt was almost overpowering.

And then, as daylight gradually began to penetrate into the Gorge, it seemed that the tower was leaning, that he, Eloy Padilla, was somehow hanging out over the remaining bottom blackness, and that inevitably he would fall and drop screaming forever down through empty space.

Alternately opening and closing his eyes, swallowing hard, clinging with desperate strength to the cold steel tower structure, he endured, and at last the torment passed. Almost.

Now, with most members of the bridge crew standing beneath the tower, every face lifted upward, voices and even some admiring laughter raised, now was his moment of triumph. He could not resist that derisive wave. It almost lost him his grip on security, and instantly he hugged the cold, solid steel to him with all of his strength, feeling again that nausea.

As before, he alternately opened and closed his eyes rapidly, and tried to concentrate on the nearby mountains. They at least did not seem to move, and he took comfort from their stability. How long it was, he had no idea, but when at last he was able, he took one more deep swallow and looked down again.

The scene had changed. The men on the ground had scattered, and two men, big anglos in hard hats, were climbing steadily toward him. They did not even look up, which somehow made their approach menacing. And one of them carried slung on his broad shoulder a coil of rope. Eloy stared at it, at first in puzzlement, then in growing fury.

That they would come for him, undoubtedly to drag him in humiliation to the ground, was bad enough. He had not anticipated this. He had not actually anticipated anything; his thinking had not gone beyond his triumphant appearance at the top of the tower when the sun rose over the eastern mountains. But that they should come for him carrying rope, obviously intending to truss him like an animal, like a calf at the roping, helpless, shamed in front of the entire world—ah, that, no! He was Eloy Padilla y Lopez and he had in his pocket a knife, and—

"Hey, kid!" One of the big climbing anglos, Pete, looking up now. "Cool it, huh?" We're going to take you down. Got it? Everything's okay."

"Leave me alone!" It was a snarl.

"No, that isn't the way it goes. You haven't got any business here, and we're just going to see that you get down. *Comprende?* We don't want any trouble. All we want is—"

Jerry, the other anglo said, his voice filled with surprise, "The little bastard's got a knife!"

"*Sí!* A knife. Leave me alone!"

"Let's hold it," Pete said, and stopped climbing. His head was perhaps ten feet below Eloy's feet. "Now, look, kid. Cool it, like I said. Going up is the easy part. Coming down, unless you do it all at once, is a little harder. What we're going to do is see you get down okay, that's all. Got it?"

"Leave me alone!"

"The record's stuck," Jerry said. His voice was weary, disgusted. "Put the goddamned knife away, kid. Use your brains, if you got any. We didn't climb up here to play games."

"Hold it," Pete said again. "Let's talk about it, kid." He felt a first, buffeting gust of wind. "Feel that? When you're up above the ground like this, that wind gets a little rough sometimes. You wouldn't know about that. We do. Maybe there're some other things we know that you don't, too. So why don't we talk things over, huh?"

On the ground, still looking upward, "Six, two and even he's a *chicano* from town," Zabrinski said. "And he isn't going to want to be touched." He glanced at Jud.

"Go ahead," Jud said. "You got an idea, say it."

Zabrinski raised his voice. "Hey, up there! What's doing?"

"Tell these mothers to leave me alone!" The boy's voice was shrill with fright, and defiance.

"Can you get down by yourself?"

"I got here, didn't I?"

"Coming down is different."

"Shit!"

"Send the hook for him," MacAndrew said.

"Okay," Jud said in sudden decision, "that's it." He raised his voice. "Those men won't touch you unless you need help. Got that? They'll climb down with you, but they'll leave you alone. *Comprende?*" He took silence for acceptance, and let out his breath in a large sigh.

"What's your name?" Zabrinski called.

"What's that to you?"

"You want it known, don't you?" Why else would he have climbed the tower, and stayed? "So what's your name?"

"Eloy Padilla." There were both pride and defiance in the tone.

"Okay, Eloy," Jud called. "Put that knife away. You'll need both hands. And let's get moving. You two, you heard me, don't touch him unless he needs help. Got that?"

"Roger." It was Pete speaking. He lowered his voice. "Okay, kid. Let's get the show on the road."

Eloy hesitated. "You mothers come close," he said, "and I'll cut you good. You hear?" He put the blade of the knife between his teeth.

"We hear you talking," Jerry said. "Now let's haul ass. This isn't my idea of fun, either."

On the ground, "Wind's coming up," Jud said in a conversational voice. He, like the rest, was looking upward, watching.

"Like I said," MacAndrew said, "devil winds. This goddamned job—"

"That's enough," Jud said. "You want to bellyache, you find somebody in a bar to listen. Don't do it here on company time."

And then, softly, his eyes still on the moving men. "Easy, goddamn it. The kid's no bridgeman."

That was obvious. A bridgeman knew where the next foothold was without looking, and the next handhold. A bridgeman moved surely and securely on a tower or a catwalk or an I-beam, and a bridgeman could look down from any height without even thinking about it. This kid was different.

Fear he would not admit showed in every stiff movement the boy made, each hesitant downward step, each hand shift, each cautious transfer of his weight. His shirttails had come out of his pants, and they flapped now in the wind, at times showing his naked, scrawny rib cage. His flared pants made popping sounds against his legs. He was scared, and stiff, and cold.

"Jesus," Jud said, assessing the situation, and raised his voice again in a shout. "Want some help?"

The boy's head waggled. The knife between his teeth was plain.

"Look, kid," Pete said, "we got a long way to go, and I think you could use a hand. Better yet, let me tie this line on you, so if you do slip—"

"I told you, goddamn!" The words came out muffled around the knife blade, but they were clear enough, angry, defiant, and frightened. "Leave me, goddamn, alone!"

"He's calling it," Jerry said. The disgust in his tone said clearly that he could not have cared less.

Pete let his breath out in slow, controlled exasperation. "Okay. We'll do it your way, kid. Slow and easy, and hang tight. You're doing okay. That goddamned wind—watch it! Oh, Jesus! I've got you, kid! For Christ sake, hold still! Jerry! Jerry, give me a hand, goddamn it!"

Seen from the ground, it was a horror play on a high stage, a senseless struggle without meaning, blind panic out of control.

Pete's voice reached the ground clearly. "Kid, for Christ sake, cut it out! We're trying to help! Hang on, and I'll just keep hold of your arm!"

Jerry said, "Hold still, you little bastard!"

"Leave me, goddamn, alone!" And the knife flashed.

"Why, you little son of a bitch!" This was Jerry's voice. "You—oh, Jesus, there he goes!"

Like a replay, Jud thought suddenly, recreation on video tape, but this time badly miscast; a scrawny kid playing Bob Anderson's burly part. But the result was the same, and the acting identical —the scream, shriek, really; the cartwheeling gyrations; the moment when the body passed the cliff edge and the screen went blank but the shriek, falling in pitch, still trailed back; then the sudden, overwhelming silence.

Daryl Chambers turned away and began to retch.

Quincy Yorke said almost inaudibly, "Lions three, Christians nothing."

"Offhand," Zabrinski said, "I'd guess that the stuff is about to hit the fan. Killing a bridgeman is one thing. Killing a local kid is something else again."

In San Francisco, Sam took the phone call sitting in Wilt Ross's big chair behind the enormous desk. He stared out the windows at the distant green hills of Marin County while he listened, expressionless, to Zabrinski's recital of the facts.

In summation, "It could have been a mistake to send the men up," Zabrinski said. "But that's hindsight. At the time it seemed the right thing to do. The kid was obviously scared spitless, and cold, and stiff, and I think Jud played it the best way he could. The only thing is, it didn't work."

"All right," Sam said. "It's done." But far from finished, he thought; in fact, probably just begun. "I'll come, but I can't be there before afternoon." In the meantime? The answer appeared at once. "Call Henry Evans," he said. "Tell him I told you to. Tell him we need his help, and ask him how he thinks we can best handle it."

He hung up and buzzed for Laura. She came in, closed the door and stood quiet while she listened. When he had finished, all she said was, "You were right about the minefield."

"Yes. Well, we're in it. Call Haskins. Tell him we're going to have legal problems."

"You're going to Tano?"

"What else?"

"I know some," Laura said, "who would bail out about now. And I wouldn't blame you, Sam."

"I would."

"Yes, you would." Her face softened. "If I were twenty years younger—" She shook her head and produced her professional smile. "Haskins. Anyone else?"

"I have a lunch date."

"With Miss Evans." Laura nodded. "I'll explain. And I'll tell Miss Lewis that you will be . . . unavailable this evening."

"You make it sound—"

"Carnal?" Laura watched him steadily. "Isn't it? Miss Lewis is a free spirit. It doesn't take special character judgment to see that. What Miss Lewis wants—"

"She gets, yes. She is spoiled rotten."

"I'm glad you see it, Sam. I was afraid you didn't." Laura turned away abruptly. At the door she stopped and faced the office again. "I'll call the airport. They'll have the jet ready." She hesitated. "Be careful. You're going to be the target for everybody in that part of the world to throw rocks at."

15.

Henry Evans listened quietly while Zabrinski gave his second recital of the accident over the phone. "I feel," Evans said when Zabrinski had finished, "like the man being ridden out of town on a rail who said that if it weren't for the honor of the occasion, he'd just as soon have walked. I am flattered by Sam Taylor's apparent confidence in my judgment, but this is a mess I would just as soon stay clear of."

"I don't blame you a bit. So would I." Zabrinski's voice contained no hint of irony. "So would anybody with a lick of sense. On the other hand—"

"Yes," Evans said, in sudden resignation, "there is frequently that other hand, isn't there? Very well. I will make some telephone calls. Friends in the newspaper and television business. And others." His voice took on authority. "My advice to you is, in that dreadful current phrase, tell it exactly like it was, in Shakespeare's far better words, 'nothing extenuate, nor set down aught in malice.' Obviously the boy was a young, *macho* fool, but that is not how he is going to be thought of by many, too many. There is, for example, a man named Trujillo—"

"I've heard of him."

"Stay away from him," Evans said promptly. "Stay as far away as you can, and tell Sam Taylor to do the same; I told Taylor once that if Joe Trujillo wanted trouble, then all of you are in the position of an isolated outpost deep in hostile territory. I'll double that now. In spades. I hope I am understood?"

"You're calling the signals," Zabrinski said, "and I go by the play book."

Evans hung up and sat for a few moments in thought. First things first, he told himself, because there was a time schedule involved. He picked up the phone again and dialed the number of his flat in San Francisco. "Be there!" he whispered as the phone began to ring. "Be there!"

Ellie was. "I heard about the accident," she said. "I have just been stood up for a luncheon date. But under the circumstances—"

Evans interrupted with uncharacteristic brusqueness. "Do you know a family in Tano named Padilla?"

"There are many Padillas in Tano, Henry. I know some of them."

"Good. Then reach Sam Taylor however you can."

"And?"

"Fly here with him. Tell him I want you here on the scene." He glared down at the light throw across his lap. "You are my legs, Ellie, and I need you."

His next call was to the governor. "You will hear soon enough, Floyd. I thought you'd better be prepared."

The governor listened. He said at last, "I've got a firm grip on what you're saying, Henry, but if there's that chain link fence like you say, and locked gates, and the boy had to climb along the cliff face in the dark just to get to the tower, how in blazes can the bridge people be held responsible in any way?"

"I am no lawyer," Evans said, "but there is a legal concept called 'an attractive nuisance' which has been known to apply to situations similar to this. The concept came into being, I am told, as a result of accidents in unfenced, unguarded and relatively easily accessible railroad roundhouses where kids would play and every now and again lose an arm or a leg, or be killed outright. The underlying theory is that kids, unlike adults, are incapable of properly assessing the hazards of a situation and must be protected. But that is only one aspect of what we have here."

"What's another?"

"Two men were sent up to get the boy. Two anglos. The boy was a *chicano*, a nuisance, and he had a knife. How do you think Joe Trujillo is going to look at what happened?"

The governor glared at the picture of Big Luke while he thought about it. "About the way a sheepman looks at a coyote, yes," he said reluctantly at last, and nodded. "You have anything in mind I can do from here, Henry?"

"Cool it, as they say," Evans said, "and point out that boys will be boys, accidents do happen, and people have fallen into the Gorge before, long before, anyone even thought of building a bridge."

"And Joe Trujillo?"

"I think in the end," Evans said, "I'll have to talk to Joe myself, or maybe Sam Taylor will, but not you, Floyd. You are a red flag to that particular bull."

"And I'm really a nice feller. When you get to know me."

Evans could smile grimly. "I doubt if that is going to come to pass," he said, and hung up to sit again for a little time in thought.

To be honest, he had to admit that he was beginning to welcome the involvement, unpleasant though it might turn out to be. He was suddenly feeling *alive*, as he had not really felt since the accident, Helen's death, and the long, sometimes painful, endlessly dreary procession of tests, diagnoses, proffers of false hope, and final, flat prognosis.

"At least you're alive," the ultimate neurologist out in California had said.

"Am I? How much of the whole can be lost before what is left is pronounced useless, as good as dead?"

"Well," the neurologist said, "that's one route you can take. Some do."

"Route to what?"

"Maudlin self-pity. Up to you."

Ellie had put it differently. "I'll sound like Pollyanna if I say that you can still do everything you've always done, except walk. But it's true. And what if you didn't have money, and couldn't afford things to occupy yourself?"

"I have never subscribed to the idea that other people's troubles make mine feel less important."

"No. You're spoiled because everything you ever tried has been successful. You've never experienced defeat, have you, Henry?"

"Have you?"

"Oh, yes. I have my private wounds. But I don't lick them in public."

"Such as?"

"No." Ellie's voice was definite. "I won't compare hurts. Isn't that just crying into your beer?"

Not a very stirring performance those first hopeless weeks, months, Evans had long since decided, but even the admission itself was entrance to a trap. It was easy enough, too easy, to look back in shame, or anger, or whatever emotion you chose, and dwell upon it, to start living in the past, rejecting the present, particularly when you had nothing of importance demanding your attention. Now, suddenly, perhaps, he had.

He consulted his private phone book and picked up the phone again. First the publisher of the one newspaper that served this northern part of the state with bilingual coverage.

"Armando? Henry Evans. There's been an accident at the bridge site. You've heard? Good. I am asking you to suspend judgment, editorial opinion, until you can talk with the man in charge, a man named Sam Taylor, who speaks for Wilt Ross out in San Francisco."

He listened in silence for a few moments. Then, "I am sorry you feel that way, Armando, and I would appreciate it if you changed your mind. . . . No, that is not a threat. Let's just say I am calling in some of the markers I've collected over the years for favors done here and there. That's all. Helping to have those trumped-up drug charges against your boy quashed, and expunged from the record, for example. How is he, by the way? I saw that he had passed the bar examination this year. . . . Good. I'm glad to hear it, Armando. He's a bright boy, and we need fresh, young blood."

TV Channel 6 next, with statewide coverage. "Bruce? You were asking last week if there was any opening for investment in that new oil shale project up near Rifle. I've thought about it, and I think there just might be. You've already made your assessment, so I won't bother to tell you how solid I think it is. . . . Fine. I'm happy to hear it. Now, it looks as if we may have a little problem up here. Yes, that bridge accident. Poor, *macho* kid. The hell of it is, Bruce, if it's handled wrong, I'm talking about publicity, newspaper, radio, and of course TV, it just could stir up a racist hornet's nest up here, and we wouldn't want that, would we? That kind of thing is worse than a range war. It spreads, and God knows where it ends. . . . I'm glad you feel that way, Bruce. I thought you would if you understood the situation. My love to Ida, and sometime this fall why don't you come up for some fishing?"

The telephone rang shortly before noon. Evans answered immediately. It was the governor. There was a trace of asperity in his voice. "Your line's been busy for two solid hours, Henry. Anything wrong with it?"

"I've been talking, Floyd." All at once, he could smile, and mean it. "I've been using up just about all the credit I have between here and the Texas line. No, not money. Personal credit. I've been spending my brownie points as if they were going out of style. And, you know what? It feels good. Like Christmas shopping."

The pilot had long understood that there were strict rules against carrying casual passengers on company aircraft, and certainly this one, driving her sports car almost out on the field, waving wildly as she braked hard, jumping out before the sports car had even stopped and running for the jet's door as if hell itself were chasing her, was about as casual as he could imagine.

But when Sam Taylor, without so much as a word of explanation, or even command, left the cockpit, went aft and opened the fuselage door to give the girl a hand up the lowered steps, then closed the door again and made a go-ahead gesture with one hand, the pilot faced forward, said, "Aye, aye, sir," to himself in a strictly inaudible voice and eased the throttles forward. Behind him the door between cockpit and main lounge closed with a snap.

Sam saw Ellie into one of the lounge chairs and made sure that she fastened her seat belt. He did the same. "I assume there's a reason," he said, "or maybe even an explanation?"

No demurral, Ellie thought, or even faint hesitation. She wondered how many would have behaved the same. "Henry called, and told me to," she said, and left it there.

"Then I can guess the rest," Sam said, and nodded, satisfied. "You suggested once that I ask his help. I didn't take your advice." He stopped there, studying the girl's face. It was suddenly tense.

The pilot had swung the jet to face the runway, already received his tower clearance, and now at full throttle was beginning his takeoff run. The jet's acceleration pushed Sam and Ellie hard into their seats.

"You're right, you know," Sam said in a conversational tone, and leaning forward, held out his hand. Unhesitatingly, the girl took it and held it tight. Sam's voice went on easily. "Takeoff is the critical time. Every flyer knows that. But it doesn't last long, and once you have a little altitude"—he glanced out the window —"a few hundred feet, as we have now, then you have some room to maneuver, and the critical part is past."

Ellie disengaged her hand. "Silly of me. But thanks."

"Everybody has his hang-ups." Sam's voice was uncharacteristically gentle. "I don't like New York elevators. As a matter of fact, I don't much like high buildings. And I won't sleep above the seventh floor in a hotel unless it has a complete sprinkler system, which damn few do."

He was deliberately making it easier for her, Ellie thought, something she would not have expected. "I flew with a boy once," she said, feeling that explanation was needed. "He was showing off. We climbed too fast on takeoff and lost control—" She managed a smile as she shook her head. "We were lucky. We crashed in a ploughed field, wiped out the undercarriage and one wing, but that was all." The smile spread. "But on every takeoff, my stomach remembers."

"I should think it might." Sam unfastened his seat belt, and with the motion dismissed the subject. "This time," he said, as if there had been no interruption, "I did take your advice. I had Zabrinski call your father. I hoped he would respond. Since you're here, obviously he has."

"I know some of the Padilla family in Tano."

"That's the boy's name? Good."

"And I have some influence with Joe Trujillo. Maybe not much, but some." Ellie shook her head. "It isn't going to be good. You know that?"

"I've guessed."

"To give you an idea," Ellie said, "a Tano boy was killed a few years back. A carful of Texans driving an enormous Cadillac. The car was parked in the public lot while the Texans had lunch in a Plaza restaurant. Somebody let air out of the tires. The *tejanos* were not happy. You couldn't blame them." Ellie watched Sam nod acknowledgment. "They said so. Loudly. When they had the tires pumped up again and drove away, some kids ran after them. You don't drive fast through Tano. You can't. So the kids could pretty well keep up. *Macho* kids, you see the picture?"

"It's building," Sam said, "yes."

"The big Cadillac filled with angry *tejanos* was the bull," Ellie said. "The kids were the matadors." Ellie was silent for a moment. "One of them ran too close. He tripped and fell." She was silent.

"And?"

"Some who said they saw it," Ellie said, "swore the driver swerved in order to hit the boy. Others said it wasn't so, there wasn't anything the driver could have done, the boy was too close. It didn't make much difference. They had to lock the Texans up overnight. For their own safety. And during the night somebody poured gasoline over the Cadillac and set fire to it."

"Offhand," Sam said, "I'd say we're going to need all the help we can get." He studied Ellie carefully. "You'll be on our side?"

"I'll help because Henry wants me to."

"That sounds less than enthusiastic."

Ellie unbuckled her own seat belt, taking a little time to it. She looked up then. "We were going to have lunch together," she said.

"And I, in effect, stood you up?" Sam's smile was mocking. "There are things in the galley here. We won't starve."

"I was going to ask you some questions," Ellie said as if he had not spoken. "I've only been in the city for a couple of days, but I know some people, and Henry knows a lot more, and I've heard quite a few things I'm not sure I like. I'm not sure Henry will like them, either."

Sam wore his poker face. "I'm an unsavory character," he said. "I could have told you that, and would have, if you'd asked."

Ellie took her time. "I'm not really interested," she said, "in your love life with Liz Lewis. Yes, as I told Henry, I know her. She is a stunner. And I've no doubt that she is very good in bed. But that's not the point."

"You call them as you see them, don't you?"

"Henry brought me up that way."

There was silence between them. It grew, and stretched, openly competitive, conflict clearly defined. Sam broke the silence. "And these things you have heard you are not sure you like?" His voice was uninflected.

"Mr. Ross."

"What about him?"

"In hospital."

"Correct."

"Incapacitated."

"More or less."

"To many people in San Francisco," Ellie said, "and probably a lot of other places as well, to many of Henry's friends, contemporaries, Mr. Ross is a—giant, somebody larger than life, the kind of person you look up to because of what he has, yes, *built* with his own hands, a worldwide business, a reputation, the kinds of accomplishments you read about in history books."

"Again, correct." Sam's face and voice were expressionless.

"He's a throwback," Ellie said, "to the days when if a man gave his word, that was it, the days when you shook hands and settled a million-dollar deal, or a ten million-dollar deal, and you didn't need squadrons of lawyers and piles of papers notarized to make it official. That's the way everyone thinks of him."

"Justifiably," Sam said. The flat muscles of his jaws worked angrily, but he said no more.

"And it's being said," Ellie said, "that you are taking advantage of him while he's helpless, you and his secretary—"

"Laura?"

"Yes."

"Advantage," Sam said, "in what way?"

"You are running things, aren't you? Everything?"

"I am."

"Do you consult him?"

"No. I haven't seen him. Laura has."

"Why haven't you seen him?"

"He hasn't sent for me."

"Would you go if he did?"

"I always have."

"Is that an answer?"

The flat jaw muscles were prominent and working, but Sam made no other move. He said nothing.

Ellie said, "I understand why you are suffering my impertinence."

"You are a guest aboard this aircraft."

"That is one reason, perhaps, but there is another."

"And it is?"

"Henry. You need his help."

"I won't deny it."

"But Henry will have the same questions. He has them already."

"So," Sam said thoughtfully. "That was why you suddenly appeared in San Francisco. I wondered. I didn't think it was entirely my charm."

"Henry has a thing about this bridge."

"He is not alone."

"I wish it had never been thought of. The bridge, I mean."

Sam's face showed nothing. He was silent.

"But it's started," Ellie said, "and it can't be stopped, not in a decent way. It can only be, as Henry says, botched, bungled, money thrown away, people killed, hopes raised and then smashed." She was silent as if waiting for an unasked question to be answered.

Still Sam said nothing.

"But you'll be paid, won't you?" Ellie said. "You'll be paid, and you'll walk away, probably without even caring. That's the part that hurts." Again she waited, and again there was no response. She lifted her hands in a gesture of helplessness, and let them fall again into her lap. "All right. I've said my piece. Now shall I say, 'Thanks for listening'?"

Sam stood up. "I'll be in the cockpit," he said, still in that uninflected, unreachable voice. "There are magazines in the rack. There is a cassette player and a collection of tapes, both classical and jazz. The john is aft, and the galley forward." He pointed to the bulkhead. "Push that button if you want me. Our ETA at Tano airport is about two o'clock, Mountain Time." He was gone.

16.

Still on the telephone to Henry Evans, the delay in reaching him already forgotten, the governor said, "I thought you'd better know, Henry, now that the bridge is off and running, regardless of that boy's accident this morning, and most of the opposition folks gone back into their holes, there is already interest in opening up that part of the state like I hoped."

The stereotypical image of the laconic westerner with his simple "yep" or "nope" was about as far from reality as most generalizations were, Evans thought. For the governor, range-bred, one word would never do when three could be made to serve. It was as if he threw up a defensive barrage of verbiage deliberately to obfuscate each subject, and perhaps it was a shrewd ploy at that, because, God knew, ambiguity was always its own possible defense. Evans had never thought of it that way before. It occurred to him that as of now he was seeing a number of things in a new light. "I'm listening, Floyd," he said.

"Eastern money," the governor said, "not local land speculators like we know all too well. These are respectable folks, far as I can see, and their representative out here is a nice feller from down Dallas way named Jones, Bobbie Jack Jones, played a lot of football when he was in college, might have gone on to the pros. You know him, by any chance, Henry? Big, good-looking feller, nose a little whopperjawed? Got it broke playing football, I gather."

"I've run into him once or twice," Evans said, and let his eyes drift to the far horizon where the mountains of the Divide rose clear and sharp against a limitless sky. Clean, uncluttered country, he thought. For how long? "But he didn't get his nose broken playing football, Floyd," he said.

"No? How so?"

"I broke it for him," Evans said, and lapsed into one of his rare uses of colloquial profanity, "when I threw him the hell off land I was leasing down near Midland. I told him if he set foot on my lease land again, I'd put him in the hospital."

There was a brief silence. Evans could almost see the governor staring across the office at the picture of Big Luke and the family ranch house while he thought it over. "Well, now," the governor said, "I don't recollect hearing about that particular dust-up, Henry. Sure you have the same feller?"

Evans did not bother to answer.

After another brief silence, "That puts it in a little different light," the governor said, "maybe a different kettle of catfish, you might say."

"These respectable eastern people," Evans said, "what do you know about them, Floyd?"

"You know, that's a funny thing," the governor said, "one of those coincidences-like. There's a smart little girl name of Perkins, sociologist, Ph.D. and all, out here to help straighten out our corrections problems, penology is her long suit—" The governor paused to draw a breath.

"And?" Evans said. "It's quite a jump from prisons to land development, Floyd."

"Yes, well, that's where the coincidence comes in, like I said, Henry." The governor's voice sounded uncertain. "What I mean is, I just happened to mention some of the names of the money people to her, and she knew about them. Never met them, she said, but she knows them by reputation. Rich people, but the kind that stay out of the headlines, you know what I mean?"

"There are such," Evans said, "yes. I went to school with some of them. Grew up with some, as far as that goes. Do you want to give me some names, Floyd? I haven't kept in touch, but maybe I could ask a few questions."

"Well, now," the governor said, "this is still in the very hush-hush stage—"

"But you called me about it."

The silence this time was longer, somehow labored. "You don't cotton to this Bobbie Jack Jones, is that it, Henry?" the governor said at last.

"That sums it up rather neatly."

"You don't trust him?"

"I might play poker with him, with my own deck, on a transparent table, but no other way."

"And these folks from the East?"

"I haven't heard any names, so I don't know anything about them, but if Jones is their front man, I'd say the knave-or-fool rule applies. And the kind of people your Dr. Perkins talks about, moneyed people who stay out of the papers, are usually not fools, or are at least surrounded by highly paid and far from foolish advice. Which they follow."

The governor said slowly, "Good, solid development could do wonders for this state, Henry."

"And carpetbaggers interested only in quick killings could only make things worse than they are." Evans's eyes were still on the mountains of the Divide. "Is Dr. Perkins pretty, Floyd?" His tone was innocent enough.

"As pretty a little heifer as—" The governor stopped. His voice altered. "You play pretty rough sometimes, Henry."

Evans sighed. "Yes. Isn't that what friends are for? Let me know if you want me to ask some questions, Floyd."

Lawyer John Haskins held one of the leather visitors' chairs for Laura, then carefully shut the door to the outer office before he took his own seat behind his desk. The desk top was uncluttered. He folded his hands on its shiny surface. "After your call," he said, "I took the liberty of telephoning the Tano bridge site. I thought it best to have a firsthand version of the accident. A man named Carl Zabrinski"—Haskins smiled faintly—"whom I used to watch knocking people down at Candlestick Park, gave me a very succinct and I think complete account."

"Sam," Laura said, "thought we will have problems."

"Understatement. But Sam will be on the scene shortly, and he can assess the situation, and let me know. But what I am concerned about primarily, Laura, is the basic situation—Wilt Ross. We can't continue this . . . charade indefinitely."

"Do you have a solution?"

Haskins leaned back in his chair, smiling. "Simple and direct," he said, "straight to the point, the question is typical of you, Laura."

"Don't make me sound like an automaton, John. I'm not. I'm close to tears most of the time. For the first time in over thirty years, I was, and I still am, disloyal to him."

"By destroying the note you told me about?"

"And ignoring his wishes concerning Sam, or at least what seemed to be his wishes."

"They were more than mere wishes, Laura," Haskins said. "He was bound and determined to get rid of Sam Taylor for good and all."

Laura blinked. It was the only sign she gave. "How do you know?"

"He called me that afternoon. He placed the call himself. He was infuriated by what he considered Sam's—disloyalty was what he called it. He wanted me to come over at once and take notes on changes to his will."

"He wasn't himself, John."

"I'm aware of it. I was then. I suggested he sleep on it. He told me I was getting too big for my britches too, that apparently he was surrounded by young whippersnappers who thought they knew it all, and, by God, he was going to show us different. My father might have calmed him down. They were young together. I—"

Haskins shook his head in slow regret. He pulled up his cuff to display a fine gold wristwatch. "He gave me this watch, Laura, when I became editor of the *Stanford Law Review*. That was thirty years ago. He talked to me on the telephone that last day as if I were still a boy at law school."

"So you're actually a part of the conspiracy too," Laura said, "not just a legal confidant. Welcome to the lodge." Her tone was bitter. She drew a deep breath. "You mentioned having him committed."

"It can be done. But not unobtrusively. Not with Wilt Ross. There would be publicity, quite a bit of publicity. There is already talk. If Ross Associates were a public corporation, God only knows what its stock would be selling for now. Probably next to nothing."

"But the banks still honor our credit."

"And will continue to as long as Sam plays the part of crown prince, heir apparent, in charge because that was how it was long planned. And as long as Sam's foot doesn't slip disastrously. A mistake Wilt Ross could make that would be overlooked because of his reputation, Sam can't afford to make. Nor can we afford an adverse comment from Wilt Ross. Either could bring down the entire company structure."

Laura was silent for a little time. She said at last, "What do we need, John?"

"Some kind of legitimating statement from the sick bed." Haskins folded his hands again on the desk top and studied them in silence for a few moments. Then he looked up, unsmiling now. "Will you talk to him, Laura? Or shall I?"

As a matter of principle, Joe Trujillo disliked all anglos, but he reserved his gut hatred for those he classed as *tejanos*, wherever they happened to come from. To Trujillo, Texans epitomized the big, solid men with their equally durable women who in the early 1800s had moved west in a vast, irresistible flood, taking what they wanted, and thought they could hold, with a ferocious ease that was insulting—worse, degrading. And ever since they had totally dominated the scene. Barbarians.

On the other hand, Joe Trujillo was first and foremost a practical man, and for the moment at least he could try to ignore Bobbie Jack Jones's easy affability, which only partly masked a bone-bred southwestern anglo sense of superiority that sang out in every twanged syllable and each open smile.

"Like I said," Bobbie Jack was saying now, "I've talked with the governor. He's a good old boy, but everybody says, 'Shucks, you want to do business up north in this state, Bobbie Jack, the man to see is Joe Trujillo, nobody else.' So here I am."

Hijo de puta, son of a whore, Trujillo thought, smiled encouragingly and said, "I'm always willing to listen."

"I heard that too," Bobbie Jack said, "that Joe Trujillo is an easy man to do business with. Now what we've got here is what I always think of as the main ingredients—opportunity, and money. When this bridge is open, and the east-west highway comes through . . ."

Trujillo tuned out the words. He had heard them all before, many times: land values would triple, quadruple; population would flow in; villages would become towns, and jobs would spring up as if by magic as goods and services were required; mineral wealth in the mountains, long considered too inaccessible, would become available for the taking; etc, etc, ad finitum, ad nauseum.

He hated it. He had fought it with every weapon he could find, or almost every weapon, and now the old dictum if-you-can't-whip-them-join-them was beginning to have appeal. If only that little *tonto*, fool, Eloy Padilla, had not climbed the bridge tower and then had the further foolishness to fall screaming into the Gorge.

Trujillo's telephone had been ringing all morning as a result, and one by one, three of the men he had sent to work on the bridge crew, dismissed for the day because of the accident, had come in to tell him in vivid, if conflicting, detail just how Eloy Padilla had met his death.

Sam Taylor was on his way from San Francisco, and it was to Sam Taylor, no one less, that Trujillo would talk about the matter. In the meantime, here was Bobbie Jack Jones holding out promises of vast riches.

"They talk about lack of water," Bobbie Jack was saying now, "but, shucks, there's always water if you drill down far enough for it. Stands to reason with these big mountains all around, snow, runoff, not to mention that big river down at the bottom of that canyon."

"And just what do you want from me?" Trujillo said.

"Why, just your support, not a blessed thing more. Once folks know Joe Trujillo thinks our development is a good idea, we'll have to fight them off with clubs."

Within bounds, the statement was true. Trujillo smiled modestly. "And what do I get in return?" he said.

"Well, now," Bobbie Jack said, and settled deeper into his chair, "that's what you might call open to negotiation. What I mean is, let's just talk a little about that, and I'm right sure we can work things out to everybody's satisfaction."

In effect, Trujillo thought, a verbal poker game to occupy the time until Sam Taylor arrived, and he, Trujillo, decided how he was going to use the fact of Eloy Padilla's death. "I'm listening," he said.

Inocencio was waiting for Ellie with one of the ranch cars when the jet taxied to a stop at the Tano airport. Zabrinski leaned hugely against the door of one of the bridge pickups.

At the foot of the fuselage steps, "Thanks for the ride," Ellie said.

Sam nodded. "*De nada.*" The coolness was still between them.

"Shall I tell Henry you'll be coming out to see him?"

Sam nodded. "But I'll go to the job first."

Ellie hesitated. "Are you thinking of seeing Joe Trujillo?"

"Among others."

"Don't." She saw instant resistance forming in Sam's eyes. "Not," she added, "until you've seen Henry, I mean. It will be better that way." She turned away to Inocencio and the ranch car. Sam walked to the pickup.

Zabrinski drove as he seemed to do most things, effortlessly. "Lawyer called from San Francisco."

"Haskins?"

Zabrinski nodded. "I gave him a blow-by-blow."

"Chambers?" Sam said. "Where is he in all this?" It ought to have been Chambers doing the talking, coming here.

"I guess upset is the word. You can't blame him. I've got a pretty thick hide, and I said I'd take over, and he said okay."

"And Jud?"

"Like I said on the phone," Zabrinski said, "Jud did what he thought best. He isn't happy, any more than I am, but he isn't hiding under the covers."

In a time of crisis, Sam thought, you got a good look at men. Some ran for cover. Others spat on their hands and went to work. He had seen it before. "Any reaction yet from the town?"

"A couple of phone calls. Anonymous. And the State fuzz came out for a report. They talked to the two men who went up after the kid. Jud took care of it." Zabrinski appeared to be weighing a decision, and the effort made his big shoulders move restlessly as if his shirt had become too small. "Old pal of mine. Pretty good quarterback. Smart boy. Broker now in the city, San Francisco." He glanced sideways at Sam. "Brokers hear things."

"Yes," Sam said, and waited in silence.

"He thought I ought to know," Zabrinski said. "Rumors. You and the old man, Wilt Ross. A hassle. Before his stroke. Maybe it even had something to do with the stroke." He glanced again at Sam's face. It was expressionless. "True?" Zabrinski said.

Inevitably there came a time, Sam thought, when your hand was called, and you had to show your cards, or fold. There was no temporizing with this big, direct, usually easygoing man. "True," he said, and waited for the reaction.

Zabrinski thought about it for a time in silence, his eyes on the road, his hands loose and easy on the wheel. "Just thought I'd ask," he said, and switched the subject with no change of tone. "Jud, Daryl, Quincy, and Frank are still at the job."

"Your doing?"

"I suggested it."

For the first time since he had left San Francisco, Sam could relax a little. Zabrinski was a man to have on your side. Comforting thought. "Thanks," he said, and meant it.

The east bridge tower loomed first, perceptibly taller than when Sam had seen it last. It rose sharp and clean and symmetrical against the bright sky, already giving promise of its eventual slender grace, its beauty, and its deceptive strength.

A case could be made, Sam thought, studying the tower, that a suspension bridge can be one of the loveliest works of man. The high bridge over the Elbe at Hamburg came to mind, or the model of the Ruck-a-Chucky Bridge; the sturdy, but graceful George Washington Bridge across the Hudson, the Golden Gate linking San Francisco to Marin County, the Verrazano Narrows giant . . .

"It's looking good," Zabrinski said. "Jud knows his job."

Sam nodded in silence.

"The hell of it is," Zabrinski said, "they're beautiful bitches, suspension bridges, but they're killers too." He glanced at Sam again. "I said that to Jud once, and he said, 'Hell's fire, they killed men building the pyramids too, and they're only piles of rock. We're bridgemen.'"

Zabrinski parked the pickup inside the gate, and Sam got out to stand for a few moments staring up at the unfinished tower, remembering the sight of Bob Anderson as he cartwheeled, screaming, down past the cliff edge and out of sight. Now this unknown, but no longer anonymous boy, Eloy Padilla, with his brief moment of triumph followed by what must have seemed almost eternal moments of disaster.

Once it had been widely thought that a human falling from great height would lose consciousness, but it was not so. Parachutists dropped thousands of feet for sheer pleasure before pulling the rip cord, achieving terminal velocity within the first few hundred as air resistance and body mass came to equilibrium with gravity. Actually, a human body in free fall achieved at most a speed less than that of a racing car.

No, both Anderson and the boy Padilla would have been acutely conscious as they fell, buffeted helplessly by the wind currents in the Gorge, perhaps striking glancing blows against the cliff face, but more likely encountering nothing but empty space until the final instant of shattering impact.

Sam started to turn away, and then stopped, his eyes again on the tower's top. "What's that up there?" he said.

Jud, emerging from his shack, heard the question. "Some rag the kid apparently tied on."

"I want it," Sam said, and looked around.

The site was deserted, as after Anderson's death the crew dismissed for the day. Machinery and equipment stood empty and idle as in a wrecker's yard. Sam looked at Jud. "Can you run the crane?" Unnecessary, almost insulting question, and he waited for no answer. "Take me up."

He stepped from the crane hook to the narrow platform at the top of the tower, and felt the buffeting of the wind. He glanced down into the Gorge and tried to imagine how Eloy Padilla must have felt when the sun rose slowly over the eastern mountains and revealed the abyss in all of its shadow and mystery.

Frightened? Without question. Terrified. But he had done it, in the darkness climbed his Everest and, as proof, left his banner for all to see. *Macho*, foolish, stupid, yes—but also in its way heroic. Sam knelt to untie the cloth.

It was a piece of bed sheeting, roughly torn, not cut. It bore in red ink the crudely drawn outline of a creature with legs and an upward curled tail, and beneath, in illiterate block lettering the single word: skorpiuns. Without doubt a local kids' gang, and the boy had carried it to this place of high visibility merely as a grand gesture.

Sam stuffed the cloth into his pocket and stepped back into the crane hook. He gave his automatic gesture to Jud in the cab of the crane, and began his descent. His eyes were still on the tower's top. Poor, proud, foolish, but somehow heroic kid, he thought. Men climbed mountains for the same motives.

17.

The governor let his hands drift pleasurably over the generous contours of Alice Perkins's naked breasts. He watched the nipples contract, as Alice's breathing quickened and turned unsteady. Her eyes were closed, and her naked pelvis began its first rhythmic stirrings.

"Honey," the governor said, "I've been thinking."

The girl's eyes opened in disbelief. She tried to keep her voice steady. "Do you have to talk about it now?"

" 'Fraid so, honey." The governor's hands now merely rested on the upthrust breasts, cupping them appreciatively. "It's about a feller I'm guessing you know. Feller named Jones, Bobbie Jack Jones. Name ring a bell?"

"Please," Alice said. "I mean, when we're here like this—" She looked down at her naked self and felt suddenly shamed to be so exposed. "Please," she said again, and tried to rise, but the hands covering her breasts restrained her with gentle, but unmistakable firmness.

"Bobbie Jack Jones," the governor repeated. "Big feller, smiles a lot. Shouldn't wonder but what he appeals quite a bit to women, like you appeal to men. And like I said, I'm guessing you know him." He was smiling, but the smile did not reach his eyes. "How about it, honey?"

"I've . . . met him."

"Smooth talking dude, wouldn't you say?"

"I . . . don't know. Please. Let me get up. I feel so . . . naked!"

"You are. And pretty as a pink turd in the snow, like I heard a feller say once. And being a sociologist and all, I'd think you'd be right interested in how a man talks, and maybe even in what he's saying."

"I told you. I only met him."

"Well, now," the governor said, "you didn't say exactly that. You only said you'd met him, but you said it in such a way that it kind of implied you didn't know him well. And I'm guessing you do. Know him well, I mean. I'm beginning to think that you imply real good. Some might even call it lying."

"Let me up. I won't answer any more questions. I don't have to—"

"Lie here and take this? Is that what you were going to say, honey? Because you're wrong, you know. It's like back East they what they call 'gentle' a horse, treat it real nice, talk to it and soothe it and gradually get it used to the idea of having a rider on its back. We do things a little different out here. We tie a horse to a snubbing post, slap a saddle on his back, climb aboard and let him know right now that being ridden, and doing what the rider wants him to do, is what he was bred for, and he'd better get used to it fast. Colts or fillies, we treat them the same way."

The governor's hands had not left her breasts, and the governor's smile had not faded, but the governor's eyes and the governor's voice made it clear that the governor wanted answers to his questions, and was determined to get them. Naked Alice Perkins swallowed hard. "What is it you want?" she said.

"Well, now, that's quite a bit better," the governor said. "Tell me about this Bobbie Jack Jones."

Sam drove the eight miles in from the highway to the ranch buildings, parked in the graveled area, got out and waited as Inocencio approached nodding gravely in greeting. "Señor Evans is expecting you," Inocencio said in Spanish, and turned to lead the way around the house.

Sam said to Inocencio's back, "The Padilla family. Do you know them?"

"Sí, señor."

"They live in town?"

"Eloy Padilla was from the town." Inocencio stopped and turned to face Sam. He had to look up to Sam's face. "Eloy Padilla was my *primo,* cousin," he said. "His mother is the youngest sister of my father."

"I am sorry," Sam said.

"That is kind of you, señor. But it does not bring my *primo* back from the Gorge."

Henry Evans was in the office-library where they had sat with coffee and cognac after dinner that first night. Somehow, in daylight, Sam thought, the room now seemed more office than library, and wondered if Evans had chosen this place for this meeting because of its feeling of formality. They shook hands as at a business interview. Sam sat in the club chair Evans indicated.

"First off," Evans said, "let me say that if I had my wits about me, I would have nothing to do with this entire unhappy affair."

Sam nodded. "Understood."

"Having said that," Evans said, "I will admit that I am involved, and as the late Mr. Gilbert wrote, 'In for a penny, in for a pound.' I will do whatever I can to keep the pot from boiling over."

Sam nodded again, and showed his faint smile. "Appreciated. We are strangers here."

"Interlopers is closer to the general view, but that is neither here nor there. Do you have any action in mind?"

Sam pulled the piece of bed sheeting from his pocket and handed it to Evans who opened it, stared at the crude drawing and the illiterate lettering for a moment, and then handed it back in silence.

"The boy tied it to the top of the tower," Sam said.

" 'A banner with the strange device, Excelsior!' " Evans said.

"Yes. Or the flag planted on the moon."

Evans's eyebrows rose. "I am pleased," he said, "and, if you will forgive me, also a little surprised that you recognize it for what it is. What do you intend to do with it?"

"Take it to his family."

Evans nodded. "A good gesture. Will you take it yourself?"

"Of course."

"It might be prudent," Evans said slowly, "if someone, perhaps Inocencio, went with you."

From the doorway out of Sam's line of sight Ellie said, "I'll go. The Padillas know me."

Sam stood up. "No. I go alone. First to deliver this, along with my sympathy. Then to see Trujillo. You agree?" He was speaking to Evans.

"I agree that Trujillo has to be seen. I don't agree that you should go into town, to the Padilla family, alone."

"Neither do I," Ellie said. "Even if I wasn't asked."

Sam raised the torn sheeting. "My flag of truce. I think they will honor it."

"You hope they will honor it," Evans said, and then shook his head, refusing further discussion. "Your decision. I will be interested to see how you make out." The interview was over.

Ellie walked with Sam back around to the parking area. From the tackroom doorway, Inocencio watched, expressionless. "Stubbornness," Ellie said to Sam, "seems to be one of your major characteristics."

"I have never pretended otherwise."

"No, that's part of it. You wouldn't. Do you even begin to see the spot you put me, us, in?"

Sam stopped and turned to face her. "You might explain that."

She too had stopped and now faced him, allowing her anger to show. "It shouldn't need explanation. It ought to be obvious. Henry spent the entire morning telephoning around the state, trying to keep feelings, emotions from getting out of hand. This is a foreign country, and you have invaded it to build a bridge a large number of people don't want. Now you kill a local boy. Never mind that it was his fault. That isn't how it is seen. It was the boy's fault with the Texans in the Cadillac, too. But if you hadn't put up your bridge tower, Eloy Padilla wouldn't be dead—that's how it's looked at, simple as that. Can you see that much?"

Sam was silent for a moment. "Go on," he said.

"You're trying in your own way to apologize," Ellie said. "I understand that. But you're about to blunder in like a bull in a china shop, and all of Henry's efforts at keeping things under control are going to be negated, wiped out because you're going to demonstrate that you are exactly what he's been saying you aren't, an unfeeling anglo, yes, a son of a bitch who does things *his* way regardless. You think I exaggerate?" She glanced toward the tackroom doorway. "Ask Inocencio. It's his family."

"I know. He told me." Sam studied the girl's face. "You lay it on the line, don't you?"

"I told you that's how Henry brought me up. And Mother. And Inocencio. And all the good, simple, honest people who work here and live here and don't have the worldliness you're used to. Maybe that makes me a freak, I don't know. Heaven knows, I've felt like one often enough, but that's neither here nor there. What is important now is what you're going to do."

Sam thought about it while the girl watched him steadily. He said at last, "Maybe I have a few things to learn here."

"You do, indeed."

"All right. You've made your point. Let's start over. You offered to go with me—"

"The offer still holds."

"Right. I accept." Sam hesitated. "With gratitude."

Ellie said slowly, "That took a lot of effort, didn't it?" But some of the edge was gone from her voice. "All right. Let's go." She raised her voice, calling in Spanish to Inocencio. "Tell the señor, please, that I am going into town with Señor Taylor—"

"No, señorita." Inocencio stepped out of the tackroom doorway and started across the gravel toward them. "One of the others will tell him. You are going to see the mother and father of Eloy? Then I will go with you also. It is better."

Ellie glanced up at Sam's face. "You understood that? Good." And she waited for his reaction.

Sam watched the small man coming toward them in his labored, bowlegged walk. He was conscious that Ellie was watching him carefully. Slowly he nodded. "Thank you, Inocencio," Sam said in Spanish. "We are grateful for your company."

Well, well, Ellie thought, there may be hope for you after all. A few moments ago I wasn't so sure.

Laura could have wept, just sitting, making herself face and talk to the shrunken old man who lay in the hospital bed. He bore little resemblance to the Wilt Ross she had known, and loved, all these years.

Oh, the eyes were still there. The lids drooped a little now, but the eyes themselves were still capable of momentary fierceness, inner fire to rouse memories. And the bony hands resting quietly on the coverlet, by their very size, proclaimed the strength that once had been in them.

But at first the voice was hoarse and labored, and the words came out indistinctly as if Ross's concentration vacillated, leaving his thinking confused.

"Until today," Ross said, "you have not even mentioned Sam."

"I know."

All at once the voice strengthened. "I found that boy. I trained him and I trusted him—"

"Listen to me. You can still trust him. You must. Because he is all you have. He *is* Ross Associates, just as you have been for all these years."

"By God, I still am. I told him—whenever it was, that day, I told him—" The voice trailed off as the mind searched for memory, and in the stillness there was only the sound of Ross's hoarse breathing.

Laura sat quiet, watching, waiting. How often, she thought suddenly, had she sat like this in Ross's presence, waiting in silence while he studied a problem, assessing it in that decisive way of his, putting together all of the pluses and minuses, the imponderables that had to be considered, constructing without hesitation or fear the pattern that was to be followed, and then in succinct, and sometimes profane, language, issued his instructions for her to implement? Dear God, how many times, how many memories to set now against this pitiful exhibition of bewilderment?

"Did Sam ask you to talk to me?" Ross said. His voice was suddenly weak, almost uncertain.

"No."

"Then it was Haskins. Wasn't it Haskins? Lawyers are always afraid. Lawyers and bankers. I've known him since he was a boy."

"I know. I remember."

"You were just a girl too," Ross said. "Once, I—" He stopped there, and rolled his head from side to side on the pillow, negating whatever thought had been in his mind. "You and Jack Haskins," he said, and his voice strengthened again. "Only he has always wanted to be called John. Okay. You and John Haskins, isn't that it? You decided between you to talk to me?"

Laura drew a deep, unsteady breath. "Yes," she said. "Because it had to be done."

"Sam's been running . . . everything?"

"As I said, he *is* Ross Associates."

"And you?"

"I do what I can. As I did for you."

"Cables in my name," Ross said, suddenly sounding almost like his old self. "Some I didn't even know about. Cancelling the whole Vera Cruz project, authorizing purchases in Venezuela, Indonesia. You took a lot on yourself over the years, Laura."

"I still do. And for the same reason. For you."

Ross leaned his head back and stared up at the ceiling. "They tell me I'll walk out of here. That's bullshit."

"Wilt!" The name slipped out. How long since she had used it? No matter. "They're doing wonderful things. You know that. They—"

"Even from you, it's bullshit," Ross said. "So cut it out." He had raised his head again, and his eyes, suddenly showing the old fierceness, the inner fire, stared hard at her. "What do you and Haskins want from me? Something to confirm Sam in complete charge? Is that it?"

"Yes."

"After that goddamn young whippersnapper defied me, actually *defied* me on the Tano bridge project?"

"He was right, Wilt." The name came out easily this time. "He said we were walking into a minefield, and—"

"That's bullshit too. That bridge is going to open up the whole area. It's going to bring—" The voice stopped suddenly, and the inner fire was gone all at once from the eyes. "I forget the details, Laura, but it's going to do wonders, and I don't want it stopped. You hear? Not for any reason. No matter what Sam Taylor—"

"He isn't stopping it," Laura said. "He's pushing it."

"How do I know that? Goddamn it, here I am tied to this goddamned bed, while God only knows what's going on. You see what I mean?"

"I see what you mean," Laura said carefully, "but you know that Sam is pushing the project because I just told you so. Or don't you trust me, either?" Tears were very close. She held them back with effort.

There was a long silence. Ross said at last in a voice that had lost its edge, "I read about it once, Laura." The words came clearly. "It's called the dementia of senility, if I remember right. Paranoia figures in it. You see enemies everywhere, family, friends, everybody. That's what you're saying, isn't it? You and Johnny Haskins? The old man's lost his marbles and he's liable to say something that'll really make the stuff hit the fan. Like he tried to fire Sam Taylor, and doesn't trust him an inch, and if he could get up from his goddamned bed—"

"Wilt, Wilt. Please."

"You know, I've never seen you cry before, Laura. I guess I've made you feel like it lots of times, but—"

"Only this time. I'm sorry."

Ross leaned his head back to stare once more at the ceiling. "There aren't even any cracks to look at," he said. "Smooth and white, and probably antiseptic too, just like this whole goddamned place." Without a change of tone, or even emphasis, he switched the subject. "Okay. You can tell Johnny Haskins that I won't blow the . . . masquerade." He brought his eyes down from the ceiling to look again at Laura. "He probably gave you a paper of some kind, didn't he? For me to sign? Goddamn lawyers, anyway. With them a man's word is no good. It's got to be on paper. In blood. Bring it over here. You've got a pen? Yes, you would have. The most efficient person I've ever known."

"My one claim to fame," Laura said. "I will treasure it."

"Now you've got your back up. Cut it out. Where do I sign? I can't read it. They fill me full of God only knows what, and my goddamned eyes won't focus close. There. Initials are all Johnny Haskins gets. They'll damn well have to be enough."

"Do you want me to read it to you, Wilt?"

"No."

Laura held out her hand. "Then a . . . handshake?"

Ross took the hand and squeezed it gently. "With you, that's good enough. Now, goddamn it, will you stop crying?"

Again Laura sat in the comfortable leather chair in John Haskin's office. The paper lay on the desk top in front of Haskins where she had dropped it. "He couldn't read it," Laura said. "I offered to read it to him, but he said he would take my word for it, and we shook hands. You have his initials. Is that enough?"

"Technically," Haskins said, "probably not, since he didn't know what he was signing. But it will have to suffice. You are a brave and good woman, Laura."

"I can't shake the feeling that there is treachery in my soul. I'll have to get used to that. If I can."

"Laura. Laura. It couldn't be helped."

"Maybe not. But you haven't seen him. I have."

Haskins studied his folded hands. He looked up. "What does that mean? I have the feeling that you aren't telling me everything, Laura."

Laura nodded, acknowledging the question. Inside, she was already in tears. "What I have not said, John, is that in the condition he is in, he can change his mind at any moment. And there is nothing we can do to prevent that."

18.

Bobbie Jack Jones drove straight back to his Tano motel after his talk with Trujillo. Things, he decided, were looking real good. He had been told, warned really, that Trujillo was not a man to underestimate, but shucks, he, Bobbie Jack, had met Trujillos before, dozens of them, and when you got right down to cases with them, they never did amount to much. It was all *latino* show, with nothing solid at its base.

And this whole Tano area had to be seen to be believed, it was that backward, so with Trujillo's help it wasn't going to be any trick at all to gather up all the land options Bobbie Jack could use for practically nothing up front, against guarantees, which like promises of marriage, cost nothing to make.

There was a telephone message for him at the motel desk, and as he walked to his room to place the return call, he wondered what Alice Perkins, that real cute little piece, had in her sociological mind.

"I'm scared," Alice Perkins said. "That's the bottom line." And humiliated, she thought, but kept that to herself. "You didn't tell me he might turn rough."

"Who?"

"The governor, that's who. Floyd Babcock."

"Why, honey," Bobbie Jack said, "he's just a good old ranch

boy. Maybe on top of a bucking horse he might look like somebody you'd best pay attention to. But walking around like everybody else, he shrinks right down to lifesize." He was frowning now. "What happened, anyway?"

Alice's voice was less than cordial. "Somebody he trusts says you even cast a crooked shadow. An interesting figure of speech, but the meaning is clear."

"And who is that somebody?"

"A man named Evans, Henry Evans. An oil man, I think."

Bobbie Jack stared at the far wall. He said automatically, "You think right. Every hole that damn eastern dude ever drilled has brought in oil or gas, or both."

"He has a ranch near Tano. And he's crippled now. He can't walk. An auto accident."

Bobbie Jack could smile happily at that. "Couldn't happen to a nicer fellow, honey." The smile spread. "I think I'll go have a little talk with him. About old times as well as new."

There were cannibalized automobile carcasses rusting in the bare dirt area behind the low adobe house. Out front burnt orange and yellow roses grew in profusion along a broken wooden fence. A bicycle with an empty front fork lay near the rutted driveway, where three cars, one battered pickup, one shiny low-slung coupe with an amputated top, and a new full-size Chrysler stood in rigid line ahead. No one was in sight, and the window curtains at the front of the house were drawn shut.

Inocencio got out of the pickup and held the door politely for Ellie. Sam came around the truck to join them. No one spoke as they started toward the house.

It was Sam who broke the silence. "You were right," he said, "it would have been a mistake to come alone." Strangely, he felt no discomfort in the admission. Nor did it occur to him to wonder how he knew with such certainty that what he said was true.

"Eloy's mother is named Viola," Ellie said, ignoring Sam's admission. She spoke in English. "She is Inocencio's aunt, even though she is younger than he is. Those are her roses. She is very proud of them. The yellow are Rose of Castile. The others are Austrian Copper. They are very common here, and frequently grow together."

It was as if she were guiding a tour, Sam thought suddenly, and realized that, as during takeoff in the airplane, Ellie's behavior was the result of sheer nervousness. He tried, and failed, to think of something to say.

One of the front window curtains parted momentarily, and then was closed again. "Bueno," Inocencio said almost inaudibly as the front door opened and a man appeared.

He was short and slight, wearing faded jeans, stout work shoes and a cotton flannel shirt. He was probably in his forties, Sam thought, but his lined face was that of a man twenty years older. He nodded politely to Ellie. "Señorita." His eyes went to Inocencio, and he nodded again, in silence this time. Then he looked at Sam.

"This is Señor Taylor," Ellie said in Spanish.

"Understood."

"He has brought you something which Eloy put on the bridge tower."

Sam held out the piece of torn bed sheeting. He watched the man unfold it with slow suspicion and stare at the drawing and the lettering. He look up, uncomprehending.

"*Escorpión,*" Sam said in translation, and not knowing which word was in local use, added, "*alacrán.*"

"I believe it is a boys' club," Ellie said. "I have heard of it."

The man looked again at the sheeting. His lips pressed together in a thin, angry line as he looked up at Sam's face. "This is all that remains," he said, a statement, no question, and yet it demanded an answer.

"That is all. If the police can recover the body of your son—"

"I know about the Gorge, señor. And the river. And we are learning about the bridge. It has now killed three, two men, and a boy. How many more will die?"

"I cannot say. None, I hope."

"Why is the bridge necessary?"

Sam shook his head gently. "That is not for me to answer, either. Your government, your legislature considered the bridge desirable, necessary. We are building it for them." There was, really, Sam thought, nothing more to be said, except the one statement he was now afraid would ring false, but nevertheless had to be spoken. "I am sorry about the boy. Your son?"

"My son, señor, yes." The man raised the piece of sheeting. "For this." His voice expressed sad anger. "Foolish, perhaps. But, to die—for mere foolishness?" He shook his head. "Is that right, señor?"

"No," Sam said, "it is not right. But it sometimes happens." He glanced at the cars in the driveway. "In one of those. In the mountains in a storm. In a river or a lake by drowning—"

"Or on a bridge where no bridge should be."

Back to square one. "I am sorry, señor," Sam said, and turned away to walk back to the pickup. The others followed.

Ellie got in beside Sam, and Inocencio after her. As they drove away, "His name is Juan Carlos," Inocencio said.

"The name," Sam said, "of the king of Spain." It was as if he had not spoken; clearly, the statement meant nothing.

"He works for the county," Inocencio said. "Don José arranged it."

"Don José," Ellie said, "is Joe Trujillo." Her tone was purely explanatory, and yet it said volumes.

"I get the message," Sam said. "It *is* a foreign country." He glanced at the girl's face. "I'm learning."

"I hope so."

Inocencio said unexpectedly, "I understand horses." He was staring straight ahead. "I do not understand politics, or why some men become rich and others die poor. I do not understand why there must always be change, new things, new ways, or why some men are never content. I understand horses, and, yes, I understand *machismo* in boys and even in some men. *Machismo* and foolishness, they are parts of the same thing, are they not?" He turned his head to look at both Ellie and Sam then. "And taken together, like some medicines I have heard about, they can kill. As they killed my *primo*, Eloy."

Ellie's voice was almost inaudible, like a whispered prayer. "Epitaph," she said.

Liz Lewis walked out on her balcony to glare at San Francisco Bay spread blue and clean and sparkling before her. The message her maid had received over the telephone from that Laura woman, Wilt Ross's executive secretary, was perfectly clear, and in its way innocuous enough. Mr. Sam Taylor had been called out of town unexpectedly, and his return was indefinite.

Now, on the FM radio news, what it was that had called Sam out of town was made clear, the death of some silly *chicano* boy in some God-forsaken spot no one had ever heard of. And Liz had had plans for tonight.

Once, in a rare moment of introspection, Liz had come up with the amusing concept that what she had going with Sam was what she understood the shrinks referred to as a love-hate relationship.

God knew, Sam could be infuriating in his arrogance and his impenetrability, if that was the word, and there were times when Liz could, and did, think that she hated him.

On the other hand, Sam was the most exciting man Liz had ever known, and she had known quite a few. Being with Sam, at dinner in a restaurant, at a concert, at a ball game, in bed, was like being with someone not far removed from the wild state, someone far larger and stronger than herself, and capable—this she somehow knew with certainty—of savagery beyond her ken.

Being with Sam was like skiing the moguls at Snow Valley right on the ragged edge of control, like driving too fast into turns in her sports car and feeling the inside wheels begin to lift, like daring a king surf in the Islands and seeing the curl of the great wave hanging over your shoulder.

With Sam, Liz could be at her most wanton best, totally without inhibitions, immersed, no, completely submerged in the pleasures of the moment. And all this, Liz supposed, was the love bit.

She had been looking forward to tonight, and now, because of some stupid boy, Sam had let her down. And Liz was not accustomed to being let down. "All right, damn you," Liz said, speaking at San Francisco Bay, but in her mind addressing Sam. She turned away then, and marched into her library to plump herself down at her desk and reach for the telephone.

To her travel agent she said, "Jenny? Do you know a place called Tano? You do? Never mind where it is. I don't care. How do I get there? Airplane, and rented car? All right. Lay it on. When? Why, as soon as you can. Call me back and let me know. I'll be packing."

The same *chicana* girl with the teased hair and the red fingernails looked up from her magazine when Sam walked into Trujillo's outer office. She hesitated momentarily before recognition came. "Okay. You're Mr. Taylor, aren't you? Okay. He's expecting you. Go on in. Okay?" She went back to her magazine.

Trujillo was sitting comfortably in his desk chair, his foot resting on the pulled-out bottom drawer. He did not get up. Sam straddled the straight visitor's chair. "You got a mess on your hands," Trujillo said. "You know that? You kill a local kid—never mind he's a jerk and never mind he was trespassing, he's dead—and that's all that counts."

Precisely what Ellie had said. Sam nodded.

"So why come see me?" Trujillo said, as if he had not anticipated the visit. "What do you think I can do?"

"Don José," Sam said. "The local squire."

"That's crap. I run an insurance business." Trujillo watched Sam's faint smile appear, the expression of a man at the poker table knowing beyond doubt that the dealer had filled his hand with the draw, or, conversely, had come up empty. "Okay," Trujillo said. "Sometimes I give people a little help here, a little there, but that's all. So what do you want me to do?"

"Keep things from getting out of hand. I've been to the Padillas'. I gave the father, Juan Carlos, the Scorpion banner the boy tied on the tower."

"The Scorpions," Trujillo said. There was contempt in his tone. "A street gang. Like in New York, Chicago. Damn fool kids. I never belonged to a gang. I—" He stopped suddenly, and sighed. "Okay," he said, "I sound like every other self-goddamn-made man, don't I, *chicano* or anglo?"

It was easy to see, Sam thought, why both Henry Evans and Ellie spoke of this man with respect if not with affection. There was no doubt that Trujillo was slippery and not to be trusted beyond his own self-interest, but there was also in him an honesty that made him look at himself and see clearly his own weaknesses, as well as his strengths. And of how many men could that be said?

"So, okay," Trujillo said. "Where are we? You want me to try to keep a lid on, cool it, look at it like a kid kills himself riding a trail bike, or taking a curve too fast in his old man's pickup. It won't be easy."

"I've gathered that."

"For one thing," Trujillo said, "just as sure as hell, you're going to get hit with a lawsuit. Some shyster will persuade Juan Carlos Padilla that he's got a big, fat case against Ross Associates and their insurance people. I know. We get it all the time."

"Understood," Sam said.

"But I can probably help some," Trujillo said. "I've got friends, people who owe me for little favors, that kind of thing."

Sam nodded. Now it came, he thought, and sat quiet, waiting.

"So what we get down to," Trujillo said, "is what's in it for me? I learned a long time ago in this anglo world only a sucker works for nothing."

Nothing changed in Sam's face. "True," he said. "Of course, the less trouble this accident causes, the better it will be for everybody, your community as well as our crew, and Ross Associates. That's something to think about."

"Like waving the flag," Trujillo said, "and, let's hear it for motherhood. You really expect me to spread myself out of the goodness of my heart?"

Again that honesty showing, Sam thought, and found it hard not to smile. "Frankly, no," he said. "I expect you would want something more tangible."

"Now," Trujillo said, "you are talking. What did you have in mind?"

"You sell insurance," Sam said.

Trujillo began to smile. "I'm listening."

"On a project the size of the bridge, we carry quite a bit of insurance."

"Better and better. Keep talking."

"It might very well be to our mutual advantage," Sam said, "to have some of our insurance placed locally. At least I think it would be well worth looking into. One of our people from San Francisco could come out here and discuss it."

Trujillo leaned back in his chair and studied Sam's face. "That's pretty vague."

Sam nodded. "It is. Deliberately so."

"You want me to take it on faith," Trujillo said slowly, carefully spelling it out, "that if I do what I can to keep this thing under control, knock myself out trying, call in some debts and some favors and ask some stiff-necked people to forget that anything much really happened—that if I do all that, then *maybe* I'll get some insurance business from you people?"

"I think you put it rather well," Sam said.

"Jesus, you've got a nerve."

Sam let his smile show once more. "I have something more than that. I have insurance business you would love to have. Just as you have local power I need used on our behalf. A stand off, isn't it? Because if you don't help us, you know you aren't going to see any insurance business from Ross Associates. That is for sure."

"And if I do help you, I haven't any guarantee that I'll get any, either."

Sam stood up. From his considerable height he looked down. "That," he said, "is the chance you have to take. Think about it. I'll be around."

Henry Evans looked up at María, the maid. "Jones?" he said, pronouncing the name in the Spanish fashion, Hones. "Roberto? A big man? Smiling?"

"That is the man."

"All right," Evans said after a moment's thought. "Tell him I am on the telephone. I will ring when I am ready to see him."

The ring came within minutes, and María led the way through the house to the west *portal* where Evans sat in his wheelchair, the light throw covering his useless legs. He did not hold out his hand. "Bobbie Jack," he said. "A long time. Perhaps not long enough. I assume you came with a purpose?"

"Why," Bobbie Jack said, "here I was right in the neighborhood, and I didn't hardly see how I could not pay an old friend a visit, now could I?"

"Considerate of you." Evans's voice was as uninflected as ever, but his eyes were cold.

"You're looking good, Henry."

"Thank you."

"In fact, I don't believe I ever did see a man who fitted a wheelchair better."

"You overwhelm me with compliments. Did you come to talk about land development? Or, more properly, some kind of real estate swindle? Because if you did, I will state my position clearly. I have some influence here, and the governor is a friend of mine. If I have anything to say about it, you will not even be allowed to operate in this state. Is that clear?"

Bobbie Jack's smile did not fade. "I hear you talking, or maybe I ought to say clicking your teeth. But maybe you aren't going to have anything to say about it. I've owed you something for a long time, Henry."

"I understand you say you broke your nose playing football. You shouldn't tell fibs."

"A long time, Henry."

"And?"

"Why, I think maybe a little tit for tat. If you rolled off this porch now in that wheelchair—"

"It would be quite unpleasant for me," Evans said. "Possibly injurious."

From the doorway Sam said unexpectedly, "Just what is going on here?" Large and suddenly grim, he walked past Ellie to stand facing Bobbie Jack. "Who the hell are you?"

"An old acquaintance of mine," Evans said. "Bobbie Jack Jones, Sam Taylor. Mr. Taylor is in charge of the bridge project." The polite tone of his voice had not altered.

"So stay with bridge-building," Bobbie Jack said, "and stay out of private business." He looked down at Evans. "I'm leaving now—"

"No," Sam said in a tone he had not used before, "I think not. Not yet."

"And who's going to stop me?"

"Why," Sam said then, and his voice had turned gentle, "I'll be delighted to."

"There is no need," Evans said. His hand came out from beneath the throw on his lap. It held the .380 automatic pistol from the table in his sitting room. He pointed it steadily at Bobbie Jack's stomach. "Once," he said, "when I was a whole man, I had no compunction about whipping you with my fists and telling you that if you came back I would put you in the hospital. You believed me then. You may believe me now when I say that I will have neither hesitation nor compunction about shooting you out of hand, as I would shoot a varmint, if you come back here again. You were very close to being shot only a few moments ago. Is all that clear?" He made a gesture of dismissal with the hand holding the gun. "Now you may go."

In the silence, "I'll see you to your car," Sam said. "Start moving."

In the graveled parking area, the bravado almost, but not quite, returned. "Now look here, goddamn it—" Bobbie Jack began.

Sam raised his hand, commanding, and getting, immediate silence. "Waggle your jaw again," he said, "and I'll be happy to break it for you. Just shut up and stand there." He raised his voice then, calling in Spanish for Inocencio. And when the little man appeared in the tackroom doorway, "Bring a rifle," Sam added in Spanish still.

He stood quiet waiting beside a silent Bobbie Jack until Inocencio reappeared with a .30-30 carbine in his hands, holding it in the ready position with easy familiarity.

"A man named Jones," Sam said then, indicating Bobbie Jack with a sideways jerk of his head. "He is not welcome here, Inocencio."

Inocencio looked carefully up at Bobbie Jack's face. His dark eyes were opaque, expressionless as if they studied an object, not a man. He made no threatening gesture with the rifle, none was needed. His finger was on the trigger, and his callused thumb rested lightly on the hammer. He nodded slowly. "Sí, señor," he said. "*Entendido,* understood. I will see to it."

"Whether you understand Spanish or not," Sam said then to Bobbie Jack, "I think you get the message. Now, beat it." He turned away before the anger he felt rose out of control. He did not look back as the car door slammed, the engine started up, the rear wheels spun angrily in the gravel and Bobbie Jack drove away.

From the head of the *portal* steps, Ellie said, "You take quite a bit on yourself, don't you?" Her voice lacked edge.

Sam looked up at her in silence.

"I have an idea that is another of your characteristics," Ellie said. And she added as she turned away, "Henry is anxious to hear how you made out with Joe Trujillo."

19.

They sat on the west *portal* facing the limitless vista, and Evans listened without comment until Sam was finished. Ellie watching both men, listening, assessing, found strangeness in the scene and in each of the players. Strangeness in her father that after what had to have been an emotional encounter right on the dangerous edge of violence, he was behaving now as if nothing at all had happened. Strangeness in Sam that within only a matter of minutes, he had displayed the subtlety with Trujillo that he was now calmly recounting, and then switched to the unmistakable fury and menace with Bobbie Jack that she had witnessed. She awaited her father's reaction with interest.

"I would say," Evans said, smiling, when Sam was done, "that you out-slickered Joe Trujillo very neatly. And Joe is not easily out-slickered." He was silent, contemplative for a few moments. "My guess is," he said at last, "that he will cooperate with you, at least to an extent. Joe keeps his eye very much on the main chance, and the prospect of a piece of the bridge insurance will be most tempting."

"I hope so," Sam said.

"Will you, in turn, honor your implied offer?"

"Of course."

Evans nodded. "Good. There is such a thing as being too . . . tricky." He was again silent, his eyes on the silhouetted mountains of the distant Divide. "One the other hand," he said, "I think it only fair to warn you that giving Joe insurance business will not necessarily neutralize him entirely. Joe is a very complex man, and he might well hold out his right hand for the business, while holding a bomb behind his back in his left."

Sam nodded. "I'll bear it in mind."

Evans looked at the automatic pistol which he had laid on the table beside him. "Now for this recent unpleasantness," he said, "my thanks for your part."

"You had it well under control."

"But you couldn't have known that any more than Bobbie Jack did."

To Ellie, Sam suddenly seemed almost uncomfortable. "We happened in at the right time," he said. "No big deal."

Evans smiled faintly and nodded. "Very well. We'll say no more about it. What are your plans now?"

Sam still did not look at ease. "Apparently there are ground rules here I'm not familiar with." He glanced at Ellie, but his words were still for Evans. "Maybe you'll tell me where you think we ought to go from here."

"I will give you my best advice," Evans said. "That will take some talk between us. Stay again for dinner. And stay for the night as well, unless you have other plans. We can make you more comfortable, I daresay, than one of the local motels, or Josie's boarding house." He looked at Ellie. "Agreed?"

"I was going to suggest it myself."

Jud and Zabrinski sat again alone at a table in Josie's bar while talk and smoke and music from Ewen McLean's piano swirled around them unnoticed. "Damn fool kid," Jud said. There was sadness rather than anger in the words.

"He could have fallen while he was climbing around on the cliff," Zabrinski said. "Would you have blamed yourself then?"

"Engineers and lawyers," Jud said. "They try to be logical. This, goddamn it, has nothing to do with logic. I let a fool *chicano* kid get himself killed on one of my bridge towers. That's what it amounts to, and I don't like it even a little bit."

"All right," Zabrinski said, unruffled, "let's forget the logic. Let's look at him as a blood sacrifice, and his death as an attempt to propitiate the gods. Maybe now there'll be no more snafus. You like that better?"

Jud shook his head in slow wonderment. "Sometimes," he said, "you sound like a man who's lost his marbles and ought to be locked up."

Zabrinski nodded, still unruffled, totally unperturbed. "It helps. I learned that a long time ago. The world itself doesn't make much sense, and there's no point in being out of step with it all the time. I used to get paid for knocking people down, which on the face of it doesn't seem very sensible, does it? Now I'm being paid to help build what a lot of people call a bridge to nowhere. Is that an improvement?" He cocked his head in a listening attitude. "That's good piano. Solid left hand. I think I used to listen to him in San Francisco. What's he doing here?"

Jud stared across the table at the big man in open, almost incredulous curiosity. "The kid doesn't get to you at all, does he?"

"Not much."

"Because you didn't know him?"

"That's probably one reason. Maybe the main one. But there are others."

"Like what?"

Zabrinski shook his head gently. "Too complicated," he said. "It gets all mixed up with religion, and mathematics. Oh, yes, they bump into each other if you go far enough out, quantum mechanics, waves and particles, closed or open universe, big bang versus solid state development, ancient oriental beliefs." The white teeth showed suddenly through the thicket of beard. "Don't let the whiskers fool you. I'm not a mystic at heart. It's just that I'm too lazy to shave." He pushed back his chair and stood up. "Be right back. We'll buy the piano player a drink and find out what the hell he's doing here." His eyes, studying Jud, showed compassion in their depths. "More interesting than brooding over a dead kid neither of us ever knew, and probably wouldn't have looked at a second time if we had known him."

Liz Lewis had driven her rented car the hundred and thirty miles from the airport to Tano in a little over two hours, miraculously avoiding speeding citations.

"I've booked you into what I understand is the best motel in town," the travel agent had told her. "It probably isn't much, but—"

"Never mind," Liz said. "I'll make out."

Knowing Liz, the travel agent was sure of it.

Liz turned her full smile on the motel desk clerk, thereby reducing him to a state of quivering adulation. He deserted his post to show her to her room, and without even being asked carried her luggage in from the car. As reward, he received another smile before he wandered, dazed, back to the motel office.

From directory assistance, Liz got the telphone number of the Ross Associates trailer office at the bridge site, and spoke with Quincy Yorke, who answered the call. Quincy was busy with tracing paper overlaid on the bridge drawing, sketching in cable-stays from the bridge towers to the roadway to add strength against sideways distortion in high winds. In his opinion, shared by Chambers, and overruled by Sam, the cable-stays were unnecessary, and merely defaced the beauty of the bridge structure. Quincy was in a fury.

"Sam? All I know is that he talked of seeing a man named Evans, Henry Evans, who has a ranch nearby." He could not resist adding, "I am sure Mr. Evans feels honored by the visit."

Sam, Liz gathered, was not spreading sweetness and light, at least not in this particular direction. She drew a perverse sense of pleasure from the thought.

Henry Evans was listed in the phone directory, as was an Eleanor Evans just above it as well, and that name rang a bell in Liz's mind. A big girl, Liz remembered, statuesque would be the word, with good legs and a full, shapely bosom, outdoorsy, probably attractive to men. Big men. Like Sam. She dialed Eleanor Evans's number.

It did not occur to her that she was being in any way intrusive. It rarely did. What Liz wanted, Liz usually got, and the means of getting it were unimportant. "Perhaps you remember me," she said when Ellie came on the line. "Liz Lewis. We have met a few times in San Francisco."

"Of course." Ellie's mind was already searching for explanation.

"I'm here in Tano," Liz said, "and I'm looking for Sam Taylor. I believe you know him?"

"He is here now."

"May I speak with him?"

Ellie hesitated. Liz Lewis in Tano, looking for Sam? It was an unlikely situation, hence, Ellie thought, interesting. In San Francisco she had been prepared, but not really anxious, to meet Liz face to face. Formidable was the word for Liz in her own surroundings. But here, in Tano? Or, even better, against the background of the ranch?

"Of course you may speak with him," Ellie said. "But if you want to see him, why don't you come out here? He's staying for dinner, and we'd be delighted if you would join us."

On my turf, she thought, and as she walked away from the phone to tell Henry and Sam that company was coming, she hoped that she had done the right thing.

The empty feeling in the pit of his stomach, brought on by the sight of the handgun Henry Evans had pointed at him and then compounded by the rifle in Inocencio's hands, had disappeared at last, and Bobbie Jack was now in a smoldering rage.

He was tempted, but not strongly enough to obey the impulse, to turn right around and drive back to the ranch. And do what? Face that rifle? Why that bowlegged little Mex would just as soon shoot him as look at him. There was nothing on earth meaner than a mean Mex. Everybody knew that. Gila monsters and rattlesnakes weren't in it by comparison.

And that big anglo bastard—what was his name, Sam Taylor? He had the red eye too, that deepset glare that said real plain that here was a man you'd best not mess with unless you had good, solid support to back you up, and then only if you were prepared to kill. There would be no give in Taylor. None.

And even Henry Evans in that wheelchair, crippled or not, had lost none of the moxie that had carried him, an eastern dude, right through the rough-and-tumble of the old oil field days when the name roughneck meant just that, and the scrambling for leverage and position resembled nothing so much as a back alley gang brawl with no holds barred. Back in those days, a man lost his footing, and the only thing he could look forward to was being trampled to death, so those very few, a mere handful like Henry Evans, who emerged triumphant, and stinking rich, were not about to be pushed around by anybody. Something to remember.

What was that saying? Don't get mad; get even. Well, maybe he, Bobbie Jack, could figure out something. He'd better, because the possibilities in land speculation up here were just too damn good to pass up, and Henry Evans had already made his position on that matter plain; he would do whatever he could to block any deals.

Bobbie Jack parked in the motel parking lot and started to walk in through the front office door just as Liz was walking out. He held the door for her, and got for his politesse the same smile that had stunned the desk clerk. He stood then, still holding the door, and turned to watch Liz walk to her rented car. The view from the rear was just as alluring as the view from the front. Bobbie Jack walked inside and straight to the front desk. He jerked a thumb over his shoulder. "Who's that?"

"A guest in the motel."

"I could have figured that, friend. Who is she, and where's she from?"

"We don't give out the names of guests, sir. Our policy—"

Bobbie Jack was still smarting from that ranch sequence, and in no mood to be trifled with. He smiled wickedly as he had smiled at an apparently helpless Henry Evans in his wheelchair. "Screw your policy," he said. "I'll ask just once more. Who is she, and where's she from?"

It was no contest. The desk clerk had to look up at Bobbie Jack's eyes, and his own fell away first. "Her name is Elizabeth Lewis and she comes from San Francisco."

Bobbie Jack turned to watch Liz's rented car drive out of the lot. "Where's she going?"

Speaking to Bobbie Jack's back was easier than speaking to his face. There was no threatening smile watching him. "All I know," the room clerk said with some asperity, "is that she asked directions to the Evans ranch."

"Is that right?" Well, well, Bobbie Jack thought, what do you know? He had no idea if Elizabeth Lewis from San Francisco might be able to provide some kind of handle, but it would be fun to find out, regardless, that was for sure. He felt better.

Of them all, it was undoubtedly Daryl Chambers who was affected most by the *chicano* boy's death. He had seen death before. Anyone who worked on large construction jobs had to be, if not familiar, at least acquainted with accidents, visible agony, helplessness and shock, and occasionally the ultimate of total destruction, a life that had been healthy and vibrant moments before, suddenly snuffed out, expunged, leaving only a broken carcass, a travesty of what had once been a man.

But, aphorism to the contrary, for Chambers familiarity did not breed contempt, nor even a callous attitude to shield emotion. A

Zabrinski could look on, apparently unmoved. Quincy Yorke could quip about the Christians versus the lions as if he were speaking of nothing more important than the Super Bowl. And Sam Taylor, arriving, granted, as quickly as he could, had nevertheless made it clear that what was important to him was not the fact of a boy's death, but merely its effect on the job.

Even Jud Wilder, whose attitude toward his crew, although he would certainly have denied it, was very much that of a father toward his children, even Jud had seemed to shrug the entire matter off as an annoying, but basically unimportant, happening.

But to Chambers, this third tragedy, for some reason even more than the first two, the truck accident and Bob Anderson's death, was a personal matter, utterly unlike anything he had experienced before. And he supposed that the reason was that on this job, for the first time, he was in charge.

And yet in a way, a very important way, he wasn't in charge, either. There was, and had been from the beginning, Sam Taylor. That matter of Chambers's hiring policy, for example, almost brutally overruled. Now the cable-stays to be added over Quincy Yorke's objections as well as his own.

Worse, Sam Taylor's attitude had seemed to indicate that afternoon when he flew in, that Chambers was derelict in his duty to command by turning this Eloy Padilla matter over to Zabrinski.

But, damn it, big, unflappable Zabrinski was better at dealing with that kind of thing than he, Daryl Chambers, was. And shouldn't the best man for the job be allowed to do it?

But that obviously wasn't how Sam Taylor saw it, and there was no way to get through to the man to convince him otherwise. He was a loner who kept his own counsel, a perfectionist who demanded perfection in others as well as in himself. He was, in short, inhuman.

But Chambers remained chief engineer, the man nominally in charge, and the *chicano* boy's death, along with the deaths of the truck driver and Bob Anderson, belonged to him. It was as simple as that.

Jesus!

20.

Henry Evans sat at the head of the polished dining table, Ellie at its foot with Sam on her right hand facing Liz. Henry's attitude was cordial, but beneath the façade, Ellie could detect his amusement and found herself vacillating between resentment of it, and understanding.

She found herself looking at Sam now too with different eyes. And then there was Liz, who was every bit as stunning and self-confident as Ellie remembered her, and she wondered if the invitation had been a mistake.

"There was a Chauncy Lewis," Henry was saying, "a banker in San Francisco. I remember hearing quite a bit about him when I first came out to the oil fields. His bank invested heavily, and very successfully, in oil and gas exploration in California."

"My grandfather," Liz said.

"Indeed?" Henry looked at Sam. "Unless I am mistaken, it was he who also provided the financing for Wilt Ross's early construction ventures."

"I've seen his name in the files," Sam said. He looked across the table at Liz. "You never told me."

"You never asked."

"You've known him then? Ross, I mean? Even before that lunch?"

"He brought me a doll once. From Tasmania. For a time it was my favorite."

"I had no idea," Henry Evans said, "that I would be awakening old memories. In the oil fields Chauncy Lewis was a name one mentioned with awe, along with Doheny, also from California, and such California oil strikes as Signal Hill and the Bakersfield-Taft area."

"And a man named Henry Evans, wildcatter in Texas and Oklahoma," Ellie said. "Don't come all over modest."

"There was a large school of thought," Evans said, tacitly accepting Ellie's statement, "that considered us freebooters, plunderers, even brigands." He turned his faint smile on Sam. "Just as you are considered here by some."

"I suppose."

Evans shook his head. "It is more than supposition. You are bringing change, just as some of us did, with all that change entails. And then, again there is a similarity; you will move on, but the problems your change has brought will remain." The smile returned. "By some it is called progress. I tend to think of an E. B. White cartoon caption: 'I say it's spinach, and I say the hell with it.' "

Liz said unexpectedly, "Is all change bad?"

Evans looked almost as if he had anticipated the question. His smile held. "As with so many situations, it depends upon your viewpoint. Mine, now, somewhat circumscribed, would prefer things to remain as they are, as I am accustomed to them."

Ellie said, "Henry sometimes plays the aging parent part to the hilt, faculties failing and all that. But you ought to play gin with him, or backgammon, or chess, your choice." She smiled fondly the length of the table. Her confidence was growing.

Sam thought of Wilt Ross, and was silent.

They had coffee and cognac in the library after dinner. The outside floodlights were turned on, showing the finely graveled and carefully tended area in which cactus grew—cholla, prickly pear, pincushion, claret cup, green torch—amidst lichen-covered volcanic rocks set seemingly at random, with an artist's eye. Three yucca plants, a large sundial mounted on a solid adobe base, and a birdbath like an oasis pool completed the foreground scene. Beyond the gravel, the piñon and juniper began, together with occasional mountain mahogany, and apache plume now in feathery flower.

"I've never seen a garden like this," Liz said.

Ellie said, "Henry's idea. And my mother's."

"Water," Evans said. "That is what governs this entire part of the country. Or should. Bernard De Voto wrote that where the annual precipitation rate falls below twenty inches, about at the hundredth meridian, is where the West begins. In Southern California, for example, they either forget that or ignore it, and they plant exotic gardens and lush lawns that demand watering for survival. Here, except when we are growing for food, we plant nothing that cannot exist on its own."

It was Ellie who broke up the group. "You two want to talk," she said, and rose from her chair. "I'll take Liz for woman chatter." The confident ease she felt with Liz here in her own surroundings was beginning to astonish her. It was all she had hoped for, and more. And it came to her unmistakably that Liz felt it too.

"I had no idea," Liz said, "that you lived on this—this feudal estate. In fact, I didn't even know such places existed outside of the sheep stations in Australia."

"There are other, even larger ranches. Not many, but some. But this was what Henry wanted. And, over the years, got; put together, rather."

"And now Sam's bridge."

Ellie nodded. "Change," she said. "We've accepted it." They sat in the living room. "Is there anything you'd like? More coffee? Wine? A drink?"

Liz shook her head. She seemed uncharacteristically subdued. "Just talk."

The new confidence asserted itself. "About Sam?"

"Since you mention it, yes."

"His interest is in Henry, what Henry knows, and can do."

Liz smiled faintly. "I doubt if that's entirely true. Sam has an eye."

"Obviously, since he's fond of you."

Liz raised one eyebrow. "You call them as you see them, don't you?"

"Do I offend you?"

"No." Here Liz took her time. "Technically, I suppose you would say," she said at last, "I have no real claim on Sam. He is very much his own man, which is one of the things I find attractive about him." She glanced around the big room. "He fits in here. But, then, he fits in almost anywhere. I think working for Wilt Ross taught him that." She smiled suddenly. "My grandfather, the one your father talked about at dinner, was a great one for aphorisms. 'A rolling stone may gather no moss,' he said, 'but it sure as hell can pick up a high polish.' He wasn't talking about Sam. He didn't ever know him. But it applies, anyway."

The sense of confident ease continued, if anything stronger even than before. "He came out of a small homestead ranch in the Nevada desert," Ellie said.

Liz experienced a sudden twinge of envy, a rare thing indeed. "You know more about his background than I do. I always thought life for Sam began in the engineering department at UC."

"He never knew his mother," Ellie said, "and his father—he lived with him in Nevada—died when he was sixteen. He's been on his own since then." She smiled suddenly, remembering her comment the night she had learned about Sam's background. "And I think," she said, "in fact, I'd bet that was exactly the way he preferred it."

Liz nodded. "It explains a lot of things."

"Such as?"

Liz smiled again. "You *are* direct, aren't you? No, again I'm not offended, just a little surprised. What I meant, among other things, was that you do not put a halter on Sam. If you even try, you are in for the shock of your life. He doesn't actually roll his eyes, but in a figurative sense which is very real, he lays back his ears and digs in his heels and will not budge. Challenge him in any way, and he will meet you head-on without a moment's hesitation. He doesn't carry a chip on his shoulder as some men, and women, do. But he is constantly and consistently vigilant in protecting his—I suppose privacy is the word. He is John Wayne walking into the strange bar, always and instantly ready to react if there is trouble. Those are some of the things I think his background explains."

Ellie said, "It must be lonely. For him, I mean."

For the third time Liz smiled, and then shook her head in wonderment. "Yours is the generous, sympathetic reaction. Mine is selfish. Sam's closed-door policy infuriates me. I read once that Goethe would actually tap out poetic rhythms with his fingers on his mistress's back while he was making love. That infuriated me, too, and for the same reason. I am not used to being only part of a man's attention, and I don't like it."

"But you're here. All the way from San Francisco."

"Because of Sam. Yes. Silly, isn't it? But from that same grandfather, who in many ways was closer to me than my parents, I learned a number of things, and one of them was that you play to win. Always."

Ellie nodded, strangely satisfied. "I will remember."

It was some little time before Sam came into the room. He looked from one woman to the other in his enigmatic way. "We've had our talk," he said. "Now Henry is asking if you'd care to join us on the *portal*."

Ellie stood up. "Henry likes an audience."

Liz rose too. "Don't we all?"

María was already setting out a tray of drinks, bourbon, scotch, port, assorted liqueurs, glasses, ice, water, soda. "Talking," Henry said, "is thirsty work. Ellie, you'll do the honors?"

To Sam, the situation was strange, but not strained, and he, too, detected Henry Evans's amusement beneath his unfailing courtesy. Ellie had as much as told Sam that she knew of his intimacy with Liz, so Sam assumed that Evans knew too, and here, of course, lay the reason for his amusement, that Ellie should have invited Liz out to the ranch.

Granted, there had been no hint of any kind of attachment between Ellie and Sam himself, but it was true that their relationship had changed with the visit to the Padilla house, the brief encounter with Bobbie Jack Jones, and Sam's account of his talk with Joe Trujillo. The change was subtle, but there, a lessening of antagonism, and the first appearance of real friendliness.

Two young women, then, both vital, attractive and unattached, and himself, obviously at least susceptible. It was no wonder that Evans was enjoying the scene as if at the theater.

"I've told Ellie," Evans said, "that she has no business being buried here in the boondocks with me. As a matter of fact she did go to San Francisco for a visit which, unfortunately, had to be cut short because of the accident at the bridge project. When the dust has settled, I hope she will go back."

Behind every word, Sam thought, there was quiet laughter, and he was sure that Ellie, at least, sensed it.

"Do you have a place to stay?" Liz said. "Because if you haven't, I have plenty of room, and I'd be delighted to put you up."

"Henry has kept a flat, and a car, in the city," Ellie said. "No problem."

"'When the dust has settled,'" Sam said. "That could take a while."

Evans nodded. "It could indeed."

"All because of a boy," Liz said, "who sneaked in and managed to get himself killed?"

Evans nodded again. "Precisely. As a matter of fact, you put it very well." Nothing in his face or in his voice betrayed his irony.

"A *chicano* boy," Ellie said, "killed on an anglo project. An Arab boy dead under unusual circumstances in Israel."

Liz looked from father to daughter. "Oh," she said in sudden comprehension, thereby raising herself several notches in Evans's estimation. "Cactus," she added thoughtfully, "great spaces and huge mountains, as much Spanish as English spoken—is it then a foreign country?"

"As I am beginning to learn," Sam said, and made an acknowledging nod in Ellie's direction. Evans, he thought, would love that.

"I grew up on the eastern seaboard," Evans said, "where we thought, no, we took for granted that this country of ours, the entire U.S.A., had its beginnings. Plymouth Rock, 1620, and, in the vernacular, all that jazz. We either did not know, or blithely ignored the fact that a man named Coronado came through these parts in 1540, eighty years earlier, claiming them for the King of Spain. He went as far east as what is now Kansas, decided that his two guides were lying to him, which they were, had them strangled, and went back to Mexico. Seventy years later, in 1610, a man named Oñate came north, founded the city of Santa Fe, and made it a Spanish capital of the New World, while the Pilgrims were still in Amsterdam wondering what to do next."

He looked from Sam to Liz, speaking to them both. "My point is that this specific area has roots that far predate the arrival of ourselves, the anglos. Roots and mores, traditions which we trample upon without even thinking. The wonder is not that we stir up resentment, but that the resentment does not get entirely out of hand. Something like this boy's tragic foolishness could be precisely the trigger that could cause an explosion." He looked again at Sam. "You resume work tomorrow?"

Sam nodded silently.

"Understandable," Evans said. "You have a schedule to maintain. On the other hand, few attitudes can rouse as much bitterness as that of business-as-usual in the face of tragedy or suffering." He made a sudden, small gesture, dismissing the entire subject. "There are other, more pleasant things to talk about. How is the new foal, Ellie?"

Ellie smiled. "Inocencio says he is going to be a big one, and a good one. You may have a champion quarter horse on your hands. Inocencio thinks so."

"Then we may indeed. Inocencio doesn't just know horses; he speaks horse." Again he looked at both Liz and Sam. "Have you seen quarter-horse races? No? Then you have a treat in store. No, a thrill. Floyd Babcock's Big Luke, for example, is in the line of a previous champion quarter horse named Hank, and resembles him in conformation, close to sixteen hands, almost fourteen hundred pounds. Watching all that horseflesh blasting out of the starting gate is almost more than one can bear. And if you blink twice, the race is over. Big Luke won his quarter of a million dollars in twenty seconds flat."

It was Liz who called a halt. "I was invited to dinner," she said, "not to spend the weekend. It is late, and I must leave."

"I fail to see why," Evans said. "Your Tano motel is hardly the Fairmont or the Palace, and I do think we can do better here. Ellie?"

"Rooms are ready." She smiled at Liz. "And there is a toothbrush in the bathroom."

"You are too kind."

"And it is a lonely drive back to town," Evans said. "So let's consider it settled. Ellie can probably provide whatever you need."

"Just a robe," Liz said, "and I'll do fine."

Sam glanced at Evans's face. It was inscrutable, the face of a man who held four aces—or a busted flush. Was there laughter in his mind? It was impossible to tell.

"I'm ready to call it quits too," Sam said. "There's a lot to do, starting early in the morning—if early is all right?"

"This," Ellie said, "is a working ranch. The kitchen will be awake by dawn, and so will I. Henry likes to sleep in, so Liz can pick her own time without trouble to anyone."

Sam awakened. Moonlight filtering through the curtains filled the room. The sound he heard was faint, stealthy, the sound of a door handle and lock turning. The door to the hall opened, and Liz stepped through and closed the door quietly behind her.

She wore the robe Ellie had lent her, and her feet were bare. "You seem surprised," she said. "Were you expecting your hostess, instead?" She moved closer to the bed. Her smile was quite plain. "Was that it?"

Sam said nothing.

"Because if you still are," Liz said, "things could be real interesting. I've never been part of a threesome, but I've heard that it can be lots of fun." She opened the robe, and let it drop to the floor. She was naked. Her flesh gleamed whitely in the filtered moonlight, enhancing the sculptured contours of her body. "Move over." She lifted the coverlet and slipped warmly in beside him.

"You," Sam said, "are something else."

"You've always said so. But our hostess looks as if she might be quite something too, don't you think? It might be fun to find out."

Sam reached for her and drew her close. "You talk too much," he said. As on the night of Bob Anderson's death, there was urgent need.

21.

Jud, driven by a compulsion he could not have explained, was at the bridge site well before sunrise, to walk around aimlessly, hands in pockets, shoulders hunched against the pre-dawn chill.

What Zabrinski, that sometime oddball, had said about the dead kid having been a blood sacrifice still stuck in Jud's mind, and would not be dislodged. Ridiculous, of course. As a matter of fact, that part about propitiating the gods, if Jud understood it correctly, wasn't even necessary. So far, the job hadn't been as tough as Jud had actually expected. And, oddly enough, he found cause for concern in that.

The truck driver and Bob Anderson had been killed, of course. But otherwise, there hadn't been any really serious injuries to raise hell with morale.

Nor had there been any bad delays in delivery of materiel, the kind of thing, like a shortage of steel, that could grind a job to a halt and leave the whole crew sitting around, doing nothing.

The inevitable snafus in design had been minor, only an occasional conflict in the drawings calling for two things to go in the same place, which couldn't be done, or some dimensions that didn't add up when you came to putting it all together; matters that could be adjusted by Quincy Yorke or Zabrinski on the spot almost without any work delay.

And there had been no real conflict between the *chicanos* and pueblo Indians on the job and the rest of the crew, mostly anglo. Jud had been prepared to bang a few heads together, if necessary, but there had been no need.

The wind was still very much with them, of course, and now, late summer approaching fall, they could probably expect the wind to pick up in those storms September always seemed to bring. But Sam had promised the safety nets by the time they started pushing steel out over the Gorge, and just the presence of the nets would probably offset any increased wind threat, so Jud anticipated no problem there.

And things in town had shaped up pretty well, considering. Some of the crew had brought their own trailers, and wives, and for the rest there was enough housing, and women, to make do. Josie's Place had become their gathering spot, and since Ross Associates had picked up the tab for the damage caused by the brawl the night Bob Anderson got it, Josie herself had turned real friendly, even buying an occasional drink on the house, which was something you didn't run into very often.

There remained, of course, the vague threat of a big wind, a real stem-winder romping down out of the surrounding mountains and catching the half-finished structures with their cable-stays down. But if a man wanted to dig that deep to find trouble lurking, he could probably find plenty else to lie awake about, too, if he really put his mind to it.

First light touched the top of the west tower across the Gorge and moved invisibly over the abyss until all at once the east tower top was clearly visible too. There was where that damn fool kid had clung yesterday morning, cold, and stiff and scared out of his wits, but defiant right down to the end. The hell of a thing, Jud told himself, kicked at a rock, and turned away to his own superintendent's shack.

He was about to walk inside when he stopped, turned, and stood for long moments, struck by a new thought, staring again at the unfinished top of the east tower now in full sunlight.

What if Zabrinski, that great hulk of oddly sensitive man, had somehow unconsciously put his finger on the truth, but backwards? What if the dead kid, instead of being the blood sacrifice to propitiate the gods like Zabrinski had said, was actually a goddamned bad omen, like having a black cat cross your path?

Nothing to it, of course. Jud didn't really believe in such things. But in years of construction work, he had to admit that there were times, some of them prolonged times, when bad luck seemed to be at full flood and you couldn't win for losing. And every now and again, it did seem that something specific kicked off the run of bad luck, and you could look back and say, "Hey, this is where it all began."

He was shaking his head in disgust with himself as he walked into the shack. He was getting to be like MacAndrew, who viewed the whole world with alarm. To his *Penthouse* nude on the wall, he said, "What I need, goddamn it, honey, is about a week in bed with somebody like you."

Ellie was up early too. In cotton flannel shirt, faded jeans and boots, she came around the corner of the bedroom wing hallway in the half-darkness just as Liz let herself out of Sam's room and started for her own, holding the borrowed robe carelessly about her. Confrontation was unavoidable.

"Good morning," Ellie said automatically, her mind instantly springing to a posture midway between anger and amusement. "I hope you slept well?"

Liz raised her shoulders and let them fall in a gesture of helplessness. She clutched the robe more tightly. "Quite," she said.

Amusement won; anger could be indulged later, in private. "I'll go along and order Sam's breakfast," Ellie said, showing not a trace of smile. "I imagine he'll be hungry."

Liz opened her mouth, thought better of it, and closed it again in silence. Her clutch on the robe tightened.

"Is there anything you need?" Ellie said, all at once the solicitous hostess.

"Not a thing, thanks."

Ellie nodded then, and walked past without another word. Amusement was overpowering control, and she was afraid she would giggle.

She was finished with her breakfast and sitting over a second cup of coffee when Sam appeared. He seemed bright-eyed and bushy-tailed, the very picture of Rhett Butler the morning after he had carried Scarlett up the stairs, Ellie thought, and again stifled mirth. "Good morning. The cook is poised. Her *huevos rancheros* are very good; fresh eggs. And we are quite proud of both our ham and our bacon, our own ranch products. Or, if you prefer steak—"

"*Huevos rancheros* would be fine. With bacon?"

Ellie rang the bell and placed the order with the maid. She spoke again to Sam. "You slept well, I hope?"

"Very."

"No . . . disturbances?"

Sam took his time. Ellie's face, he decided, betrayed no more than her father's did when he chose to hide his thoughts. "None that I recall," he said. "Is that the proper answer?"

Liz had been right, Ellie thought, Sam did respond immediately to challenge. She said without emphasis, "I met Liz in the hallway. No doubt she will tell you herself. And I took the liberty of ordering coffee immediately. And juice."

Sam thought about it. He said, after a pause, "It was slated to happen, of course. Whoever arranges these things must have found it irresistible. We, Liz and I—"

"A man I knew once," Ellie said, "told me never to apologize and never explain. I won't go quite that far, but it does seem to me that there are times when the dictum can be applied. With profit. Here is your coffee. Do you take it black? And I hope orange juice is right?"

Sam leaned back in his chair to study her. "You're enjoying yourself, aren't you?"

Expressionless still, Ellie sipped her own coffee. She set the cup down with deliberate care and looked straight at Sam. "As a matter of fact," she said, "I am. I don't think you take pratfalls very often. So I am enjoying the spectacle of this one."

Sam considered the words, and the situation. He thought of Henry Evans last night, and of his quiet amusement. Was there any difference now? He shook his head slowly at last, his eyes still on Ellie's face. "You know," he said, "I can't say I blame you. Not even a little bit." The reaction was remarkable.

Ellie blinked, but her eyes remained steady. Her expression softened. "At this moment," she said truthfully in a new, friendlier voice, "I think I like you better than I ever have before. Drink your juice. Or your coffee. One."

When Chambers walked into the trailer that morning, Zabrinski was looking over Quincy Yorke's shoulder and nodding solemn approval as he studied the sketched-in cable-stays on the transparent overlay of the bridge drawing. "It has the right look and the right feel," Zabrinski said, "and I'll be willing to bet the calculations will agree."

"Unnecessary, unsightly and a waste of money and materiel," Quincy Yorke said. "But Sam Taylor"—he turned to glare up at Zabrinski—"aided and abetted by you, you huge monster, has decreed, and what can I do but obey?"

Business as usual, Chambers thought with some bitterness, having not yet shaken the memory of the Padilla boy. He nodded his good morning to both men and walked into his own tiny office.

For reasons he could not now fathom, he found his thoughts going to that Bohemian Club lunch with Wilt Ross, so long ago it seemed. Had the old man already been a trifle off his rocker then, as Chambers had heard that he was now? Had there been telltale traces of senility that he, Chambers, had missed and ought to have caught and taken into consideration? Because certainly things had not worked out as he had anticipated they would. Not by a long shot.

"There's a qualitative difference," Ross had said, "between being number two and being number one on a job. When you're number two, no matter how much responsibility you may seem to have, you always have somebody to lean on, to back you up, and that makes a difference in your thinking, whether you realize it or not.

"But when you're number one, you're out front, leading the parade, in the final analysis making all the important decisions, taking the blame, and sometimes even getting the credit. You think you want that, do you?"

"Yes, sir. Very much."

"We always need good men who can run a job," Ross had said then. "Engineers, technicians, mechanics—we can hire them by the gross. What we never can find enough of are those who can pick a job up by the scruff of the neck, shake it until its teeth rattle, and then put it on course and keep it there. Men like that don't come along often. Now, where were we?"

God, was that the tip-off he had missed? "We were talking about the Tano Gorge bridge project," Chambers had said.

"Right." Ross's focus was clear again. "You want it. Okay, it's yours. I've looked over the planning and the scheduling and the design and all the rest of it, and they're sound. We've got some weak sisters, computer jockeys and pencil pushers, who don't agree, but I say different. The job's yours. Think you can cut it?"

"Yes, sir!"

A brave beginning, but somehow Chambers had not quite realized how it was going to come out. Oh, the project *was* moving along. You had only to look at the two proud tower structures rising to realize that. But what he had not anticipated was the impact he felt from the three deaths so far, nor the sense of frustration that came from feeling that Sam Taylor was omnipresent and looking over his shoulder, nor the growing belief that while he was technically in charge, he really was not, that Jud Wilder and Carl Zabrinski, let alone Sam Taylor, went their own ways regardless of what Daryl Chambers might think.

The ringing telephone broke his thought pattern. He picked up the phone and spoke his name.

"State Police here," the voice on the phone said. "Agua Blanca station. You're in charge on that bridge project?"

"I'll do. What's up?"

"A long shot hunch," the voice said, and settled down to detailed explanation. "Week, ten days ago one of the local kids turned up wearing a hard hat. Ross Associates, the hat was marked. Kid said he hauled it out of the river when he was fishing. Finders keepers, you know what I mean?"

"I don't think we'll sue."

"Yeah. Well, now maybe we got a body that goes with the hat. Could be? We had a bulletin some time back saying a man of yours was missing."

The picture in his mind was unnerving—Bob Anderson cartwheeling. "We lost a man into the Gorge. We reported it."

"Yeah. Well, I'll tell you. It's a funny damn thing, but when they hit that river, you never know where they're going to turn up, or when, or even if. One of those white-water rafting trips a while back, the raft flipped over. They lost three. Only one ever turned up. Depends how the bodies go, you know what I mean?"

Chambers held himself stiffly under control. "I think I follow you." He wished the man would not be so damned graphic.

"This stretch down here is called Agua Blanca. That means white water, and it damn well is, white and rough, narrow, fast and full of big rocks. What I'm working up to is this body's been in the water for quite a spell, and it's been through our rapids, and maybe it was hung up somewhere and banged around first, I don't know, doesn't much matter. But what I'm saying is you'd best send somebody down here to try to get a fix, an identification, which isn't going to be the easiest thing in the world to do, because what's left doesn't look like much. The hard hat's okay, if that helps any, though there isn't any name in it. And the body's still wearing one shoe. Maybe that'll do some good. Okay?"

Chambers closed his eyes briefly. It was bad enough watching Bob Anderson fall and hearing him scream. But it was something else again to think now of what someone would have to face in order to try to make identification.

"You still there?" the policeman's voice said.

"I'm here. I'm wondering who to send."

"Somebody who knew your guy, that's for sure. And even then it isn't going to be—"

"Okay, I heard you." I knew him, damn it, Chambers thought. I saw him every day. I knew him, and I have a good, a too goddamned good memory for people, faces—if there is a face. And—

"We want somebody responsible," the policeman said, "not just some guy who'll say, 'sure, it's him,' without giving much of a damn whether it is or not. You know what I mean? If we notify next of kin, we want to be damn sure what we tell them is a fact, not just somebody's half-assed guess. You're in charge? Then how about you? Did you know this guy you lost?"

"I knew him."

"Okay, then how about it? We don't want to keep him laying around too long. Not in the shape he's in. This warm weather—"

"Okay!" Anything to stop this grisly conversation. "I'll come down! How far is it?"

"By river, about a hundred miles. By road a little less."

Chambers hung up and sat for a few moments motionless. It was strangely quiet, and through the doorway of his tiny office when he looked up he saw Quincy Yorke, Zabrinski and Frank Miller all watching him. Zabrinski said, "A body? Where?"

They all listened as he told them.

"Nice assignment," Zabrinski said. "Want me to go along?"

The temptation was there, sudden, strong, almost overwhelming. The mere presence of Zabrinski would be a steadying force, something to brace against. In short, Chambers told himself sternly, a crutch. He remembered Ross's explanation of the difference between being number two and number one. And I am supposed to be number one, he told himself. "Did you know Anderson, Carl?"

"I suppose so. I must have seen him."

"No," Chambers shook his head in sudden decision. "Not good

enough, but thanks. I'll go. Tell Sam when he comes in." He stood up and walked out before he changed his mind.

He was in his car, turning the ignition key with reluctant fingers, when the far door opened, Jud Wilder slid into the seat and started to close the door.

Chambers said, "Did Zabrinski call you?" There was no other explanation.

"My men," Jud said. "I do what I can for them."

"Get out." An order, sharp, almost angry.

Jud looked at Chambers for a moment in silence. "You know," he said slowly, "most people don't talk to me like that."

"I did. And I am. Get out. You're running a construction job. Get back and run it. I'll do what I can for your man." And then, in a higher-pitched tone, but his voice now little more than a hoarse whisper, "Goddamn it, can't you see this is something I've got to do myself?"

There was another short silence. "You may have a point," Jud said gently, got out and closed the door with care.

He watched the car drive out through the gate. Men came of age in different ways, he thought, and sometimes practically all at once. Watching the metamorphosis was always something of a surprise.

There was no point skulking in her rooms, Liz told herself, now showered, dressed and ready for the day. Sooner or later she was going to have to emerge, and the longer she postponed the inevitable second meeting with Ellie, as well as the first meeting of the day with Henry Evans and his quiet, not quite concealed amusement, the worse it was going to be.

The question of morality did not enter. Liz could not have cared less what Ellie, Henry Evans or anyone else thought about her going to bed with Sam. Hester Prynne and her ridiculous scarlet letter were of a different age, a different world. Sex had come out of the closet and was not about to be shut back in.

No, it was purely and simply the circumstances surrounding her night's activities that were awkward, and even—a rare situation indeed for Liz—embarrassing. Because with fun and games, as with all sports, there were rules, and she had flouted them.

She was a guest in this house, and being a guest imposed responsibilities. There were certain things one did not do, or if one did, one made damn sure he or she was not caught at it. And that encounter with Ellie in the hallway had made Liz feel as if she had been surprised stealing the silverware.

If it had been Sam coming out of her room, all would have been different. Regardless of the facts of the matter, men were still considered to be the irresponsible, lusting gender, and the boys-will-be-boys rule was still tolerantly applied. Women displaying the same tendencies were either mercenary or just plain gauche.

There was the root of the matter, the unforgivable sin, to be caught behaving in a gauche manner, seen in public with your hair up in curlers, or your slip showing, or your eye makeup a mess from recent and obvious tears.

Liz studied herself in the mirror, and found herself suddenly laughing. "You silly bitch," she said, stood up, walked out of the room and down the hallway. The tune of "La Donna è mobile" (The Lady Is Fickle) from *Rigoletto* popped into her mind, and she began to hum it as she walked.

Ellie, from her desk in the library-office, saw Liz come into the breakfast room and went in to greet her. She rang the small, silver table bell, and María appeared at once. "I've had breakfast," Ellie said to Liz, "but if you like, I'll have a cup of coffee to keep you company. I hate to eat alone."

Without guile, Liz thought; and smiled. "Please do."

They sat facing one another at the polished table. Light, the dramatic high-mesa light that has intrigued artists of four civilizations, poured in through the east windows, highlighting the gleaming brick floor, the solid, handmade furniture, the heavy silverware on table and sideboard.

Opulence and taste, Liz thought, and Ellie, even in flannel shirt, jeans, and dusty boots, still managed somehow to fit the setting. Strange. She found herself studying Ellie as, despite her remarks to Sam last night, she had not done before.

Ellie was poised and at ease, Liz thought, mistress of the situation. Large, but all in proportion, proud neck, solid shoulders, splendid breasts, trim, undoubtedly firm waist, long, lithe legs. And when she smiled, as now, Ellie was almost beautiful.

"A working ranch, as I said last night," Ellie said, indicating her clothing with a casual gesture. "I've been out to see the foal, and I've ridden over to the Gorge to check on my eagle eyrie. And one or two other odd little chores."

"While I lay slug-abed."

"Our elevation sometimes affects people for the first day or two. We're a little over seven thousand feet here at the house." An attempt to put a guest at ease.

Still without guile, Liz thought, and with no apparent irony, either. But the subject had to be explored, if only briefly. "Have you seen Sam?"

"I sat with him at breakfast too. He had juice, *huevos rancheros*, bacon and coffee."

Nothing had altered in Ellie's face or in her tone, and Liz decided, as Sam had before her, that like father, like daughter, when the Evanses chose to keep their thoughts, and perhaps feelings as well, hidden from view, they did it with ease. Liz felt vaguely outmaneuvered.

"As far as I know," Ellie said, "Sam has gone to the bridge site. And where from there, I have no idea."

"He will be coming back here?"

"Until this Eloy Padilla matter is laid to rest," Ellie said, "he and Henry will want to compare notes, and ideas. So Sam will stay here as long as he stays in Tano." And just maybe, she thought with no change of expression, one of these mornings I will be the one leaving his room, or he mine. And how would you like that, Miss Lewis?

Something of the same thought was going through Liz's mind. "I'm sure he and your father will find much to talk about," she said.

Ellie leaned back in her chair, hooked her thumbs in her silver and turquoise decorated belt and studied Liz quietly. "I've always found," she had heard Henry Evans say once, "that if confrontation is inevitable, there is rarely any point in postponing it. The first punch is frequently decisive." And Henry, Ellie had long ago decided, was far more often right than wrong.

"Since Sam is your reason for coming to Tano," she said, "why don't you stay here too for as long as you care to?"

Liz concealed her surprise with effort. "You are too generous."

Ellie said nothing. Thumbs still comfortably hooked in her belt, she continued to study Liz without expression.

"You are sure I won't be too much trouble?"

Ellie's face softened and the smile began to appear. "I think we'll manage."

"Generous *is* the word," Liz said. "You don't press your advantage." And then, although she had not intended to raise the subject, "Last night—"

"Last night," Ellie said, "was between you and Sam. I believe the phrase is 'consenting adults'? More coffee?"

On the surface, but only on the surface, dinner at the ranch that night was a replay of the night before. At first, Sam, watching the two women closely, was impressed by their remarkable mutual cordiality.

That afternoon, while Sam was gone and Evans was busy on the telephone to his many enterprises, the two had gone horseback riding. Ellie had ridden the big buckskin, and her usual heavy, western roping saddle.

"But that wonderful little man," Liz said, "Inocencio, I think is his name, produced a beautiful flat saddle for me, and a lovely mare who would have been quite in tune in Central Park or on one of the bridle paths around the parks in London."

"My mother's saddle and mare," Ellie said. "She hasn't been ridden much, and I must say you handled her beautifully."

Later, when Sam and Evans sat alone on the *portal* and talked of the continuing local feeling concerning Eloy Padilla, Evans, without preamble, digressed from the subject.

"I once had the dubious pleasure," he said, "of serving on the board of a hospital. There were two women on the board, both in their late fifties or early sixties, who disliked each other intensely. Had they been men, one would have said they hated each other's guts. But in board meetings they smiled and smiled and smiled, displaying expensive dental work, and they spoke to each other with intense cordiality and extreme politesse. There was only one clue to their real feelings. One inevitably called the other by her given name, which was Phyllis. And Phyllis just as inevitably called the other by her formal title, *Mrs.* Swanson." He sat silent then, sipping his glass of port.

"I see," Sam said. And then he shook his head, correcting himself. "No, I don't see. I think you're talking about Ellie and Liz, in fact I'm sure you are." He saw confirmation, almost imperceptible, in Evans's face. "But I sure as hell don't see why they behave like that. Like sisters."

"Good man," Evans said, and allowed a faint smile to show. "Admission of ignorance is the first step toward wisdom."

Sam slept well that night. Undisturbed.

22.

The bilingual paper in this northern part of the state was called *La Prensa*, Armando Baca, Editor and Publisher. Summoned, Baca sat now in Joe Trujillo's insurance office. "They call you Don José," Baca said in Spanish, scorn heavy in his voice. He switched to effortless English. "Philanthropist and public-minded citizen. Shit. You see a buck, and that's all you see."

"And you only see headlines to sell papers. You *want* to stir up trouble, don't you?"

"When it's deserved. An anglo bridge company not even from in state. From California, for Christ's sake. And they let a kid climb around on their goddamned bridge tower and get himself killed. Or was he pushed? Way I get it, they sent up two goons in hard hats, and the kid didn't have a chance."

"You said Henry Evans called you."

"That's right. He wanted me to lay off the story."

"Maybe he pointed out how he'd kept your kid out of the slammer? And had his record wiped clean? Maybe he figured you owed him one?"

"He laid it on that way, yes. But, goddamn it—"

"With you," Trujillo said, "integrity comes first, no? You'd rather be right than be president, particularly if by claiming you're right, you can sell more papers and more advertising and sound like you're gung ho for the little man. Screw the big landowners and the out-of-state construction companies, they're anglos. Isn't that it?"

Baca leaned back in the straight chair and took his time. He said at last, "You don't care what you say, do you, Joe? Okay, so you're an important fellow. But once upon a time a *chico* like Eloy Padilla wasn't just a statistic to you, like they say. He was the same kind of raggedy-assed damn fool kid you were once, and I was, and that meant something to you. Now do you give even a small goddamn that he's dead? It doesn't sound like it."

Trujillo said almost wearily, "Suppose you kick up a big fuss, get everybody up and stomping around yelling for blood like in those TV pictures from Iran? Will it change anything? Will it bring the damn fool *macho* kid back from the Gorge? Will it keep other kids from thinking about trying it? And who's at fault, anyway? Tell me that."

Baca shook his head in exasperation.

"Have you got another way to handle the story that will do some good for somebody? No? Then how about handling it so it won't do a lot of harm? Remember that kid and the Texans in the Cadillac?"

"The bastards."

"Maybe. But all you accomplished by playing the story big and tough, you and the TV news reports between you, was you got the Cadillac burned up, and the Texans held in the slammer overnight, and on their way back to Texas in the morning. Big deal. In your editorial you sounded like you'd defeated the whole state of Texas. This time you're taking on California, is that it? Another big deal?"

Trujillo sat on alone after Baca had left, his foot propped on the pulled-out bottom drawer of his desk, his eyes fixed on the empty visitor's chair. Now why did I do that? he asked himself. And what the hell did I accomplish? He heard no answers.

The goddamn trouble, he was coming to believe, was that he, José María Trujillo Sanchez, raggedy-assed damn fool kid like Armando had said, had moved too far from his beginnings, lost the fine, eager, unhesitating fighting edge that had been his when he was lean and hungry, and reached the point where he saw, not one side of a question, but many sides, as if every situation was surrounded by mirrors reflecting different goddamn versions of the truth. Worse, all the versions were convincing.

And the sorry fact was that no matter which of the many possible positions he took, he could no longer feel entirely comfortable with any of them. And that, *sin duda,* without doubt, was just the hell of a thing, no?

What was more, he was also beginning to believe that at the root of this major change in himself, somehow inextricably entangled, was that goddamned bridge, Floyd Babcock's bridge.

The governor too was thinking long and hard about the bridge. It wasn't that he was beginning to wish he'd never started pushing the idea in the first place. Not exactly. But like after anteing up with an inside straight in your hand, drawing your card and finding what you damn well ought to have known from the start, that the odds were long, too long against drawing the one card that would fill the gap, you then had your choice of tossing in your worthless hand or trying to run a bluff, and neither course of action was what you might call downright appealing.

Henry Evans had been right, as usual, predicting that there would be a stink because of the death of a single, scrawny, no-account *chicano* kid who had no business on bridge property in the first place. The governor's phone had been ringing itself almost off the hook these last twenty-four, thirty hours, and a lot more calls had been stopped and not put through by Betty Jo out in the reception office.

Now came Sam Taylor in person, and Betty Jo stood just inside the closed door waiting for decision. "Oh, hell, show him in," the governor said. "I'd better see him."

"Henry Evans thought I'd do well to touch base with you, Governor," Sam said, and smiled faintly, without amusement. "And I've found Henry more often right than wrong."

"It's a habit with him," the governor said. They shook hands. He indicated two leather club chairs and they sat down.

"The bridge progresses," Sam said. "We're back at work this morning. We'll have both towers finished in forty-five days, and then there'll be something to see when we start cantilevering the roadway out over the Gorge. You'll have your bridge. On schedule."

The governor took his time. "I've played a little poker myself," he said at last. "And you get kind of a feel for the game. And for the men sitting around the table." He looked shrewdly at Sam. "You're talking a little different from what you were last time we got together. You were a little cagier then."

"I'm always cautious at the start of a project."

The governor nodded. "Makes sense. Whipped all your problems now, have you?"

"Those we know about."

"Including those in San Francisco? Wilt Ross?"

"We miss him, but he's no problem."

"Sure about that, son? Even out here in the boonies, we hear stories."

"Unless I know what they are," Sam said, "I can't refute them. Or affirm them."

Again the governor took his time. He said, as if in decision, "You're running things?"

"I'm running things."

"Including the bridge?"

"I'll give the bridge all the time it needs."

"That may stretch you out a mite."

"You have my word, Governor."

The governor thought about it. "Seems to me," he said slowly, "that you've turned into a true believer, a real, honest-to-God, born-again bridge gospel singer, preaching the Word in the wilderness. What changed you?"

He had not really examined the reasons, Sam thought, although he had been aware that his attitude toward the bridge had indeed been changing. "Part stubbornness, I suppose," he said.

"Dwell on that."

He tried to sort it out, but it was all a jumble—Wilt Ross, Jud Wilder, Bob Anderson, now Eloy Padilla, Zabrinski, waspish little Quincy Yorke, even Daryl Chambers, yes, and Evans and Ellie, and Liz on the scene . . . There was no clearcut answer, but clearly the governor needed reassurance to continue his staunch support.

"You start a job," Sam said, "and it's just something on paper. Then it begins to be people, and structure, something you can see and touch. It doesn't come easy. It never does. You kill a man—that truckdriver."

"Seems to me he killed himself."

"But on the job. There's a difference. Bob Anderson. Now this *chicano* kid. And there'll be others. I guess the thing is, you invest more than money in a job. You invest part of yourself, as well as the lives of others, and finally you reach the point where you're sure as hell not about to let all that investment go down the tubes. I'm not all that good at explanations, and that's the best I can do."

The governor thought about that too, and in the end nodded. "That's good enough for now." He stood up. Sam rose with him. They were about of a size, big, solid men both. "You know," the governor said, "I'm beginning to feel about this bridge the way the Arabs probably feel about the camel who pokes his head inside the tent. First thing you know, the camel's right in the middle of everything, affecting everybody. All you can see, or feel or think, is camel."

"I think I know what you mean," Sam said.

Betty Jo stopped him in the outer office and held out a While You Were Gone form filled out in her neat hand. "I didn't want to interrupt you and the governor," she said. "But the lady did say it was urgent."

Sam looked at the form. Laura. And the message of urgency was not needed. Laura would never call him with anything trivial.

There was a public phone in the hall. Sam placed a credit card call, and as he waited he wondered. Ross? Comment from Haskins? Materiel problems? "Laura," he said when she answered; and stood quiet and expressionless while he listened.

"I've tried to keep it from you, Sam." Laura's voice was tightly controlled. "But I'm afraid it's beyond me now. Jim Hardy's in hospital in San Juan. Malaria. Bad. He's been there over a week now, and the Cul de Sac job in Haiti is coming apart without him. I talked with Leclerc an hour ago. He's Jim's number two in Port au Prince. I've talked with him every day. But now he talks of problems and delays and major difficulties as if the world were coming to an end. And I gather that for him it might as well be doing just that. He can't cope, Sam. I've heard too many like him, in over their heads and just giving up."

Sam closed his eyes briefly. "I'm not twins, Laura." The words came out before he knew it.

"I realize that. And if I thought it would help, I'd fly to Haiti myself."

You would, too, Sam thought, suddenly shamed. "All right," he said, "I'll see what I can figure out and get back to you by this afternoon. There are a couple of things here—"

"I'm sorry, Sam."

"I know."

"You don't even think of malaria until it happens. *Anopheles* mosquito, isn't it? And female at that?" Her voice was tight. "Wilt has had it off and on for years."

It was the first time Sam had ever heard her refer to Ross by his first name. "Easy, Laura. We'll figure it out."

"There's a deadline, Sam. On the Cul de Sac job, I mean."

"There always is."

"And bad penalties. I checked with John Haskins."

"Laura. I'll get back to you. Have some lunch. And a drink first. A stiff martini."

"Now you sound just like Wilt."

Sam smiled wryly at the wall. "I guess I'm trying to," he said, and hung up.

There were four men standing beside the Ross Associates pickup in the capitol parking lot when Sam came out of the building. They watched him as he approached, and when he was close, one of the men spat on the pavement directly in his path.

Sam hesitated. With the mounting sense of frustration he felt, nothing would have suited him more than action, a sudden throwing off of the restraints he realized he had been under, a return to other, younger, yes, and less responsible, times. Only two quick punches, that was all it would take, one a left hook to the belly, high up just beneath the sternum, and the other, a straight right hand to the side of the jaw as the man bent inevitably forward, punches with all the energy that had been building in his mind behind them. Once, he would not even have hesitated.

He put it behind him and continued walking straight for the pickup, through the four men who grudgingly stepped aside to give him passage. He got into the cab, started the engine and drove off without a word. In the outside rear mirror he saw the men staring after him.

The name on the door of the pickup must have caught their eye, he thought, and the fact that they had seen fit to stand beside it, apparently waiting for whoever had driven it, testified to the depth of their feelings about Eloy Padilla's death.

Hard to believe that anger, or resentment, or whatever it was had gone so deep. Yes. But it had, and, understanding that, it was not hard to see why the governor was having second thoughts about the entire bridge project.

But it is too late to stop it, Sam told himself, even if we

wanted to, and we, or at least I, don't. No way. We barge ahead, regardless.

When he reached the bridge site, he went first to Jud's superintendent's shack. It was empty. Then behind him in the doorway Jud said, "I saw you heading here and figured you had something on your mind."

Sam nodded. Through the open doorway, sounds of construction were plain, the racket of the crane's engine powering its hydraulic muscle, the staccato chatter of rivet guns, jackhammers pounding away at bedrock, opening holes for eyebolt anchorages. A truck engine started up with a roar. A backhoe flexed its mechanical claw, and the clatter of its exhaust rose in pitch.

A construction symphony, Sam thought, and watched Jud's face which seemed to indicate that he was unaware of the noise. But he is, Sam told himself, and if a single false note is struck, he will hear it on the instant as surely as a Barenboim or a Mehta or a Bernstein would detect even a minute error deep in the string section or among the woodwinds.

"What would you say," Sam said, "if I put you in charge here? Total charge?"

Jud stared at him for a moment in silence. "I'd say you'd lost your fucking mind," he said.

"Tell me why."

Jud spread his hands. "I'm a working stiff. I can run a construction job, but I'm no engineer, no planner. If you don't think Chambers can cut it, put Zabrinski in charge, or bring in somebody from San Francisco. Don't even think of me. Anyway, you've been running the show yourself, even if it has been from long distance. I'd say it's the hell of a way to run a railroad, but that's your business, not mine."

For Jud it was a long speech, and there remained a great deal behind the words unsaid, Sam thought, and he wanted to know what. "You've been saving this up? Spill it."

Jud looked up at the nude on the wall. "Honey, the man's asking. You heard him." He looked at Sam again. "Okay." His voice was reluctant, but determined. "I never did know Wilt Ross well. Met him a few times, that's all. And I never even saw that office of his in San Francisco, but the way I always thought it would be, he'd have his ass in a big chair all day every day, with paperwork and cables and telex and phone calls coming in from wherever Ross Associates was busy doing something."

Sam nodded, "You're right so far."

"Long as everything was going fine," Jud said, more sure of his thoughts now, "all he'd do was read the reports and look at the figures and maybe send out a cable or two himself, or make a phone call. Am I still right?"

Sam nodded in silence.

"But if something went wrong, he'd call you in and tell you to get the hell out to that particular job and shake it until its teeth rattled, fire whoever needed firing, hire whoever you needed, get the job back in line and then come back to San Francisco and report. No?"

"Close enough," Sam said.

"But he didn't go out himself," Jud said. "Know why? Not because he was getting old, or tired. He didn't go himself because he was needed right where he was, right in the center of things, keeping all the colored balls in the air at once. You said it yourself that first day here. You can't sit in the stands and still call the signals. But you can sit on the bench and send in the plays. You don't have to go out and play them yourself. And that's what you've been doing, running here in that fancy jet, doing the job Chambers was hired to do, doing it better than he could, I'll admit, but the point is, you haven't any goddamn right doing it at all. You belong with your ass in the big chair, making the big decisions, not here on the job riding a crane hook to see how my men are doing on the top of the tower."

Sam sat quiet, thinking about it. More introspection, he told himself. This seemed to be his day for it.

"You asked," Jud said, suddenly uneasy after the long speech. "Otherwise I wouldn't have sounded off."

Sam gestured briefly, brushing aside the implied apology. "You suggested Zabrinski," he said. "He's a stress engineer."

"He's the hell of a good man, Sam."

"Could he run this show?"

"Better than Chambers. Not as good as you. But give him a little time and he'll be a top hand. Chambers—" Jud shook his head. He was thinking of that brief scene in Chambers's car, and his fleeting idea that the man might at last have come of age.

"What about him?"

"I don't want to sound like a damn shrink, Sam, but he never had a chance here from the start. You came in and pushed him aside, and Chambers couldn't take it. I don't think he could grab hold again here after that. He'd always be looking over his shoulder for you." Jud hesitated. "But I think he has the makings. If you'd give him a job and leave him alone. Jesus, talking's thirsty work! I could use a shot and a beer right now!"

23.

All during the drive back from Agua Blanca and that devastating glimpse of the body that had been pulled out of the river (his immediate reaction: a swallow, a nod, another swallow, and then the words blurted out, too loud, too fast, almost incomprehensible but mercifully sufficient, "Bob Anderson. Yes!") Daryl Chambers seemed to be seeing things, everything, as he had not seen them before.

Colors were brighter, shapes more real, the late summer cumulus clouds in the limitless sky far more beautiful than he had ever seen them. He passed a cluster of adobe houses against whose walls long *ristras*, strings, of red chili peppers hung drying, their shapes and colors brave against the roughness of the wall surfaces. He wondered if he had ever seen such a sight before, which was ridiculous, of course, because he must have. He just hadn't been noticing. Now he was.

The difference, of course, was the difference between life and the fact of death, from which he had fled as fast as he could. The air he breathed seemed sweeter, a tonic, and the feel of the sun's warmth through the car's glass pushed back into darkness and oblivion what the fall, the cold river and its rock had done to what had once been a man.

There were changes in thought, too, and if the new attitudes turned out not to stand the test of time, they were real enough right now, and that was what mattered. He was Daryl Chambers again, alive, well, competent, knowledgeable, all of the things he once in his private thoughts had listed on the plus side of his personal ledger, but recently had come to doubt.

What had happened to Bob Anderson, and probably to Eloy Padilla too, made other failures, defeats, call them what you would, shrink into insignificance by comparison. So Sam Taylor had overshadowed him on the job? Far worse things could happen, and only death was irreversible.

It was in this mood, not of buoyancy but, rather, of determination, that he reached the bridge site again. The familiar rivet guns were chattering, and the crane was swinging another I-beam up to the connecting gang on the tower platform. Strange, but when Chambers looked up to watch, he no longer saw Eloy Padilla, and no longer heard his screams. He had seen the results, and against that, all that had gone before was mere prelude.

The pickup Sam Taylor was using was back, he noticed, which probably meant that Sam was in the headquarters trailer, giving orders, as usual. Chambers went to see.

Sam was there, in the middle of the large room of the trailer, as usual seeming larger than lifesize, dominating the scene. Quincy Yorke and Frank Miller watched him in silence, and even Zabrinski seemed somewhat subdued. Nobody noticed Chambers in the doorway.

"I'll tell you straight out," Sam said, "I offered the job to Jud Wilder. He has more experience than anyone here, including me."

"Jud's a good man," Zabrinski said. "You could go a long way and do far worse."

Sam's smile was crooked. "He told me I'd lost my mind. He knows his limitations, and he's right. Running the actual job, as he is, he's the best possible support for whoever sits on top in here. He knows it, and that's the way he wants to keep it. I agree."

Quincy Yorke said, "Are you going to make us privy to your further thinking?"

Sam smiled again. "I am. Carl here is going to take over."

There was silence. Quincy Yorke said at last, "And what, pray, of Daryl?"

Zabrinski said, "I don't think I want to—"

"I need him elsewhere," Sam said. "He's going back to San Francisco with me."

Too much. Entirely too goddamn much, "The hell he is," Chambers said loudly, and all eyes turned to see him for the first time. "I was hired to do this job." There was a sudden luxury in expressed anger. "You can fire me. Okay." Chambers shook his head suddenly as he changed his mind. "No, you can't. I just quit." He turned away and walked out of the trailer.

Quincy Yorke said, "I do think you touched a raw spot."

Zabrinski said, "I don't know what you have in mind, Sam, but do you want me to talk to him?"

"No," Sam said, all at once angrier with himself than he could remember. "I blew it. I'll try to put it right." He started to turn away and then stopped. He spoke to Zabrinski. "It's all yours, lock, stock, and barrel. I want to be kept informed, but unless there's a crisis, I won't interfere. Just remember that if you have troubles, there's a phone line to San Francisco." He looked at Yorke and Miller and awaited reaction.

Quincy Yorke said, "Taking orders from this great shaggy monster will take some getting used to"—he shrugged his slim shoulders—"but I believe I can manage."

Frank Miller nodded.

"Right," Sam said, and left the trailer.

Chambers was in his car, and starting to pull out through the gate. Sam waved him down by stepping deliberately into the car's path. It stopped with the bumper almost touching his legs. He walked around, opened the offside door and slid into the seat. "Let's take a drive," he said.

"Where?"

"It doesn't matter. Your choice."

"You may have a long walk back."

Sam shrugged. "I'll take the chance."

Chambers hesitated, then put the car in gear again and drove off slowly. From the doorway of his shack, Jud watched without expression.

"You weren't supposed to hear that back in the trailer," Sam said.

"Why not?"

"Because I wanted to talk to you alone."

"To cut me down to size gently, in private?"

Sam turned to look at the man. He was changed, he thought,

and wondered why, or by what. "You've got a chip on your shoulder," he said. "How about taking it off for a few minutes?"

"Or you'll knock it off? Is that what you're waiting for, a chance to flex your muscles?"

"When I was a kid," Sam said, "a man I knew and didn't particularly like wanted to tell me something and I didn't want to listen. I don't even remember now what it was. But I remember what he said about listening to it. 'You can have it however you like,' he told me. 'You can listen sitting in a chair like a normal human being. Or you can listen lying on the floor with me sitting on your chest. Your choice.'" He glanced again at Chambers. "Well?"

Chambers thought about it. Staring angrily at the road straight ahead, he said at last, "What the hell am I supposed to say? I'm —outnumbered."

Sam nodded. "That's good enough. Why don't you pull off in this wide spot?" And when the car was stopped and the engine turned off, "I've got a new job for you," Sam said.

"I'll bet."

"Just save the comments until you know what you're talking about. Do you know anything about dams?"

"They hold water. Usually."

"Have you ever worked outside the country?"

Chambers turned in surprise. He studied Sam's face.

"When we send somebody out of the country," Sam said, "it costs us money. So we pick and choose pretty carefully. We've got a good man in charge of this dam project, and he's flat on his back in a hospital a hundred miles or so from the job and in another country. And his number two can't cut it."

Chambers opened his mouth as if to speak, thought better of it, and sat silent, still studying Sam's face, still showing his surprise.

"I'd go myself," Sam said, "except that it's been pointed out to me that I can't be in a number of places at once, and I haven't any business being in any of them, anyway. I should have seen that without being told. Somebody has to sit on his ass in an office and call the shots and attend to the detail and be available." Echoes of Wilt Ross's words that last day. "So I want Zabrinski here where he's familiar with the problems, and I want you in Haiti taking over cold turkey."

Chambers shook his head. "I'm not good enough to stay here and run this job, but—"

"Something else was pointed out to me," Sam said. Jud saw deep. And it was galling to have to admit that Jud was right. "I came down on you here," Sam said. "I spoiled whatever chance you had to run the project right, and it's too late now to back up and start over. Zabrinski can carry on. I don't think you could. Or would."

For long moments Chambers sat motionless, and silent. Then he spread his hands in a gesture of uncertainty, and let them fall to the steering wheel. "Go on," he said.

"The old man picked you," Sam said. "He had faith or at least hope that you could cut it here. I'll do the same in Haiti. Fresh start. You go in cold, and you cut it, or you fall on your face." And if you fall on your face, he thought, you take me, and probably Ross Associates as well, down with you. He knew about the dam job, and it was important, but his expression showed nothing of these thoughts. "Well?" he said.

"You," Chambers said, "are the damndest. One minute you—" He shook his head. "How do I know you won't change your mind again tomorrow? Or next week? Or whenever I get to this new job?"

"I won't," Sam said. "Not this time." Because this time, he thought, it's sink or swim for sure, and I can't even help except from the office in San Francisco. Because the next trouble will come from maybe Indonesia, or Alaska, or Saudi Arabia, or someplace else, and Jud was right, too damn right. Like the old man, I've got to stay out of the action, and just send in the plays and hope. "Okay?"

Chambers shrugged. "I don't even know what language they speak in Haiti."

"Your number two does. French, English, and Creole. He can handle them all."

Chambers spread his hands again, and this time studied them for a time in silence. Then he looked at Sam. "You're taking a chance, aren't you?" The question brought the first real smile he had ever seen on Sam's face.

"I'm betting the bundle," Sam said. "And, you know what? It feels good to have it right out on the table at last."

One more base to touch, Sam decided, before he and Daryl Chambers got into the Ross Associates jet and sped back to San

Francisco. Precisely how Henry Evans and his opinions had become so important to him, Sam could not have explained in detail, but it was so, and he felt no sense of pain in the admission.

Henry, in his wheelchair, was on the west *portal*, far enough back toward the wall of the house that the roof overhang shaded him from the sun. "You saw Floyd," he said, and nodded. "He called me. You are taking over the bridge project yourself?"

In Evans's quiet, almost uninflected manner of speech, it was difficult to detect overtones, but beneath the words there lay a definite opinion of some kind. Of that, Sam was sure. "Not exactly," he said. "There are—complications." He began with Laura's telephone message, went through his own talk with Jud, and explained his decisions regarding Zabrinski and Daryl Chambers.

Evans listened quietly, showing no reaction. In the end, he nodded. "I think you have made the right choice. Not necessarily the easy choice, but the right one." He smiled briefly. "And I should very much like to meet your man Jud, who apparently sees matters with great clarity. Lack of technical knowledge is not necessarily a limitation. Henry Ford began as a bicycle mechanic, and so did the Wright brothers."

Sam wondered how Jud would react to that concept. Probably with scorn, he thought, and smiled inwardly.

"But your—transition," Evans said, "is going to take getting used to. It is very difficult to watch others doing jobs you could probably do better, and still keep your hands in your pockets where they belong. Is the Haitian project critical?"

"Important enough."

"Then I applaud your courage in putting Chambers in charge."

"No choice. And I had Ross's assessment of him to go on. He made one mistake here, hiring only anglos, and I never let him make any more decisions."

Evans nodded agreement. "Your plans now? Back to San Francisco?"

"As soon as I leave here."

Again Evans nodded. "Tell your man Zabrinski that I will be here, and available, if there are further repercussions from Eloy Padilla's death. And I think you can expect that there will be."

"Maybe you'd like to meet him?"

"I would. He is, Ellie tells me, aptly named by the *chicanos* on the bridge crew *el oso pardo*."

" 'The grizzly bear,' " Sam translated, and smiled. "It fits. Big, solid and powerful, also unflappable."

"Better and better." Evans held out his hand. "I wish you luck. Total command is a lonely business. But in time, one can become used to it. And you might remember that to anyone, the command position is inevitably strange at first. I'm sure it was to Wilt Ross. It certainly was to me."

Ellie was waiting beside the pickup. "If you want to see Liz, you'll have to wait. She's gone into town."

"Tell her I've gone back to the city. Your father can explain."

Ellie shook her head. "I'm not sure Liz will like that."

"Can't be helped."

"Shall I say, 'Slam-bam, thank you, ma'am'?" Ellie watched closely for his reaction to the teasing.

"I guess I deserve that," Sam said slowly, nodded, and could even smile. He held out his hand. "*Hasta luego*."

" 'Until then,' " Ellie translated, "not goodbye." And she too nodded. Her handshake was firm.

In the pickup's outside rear-view mirror, Sam could see her standing there, watching after him as he drove away.

In the executive jet, "I'll take her," Sam told the pilot, and with brakes locked, advanced both throttles until the aircraft quivered with eagerness. He released the brakes and used no more than half the runway before he lifted off, tucked up the gear and pointed west, tearing a hole in the sky.

"I'll be in early tonight," he had told Laura on the phone.

"I'll wait at the office."

"No need."

"Yes there is, Sam. I want to see you, and talk to you, and know your reasons."

"You disagree?"

"Not at all. You are doing what I've been wanting to suggest. But I want to know why. And so will Wilt."

"That means what?"

"Sooner or later, Sam, you and he are going to have to have your confrontation. Unless you walk away first. And that you won't do. So I'll be waiting."

"You're the boss."

"Definitely not. You are the boss. I am merely playing the part of your conscience. Jiminy Cricket."

She was waiting in the large silent office, wearing her professional smile, but with warmth in her eyes showing plain. And in greeting she did what she had never done before, rose on tiptoe to kiss his cheek. "Welcome safe back from the wolves," she said.

Sam thought of the four men standing beside the pickup. Wolves? No. Coyotes, but significant nevertheless. And I left Zabrinski to handle the situation, he thought. It was a command decision, the kind of thing one had to do, and then live with. This was what Evans had meant. Part of it, anyway. "Where do you want to begin, Laura?" Her answer surprised him.

"With Miss Lewis. Her maid told me she had gone off to a place called Tano."

Sam thought of Liz as, naked, she had climbed out of his bed in the early dawn, wrapped the borrowed robe around her loveliness, and, smiling, left the room. He tried to picture her meeting with Ellie in the hallway, and found that he could not imagine clearly the reaction of either woman. Meanwhile, Laura watched him steadily. "I saw her," Sam said.

"None of my business," Laura said, "but—" and left the sentence hanging.

Sam perched on a corner of the big desk to think about it. "I think I understand what you're saying," he said after a few moments. As I have not completely understood the situation before, he thought. "I'm running the show here only temporarily, and in a rearguard holding action. With you. We are caretakers, or at least we're trying to be. If I were in total command, Liz would not be any of your business. But since we're in this together, she is. Right?"

"I'm sorry, Sam."

"Yes, I think you are. I also think you're aware that your opposition to Liz, yours and Ross's, might very well push me right at her, assuming I need pushing."

"She is a very attractive woman," Laura said. "I'd imagine that to a man the word for her would be 'desirable.'"

"Would be, and is."

"They talk about the battle of the sexes," Laura said. "More often it is internecine warfare, between women. All right, I've made my point. Now what about Daryl Chambers? Can he make it?"

"We'll find out."

"Sam—" Laura shook her head. "No. Ignore me. You have Wilt's boldness, which is as it should be. I would choose the timid way. And fail. I will say it again, Sam, you are the boss. I am Jiminy Cricket. Zabrinski?"

"Henry Evans will back him up. And Jud Wilder. Together they'll do as well as I could, maybe better. It's still a minefield" —Sam spread his hands—"and I don't like walking away from it."

"But your place is here," Laùra said, and nodded in understanding. "I hoped you'd come to realize that."

PART III

24.

Jud and Zabrinski together rode the cable tramcar across the Gorge to the west site. Suspended now from three cables, it was more stable by far in passage than it had been on Jud's first trip, but, as Zabrinski pointed out, "She still makes sure you know you're having a ride, doesn't she?" He had a firm grip with both huge hands on the tramcar's gunwales.

"From out here," Jud said, looking both ways at the two rising towers, "it's almost beginning to look like we've got ourselves a bridge, or at least a good start on one."

The uneven legs of the east tower were set into the rock contours as if they had grown there. Tall and straight, the structure itself rose, gray and dirty metal-colored now, but its skeletal form unmistakably strong, graceful, light, airy, reaching for the sky in its angular, geometrical, otherworldly way to dwarf the surrounding countryside and its gently rolling landscape.

"We'll start spinning in about a week," Jud said.

Zabrinski nodded approvingly. "You're reading my mind. And Henry Evans's. He asked me about that last night."

They had been sitting on the west *portal* of the ranchhouse, pre-dinner drinks in hand, watching the sunset fade and then slowly brighten with the afterglow which frequently produced the brilliant color effects.

"I understand your construction of the towers," Henry Evans

said, "and how you cantilever out the roadway from each side until it finally joins at mid-point. What I don't understand is how you get those big cables up over the towers. I've driven across the Golden Gate Bridge, and the George Washington and a number of others. Those main cables must be a full yard in diameter."

"I've been wondering about that too," Ellie said. She found Carl Zabrinski fascinating, docile as a teddy bear, but with an unmistakable impression of power that could break through walls or uproot trees like some massive piece of mechanical ranch equipment. And a mind, knowledgeable, quick, strangely gentle and possessed of an almost feminine sensitivity. Strange mixture.

"The Golden Gate Bridge is a hobby of mine," Zabrinski said. "And you have a good eye for the cables' size. Each one is exactly thirty-six and three-eighths inches in diameter. And, to give you some of the rest of the statistics, the cables are each seven thousand seven hundred and sixty feet long, that's almost a mile and a half; and together they weigh well over twenty thousand tons. So you don't just pick up one end of a cable and carry it over the towers like a clothesline. No. You spin it, four strands of small wire at a time."

He put down his glass to free his hands for gestures. "John Roebling and his son Washington, who built the Brooklyn Bridge one hundred years ago," he said, "invented the system that's been used ever since. Visualize a pulley block mounted beneath the window of an apartment house. Now visualize another, identical pulley mounted beneath the window of a neighbor just across the airshaft. There is an endless clothesline stretched around those two pulleys. When neighbor A pulls her clothes in on one side of the line, the clothes on the other side move toward neighbor B, correct?"

"I'm with you so far," Ellie said.

"Now instead of a clothesline," Zabrinski said, "we have an endless rope stretched from a pulley on the ground on one side of the Gorge, up and over the bridge towers and down to another pulley on the ground on the other side. And instead of clothes on that endless rope, we have two sheaves, rollers; and they are fixed, one on either side of the endless rope. Around each roller you loop a strand of small wire. One end of the wire is secured to an eyebolt set in concrete so it can't move. The other end of the wire is free to unwind from a supply bobbin. Okay so far?"

"I think so," Ellie said. Evans listened in silence.

"Then when you pull one side of the line with its fixed roller east," Zabrinski said, "just the way neighbor A pulls her clothes, the other side with *its* roller and looped wire goes west, right?"

"And so," Evans said in his quiet way, "you are carrying four strands of wire from side to side at the same time in opposite directions. Ingenious."

Zabrinski nodded. "Exactly. Then you cut the wires, fasten the loose ends to anchored eyebolts, loop more wire around each roller and repeat the performance. Each of our cables will be made up of eleven thousand five hundred sixty-four of those small wires, by the way, which means that we will make two thousand eight hundred ninety-one traverses, carrying four wires each time. Then we compress the wires into a solid bundle hydraulically, and wrap them with more wire the way you'd wrap a trout rod."

"The cables," Evans said, "are the heart and soul of a suspension bridge?"

Zabrinski thought about it. "Yes, and no," he said. "There are three major components, and each is indispensable. Without the roadway structure, you have no bridge. Without the towers, you have no means of supporting the cables across the span. And without the cables to support it, the roadway structure can carry no load."

"So what it amounts to," Evans said, "is that the towers hold up the cables. And the cables hold up the roadway. And the roadway is the reason for the entire structure."

"Exactly. All parts are interdependent."

Now, swinging in the cable tramcar almost one thousand feet above the bottom of the Gorge and midway between the two towers, "Plenty wide enough, no?" he said to Jud.

Jud looked over the side and down into the emptiness. He nodded. "Farther across than a man can spit," he said, "and just about as deep as you'd crave to have it."

A pair of ravens performed their aerial acrobatics not far away, diving, zooming, doing wingovers and whip stalls and giving out their harsh cries of what had to be excitement and sheer ebullience. Zabrinski watched them thoughtfully for a few moments, but said nothing until he and Jud reached the west cable car terminus and clambered out on solid ground.

Jud said, "You're chawing awful hard on something. Those birds?"

Zabrinski shook his head. "I've never been down inside the Gorge, have you?"

"Never thought about it."

"When we finish here, let's take a walk."

The west tower was a mirror image of the east, except for the uneven legs. Jud rode the crane hook to the top, prowled the narrow platform, spoke to the connecting gang and the riveters, and stood for a time looking back across the Gorge, picturing how it would be when the towers were completed, the great cables dipping in their graceful catenary curves, and the roadway, the sole reason for all this construction, spanning the chasm and its winds, defying its myths and its evil spirits, and carrying unfeeling tourists in smooth comfort at whatever speeds they chose.

He was not an introspective man, but there were times, as now, when he wondered why he spent his life building magnificent structures such as this for such trivial purposes. There was no sensible answer, he decided, as he turned away and signaled for the hook to come fetch him down again.

The walking boss on this part of the job was Gus Oliver, a small, leathery man, still active as a squirrel in his fifties, and as quick in his movements. He was talking with massive Zabrinski. "We're going ahead with cable-stays?" he said.

"We are."

"No skin off my ass," Oliver said. "It's all work. But tell me why. Wind?"

"That's it."

"Yeah." Oliver turned to stare out over the Gorge. "Night before last," he said. "After quitting time. I was still here." He shrugged. "No reason."

Jud said, with full understanding. "You just didn't have the sense to leave, isn't that it?" There was no explaining the fascination of a job when you had pushed it and driven it and wheedled it and watched it grow. You hated to leave it. You just wanted to stand and look, and touch, and make sure that everything was real, and right, because, by God, it was part of you, and when you finally hung up your hard hat and settled into whatever time you had left, you wanted to have a few jobs of work well done because you had cared about them, to look back on and feel good about. "So you were just standing around like the drunk outside the bar, is that how it was?"

Zabrinski said, "What happened?"

Nothing changed in Oliver's face. "A two-by-six damn near cold-cocked me."

Both men stared at him. Jud said, "Dwell on that, Gus."

Oliver pointed, a quick motion matching his words. "It was lying over there. Not on a pile. All by itself where someone had dropped it. I ate the pusher's ass out yesterday."

Zabrinski said, "We were talking about wind. That's what did it?"

Oliver nodded. "Like a dust devil, I guess, only there wasn't any dust. I saw that damn piece of lumber begin to move—begin to move, hell, it jumped, and whirled, and came right at me. I didn't argue with it. I hit the ground, and it went *whoosh* right over me and slammed into the side of the shack." He pointed again. "See the cracked boards?"

Zabrinski and Jud finished their tour of inspection. "Nothing in particular," Zabrinski told Oliver. "We just wanted a look around."

"You're three–four days behind the other side," Jud said, "but maybe you'll catch up."

"Shit," Oliver said, and both men smiled.

"Now let's walk," Zabrinski said, and he and Jud started for the old road that clawed its way down the cliff face.

Jud said, "What do you think of that two-by flying around?"

Zabrinski nodded. "Same with the birds. And with the tram. There's turbulence down in that ditch, churning away and every now and again spilling up and over—"

"No structural problem so far. We're building strong and tough."

"Yeah." Zabrinski walked a few more paces down the road in silence. He said at last, "Every piece of steel we rivet in place adds to the frontal area, the windage. The cables will add more. And so will the roadway, particularly the roadway, and the roadway stiffening even if it is open truss. And God save us if we get harmonics."

"Now you dwell on that."

"Vibrations," the big man said. He used his hands to illustrate. "You know about a violin breaking a wineglass across the room? Well, that's what I mean. The wineglass is resonant to a particular pitch of music, and that pitch sets the glass into harmonic motion, vibration. And because the musical note continues, each harmonic motion is amplified by the next, in phase, increasing in force exponentially until finally the glass breaks."

Jud stared up at Zabrinski's face. "And you're talking about a bridge behaving like a wineglass?"

"When soldiers march across a bridge," Zabrinski said, "any bridge, they break step, deliberately. That's so their cadence won't set up harmonic vibrations that, because of the rhythm of their marching, build in amplitude until the bridge, like the wineglass, can't stand the stresses that are set up."

Jud thought about it, trudging down the narrow road in silence. "Okay," he said at last, "so how do you go about making sure wind can't cause it?"

"We could pray," Zabrinski said. The funny thing was, he almost sounded as if he meant it.

Midway down the cliff face, Zabrinski stopped and turned his head this way and that as if sniffing the air. Jud watched. "You can feel the wind here," Zabrinski said, "but my guess is that because of drag against the Gorge walls, friction, the wind currents here at the side are dampened. Like a stream that flows faster out in the center than along the shores. Let's see if we can tell."

He bent to pick up a flat piece of broken rock, and with a sharp underhand flip sent it sailing into space. For a few feet its course was smoothly curved in a nearly flat trajectory, but all at once it seemed to jump and then flip over, lost speed and began to fall sharply. They watched its erratic course, swinging this way and that in no rhythmical sequence until it disappeared into the river.

Jud said, "I see what you mean."

"Like that river down there," Zabrinski said. "That's a lousy analogy, but in a vague way, it's apt. The water churns around because of the rocks. There aren't any rocks in the air, of course, but there are currents and crosscurrents, real honest-to-God turbulence probably caused by the confined space of the Gorge and the unevenness of the Gorge walls. It would be suicide, for example, to try to fly a chopper through here—remember that chopper carrying that line?—and even those ravens, you'll notice, good as they are, don't come far down into the Gorge itself. They get their jollies in the turbulence that spills out over the top."

They were no more than fifty feet above the river and the

rickety bridge when Jud stopped, and pointed upstream. "For God's sake, will you look there!"

A double-ended rubber raft was coming down through the white water, two men at the oars bending hard into their work, maneuvering around a standing rock, heeling the raft dangerously and righting it only just in time as they streamed into the next crest of angry foam.

Jud had to shout above the sound of the water. "Some people need their heads examined!" And then, with a quick, measuring glance, "Jesus, can they clear that bridge?"

The raft mounted one crest and pitched down the far side. It heeled, partly righted itself, slammed into relative flat water, and then, entering the next white water area of turbulence, threw its bow high, seemed to shake itself, and, already off-balance, flipped over.

Zabrinski's voice, large as the man himself, roared, "Academic! Come on!" And he ran down the remaining few feet of roadway like a charging buffalo.

Unmanned now, the raft tumbled and tossed, slammed into rocks, somehow wrenched loose and swept past them. Zabrinski reached the water's edge and took one step down, found bottom, with outspread arms adjusted his balance and took another step.

Water rose to his waist and formed a standing wave ahead of him. Behind, aerated water streamed in a turbulent wake. The big man moved another step forward, planted his legs like massive bridge supports and reached out as far as he could with one hand.

He made a sharp, incredibly fast grabbing motion, plunging his arm into the water up to his biceps, and heaving back with all his enormous strength. His hand emerged, holding one of the men by his life jacket, and with a second giant effort he tossed him back over his shoulder like a sack of grain for Jud to seize and drag ashore.

The orange of the other man's life jacket showed briefly, still upstream, slamming its way down through a rocky chute. The man's arms flailed in sheer futility, he disappeared, and then emerged flailing no longer, bobbing around in the turbulent water like a doll unhinged.

Zabrinski took another long step, reached, grabbed, and caught the man's arm. Water churned against Zabrinski's chest and threatened to tear the man from his grasp.

One small step at a time, Zabrinski retreated, braced against the foaming current, holding the man's arm and dragging him as one might drag a half-submerged log.

Zabrinski's foot slipped and instantly recovered, and Jud, himself now in water to his knees, held his breath. Zabrinski took another step, and another. The water was now down to his waist, but it was obvious that even his enormous strength could not hold out indefinitely.

"Give me your hand!" Jud shouted and lunged forward, feeling the force of the current threatening to sweep him away. "Your hand, goddamn it!"

Zabrinski reached back with his free hand as far as he could. Jud caught it, and with his other hand reached for and caught a timber of the rickety bridge. "Heave!" he shouted, and repeated in cadence, "Heave! Heave! Heave!" Until his feet found the shore edge, and he could catch Zabrinski's hand with both of his and haul the big man and his limp burden to safety.

The first man was trying to sit up, and was unable to make it. Laboriously he rolled on his side, propped himself on one elbow and began to retch in deep, painful spasms.

Zabrinski turned the second man on his face, grabbed him with both hands just below the knees and, lifting him off the ground, shook him as one would shake a container to empty it. Water poured out of the man's mouth, and after a few moments Zabrinski lowered him gently, turned him on his back, and kneeling, began to give mouth-to-mouth resuscitation.

"The Zabrinski treatment," Jud said, "but, what the hell, it seems to work. You stay here. I'll go for help." He set off up the narrow road.

25.

"So they're both all right," Zabrinski said over the phone to Sam, "and they'll live to try some other damn fool stunt like maybe going over Niagara Falls in a bathtub. Nobody really got skinned up."

"Anglos," Sam said.

Zabrinski's voice was regretful. "Pity too. If even one of them had a Spanish surname, it might have improved our standing in the community."

"Which still isn't good?"

"Coronado came through here four hundred and fifty years ago," Zabrinski said, "and some people haven't forgotten that yet. How's Daryl Chambers doing in Haiti?"

As far as he could tell, Sam thought as he hung up, Chambers was doing all right. But what he was discovering, sitting in this big office overlooking the Bay, manipulating the levers of power, was that eyeballing a job yourself and following its progress by remote control were two very different things indeed. Decisions that had to be made were sometimes almost blind decisions, and that was not comfortable.

Jim Hardy's call from the Hospital for Tropical Diseases in San Juan, for example. "Who's that character you've got ramrodding my Cul de Sac job?" Hardy wanted to know.

Sam explained who Chambers was, and why he was there.

"Well, I'm fit enough to go back, damn it. If not today, then tomorrow. So why don't you recall him before he louses everything up?"

"You stay where you are and enjoy the sunshine and the tradewinds. Go back too soon, and you'll just crack up again."

"Now, look here, Sam—"

"No. You look here. You've got the hell of a good man keeping your job moving until you're well enough to go back and take over again and finish the project." I hope, Sam thought. "So I don't want to hear any more about it, *entendido?* Understood?"

Hardy's voice held grudging acceptance. "You're a hard-nosed bastard. You always were. How's the old man?"

"He's coming along." And maybe that was a lie, and maybe it wasn't, Sam really didn't know.

"I can't tell you when it will be best to see him," Laura had said. "He's up, and he's down, but he's down more than he's up, and when you finally do see him, it's going to have to be right. Do you see what I mean?"

"One chance," Sam said. "Is that it?"

"Exactly. John Haskins agrees."

"If I blow that one chance, then it's blown for good?"

"I'm sorry, Sam, but that's the way it is. We're trying as hard as we can to set it up."

"Does he know about Jim Hardy?"

"No. And he doesn't know about that boy killed on the bridge job, either. You're in sole command, Sam, as I think you're beginning to find out."

"Thanks a lot."

"You could chuck it, Sam."

"Could I?"

"Just walk away. Maybe with Miss Lewis. She's back from Tano."

"That's just dandy. And who's waiting in your office outside?"

"Charley Webster, with the bridge cost overrun figures."

Charley had papers. Charley always had papers, and his hand-calculator. He would sooner have been naked than without both. "I really don't know what you're thinking of, Sam," Charley said. "Safety nets. Why? And additional cables—for what?"

"The answer to both is one word. Wind. I watched one man die—"

"We've taken care of that with insurance. The family is paid off. And there are always deaths or injuries on any large job. You know that. I just wish the deaths would happen late in the day so we wouldn't lose so much work time when the crew is laid off."

"I'll see if I can arrange it with the next one."

"There is no need for sarcasm. Honestly, Sam, I really don't think Mr. Ross will approve these—extravagant extras. Our profit margin was slim enough to begin with. Now, would you care to see the figures?"

"I'll take your word for them, Charley."

Charley stared glumly at his papers. He looked up and said at last, "You don't like me much, do you, Sam? You never have. I'm a pencil-pusher and a paper-shuffler, and you're like Mr. Ross, you're both men who *do* things. I understand that. I'm just the one who tries to put what you do into some kind of financial order. I don't get my name on the bronze plaque on the dam or the bridge or the irrigation project or whatever. But when I talk of figures, Sam, I know whereof I speak. So it really does behoove you to listen. And I suggest you stop playing fast and loose with the Tano bridge project. Too much is at stake."

When Charley was gone, Sam sat for a little time just staring at nothing. Charley was an old woman. In happier times, Wilt Ross had agreed with that assessment. But Charley was right when he said that he knew whereof he spoke when it came to figures. And if playing fast and loose was not precisely the way to describe the handling of the Tano bridge project, why, it wouldn't really be fair to say that everything was ginger-peachy, either.

Zabrinski was a good man, of that Sam had no doubt. But if he himself were on the job, then he would *know* that everything possible was being done to stay on schedule, maybe even a little ahead, and somehow manage to absorb the additional cost of the safety nets, and both the added cost and the added work of the cable-stays.

The intercom buzzed on his desk. Laura's voice said, "Ben Knopf is here. You're running a little late in seeing him."

"Send him in," Sam said. He stood up to move to one of the leather club chairs for a powwow, feeling like a man in handcuffs.

Ben was tall, plump, impeccably tailored and deeply tanned. He spoke six languages, and could wheel-and-deal in them all. He was the Ross Associates roving negotiator. He sank into the club chair and lighted a cigarette from a silver case.

"It's that madman in Brazil with his paper mill," he said. "He's mad about the way a fox is. The point is, do we want to get into it with him on his new hydroelectric project? If we do, we're going to have to move fast. I talked to Ross about it. Before his stroke, of course. And he said he'd think about it, which probably meant he'd send you down to have a look."

It seemed years, instead of scant months, ago when that close relationship between himself and Ross had existed, Sam thought, when Ross would summon him and they would sit in these same two chairs, Laura in the outside office preventing interruptions. One of two phrases would be the reason for the talk:

"Go down and bird-dog it," Ross would say in summation, or, "Go down and straighten it out."

Bird-dogging meant looking into feasibility and desirability of a potential new job; situation, background, backing, availability of transportation, labor, equipment and materiel, political stability, and anything else that could possibly affect a decision to go, or not go.

Bird-dogging was all-inclusive and decisive. "Yes, or no?" Ross would ask when Sam returned. "Either way, tell me why." And after minutes, sometimes even hours, of listening and probing, a nod of Ross's head, and the verdict. "Okay. Have Ben Knopf set it up." Or, "Right. Tell them we're not interested."

"Straighten it out" meant carte blanche to come down on an ailing project, as Ross had once described it, "like a ghost on a frame house," to fire anybody from chief engineer on down, hire anybody necessary, make whatever local arrangements would bring the job back on track and on schedule, and not return to San Francisco until he could report that, "the job is marching again."

Those were the simple days, Sam thought now, when he had one task at a time and could put his hands to it on the scene, rather than by remote control, rely on himself and not on his judgment of others, eat and sleep the task he had been assigned, and wrap it up to be put aside and forgotten.

Of course, and this he had not really appreciated until now, Ross himself would then take over all responsibility, and from his desk here in this office keep an eye on each project in the far-flung operations of Ross Associates, keep, as Jud had pointed out, all the colored balls in the air at once, and bring Sam in only at need.

"I'll find somebody to go down with you and bird-dog it," he told Ben Knopf, unaware that already he was using Ross's terminology. "Then we'll lay it all out here and have a look at it." He saw impatience for a definite answer in Ben's face, and took issue with that feeling immediately. "If there isn't time for a complete look-see," he said, "then we're not interested. We aren't going into anything blind." As we damn well did on the Tano bridge.

"Ross seemed to think—" Ben began.

"I'm the one who's doing the thinking now," Sam said. There was finality in his tone.

Laura buzzed again as the door closed behind Ben Knopf. Laura's voice was expressionless. "Miss Evans is on line one."

It was strange, but Ellie's voice, like the memory of his close relationship with Ross, seemed something out of the past, a different world. "Henry," Ellie said, "is determined that I won't rot out in the boonies, so I'm here again. And you owe me a lunch."

"At least. But we'll start with that." She would wear no faded jeans or dusty boots here in the city, Sam thought, but the breezy Evans self-assurance and the aura of big mountains and limitless vistas would still be very much a part of her. He found that he was looking forward to their meeting.

He stood up at the small table when she entered the restaurant almost precisely on time, and he noticed with pleasure that, as with Liz, eyes turned to watch her progress across the room. As on that last day at the ranch in Tano, her handshake was firm, and her greeting smile was guileless.

Seated and smiling still, "Responsibility seems to agree with you," Ellie said.

"I'm not sure it does. Or, the other way around." Henry Evans would have explained to her, as he had suggested, the reasons for his abrupt departure for San Francisco. "The returns are far from in," Sam said.

"Carl Zabrinski seems to be doing well. Even aside from his heroics in the river."

"He's a good man. And so is Jud. None better."

"Except you?"

Ordered drinks appeared while the question still hung, unanswered. Sam sipped slowly, set his glass down.

"That means what?"

"Liz was right," Ellie said, smiling again. "You respond at once to challenge, don't you? Even when it isn't real. Henry said you were going to find it hard to keep your hands off and let others do the job because you would always think you could do it better. He recognized that in you, he said, because he had always felt the same. Does that explain the question?"

Somewhat mollified, Sam thought about it. "I suppose it does. I suppose everybody feels that way."

"No. Only the good ones. They're the ones who are hard to get along with. Have you seen Liz?"

Sam shook his head slowly. "You have a trick of ending with a change of subject. I've noticed before. No, I haven't seen Liz. I've been too busy. Liz won't pine away. How are your eagles?"

Ellie's laughter was totally without self-consciousness. It caused heads at nearby tables to turn again. "Now you're doing it," Ellie said. "Change of subject upon change of subject. Obfuscation rampant. My eagles are fine. One of the nestlings has soloed. And how is poor Daryl Chambers in the wilds of Haiti?"

"He'll survive. I hope."

Ellie sipped her drink, watching Sam thoughtfully over the rim of the glass. She set it down at last, and resumed her smile, but its quality had changed. "You do worry, don't you?" she said. "Henry said you would. I disagreed."

"Henry is too damn right too often."

"Not always. He killed Mother and almost killed himself through carelessness. He hasn't forgotten that. Are you going down to Haiti?"

He had considered it, and been strongly tempted. A quick flying visit, a look around in all directions, a little talk here and a little there, and above all a chance, however brief, to watch the job itself in progress, to judge for himself the temper of the men, the tempo and quality of their work; in short, to get the *feel* of the project to take back to San Francisco, data stored in memory as in a computer bank, against which future reports could be weighed and evaluated.

But he had done that once to Chambers, and the results had not been good. He would not make the same mistake again.

"There is always the telephone," Laura had said. "He can't feel overpowered if all he gets are phone calls from the home office every now and again. Wilt always kept in touch."

It wasn't the same as seeing for himself, of course, but the telephone was better than nothing. "Henri Leclerc and I get along fine," Chambers had reported. "He just doesn't like to stick his neck out, is all. How's Jim Hardy? I thought I might fly over to San Juan and see him."

"Why?"

"Well, you know, there are always a couple of vague ideas a man carries around in his mind and doesn't bother to put down on paper. Maybe he can give me some tips or shortcuts he's thought of. Okay?"

You gave a man a job, Sam thought, and you had damn well better let him do it his way. "You're calling the shots. Just keep me posted."

"Will do." Was there unspoken relief beneath those last two words?

"To answer your question," Sam said now, conscious that he had taken time with his thoughts, "no, I'm not going down to Haiti. At least not right away. How's that foal coming?"

"Stupendously. He's all Inocencio can talk about."

"And that character, Jones? Bobbie Jack, wasn't it?"

"He's still around."

To hell with Bobbie Jack, Sam thought. The here and now were more important.

"Are you busy tonight? Dinner? The Guarneri Quartet is in town—" Sam saw the surprise on her face. "No," he said, "there were no concerts on that postage stamp ranch in Nevada. All I ever heard was country and western music. I met the other when I came to Berkeley. I met a number of things I'd never heard of."

"I think," Ellie said slowly, "that I'm beginning to see it now, why Liz thought you began life in the engineering lab at UC. You never talked about the other to her."

"Patched jeans," Sam said, "rundown boots, sagebrush, jackrabbits and horny toads—that isn't Liz's kind of world, and you don't talk about color to the blind."

"I am not busy tonight," Ellie said. "And I happen to love the Guarneri Quartet."

26.

Zabrinski stood with Jud and Quincy Yorke while a crew rigged a portion of the new safety net on two supports projected out over the Gorge from the base of the east tower, and supported from above by light cables attached to the upper tower structure. Quincy Yorke's design.

Zabrinski patted the top of Quincy Yorke's head. To Jud, he said, "He's an ingenious little rascal, isn't he, when he puts his mind to it?"

"It would be all the same to me," Quincy said, "if every one of your Neanderthal bridgemen disappeared into the Gorge in sequence, performing forward three-and-a-half layouts with full twists while singing falsetto. But Sam Taylor pronounced, and made it clear that his will had damned well better be done. So, voilà!"

Jud said, "It will pay off." He looked at Zabrinski. "I'm thinking of that rock you tossed out from the road."

"On your way down to your act of derring-do?" This was Quincy again.

Zabrinski grinned. "That's it, little man. We knew all along that raft was coming."

"Sturdily breasting the mighty torrent," Quincy said, "he defied the gods and the elements and plucked two souls from the flood. Blind Homer could have done well with that theme."

Jud said, "I want to see what it looks like from above." He left them abruptly.

They watched him ride the crane hook to the top tower level, step off on the narrow platform and walk unconcerned to its edge to peer down in contemplation.

Quincy said suddenly, "Is it sheer bravado, or does he indeed feel no fear?" For once there was no artificial emphasis in his voice. He looked up at Zabrinski in genuine question.

"I wouldn't know," Zabrinski said. "I honestly wouldn't."

"You go up there yourself. It doesn't appear to bother you in the slightest."

"Every now and again I get my butterflies."

"With your volume, they would have to be the size of eagles to be felt."

Zabrinski grinned again. "Now you sound natural."

Quincy said, again without artificial emphasis on the key words, "I simply do not comprehend men like you and Jud, yes, and Sam Taylor too. I do not comprehend boxers and wrestlers either, of course, men who deliberately harm one another for money. But you and Jud and Sam do have at least a modicum of intelligence, which means imagination, and that ought to make some difference. When you are up there, or riding that unspeakable cable tramcar across that bottomless chasm, does it never occur to you what it might be like to—fall? Perhaps shrieking your exit lines as both the big man and the boy did?" He shuddered, remembering.

"I don't lie awake nights about it," Zabrinski said.

"I do." In the two words there was revealing honesty. "Silly of me, isn't it?"

"Your specialty," Zabrinski said, "is designing, and you do just the hell of a job of it."

"I don't need reassurance," Quincy's voice was its normal, defensive self. "I have Valium for that. What I am asking is explanation. What kind of men are you to ignore such basic human frailties as vertigo, to flirt with the laws of gravity as if they were about to be repealed, to stand unconcerned on the brink of absolutely nothing as Jud up there is doing now, and think calmly and logically about the number of lives and man hours of work this net is going to save, and whether in dollars and cents it will be worth it?"

"I'll tell you the secret," Zabrinski said. "It's all really just showbiz when you come right down to it, all done with mirrors. And the show must go on. You dig?"

Quincy nodded, his smile quiet and subdued. "I asked for that, didn't I?"

The governor said, "It's strictly up to you, honey. To me, it makes no never mind. You're being paid per diem on a consulting basis, and that can stop any time you or we decide to stop it."

Alice Perkins, primly dressed and clutching her slim attaché case in her lap said, "You—" and shook her head.

"You're a penologist," the governor said. "You've turned in this here report which I happen to think is a good one. Put in practice, it might solve some, maybe even most, of our problems. And it might do quite a bit for your professional reputation too. You want that, do you?"

"Of course. But—"

"Honey," the governor interrupted, "let's get a couple of things straight. I don't like to hold grudges. Takes too much time and energy. I don't say I might not skin your friend Bobbie Jack up a bit for lying to me, and maybe stomp on him some if the opportunity just happened by, but I'm not going out of my way to hammer him down to size, and I'm not going to hold it against you that you stretched the truth a mite when you built him up for my benefit. Nobody really got skinned up because of it. So if you want to stay here, and see if what you recommend in this here report will work, why, that's fine with me, and I'll tell the Corrections people to give it a good try or else come up to this office and explain to me why they didn't. You hear?"

"I'm grateful. But—"

"But you want to know what the price tag is? Well, I'll tell you. There isn't any. You and I got along real fine for a time. That's nice to remember. And if we got around to thinking we might give it another whirl, why, that would be real fine too. But I'm not making that any kind of condition, or even hinting at it. Some folks don't believe it, but for all my faults, I do intend to leave some things accomplished when I walk out of this office. And this here penal reform just might be one of them. It, and the

Tano bridge." The governor paused for emphasis. "Have we got a deal?"

Alice Perkins swallowed. "Yes," she said. And she added, "Thank you, Governor."

Chambers's telephone call came late in the afternoon, San Francisco time. "I'm in Puerto Rico," he said, "San Juan. I've just seen Jim Hardy, but that wasn't the only reason I came over here. We may be running into trouble in Port au Prince."

"What kind of trouble," Sam said.

"The worst kind. Political."

"Oh," Sam said, and instantly all was clear. "Your phone line in Haiti is tapped?"

"Leclerc says it is. I didn't want to take the chance, so I flew over here to call you."

"Good thinking. What does Jim Hardy say?"

"Maybe yes, maybe no."

"He's a good man. Has he had trouble?"

"He's been playing it cagey."

"Meaning what?"

"It hasn't been too bad, he says, so he's gone along."

"Being squeezed? Paying off?"

"That seems to be it."

Sam sat silent for long moments, staring at the windows overlooking the Bay. A ship whistled, two blasts, and two blasts answered indicating agreement on a distant starboard-to-starboard crossing. Sam scarcely heard. "I don't like that one damn little bit," he said.

"I had an idea you might not." This was a confident Chambers, standing on his own, speaking as an equal.

"We've bent the rules on occasion," Sam said. "Our own rules, I mean. But the occasions have been damned few and far between, and the reasons have been overriding. Jim knows that."

Chambers said nothing.

"You've had threats of some kind?" Sam said.

"Only indirectly. They put the pressure on Leclerc. He's Haitian, and they can bear down on him a lot easier than they can bear down on me. On him, and his family, and, of course, basically on the job itself too. There have been accidents, equipment breakdowns, the kind of thing you might expect. I think that's why Leclerc desperately wanted someone to replace Hardy, someone to pass the buck to."

It made sense, too damned much sense. "Do you want me to come down?" Sam said.

The answer was immediate. "No. You gave me the job. You told me to stay in touch. I am. You've made it clear how you, how the company feels."

"We don't like to be shaken down. We'll go to almost any lengths to fight it. That's our reputation, worldwide, and that's how we want to keep it. But if you feel you need help on this—"

"I told you, no. If you want to give me specific orders—"

"At this distance, that would be just plain silly."

"Then I'll handle it my way."

"And if you blow it?"

"Then I'll be looking for a job. But I don't intend to blow it."

This was not the Chambers he had seen on the Tano job, Sam thought, and could not escape a feeling of satisfaction, almost of triumph, that it was so. Jud had been right again, predicting that given the chance and handled properly, Chambers might very well turn into a good man, a man to have around. And Wilt Ross's assessment of the man was being justified.

"Well?" Chambers said. His tone was not pugnacious, but neither was it timid.

Now it's my turn for decision, Sam thought, and found himself smiling at the windows. "It's your baby," he said at last. "Handle it your way. As you can, keep me posted." How often had Wilt Ross, from this same chair, issued identical directions to him? "What I'm saying," he said, "is handle it your own way, but make damned sure it works out right." And again he found himself using Wilt Ross's words. "Or it's your ass. Understood?"

"Understood. And—thanks." The line went dead.

Sam did not hang up. Into the phone he said, "You got all that, Laura?"

"It's all taped. And, Sam?"

"Right here."

"You handled it well. Exactly as Wilt would have done."

He hung up then, got out of the chair and walked to the windows. Standing there, looking down at the water, the ships, at the tiny, scurrying pleasure craft, both power and sail, thinking back over the entire conversation with all of its nuances and its implications, he was conscious of a warm sense of satisfaction, even of pride brought on by Laura's praise and her comparison of him with Ross. Maybe both Chambers and I are learning some things, he thought.

Ellie, greeting him that evening at her apartment door, said, "The cream is visible on your whiskers. Did you score a coup this afternoon?"

You could take the girl out of the country, Sam thought, but you could not take the country out of the girl. There was the kind of open directness in her that was in her father, that was, really, a western tradition. The instant invitation, "'Light, stranger, and set a spell. We're just fixing to eat," came to mind again.

"No coup," he said. "Actually, I just rolled the dice, and I haven't seen yet how they come up."

Ellie's eyes searched his face. "Do you want to tell me about it?"

"At dinner. Over a drink."

Ellie was a good listener. Again, like her father, Sam thought. And she had, too, Henry Evans's acuity, his ear for the unspoken. "Hasn't he changed since Tano?" she said. "Daryl Chambers, I mean? He sounds self-reliant now, which wasn't the way you spoke about him before."

"I think, I hope you're right. We'll see. Now, what's the news of Trujillo? The Padillas? General feeling in Tano? We didn't get into that at lunch."

"You wouldn't win any popularity contests." Her sudden smile appeared. "But, then, that's never been a worry of yours, has it?"

"We're building a bridge, not running for office."

"Carl Zabrinski's river rescue has had an effect. The local paper played it up, and the TV news programs as well. They emphasized the heroics. Strangely enough, it's had a reverse effect, too. The young ones, the wild ones in Tano, the Eloy Padilla-types resent Carl. He's a stranger, an anglo, bigger and stronger than any two of them, and now he's a hero as well, and they feel put down. Can you understand that?"

"I'm trying."

"Yes." Ellie nodded. "You do try. I'm beginning to understand that."

"I think Carl can take care of himself."

"So does Henry. But he's made a point of telling Carl what the feelings are. He even quoted Latin to him. *Praemonitus, praemun-*

itus; forewarned, forearmed. I think it's all the Latin Henry knows."

"It's more than I know. Shall we order?"

They walked to the concert after dinner. "I know two of the works on the program," Sam said, "the Schubert A Minor Quartet, and the Mozart B Flat. I have the Guarneri recording of both. The rest I'm not familiar with."

Ellie said, "You're a continual surprise. I wouldn't associate you with chamber music. Huge symphonies, perhaps, or big, tuneful operas—"

"Or maybe cowboy laments? 'The Streets of Laredo'?"

"And your skin isn't as thick as you like to pretend, is it?"

"Is yours?"

"No." Simple honesty, "I'm an oversized girl—"

"You're a stunning woman."

Ellie stopped walking, and faced him squarely. "I wasn't fishing for that."

Sam too had stopped. "If I had thought you were, I wouldn't have said it."

"No, you wouldn't, would you? There is a perversity in you—" The words stopped, as Ellie shook her head angrily. "Why do we strike sparks? Do you strike them with Liz?"

"What does she have to do with it? She isn't here, except when you bring her up."

"My gaucheness is showing. Or is it gaucherie?"

"Your choice."

"Of weapons? That's what it sounded like." She stared at him. "Now what are you smiling about?"

"Guess."

There was silence between them that grew and stretched. Ellie took a deep breath, and slowly the stiffness went out of her shoulders. She managed a smile at last. "Me," she said. "I'm wearing a chip on my shoulder. I'm afraid I have to admit it. Sorry."

"Let's start over. I admit to a liking for John Philip Sousa—"

"As well as Schubert and Mozart chamber music." Her smile was fullblown now. "Understood." She tucked her arm through his. "Let's go hear some."

They stood at Ellie's apartment door. "Aside from one brief interruption," Ellie said, smiling again, "it was a lovely evening. Thank you. Will you come in for a drink?"

"Work tomorrow. Early."

"Decisions?"

"Probably."

"Do you enjoy it?"

"Funny question."

"Is it?"

Sam thought about it. "Maybe not. If I don't enjoy it, why do I do it?"

"I think that's the question, yes."

"That implies a lot of freedom to maneuver. Most don't have it."

"I think you do."

"I'll ponder it," Sam said. "Good night."

27.

Sam was down at the office early and on the telephone by 7 A.M. to escape the sometimes heavy daytime international telephone traffic. This was a weekly person-to-person report he had initiated for some of the major Ross Associates projects around the world. "More psychological than anything else," he had told Laura and John Haskins in the beginning, and both had nodded agreement.

Even Charley Webster, papers in hand and small calculator at the ready, had concurred. "Seven dollars and eighty cents plus tax for the most distant call," Charley had said, "seems a worthwhile bargain. Since you ask, that is." His voice expressed his gratitude that Sam had even bothered to consult with him.

It was ten o'clock at night in Malaysia. "All serene," Bob George in Kuala Lumpur said, "but you do make my evenings begin late. I can't even get to work on the girl until I hang up."

"With your blitz tactics," Sam said, "the later you start, the better. Think anticipation. Your steel is on the way. You had my cable?"

"Affirmative. What about the cement?"

"You'll have it. Anything else?"

"One of Vanessi's good steaks, preceded by two or three proper martinis. It's thoughts like that that keep me whipping asses and driving the schedule."

"Stay at it. I've got Charley Webster working on a bonus system."

"A what?"

Sam smiled. "I thought that might catch your attention. Beat your schedule and your budget and there'll be something a little extra in your stocking. Provided, of course, that your roadway doesn't fall down before you finish it."

Bob George whistled softly. "Does the old man know about this?"

"He and I have talked about it." Many times. Before his stroke, of course. And Wilt Ross's views had never altered.

"Goddamn it," Ross had said, setting forth his position with emphasis, "we pay top wages for top men to do top-flight jobs. Why the hell should we give them something extra just for doing what they're hired to do? Answer me that."

"If they turn in a better performance than is expected—"

"Then the goddamned scheduling and estimating were wrong to begin with. Nobody ever held out a lollipop to me, and I'm not going to start doing it to grown men who work for me. You included."

"You already pay me more than I ever expected to earn."

"Because sometimes you're worth it. But not this time."

"So bear it in mind, Bob," Sam said now.

"There'll be some sore asses tomorrow night, and I'll probably have a sore foot from kicking them."

Bill Nevers in Riyadh said, "It's six o'clock here. Another day ended, Sam. I've been looking forward to this call."

"That sounds a little . . . ominous. What's up?"

"Nothing specific. You have my last cabled report. We're on schedule. No shortages to speak of. Nobody's getting openly drunk, thank God, or they'll land in the slammer at least. And nobody's fooling around with any Saudi wives, at least not that I know of, because adultery's the big no-no. Still."

"The job getting to you, Bill?" It happened, Sam thought, and sometimes you couldn't even put a reason to it, or place a blame. Living overseas sounded romantic to some, but at times it could be murder.

"That isn't it," Bill said. "Hell, I haven't been unpacked permanently in years, and I don't think I'd know how to behave if it happened. No, it's the waiting, Sam. And I'm not the only one who's jumpy. I hate like hell to talk about powder kegs, but this part of the world isn't exactly inert, you know, not with Israelis, Arabs, and Palestinians snarling and snapping at each other, Iran and Iraq still shooting, Syria and Libya not all that far away, and Lebanon, which they used to call the Switzerland of the Middle East, still tearing itself apart."

"Do you want to be relieved?"

"Hell, no. I just want to bitch to somebody like you who won't carry gossip into town here, get the job done as fast as I can, and then get the hell out."

"Fair enough."

"You know what, Sam? It just could be that some day we, Ross Associates or somebody like us, will come back in here in order to rebuild what we're building now. If anything really happens, that is, and if there's anything left to rebuild, or anybody left to rebuild for. That would be a joke, wouldn't it?"

"A real thigh-slapper," Sam said.

It was 5:15 A.M. in Anchorage. Walt Fisher said, "It gets early in the day real fast in Alaska, you know that, Sam? Never mind. I've been up a couple hours. Heard what sounded like a moose and went out back to see, hoping to hell it wasn't a bear instead. By the way, I took a fifteen-pound rainbow day before yesterday in the east fork. How about that?"

Sam was smiling. "Have you been anywhere near the job?"

"Oh, that, sure. It runs itself. We've got a crackerjack crew, hand-picked, guys who came up to work the pipeline, and stayed, top-hands, every one. Don't you worry about us. I know, it wasn't always that way. But you kicked out a few asses, and straightened things around, and when you handed over to me, why, hell, all I had to do was get in the driver's seat and sit there."

"Keep it that way."

"You've seen my reports."

"And I can't complain even a little bit, Walt. Hang in there."

"Flying out west this weekend. Going to get me one of those big browns. Related to grizzlies, they say. And big as the side of a barn."

"Don't let him get you first."

Sam hung up. What had he accomplished? He doubted if he would have been able to explain, but the accomplishment was real, and good, and important; mail from home, only better because it was immediate, not stale, a living, breathing, talking touch with familiarity, proof that you, as a person in a far place, were not out of mind, that the front office actually wanted to know what you were doing and feeling. And for that, Sam knew from experience, there was no substitute.

His name was Pete Harmon, and he had begun work on the Tano bridge job side by side with Bob Anderson whom he had run into here and there on other construction jobs. He could still remember vividly lying stretched out on that I-beam, reaching down as far as he could, maybe a little farther than was safe, but the hell with that, trying to catch Bob's hand—and missing. And he could remember what happened next, in full sound and living color and seemingly slow motion.

They were higher now by far than they had been when Bob Anderson fell, with maybe only thirty feet of tower left to go. And down near the base of the tower structure, other connecting and riveting gangs were already beginning to cantilever out the roadway structure, the first direct attack upon the emptiness of the Gorge itself.

To Pete, all bridges, and suspension bridges in particular, had a special meaning he would never, never have talked about to anyone. Because bridges played a big part in your life, in everybody's life. On a bridge, you crossed over from side to side, that was what it was, although he had never quite gotten it straight in his own mind. Like when you were born, you crossed a bridge into life; and when you died, you crossed another into who the hell knew what? And all through your life you were crossing real bridges, over rivers, over canyons, even in some of those New York skyscrapers, over the street to connecting buildings, as well as imaginary bridges like from job to job.

Bridges were important, and he liked working on them. He always referred to this one as, "the bitch," but there was affection in his voice. "The bitch is coming along," he would say over a drink at Josie's Place in town. "If they keep getting us the steel on time, we'll have her whipped into shape right back on schedule. I think she knows we aren't fooling around with her, we mean business."

Usually here in this high mesa country, the sun was bright enough to blind a man, but on this morning there were clouds scudding across the sky, and when one of them swept across the sun's face, the temperature dropped instantly, and it was almost as if the lights had been turned off by a switch. Maybe that was what did it. Maybe.

Pete and Stoney Jackson had maneuvered a flanged beam into place as it hung from its sling on the crane, and Stoney was working with his bull's prick to line up the pre-drilled holes, when Pete, for no reason at all, just stepped out into space.

His first thought was total, instantaneous and incredulous disbelief. His lurching grab for support was purely reflexive. It was also futile. His gloved fingertips brushed one of the tower cross-members, but that was as close as he came. Gravity and wind had already taken over.

Pete's voice came out in a great shout, "Jeee—sus Christ!"

His body cartwheeled, and his hard hat came off to fall, planing in the air currents at its own pace.

"No, goddamn it!" Pete's voice roared in protest. "No!"

As the crew stopped whatever they were doing to watch helplessly, Pete's arms and legs flailed wildly as he fell, for support that did not exist.

For moments it looked as if his fall would clear the end of the projecting roadway stub, but the vagaries of the Gorge's updrafting air currents threw him toward the cliff face, and for another moment he seemed about to crash right into that unyielding steel roadway structure, and those watching, braced themselves for the crunch.

But again the wind played its tricks, and, like a diver off the three meter springboard, Pete's body twisted and changed direction enough to clear the end of the steel—almost.

One shoulder brushed the tip of the last projecting steel beam, scarcely slowing his accelerating fall, but giving a little more rotating momentum to his cartwheeling body.

The cry he let out at the impact was half scream and half deep, gurgling grunt of pain, and then in total silence he continued to fall—into the safety net.

The three-eighths inch nylon lines forming the net stretched with the sudden load. Quincy Yorke's ingenious framework of net support projecting out from the tower's base quivered as it took the sudden weight, but held. The nylon sprang back to its original shape, and Pete lay motionless, huddled, suspended, swaying a thousand feet above the bottom of the Gorge, safe.

Jud's voice rose in a roar. "Cut loose that steel in the sling, and get the crane hook to him!" Pete had not moved. "With a man in the hook!" Jud added. "Move it, goddamn it!"

It was Stoney Jackson who stepped into the hook of the crane's cable and rode it down to dangle precisely beside the obviously unconscious man. Stoney surveyed the situation while the watching crew held its breath.

Pete was hurt; he hadn't just passed out; that was obvious. And probably what was best was to call in an ambulance crew, Stoney thought, as he had once upon a time been taught, and let experienced paramedics handle the damaged body.

Then he took a single look down through the mesh at the bottom of the Gorge, and thought, screw the ambulance crew and all their knowledge, they'd be scared shitless out here and the first thing to do was get the son of a bitch back to solid ground.

Telling about it in Josie's Place that night, "He's a heavy bastard, you know what I mean? Maybe two hundred pounds. And all I knew was what they call fireman's lift. Would you believe it, I was a Boy Scout once? It was just damn lucky that the arm I grabbed when I hoisted him was the good arm, not the one with the busted shoulder. Jesus, I might of hurt him bad!"

Joe Trujillo again drove his great, dusty Cadillac in from the highway to the Evans ranch house, on invitation this time. Inocencio was in the parking area to meet him, and led the way around the gallery to the west *portal*, where Henry Evans waited.

"Thank you for coming, Joe," Evans said, and, shrewdly assessing Trujillo's suspicious thoughts, added, "No, I'm not going to try to out-slicker you. I just want to talk. A drink?"

Trujillo sat down. "Maybe a beer."

"I'll join you." Evans rang for the maid and gave the order. He took his time then, as if setting his thoughts in order. Trujillo waited in silence.

"You persuaded Armando Baca to downplay the Eloy Padilla story," Evans said at last. "Do you mind telling me why?"

The beers arrived. Trujillo took his, tasted it, nodded approval, and set it down. "You ask the damndest questions," he said.

Evans smiled, and sipped his own beer in silence.

"Okay," Trujillo said, and shrugged. "The thing is, I've been asking myself the same question ever since. And I don't know the goddamn answer."

"Perhaps it could be," Evans said, "that now you want the bridge?"

"Could be. If you can't whip them, join them. That kind of thing."

"With a man named Bobbie Jack Jones?"

Trujillo had his beer halfway to his mouth. He set it down untouched. "Is that what we're getting at? Him?"

"No doubt he promised you quite a bit," Evans said. "And who knows? You might even get some of it."

"But what?"

"When you came here last, Joe," Evans said, "you professed a concern for the people of this county. Your people, your county."

"Are you waving the flag, Henry?"

"In a way."

"You've got a goddamn nerve."

"That was what you told Sam Taylor, too, wasn't it?"

"And then he gave me a look at his hole card, insurance business I wouldn't mind having."

Evans nodded. "You will get it, too, Joe. He has assured me of that."

"I'll believe it when I see it on paper. Notarized."

Evans nodded again. "Suit yourself. But I can understand your attitude. I used to believe my geologists, too—after we finally found the oil they said was there."

Trujillo settled deeper into his chair. "You're working up to something," he said.

Evans smiled. "You are an astute man, Joe. I have never underestimated you."

"Okay, so what is it? Something to do with the Jones dude?"

"Exactly. He will be buying up land options. Cheap. Isn't that his idea?"

Trujillo thought about it. "Could be." His face and his voice were expressionless.

"And with your prestige behind him, he will have no trouble at all."

Trujillo thought about it some more. "What's the point?"

"I will not only match his every offer for options, Joe," Evans said, "I will raise the ante as much as necessary to get them before he does."

Trujillo picked up his beer, drank, and set the glass down again without ever taking his eyes from Evans's face. He said at last, "I guess you could do it, too, Henry, if you really wanted to."

"I can. And I will."

"Why tell me?"

Evans smiled again. "I think you know the answer. I think you just want it out in the open. I want your prestige on my side, Joe, instead of his. I want you to act as my agent in the matter. As agent, you will of course deserve recompense, a commission, which I will guarantee."

Trujillo shook his head in slow wonder. "You hate my guts, Henry. You always have."

"No. You have always hated mine, and so you have imputed to me your own feelings. I told you once that I find you a very complex man. I do. You have many qualities I admire, and a number I do not particularly like. But no one can accuse you of stupidity. And working with me will benefit you considerably more than working with Bobbie Jack Jones."

Trujillo shook his head gently. He was frowning, puzzled. "What's in it for you?" he said. "That's what stumps me."

"Now it is you asking the damndest questions. You embarrass me."

"With land options in your pocket," Trujillo said, "you stand to make a bundle with a quick turnover to speculators as soon as the road comes through. No fuss, no muss, no bother at all."

"That is precisely what Bobbie Jack has in mind," Evans said. "Do you impute the same motives to me?"

"That's what bothers me. That isn't your style."

"Thank you, Joe, for that. I appreciate it."

"All right, then, goddamn it, are you trying to tell me you're doing it just to keep Jones from ripping off half the county?"

Evans sipped his beer in silence. He set his glass down with great care. He looked at Trujillo, and waited.

Trujillo said, "I guess maybe you're just crazy enough to do it. You goddamned anglos get the wildest ideas. You are waving the flag, aren't you? Up, motherhood! You're fixing to do exactly what I said I wanted to do last time I was here—keep people from being ripped off. And you'll put up your own money to do it. Do you figure to get it back?"

"Possibly. I would judge the odds to be about even."

"Something else you're doing too, of course," Trujillo said.

"You're putting me right down in favor of the bridge, aren't you? Floyd Babcock's goddamn bridge?"

Evans allowed that faint smile of his to show briefly. "So you see, Joe, my motives are not wholly eleemosynary."

"Whatever the hell that means. But I guess I get the idea."

"So do you represent me as my agent? I said once we would make a strange team. But I think the time may have come."

Trujillo lifted his hands, and let them fall helplessly. "Like you said," he said, "I can recognize a good deal when it steps up and slaps me in the face."

Evans nodded, smiling again. "Fine. Another beer? Or perhaps a glass of brandy, to toast our new relationship?"

Bobbie Jack Jones got a version of the news in roundabout fashion through the real estate gossip line that recognizes neither county nor state boundaries. He headed immediately for Joe Trujillo's office to straighten Trujillo out. That was the damned trouble with these Mexes, he told himself, they couldn't be trusted to stay bought. He came right to the point.

"You're working for me," he said. "I thought we had that understood."

The only visible change in Trujillo was deep in his eyes, which changed in opacity as the sky changes when thunderstorms form on the horizon. "Wrong," he said. "I don't work *for* anybody. Sometimes I work *with* people. There's a difference." And the difference, he thought, between working with an *hijo de puta*, son of a whore, like you, and an *hidalgo*, a grandee, like Henry Evans is so vast that there is no possible comparison.

"Call it what you want," Bobbie Jack said, "we had an understanding, didn't we?"

"A tentative understanding, yes."

"Where I come from, by God, a handshake is as good as a contract."

"In the insurance business, I learned that it isn't."

"I showed you how we could clean up," Bobbie Jack said, "and split the loot. Now you're going off on your own to try to take it all, is that it? Well, that's not the kind of thing I take laying down. I've got money behind me, enough to buy you and sell you half a dozen times over."

"Then you haven't got anything to worry about, have you?" Trujillo said. His voice was still soft, but the thunderstorms in his eyes were menacing.

"Look," Bobbie Jack said, suddenly switching tactics, "it don't make any sense at all for you and me to squabble, now, does it? Shucks, we had a good thing lined up. You try to handle it all by your lonesome, and—"

"I'm not working alone," Trujillo said.

"No? Then who you working for? With?"

"Henry Evans."

For as long as it might take to count slowly to ten, Bobbie Jack was silent. His mouth opened and closed in spasms like the mouth of a fish landed on the bank. His breathing was deep, and not entirely steady. He said at last, "Why, that son of a bitch already has more dollars than Carter has liver pills; oil and gas royalties, uranium holdings, God only knows what all, and now he wants to screw me out of this as well? Well, by God—"

"Do you want to know what I think you ought to do?" Trujillo said. He watched Bobbie Jack's attention come back into focus. "Go back to Texas," Trujillo said. "And stay there."

"The hell," Bobbie Jack said, got up from his chair and marched out of the office.

Trujillo heard the front door of the building slam, and leaned back in his chair. After long moments, he sat up again, and reached for the phone to call Henry Evans at the ranch.

"He's good and mad," Trujillo told Evans. "Whether he's mad enough to try something crazy, I don't know, but if it was me, I wouldn't let him get behind me."

"I appreciate the warning, Joe."

"He may do like I said, and give up the whole idea."

"If it isn't he, it will be someone else. Speculation is inevitable."

"Does that mean you want to go ahead, no matter?"

"I'm afraid it does, Joe."

"What was that word you used? Elee—something?"

"Eleemosynary. It means, well, charitable; in this instance maybe philanthropic. And it is not a position in which I find myself comfortable—"

"The hell you don't, Henry. I never really believed it before, but I guess what they say is true after all, and there are people like that, like you. Okay, we'll tie up this whole damn end of the county in options to buy. Then what?"

"Then we will be able to exercise some control over the eventual sales, and over the direction and rate of growth."

Trujillo smiled. The thunderstorms had disappeared from his

eyes. "I looked up a couple of words you called me once, Henry," he said. "Seems to me they apply more to you."

"What were the words?"

"Benevolent despot. You said they were out of style."

"Together," Evans said, "and only temporarily, we will restore the monarchy. Agreed?"

Bobbie Jack drove straight back to his motel from Trujillo's office to think over this new turn of events. No matter how he looked at it, he saw only bad news. Henry Evans was not someone you could discount. Aside from the money he controlled, which was almost, but not quite, unlimited, there was the man himself, who, crippled or not, was still a force to be reckoned with. If he set his hand to something, and it did not even occur to Bobbie Jack to doubt Trujillo's word that Evans was involved, then that something was going to be accomplished come hell or high water. That was the man's reputation, and Bobbie Jack knew of no instance in which it had not been lived up to.

That unpleasant scene out at the ranch had demonstrated what could happen if you treated Evans with less than great care. Bobbie Jack could still see that handgun pointed right at his stomach, as unmoving as if it had been in a steadyrest; and he could still hear what was in Evans's voice when he issued his warning. Henry Evans was one of the few who said what he meant, and meant what he said right down to the last syllable.

The fact of the matter was that what ought to have been a simple, straightforward piece of land business had turned out now to be damned near impossible. Without Trujillo, who was widely trusted in these parts, he, Bobbie Jack, anglo from Texas, stood just about as much chance as a snowball in hell in dealing with the locals. And that was something he'd better face up to. Tough tit, but there it was.

Reluctantly, he picked up the bedside telephone, and placed a call to Houston. "Jones here," he said.

"Bobbie Jack, baby. How's the boy?"

"Not too good." He went on to explain, and when he was done, the telephone was silent for long, somehow ominous moments.

"Bobbie Jack, baby," the voice said at last in a new, quite different tone. "That is bad news. Very bad news."

"Can't be helped."

"Correction. It has to be helped. Do you follow my meaning?"

"There's just no way—"

"Then you'll just have to find a way. This was your idea, your project. And we have plans for it. Do you follow my meaning? Since you pointed the opportunity out to us, we have given the matter a great deal of thought, and research, which costs, you know what I mean? And the area looks better and better."

"But—"

"The area is virgin territory, Bobbie Jack, baby, where in a manner of speaking no human eye has ever set foot. Mexes and Indians don't count. And virgin territory is hard to come by, just about as hard as the real thing. So now what you do is you sit down and use all that college learning they gave you for playing football, and you figure out just how we go ahead as planned. Because if you don't, some people are going to be real disappointed, do you follow my meaning?"

The trouble was, Bobbie Jack thought as he hung up, he followed the meaning all too clearly. It was as if it were written large on the wall in letters of fire. Or doom. He was caught right between a rock and a hard place, and he didn't like the feeling it gave him in the pit of his stomach. It was, in short, a situation he would wish on no one, except perhaps Henry Evans, who was really the cause of it all.

How long he sat on the bed trying to think, he didn't know. He considered defiance, which was merely another way of saying suicide. He thought of appealing to Trujillo, or even to Henry Evans, both of which ideas were plainly ridiculous. He wondered how life in Australia might be, and decided that was no answer either. In the end he picked up the phone again, and put a call through to Alice Perkins who was hard at work in the state's Department of Corrections.

"I need a favor, honey," Bobbie Jack told her.

"Ever since I've known you, you've needed favors."

"This is a big one. And it's important," Bobbie Jack's voice took on a contrite tone. "I know, I've thrown you some curves."

"You have indeed."

"But this may be the last favor I'll ask. Of you, or of anybody."

"And just what does that mean?"

"It means, honey, that if I don't get this one, I may not be around very long to ask for others."

"Now I know you're kidding."

Bobbie Jack was silent.

"Aren't you?" Alice Perkins said. "Kidding, I mean?"

"Honey, I'm in a jam. That's fact, not fiction."

"What kind of a jam?"

Bobbie Jack took a deep breath. "I promised some people something and now I can't come through. And they're not the kind of people who smile, and say, 'Forget it.' That's fact, too."

There was a short silence. Alice Perkins's voice rose perceptibly. "Oh, damn you, Bobbie Jack! When you got out of college, you had the world by the tail with a downhill pull—"

"I know. I let it get away."

"And that is fake contrition if I ever heard it, and I have. All right. What do you want me to do?"

"I want to talk to the governor."

The silence this time was long. Alice Perkins said at last, "Do you know what you're asking? Yes, you do. You know perfectly well, and you simply don't care. As long as Bobbie Jack Jones gets what he wants, nothing else matters, does it?"

"You were friendly with him once."

"I liked him."

"And he was in a position to do things for you, wasn't he? Didn't you have a little bit of that in mind too? You know me, honey, but I know you just as well."

"That's a cheap shot."

"I don't think so. Pragmatism, isn't that the word? We talked about it two, three times, I do recall, back when we had something going between us, about how a woman needs all the weapons she can find just to get along, isn't that how it was?"

"All you want me to do," Alice Perkins said, "is cozy up to Floyd Babcock and persuade him that you're really a fine fellow, just misjudged by some people, is that it?"

"I've got a couple things to tell him he'll be real interested to hear."

"What kind of things?"

Bobbie Jack shook his head with emphasis. "No. You don't want to know, honey. I'm not going to put you in the middle, and you can believe that too." His voice changed again. "Will you help me?"

This third pause was the longest of all. At last, "I'll think about it," Alice Perkins said.

28.

The governor arrived without warning at the bridge site. To Pepe, his driver, he said as he got out of the car, "The new honcho here—what's his name?"

Of all the politicos Pepe had ever known, this one had the worst memory for names. "Zabrinski," Pepe said. "Carl Zabrinski. Biggern'n either of us, Governor. They call him the *oso pardo*."

"Zabrinski. Got it," the governor said. "Make yourself comfortable. I may be a spell."

All this construction was strange to him, the governor thought as he looked slowly around, but after he'd studied on it a little while, he began to see organization in the confusion, and in the noise. And the sheer dimensions were almost overpowering, like the huge buildings that lined Park Avenue in New York.

Those towers, now, one on each side of the Gorge, which of course made sense. The near one gave you a crick in the neck just looking up at its top, where men moved around as if there wasn't any drop-off, let alone all that distance to fall if they didn't mind their step.

It was easier to get the whole picture looking across at the west tower, seeing the thing in one piece, anchored solidly into the rock, tapering up from spread legs almost like pictures he had seen of that Eiffel Tower in Paris, France.

When you looked at this structure, you had a feeling of enormous strength, and yet lightness too, the feeling you sometimes got from looking at a fine horse, muscled and powerful and yet agile enough to turn on a dime and give a nickel back in change. Big Luke blasting out of the starting gate came to mind.

And those three cables strung across the Gorge looked about as fragile as spiderwebs, but that was a pretty fair-sized tramcar affair they supported, so the governor supposed they were stronger than they looked. Had to be, because that tramcar crow-hopped and buck-jumped as he watched it creep out over the middle of the Gorge, until the governor could almost feel the twist and the shake and the solid jar a rider had to anticipate when first he turned an unbroken horse loose from the snubbing post.

"You're the governor, aren't you?"

The governor turned and had to look up at the shaggy head. "Zabrinski," he said, for a wonder remembering the name. "Has to be. There won't be two your size in one place." They shook hands. "Just thought I'd come up and have a look for myself," the governor said. "This here's kind of a pet project of mine."

"Be glad to show you around, Governor."

"Well, now, that's right nice of you."

They inspected the tower foundations set deep, plumb, level and solid in bedrock and concrete. They examined the steel itself that made up the lacework of the massive tower structure.

"It'll be painted red," Zabrinski said, "like the Golden Gate Bridge. Go well with the earth tones of this country."

The governor caught the feeling behind the words. "You an artist?"

Zabrinski smiled and waved one big hand in a deprecating gesture. "Just watercolors. Strictly amateur."

They visited the shops and the storerooms and peered down into the cable anchorage preparations, again bedrock and concrete and steel. They looked at the huge reels of wire, the spindles from which the strands of the main cables would be spun, four strands, as Zabrinski explained, at each traverse of the two sheaves.

They walked to the edge of the Gorge to look out at the safety nets already in place, and to look up at the beginnings of the roadway stubs jutting out into space above the nets. The governor recalled the stories he had read in the newspapers about the lives those nets had already saved.

"Knew a cowboy once," the governor said, pitching his voice

over the clatter of rivet guns, "who claimed he could take a horse just about any place a man could go on foot. Used to feel the same way myself. But out over that gorge on one of those skinny little steel beams—" He shook his head. "Not for me, with or without a horse." He looked again at Zabrinski. "Much obliged for the tour. Now let's go some place and set a spell and talk a bit. How about the back seat of my car?"

It was quieter there, and with the engine turned on and the air-conditioner going, there was complete privacy. Pepe leaned against the fender of a truck nearby.

"I kind of expected trouble up here over that local boy," the governor said. "Forget his name. Doesn't matter. But it kind of blew over, didn't it?"

"No trouble yet," Zabrinski said. "Henry Evans has had a lot to do with that, I think."

"Henry's the kind of man you'd admire to ride fence with. Or go out hunting bear." The governor's voice seemed preoccupied, as if the words were automatic. "What about your schedule?"

"We're just about on it."

"And cost?"

"They work up the cost figures in San Francisco, but I haven't heard any screams, so I figure we're in line."

"What will those cable-stays you're adding do? And those safety nets you've added?" The governor watched Zabrinski's eyebrows rise in surprise, and he smiled faintly. "First thing you learn in politics," the governor said, "is you better keep informed. I do pretty well. And I've been waiting for what's-his-name, Sam Taylor to come around and talk to me about those cable-stays. You're afraid of wind? That it?"

"Basically, yes."

"Farmers and ranchers," the governor said, "and I guess sailors too think quite a bit about the weather. You watch it year in and year out, maybe keep records, and you see it change." He was watching Zabrinski's face steadily. "When I heard about the cable-stays being added, I thought maybe somebody hadn't done his homework first, and only just now was beginning to start to worry about the kinds of winds we've been getting these last two, three years. Is that how it was?"

"Not exactly."

He listened with quiet attention until Zabrinski was through. Then he thought about it for a time, still in silence. "The way I get it," he said at last, "is if we catch here the kind of windstorm they had up in Cheyenne or down in Silver City, a real tornado, or maybe even like that one not quite so bad over in Pojaque, then we might have big trouble?"

Zabrinski spread his hands and shrugged massively. "There's no way of telling, but, *if* we caught a big wind, a tornado, say, *before* we got the cable-stays in place, then, yes, we could have trouble."

"And you kind of think the Gorge might be what you could call vulnerable? Your what-you-call-it Venturi tube effect?"

"I don't think there's any way of predicting that. Or refuting it."

The governor leaned back in the seat and pushed his hat up a little from his brow with a long forefinger. "Cost overruns we don't need," he said. "You might tell Sam Taylor that, if he doesn't know it already. Or delays in completion. And the cable-stays will likely produce both, isn't that about it?"

"We'll try to avoid both."

"But," the governor said as if he had not heard, "the thing we don't need most is for this Tinkertoy structure to fall down, no matter what kind of wind we get. There was that bridge out Tacoma, Washington way—"

"Galloping Gertie, yes. We've designed in none of the faults that one had."

"Well, I'll tell you," the governor said, "I've kind of pushed all my chips right out to the middle of the table on this here structure. I'm not betting show or place or any combination. I've put my bet right on the nose to win. Big."

"And you don't like to lose," Zabrinski said.

"Exactly."

Zabrinski nodded. "Neither do I. And neither does Sam."

The governor nodded in return. "I guess we understand each other," he said.

From the bridge, the governor had Pepe drive him to the ranch, where, stretched out in a chair, a drink of Evans's fine bourbon at his elbow, he stared at the distant mountains of the Divide and felt himself relax as he had not relaxed in some time.

"If I had the brains God gave a chipmunk," he told Henry Evans, "I'd stay home on my own spread, tending to ranching and nothing else, and let the piss-ants in the capitol, both of them, this here one *and* the one in Washington, screw up without any help from me. Or hindrance, as the case may be."

"But you're an ambitious man," Evans said in his quiet, controlled way, "so if you remain idle, you itch."

"Isn't that the damn truth? And why it has to be I'm damned if I know."

Evans smiled faintly and changed the subject. "What does your Denver gossip tell you about Wilt Ross in San Francisco?"

"Holding his own. Maybe even gaining a mite."

"Will he go back to work?"

"From all I hear, no. Not even at an easy lope instead of a dead run."

Evans, too, stared at the distant mountains. From talk of Wilt Ross it was a short step to thoughts of Ellie, and her telephone call the morning after her first date with Sam. "I've taken the chip off my shoulder," Ellie had told him, "and Sam has even gotten around to laughing, not often, but on selected occasions."

That single sentence, Evans thought, told volumes. It said that Ellie and Sam had stopped walking around one another like a couple of strange dogs. And once that change had taken place, anything could happen.

He had no business extrapolating from this new situation, Evans told himself, and he certainly had no business even thinking of trying to exert influence. Ellie was a grown woman, perfectly capable of making up her own mind and guiding her own behavior. Being Evans's daughter, she was under a kind of curse, true, that of considering overachievement a normal way of life, but she was also of a generation that had largely embraced hedonism, and somewhere down the line there was going to be conflict.

Sam Taylor was settling into the pattern Wilt Ross had established, and, being Sam, would probably fit it as a hand fits a glove. The job would be always paramount in his mind. And it followed that Ellie, if indeed she were to become part of his life, would take second place.

"They don't pay off for second place." How often had he, Henry Evans, heard himself saying that in Ellie's presence, and how deeply ingrained in her thinking had the aphorism become?

The governor said, almost as if he had been reading Evans's thoughts, "You know, you need a foreman on this spread, Henry, somebody who knows his business and can work at it full time."

"Someone not in a wheelchair, you mean," Evans said, and instantly regretted it.

"You gave up being a tool-pusher yourself a long time ago," the governor said without change of tone, "and took to driving around, or flying your own plane from lease to lease just checking up on how the folks who worked for you were doing. You can run this spread from that chair easy, if you got somebody to take orders and report back."

Evans had a sip of his bourbon. Its smooth taste rested well on his tongue. "You have someone in mind?"

"Well, now," the governor said, and smiled. "I met that feller Zabrinski for the first time. He strikes me like a man who'd do well at any job he put his hand and his mind to. How does he get along with Ellie?" He smiled again. "Course, you'd have to set him up a *remuda* of Percherons or Clydesdales or those big Belgians to ride. Nothing smaller could carry him."

"Carl's a good man."

"Then," the governor said, "there's Sam Taylor. He know anything about ranching?"

"He has his hands full running Ross Associates and seeing, among myriad other things, that your bridge gets built."

"He and Ellie get along?"

Evans produced another of his rare smiles. "When you get the bit in your teeth, Floyd, you're a hard horse to stop."

Long after the governor had disappeared around the corner of the gallery walking with the choppy stride of a man who has grown up wearing heeled boots, Evans sat quiet, staring out at the distant horizon and letting his mind wander as it would.

Those who considered Floyd Babcock no more than a bucolic boob, he thought as he had thought many times before, were fools. The governor saw clearly, and he saw deep, sometimes uncomfortably deep.

Sam Taylor and Ellie—of course Evans was already thinking about that. And there was growing within him an almost overpowering desire to meddle. Invalid and tyrant, he was coming to believe, were almost synonymous words. He wondered if any of the deep-think psychologists appreciated the fact.

When you were no longer able to cope with the world on its own physical terms as you always had, then the temptation was to remake that world, or at least whatever part of it you could conceivably control, into a form you could meet on equal terms; and because your need seemed urgent, normal rules of considerate behavior no longer applied. It was as simple, and as selfish, as that.

As he had told Sam, he wanted Ellie here on the ranch, close, a young, vibrant, cheerful presence from whom he could draw affection and concern. Of course that was selfish, but he didn't seem to be able to help it.

And, as the governor had pointed out, the big ranch needed someone who could give it personal direction, acting, of course, on orders from Evans. Zabrinski or someone of similar caliber could do the job, but as long as he, Henry Evans, was arranging matters anyway, or trying to, why should he settle for anything less than the first string? And that meant Sam Taylor. The governor had seen that just as clearly as he did, even if he hadn't said so.

So? Evans sat quiet, looking out at the limitless vista, and thinking about ways and means.

Laura knocked, and came into the big office. Sam was behind the desk studying a folded computer print-out. He did not look up.

"You have a date," Laura said to the top of his head. "And you're going to be late. And I've been wanting to talk to you all day. Must I stamp my foot to get your attention?"

Sam put down the folded print-out, and leaned back in his chair. "Kuala Lumpur's going fine." He was stating a fact, not emphasizing a point, but there was in his voice an underlying note of reproach. "So are Riyadh and Anchorage, in good shape, in good hands. But I don't like the feel of Port au Prince, and Tano is still in a minefield. That's only counting the big jobs. I haven't even been able to look into the little ones."

"You're doing fine," Laura said. "Better than fine. But if you aren't careful, you'll end up where Wilt is. In the hospital. All alone."

"Yes, ma'am."

Laura shook her head. "Don't do that to me, Sam. Wilt did it for too long. Until I stopped even trying to get him to cut down. I'll call Miss Evans and tell her you were detained, but that you've already left, hurrying."

"What did you want to talk to me about?"

"It can wait. It will have to." She saw the refusal forming in his face, and she did stamp her foot. "Damn you, Sam!" It was almost a cry. "You're just as stubborn as he was. All right. It's about him. He has agreed to see you. Alone."

"When?"

"As soon as possible. Shall I tell you how he put it in words?"

Sam's faint smile appeared. "I can guess. He probably said, 'All right, goddamn it, I'll see him. Tell him to haul his ass over here on the double.' Right?"

Laura closed her eyes. Tears stung her lids. She blinked them back. "Exact," she said. "Now, go off on your date."

29.

Over cocktails, the governor studied Alice Perkins across the restaurant booth. "I like things spelled out plain, honey," he said, "like who's doing what to who, and why. You want me to see this here Bobbie Jack Jones again."

"He wants to see you. And if he just called your office, you'd have him brushed off, wouldn't you?"

"Likely. So he sends you. Like an ambassador?"

"You frightened me once," Alice Perkins said, remembering that painful naked scene. "Please don't do it again."

"Well, now," the governor said, "that time I meant to. This time I don't. This time I'm just plain curious. Why does he want to see me?"

"He's in some kind of trouble."

"And he thinks I can help him?" The governor shook his head. "I said I don't hold grudges, but I don't always do what the Bible says about forgiving and forgetting, either. I don't figure I owe your Bobbie Jack any favors, honey."

"He says he has a couple of things to tell you you'll be interested to hear." She anticipated the governor's query. "He wouldn't tell me what kind of things. He said he wasn't going to put me in the middle, whatever that means. I thought you might understand."

"Honey, you're an enigma wrapped in a riddle, like somebody said once," the governor said. "Looks to me like your friend Bobbie Jack covers a lot of territory swinging a real wide loop, and, from what Henry Evans says, casting a crooked shadow while he's doing it. Are you and he kin?"

"He was a big man on the college campus. I was drab little Alice Perkins."

"He surely blossomed you out then. Or somebody did."

"He could have been anything he wanted to be. Anything." And I have never really gotten over him, she thought.

"Like a lot of the fellers in the jails you're such an expert on."

Alice Perkins closed her eyes. When she opened them again, there was sadness in their depths. "Yes," she said. "He—always looks for the easy way too. Will you see him?"

"Aren't you sort of dangling yourself as bait?"

"I suppose I am. If that's the way you want it."

"No." The governor shook his head. "That isn't how I play. When I go hunting, I don't pick on cripples. Drink your drink, and we'll see about some food. I'll see your Bobbie Jack. Tell him to call for an appointment. Now, how are you and my Department of Corrections making out? You getting the cooperation you need? If you aren't, I want to know about it, and I'll bang a few heads together."

Ellie answered the doorbell wearing black trousers and a creamy blouse. She was smiling as she held the door for Sam. "A slight change of plan," she said. "I want to know if you're capable of flexibility."

"That depends."

"I thought dinner here."

"I've booked a booth at Ernie's."

"So now you see how the word 'flexibility' comes in." Her smile did not change. "And while decisions are being made, I'll fix you a drink. Bourbon?" She turned away then and walked toward the bar tray.

Sam stood silent, watching her and the way she moved, easily, with grace, the black trousers concealing none of her rounded shapeliness and strength.

He was vaguely annoyed. He admitted it. She was forcing a confrontation, and he was and had always been instantly ready to accept a dare. It was, he thought, something Ellie had better understand, except that he had the sudden feeling that she already did.

It was, then, foolish as it might seem, a deliberate test of strength between them, annoying concept, and there could only be one outcome. He watched Ellie reach the bar tray, stop, turn, and stand watching him, smiling still.

"The male dominant?" she said. "It's the view Henry holds, even though he tries to hide it. I'll repeat my question—bourbon?"

"I thought we got rid of that chip on the shoulder."

"We did. Once and for all."

"Then?"

"This is wholly different. You ought to be able to see that for yourself. You disappoint me if you don't."

Sam thought about it. Slowly he nodded. "I see your point. This is not—defensive."

"Exactly."

"What you want is equality."

"You put it very well."

"You have all the Evans arrogance."

Ellie nodded. Her smile held steady. "To match yours. One more time, bourbon?"

Sam hesitated, poised midway between anger and incredulity at being challenged so. Time stretched in silence. And then, all at once, he found himself smiling and shaking his head in slow wonderment. Out-faced, he thought, out-matched. And, astonishingly, suddenly loose and easy, he found no pain in the admission. He took his time, savoring the moment.

"No," he said at last. "Bourbon is for earlier. And later. When dinner is imminent, I prefer a martini. On the rocks, very dry, with just a twist of lemon peel."

Ellie's instant relaxation was palpable. Tenseness flowed from her body, and the quality of her smile changed until it seemed to brighten hidden lights within her eyes. "Coming up," she said as she turned to the tray. And over her shoulder, in a different softer voice she added, "I hoped it would be this way, Sam. I gambled on it." Admission.

"I'll call Ernie's and cancel the booking," Sam said.

It would be a long time, if ever, before Sam would forget that evening. There was about it a quality, the essence of which was intimacy, far different from anything he had known before, as if the barriers between Ellie and him had not only been lowered, they had been destroyed, and it was as if they had never existed.

Drink in hand, and the smile still lighting the hidden depths in her eyes, "A steak," Ellie said, "and I pride myself on my Caesar salad. Garlic French bread, and a bottle of Monterey Cabernet Sauvignon, with apple and cheese to follow. Satisfactory?"

Sam was smiling too. "Eminently."

"We'll charcoal-broil the steak, of course." Her smile spread. "If you're wondering about the time a charcoal fire takes, it's already lighted. It has been for forty minutes."

"You were that sure of me?" Strangely, he felt no resentment.

"No." Ellie shook her head. Her eyes did not leave his. "I told you. I gambled. I don't gamble often, as Henry does. But this time I thought it was worth it. Am I blushing?"

"Whatever it is," Sam said, "it becomes you."

Ellie walked to the windows and stood looking out over the formless pattern of the lights of the city, the regularity of the twin row of lights on the Bay Bridge like a necklace extended, the vague shape of the Berkeley hills across the water. "This was Henry's and Mother's pied-à-terre," she said, turning. "They enjoyed it, but they never stayed here more than a week at a time. Henry is claustrophobic about cities. Are you?"

"In a way." It was an admission he had never spoken aloud before. "I grew up looking at the big mountains. Big buildings are no substitute. They close you in."

"But you're tied here, aren't you?"

Sam thought of Wilt Ross's summons. "Maybe. Maybe not. I'll have the verdict tomorrow."

She understood instantly. "You are going to see Mr. Ross? He's sent for you?"

"Laura's doing."

Ellie's eyes seemed to scrutinize his face and probe into his thoughts. "And which way do you hope the verdict will go?"

"I wish I knew." And this was strange, too, because until this moment he had not questioned his destiny. "I'm an engineer. I build things. I'm good at that."

"But?"

"I'm finding out what Ross has had to put up with, and I'm not sure I like it. You're a man in a cage. Problems are handed in to you through the bars, and you pass the answers back out, but you're not able to see the results, only the balance sheets. You pull the levers and push the buttons, but it's all remote control, somehow unreal." Never, never, could he have imagined himself talking like this to anyone, let alone a woman. He wondered if Ellie understood even vaguely what he was saying.

She surprised him. "I've heard Henry say the same thing," she said. "Bringing in a successful well was always a thrill when he had a hand in drilling it. But hearing over the phone that they had hit another big one meant nothing, except more money in the bank. It doesn't compare to something close, and tangible, like the new foal Inocencio is so crazy about."

Sam's thoughts went off in a new direction. "And what do you want?"

"I'm as bad as you are." She was smiling again. "I don't know what I want. Maybe some day I'll meet it, or him, face to face, and then I'll know. Henry needs me. Correction. Henry wants me near."

"And you love the ranch."

"It is home. But I could leave it—if there were good reason."

"And live in a city? Like this?"

Her smile turned gentle. "I'm claustrophobic too. Let's make another drink, and see how the fire is doing."

"I suppose the table is all set too?" Again, he felt no resentment, only curiosity.

"It is. When I do gamble," Ellie said, "I bet to win. I'm not interested in place or show."

The steak was superlative, marbled, tender, flavorful. "Our own beef," Ellie said. "Still Henry is not satisfied. He never will be. Sometimes that used to drive Mother wild."

"Not you?"

"I was brought up to believe that excellence isn't enough. You should look beyond. Maybe that's why I'm twenty-nine and still unattached."

Sam put down his knife and fork. "And does that bother you?" His was, he thought suddenly, no idle curiosity. He had a real desire to learn the answer.

"Sometimes."

"Tell me why."

Ellie picked up her wineglass and studied it while she considered the matter. She sipped slowly, and set the glass down again. "Few things bore me more," she said, "than talk of somebody's 'identity crisis' or somebody else going off to exotic places to 'find herself,' but I suppose in a way I'm saying the same thing. I'm . . . incomplete. I don't mean that just because there are male and female, everybody has a biological duty to pair up. I don't think in big generalities like that. What I do mean is that I, Ellie Evans, need a man, one man, to help me fit together all my pieces, my abilities, my enthusiasms, my animal desires, and, of course, my love. And in return, I'll fill in the gaps that are in him. Then, I think, I'll be able to set aside that feeling that I'm just an accident that happened to be born, and there really isn't any place for me in the scheme of things. If there is a scheme." Her sudden smile was brilliant. "You ask a silly question, and that's the answer you get."

"Quite an answer," Sam's voice was noncommittal. And, in a quick change of pace, "You deserve to be proud of your Caesar salad."

Ellie studied him quietly, the brilliant smile wiped clean. "Did I touch a nerve?"

Sam considered evasion, and rejected it. Right up to you, he told himself, and found that he could smile after all. "I suppose so."

"I'm listening."

Still he tried to avoid commitment. "This is the kind of thing you talk about freshman year at college."

"Somehow I can't see you doing that. Did you?"

Sam shook his head, smiling still. "No. You Evanses, father and daughter, you keep boring in, don't you?"

"When we sense pay dirt. You're a loner too. Why?"

"My life story. All forty years of it."

"We have lots of time to talk about it." Her eyes, fixed on his, were somehow open, revealing even more of their intimate depths. "All night, if you like."

Another dare, Sam thought, another confrontation, but this time the decision was never in question. "I accept with pleasure," he said. "Great pleasure." They smiled across the table at each other.

Yes, it was an evening he would long remember.

He was at the office early the next morning. Laura, as always, was ahead of him. She followed him into the big inner office, closed the door, and studied him, smiling.

"Something obviously agrees with you," she said, "and I won't even try to guess what it is." The smile disappeared. "I saw Wilt last night. He will see you at ten o'clock, after his morning routine."

Sam nodded. There was no need to check his appointment book. Laura would already have done that.

"Daryl Chambers called," Laura said.

"From Puerto Rico again?"

"No. This time from Haiti. Port au Prince. He wants you to call him."

"Anything else?"

"I've only begun. Carl Zabrinski just hung up. Bad news. They've killed another."

"Anglo?" It was the hell of a question, Sam thought, but the answer could make all the difference.

"No. *Chicano*. One of the crew this time."

"Damn it," Sam said, "they're supposed to stay on the ground. They're not bridgemen."

"It was on the ground. A cable broke, under tension. He caught the backlash."

Sam had seen it. Who, working on construction jobs, had not? A cable failing under enormous tension instantly became a mad, uncontrollable, whipping, flailing weapon, despite its diameter and because of its speed of travel capable of cutting like a giant scythe. Through masonry. Through steel itself. Through a man's body without even slowing.

"All right," Sam said. "I'll call him."

"He'll be with Henry Evans."

Good. Sam nodded. "What else?"

"Miss Lewis called. Last night, just after you had left. She said she would call you later at your apartment. Did she reach you?"

"No. I wasn't there."

"Shall I call her and say you are very busy this morning?"

"No." Sam walked to the desk chair and dropped into it. "I'll find time to call her." He considered priorities. "Zabrinski first."

Evans answered the phone. "I hear we have troubles," Sam said.

"So it would appear. Carl is right here."

Zabrinski said, "Routine, but a freak too. Cable from the power takeoff on a cat hooked to a big rock pulling it out of the west cable anchorage area. The punk was behind the cat where he ought to have been safe, but the broken part of the cable was long enough to whip around and catch him good. Two pieces. Quite a mess."

"Hazards of the job," Sam said. "You can play that up. It's different from the Padilla kid."

"Henry thinks the same. We'll work on those lines."

"Let me speak to Henry," Sam said, and waited until the quiet, calm voice was again on the line. "What do you think?" Sam said then.

"Unfortunate, but the kind of accident that can always happen on the best-run jobs."

"Can Carl sell that?"

"With help, I think yes. And I will give him what help I can."

"We ought to put you on the payroll as consultant."

"I have considered it." There was a smile beneath the words. "We will keep you posted."

Daryl Chambers in Haiti next.

"I'm taking a gamble," Chambers said. "I wanted you to know."

"You're not going over to San Juan soon?"

"Calling from here is part of the gamble. I don't think our threat is political at all. I think it's Leclerc himself, all by himself. You remember I said they always put the pressure on him, instead of Jim Hardy? Well, I got to thinking about that, so I told Leclerc that I'd deal personally with the next attempt at shakedown."

Sam began to smile.

"He didn't like that," Chambers said, "but he agreed it was okay, except that I'd have to have him translate for me because I don't speak French or Creole."

Sam nodded. "What did you say to that?"

"I said that would be all right, but maybe it would be better if I asked somebody from the embassy to act for me."

"And?"

"He didn't like that at all. And I've been waiting, but there's been no shakedown attempt and according to Hardy we're overdue."

Sam leaned back in his chair and thought about it. In a nasty sort of way, it made sense. Leclerc merely pretending to receive threats, reporting them, and making whatever payoff Jim Hardy had authorized straight into his own pocket. Simple. And almost impossible to prove. Almost. "And what now?"

"That's the gamble." The deep breath Chambers took was clearly audible on the phone. "If you okay it, I'll go to the embassy, tell them what I believe about Leclerc, and get someone to go with me straight to the Minister of Interior. They need this dam, and they want it bad. That's been made clear to me. And if one of their own nationals has been lousing up the project, strictly on his own—"

"They'll take action," Sam said. "Yes. On the other hand, if someone in government has been involved too, you may be asking for trouble."

"I understand that."

"Still you want to go ahead." Sam nodded. "But don't for the moment. This is what we have Ben Knopf for. He has the languages, and the connections. I'll send him down, and he'll work with you."

There was a silence. "Okay," Chambers said at last. "You're the boss."

"Hold it," Sam said. "I'm not through. A couple more things. First, you're doing fine." When had he last said something like that? But it was true, and deserved to be said. Even Wilt Ross had passed out compliments on occasion. Something to remember. "The second is that if you and Ben do blow the whistle on Leclerc, and it is as you think it is, all his own idea, then the government won't play around, Leclerc will have had it. Their ideas of crime and punishment are different from ours. Do you want him dead?"

"That's their business. I mean—" There was a silence. Sam waited patiently. "No," Chambers said at last, "I don't want him dead. He's useful. He knows the project. And the men. He—"

"Good for you," Sam said. Two compliments in one conversation. Unheard of. "Keep him. Hold it over his head to keep him in line, and knowledge that you can and will go to the government *will* keep him in line, and keep him working."

There was another silence. Chambers said in a new, different voice, "Is that how these things are done?"

"You're learning," Sam said. "You're learning fast." As I learned from Wilt Ross, he thought as he hung up.

30.

Liz Lewis was furious. If she had been asked, it is possible she would have admitted that she was not acting in a wholly rational manner, but neither would she have given a damn.

She was long returned from Tano and Santa Fe, and not a word from Sam, who must have been aware that she was back. Last night's call to his office would have made clear to him that she was not amused by his silence. That she had not been able to reach him with the call merely increased her displeasure.

At midnight, ready for bed, she had called his apartment again without success. At five o'clock in the morning, unaccountably awake, she had decided that it would serve him right if she awakened him too. Although the telephone rang and rang long past the six rings Liz had heard once that Pacific Telephone recommended, there was no answer. And that, Liz decided on the basis of her own proclivities, could only mean one thing. Sam was somewhere in bed with some woman.

By seven o'clock, still awake and sipping on a cup of coffee, she had gone through the list of females she knew that Sam also knew, and come up with only one likely name, Ellie Evans, last seen at the Evans ranch. But she might by now have returned to the San Francisco apartment Ellie had told her that Henry Evans still maintained.

There were a number of Henry Evanses in the telephone book, and Liz considered calling all of them, but decided that it would be simpler to call the Tano ranch and ask where Ellie was, which she did, and spoke to María, the maid.

"The señorita," María said, "is in San Francisco."

Aha! "Do you know the telephone number here?" Liz said.

"It is a how-do-you-say, not listed number, señorita."

"Never mind." Liz's voice was imperious. "I need to talk with her."

It was an unequal contest of wills. Eventually, Liz wrote down the phone number, thanked the girl, and hung up. Then she sipped her coffee and pondered the situation. By eight o'clock, at which time Sam was already at the office, her mind was made up, and she called Ellie's apartment.

"I'm looking for Sam," she said.

Ellie was first annoyed, and then amused. "I don't have him." I did, she thought smiling, and in a larger sense, I may still. But she let the answer stand.

"But you have seen him?"

"Why, yes. We went to hear the Guarneri Quartet the other night. Do you know them?"

"Of course."

"Do you like them?"

"I'm interested in Sam."

"I gathered that."

That painful early morning scene was still vivid in Liz's mind. "Never mind," she said. "Do you know where he is?"

"I should think he's at the office. I understand he goes down early."

Straight from your bed, no doubt, Liz thought, and found the concept infuriating. "You and I must have a talk," she said.

"Isn't that what this is?"

"I mean face to face."

Too much, Ellie thought, and tried not to giggle. Sunlight was streaming in the windows, the sky was a vivid blue above the sparkling Bay, and it was altogether a lovely day to be young and alive and as filled with *joie de vivre* as she was. "Face to face," she repeated with mock solemnity. "Do I have choice of weapons? My preference is for rifles. At about a hundred yards. Is that suitable?"

"Damn it," Liz said. "I'm serious. How about lunch?"

"When?"

"Today. Then we can talk, and—"

"I'm sorry," Ellie said. "I have a lunch date." She tried, and failed, to keep the triumph out of her voice.

Sam had a healthy man's dislike of hospitals. Worse, when he was visiting one, he felt that he, hale and hearty, could only be an affront to those who were confined, and the temptation was to sneak in and sneak out as unobtrusively as possible, like a thief in an apartment house.

Wilt Ross's door was open. Sam hesitated, knocked once and then walked in. Despite what Laura had told him, he was not prepared for the sight of the man in the bed.

Ross's thinning hair was neatly combed, and he was clean-shaven, but the skin of his face and throat hung in folds, and there was a perceptible tremble in the big, bony hands that lay on the coverlet. Only the eyes, dark and sunken, nevertheless held fire in their depths, constant reminder of the man that had been.

For a few moments neither spoke. It was Ross who broke the silence. "You might as well sit down." His voice was clear, but uncharacteristically querulous. "It looks as if usurping my command agrees with you. Goddamn it, who gave you the right? I was going to fire you for insubordination. Treachery. That's what it was. Well? What have you got to say for yourself?"

"I'm not taking your place," Sam said. "Nobody can do that. I'm filling in."

"Until I get back? That's poppycock. I won't leave here except in a box. Laura keeps up the brave little woman act and tells me I'm doing fine, but I know better." He added vaguely, "Where were we?"

"What have I got to say for myself?" Sam said. He raised his hands and let them fall. "Not much of anything."

"Humility never did become you." The voice was stronger now, suddenly no longer querulous and petulant. "Laura says you're doing a good job. So does Johnny Haskins. I have to believe them. The Tano bridge?"

"We've had troubles. But we're—"

"What kind of troubles? Delays in deliveries? Design problems? That Chambers fellow isn't working out?"

"I replaced him," Sam said, "with Zabrinski, the stress engineer. Chambers is in Haiti standing in for Jim Hardy who's in hospital in Puerto Rico. Chambers is doing fine."

"But the Tano bridge isn't. Why?"

Right now, Sam thought, the old man seemed as sharp as ever, as attuned to subtleties. Attempt at evasion would be futile, and probably infuriating as well. "The bridge is doing all right," he said, "on paper. But the problem we have is wind, and that's what has us . . . worried." He braced himself for a tirade on the practice of finding dangers that did not exist.

Instead, Ross looked up at the ceiling in silence for a few moments, and then nodded. "Could be." He was looking at Sam again. "In narrow passes, narrow gorges in mountain country you can get winds you wouldn't believe. I've seen it in the Andes. Other places. What're you doing about it?"

"Safety nets." Again, Sam waited for an explosion, but the only reaction was a question.

"What else?"

"We're adding cable-stays from the towers to the roadway."

"Steinmann, and the Bronx-Whitestone." Again Ross nodded. "Will that do it?"

"We think so."

"And cost?"

Sam shrugged. "A problem."

Again there was silence as the old man's eyes returned to the ceiling. When he spoke again, his voice had altered. It now contained a wistful note. "Goddamn it, boy, I found you, and I raised you, and you went behind my back. That hurt. It still does." He was looking straight at Sam again. "I've had a lot of time to think just lying here, and maybe you were right, maybe we jumped into that project too fast. My fault. You tried to tell me. I'll give you that." His voice grew stronger. "But then, goddamn it, you sneaked off without a word. Or a nod. You took it on yourself to try to correct a senile old man's mistake, and that, by God, I was not about to take lying down. You hear me?"

Sam glanced automatically at the open door. "I hear," he said.

"And maybe they're hearing me out on the street too," Ross said. "Not that I give a damn." In a different, quieter tone, "What am I going to do with you, boy?"

"That's up to you."

"I know it is. You don't need to tell me. You've been sitting in my chair how long now? Time runs together here. Never mind. You've been there long enough to get the taste of it. Do you like it?"

Sam thought of his talk with Ellie last night, much talk at intervals during the long, lovely hours. "Not much," he said.

Surprisingly, once again Ross merely nodded. "You're honest, anyway. The job's a ball-breaker, I'll admit it. Laura tried to tell me that for years. But the thing is, the job sneaks up on you, and the first thing you know, you're in so deep you can't get out. Too many people in too many places depend on you. You finish one job, and here comes another that, by God, you know you can do better than anybody else. So you take it. It goes on and on, and there never comes that time when you just cash in your chips and walk away from the game. Do you know what I mean?"

"I think I'm beginning to."

"So," Ross said as if in summation, "maybe it isn't a question of what I'm going to do with you. Maybe it's a question of what you're going to do to me, not that I matter much anymore, and what you're going to do to Ross Associates. My Ross Associates. Had you thought of it that way?" He was silent then, the dark, sunken eyes fixed on Sam's face.

"I'll see the Tano bridge finished," Sam said.

"And after that?" The old man waggled his head on the pillow in instant negation. "No. You don't have to answer that. You probably don't know the answer. We'll stick to the Tano project. It was a mistake. Mine. I admit it. Can you bring it off successfully?"

"We have to. We will."

Slowly, Ross nodded then. "So now beat it," he said. "I'm supposed to rest. God knows why. Pretty soon I'll have all of eternity to rest in, no matter what the silly doctors say."

Sam walked down the silent hospital corridor and out into the bright day. He felt let down, almost physically tired, and the normal sights and sounds of the city seemed oppressive.

Ross's words kept repeating themselves in his mind: "Goddamn it, boy, I found you and I raised you, and you went behind my back. That hurt. It still does."

Well, it was true. Ross had found him, fresh out of UC Engineering. And in a very real sense Ross had raised him, bringing him along from job to job with increasing responsibilities, increasing authority; like a good manager with a talented but inexperienced boxer, pushing him, but never over-matching him. "I don't want you to fall flat on your face," Ross had said once in a rare moment of explanation. "That takes something out of a man. I've seen it. Your foot will slip sometimes, but I want it to be for a goddamned good reason, not just because the job was too much for you."

A good manager, or a good substitute for the ineffectual, alcoholic father in the Nevada desert. I owe him a lot more, Sam thought, than I'll ever be able to pay. Unpleasantly guilty concept. He walked on, back to the office.

Laura got up from her desk and followed him inside. She closed the door and stood against it, hands behind her back, while her eyes searched Sam's face in question.

"You'll have to check it out," Sam said, "you and Haskins between you, but as far as I can see, he's leaving it all up to me." He smiled with wry amusement. "Or, rather, leaving it in my lap."

Laura let her breath out slowly. She nodded. "As it had been planned for a long time. Are you sure it's what you want, Sam?"

"He asked almost the same question. And I don't know the answer."

Laura nodded again. "I can't help you make up your mind." Her voice was sad. "I don't think anybody can."

31.

There had been lingering September days of idyllic weather, pleasant days, cool nights, low humidity, unlimited visibility, making the distant mountains of the Divide seem close enough to walk to for a noonday picnic.

"September summer, folks," weatherman Carruthers told his statewide audience on the TV6 evening news. "Make the most of it." And then, lapsing into his homey approach that lectured without really seeming to, "September is kind of special, you know. That's when we get what they call the autumnal equinox, when the sun, going south for the winter, is dead smack over the equator and the days and nights are the same length.

"Well, sir, it used to be that people expected storms about then, what they called equinoctial storms. Everybody knew about them. But nowadays, meteorologists don't put much stock in that idea." Carruthers was a meteorologist himself, not merely a reader of Weather Service bulletins. "But, you know, the funny thing is, our local records do show more and heavier storm activity in these parts toward the end of September than you can readily account for, no matter what the bigwig weather folks say, and that's why I tell you-all to enjoy the kind of weather we been having while we can. And there'll be more of it tomorrow, too. See you then."

When the red camera lights went off, anchorman Phillips, TV6 news editor, took off his tieclip mike and gathered up his copy. "Every year about this time, rainmaker," he said to Carruthers, "you seem to give out with the same spiel."

"Ain't it the truth? The kind of weather we've been having, there's nothing else to talk about. But one of these years—" Carruthers shook his head, smiling. "See you tomorrow."

On the morrow, which was Tuesday, "I can promise you at least one more day of hiking, swimming, picnicking and fishing weather, folks," Carruthers said on camera. "After that—well, we'll just have to see."

"What's up?" anchorman Phillips said, when the camera lights were off. "Are you hinting at something?"

"Call it at least half-hunch. Maybe nothing to it."

"Now you're being mysterious."

Weatherman Carruthers tried to explain. "You look at the satellite pictures," he said, "and at the millibar charts and the wind direction and velocity data, and a few other little tidbits of information, and you add them up one way and get one result, add them up another and get something entirely different. The trouble is, the more we know, the more we see we don't know. If you see what I mean."

"Perfectly clear," anchorman Phillips said. "Absolutely lucid." He was smiling. "When you've got something that makes sense, how's to share it with the rest of us?"

Weatherman Carruthers was late for Wednesday's news show, something that had never happened before. Anchorman Phillips, annoyed, switched sportscaster Baca into the normal weather segment, and during a commercial break told the director to hunt up a copy of the evening newspaper so they'd have some kind of weather report to read when Baca was finished.

But weatherman Carruthers, breathless, slid into his seat just as the cameras came back on for the final segment of the show. On cue from Phillips, he stood up and pulled a large weather map from behind the curtain. The date was September 22.

He wasted no time. "That fine weather we been having, folks," he said, pointing, "is because of this here stationary high, a weather mass that's just been sitting right on top of the whole northern part of the state. Well, we're in for a change, and here's how she goes.

"Up here"—his hand moved northward on the weather map,

across the state line toward the Canadian border—"we've got a whole different ball game. Daytime temperatures up here, instead of being in the seventies and low eighties like we been having it, are in the middle and low thirties, just barely above freezing. What's more, that cold air mass is beginning to move south, arctic air coming right down at us out of Canada. But that isn't all. Not by a long shot, and that's what makes the situation right interesting, to say the least."

His pointing hand moved southward, toward Mexico. "Because down here, romping up right out of the Gulf, snortin' and stompin' like a herd of Texas cattle, is a warm, moist, high-pressure mass heading north, just itching to tangle with anything in its path. We been watching it, wondering what it might do, and now it's made up its mind, and it's on the move.

"Now, meteorologically speaking, like we say, we get a real humdinger of a triple threat like this, a stationary moderate high, a dry cold front coming down on it from above, and a warm, moist front moving up on it from below, a real stemwinder of a confrontation about to occur. We get this kind of situation in these parts, up north in the mountains and all, maybe once in a blue moon, maybe once in two or three. Our records don't go back far enough to show. And all we can do is guess what is going to happen. But it'll be something. That's the bad news.

"Now for the good news. Thanks to our eye-in-the-sky satellite, looking down from twenty-two thousand three hundred miles and not even blinking, we're going to be able to watch the whole performance when they all do meet, somewhere up here in the northern part of the state." He put his hand over the Tano area. "One thing I can tell you. It'll be better than the 'Late Late Show.' "

Coming off the cluttered, darkened soundstage, anchorman Phillips said, "Buy you a beer, rainmaker. I want to hear more about that scenario you sketched in."

Across the street, in a tavern booth, "Now, what's the real story? You've been hinting. But what's going to happen? Do we need news coverage up north? And where? How? The chopper?"

Carruthers said, "Keep the chopper down here where it's safe. If what I think is right, the chopper'd have about as much chance as a fart in a whirlwind. Things are going to *happen*, friend. Look." He bent forward and began to sketch with his finger in the beer spills on the table. "Here's the stationary high, fat and happy, just sitting there. Here's the cold air coming down and here's the warm, moist air coming north. There's one Christ-awful amount of energy that's going to be released when they all meet because of the heat differentials, you know what I mean?"

"Vaguely."

"Okay. Heat, which *is* energy, only flows one way. That's the law of thermodynamics that makes everything tick. Everything. And everything contains energy, heat. You touch a match to a pile of paper, the paper absorbs the heat of the burning match until it reaches its point of combustion, then it bursts into flame, oxidizes, really, and in turn begins to release some of the energy it has been holding, are you with me?"

"I'm hanging on. Keep going."

"Okay, all three of those air masses contain heat, energy. The warm air coming up from the Gulf contains most, probably, but even the cold arctic air contains just the hell of a lot. If it, for example, at a temperature of just above freezing, ran suddenly into some air that was only, say, twenty below, there'd be a heat flow, warm to colder, the only way heat flows, and in the process there'd be energy released probably in the form of wind. Now do you see what I mean?"

"I'm afraid I'm beginning to."

"Okay. The textbook situation is a warm air mass and a cold air mass colliding, and turbulence produced because of the heat flow, warm to colder. Turbulence can lead to thunderstorms, rain, hail, that kind of thing. Happens every summer day somewhere. Enough turbulence, and the right conditions, and the thunderstorms produced can spawn tornadoes. Ask anybody from Kansas, Oklahoma, the Texas Panhandle. But that's open country. What we're watching up in the Tano area is different."

"How so?"

"You've got high, almost flat mesa land sitting between two mountain ranges. Usually those mountains are some protection. They break up approaching fronts, make them precipitate their moisture, dissipate some of their energy in rain or snow. This time they haven't."

Carruthers sucked thoughtfully on his beer-soaked forefinger that had served again as a crayon. "What you've got this time is like a mixing bowl into which all these explosive ingredients are being poured, see what I mean? A nitroglycerin brew on the burner with the heat turned up, just dangerous as hell. And unless I'm wrong—and I don't think I am and neither does the Weather Service—when things start to happen and all that energy starts trying to get itself leveled out, why—" He spread his hands and shook his head. "I want to watch it by satellite pictures. I don't want to be there. That's what I'm talking about."

The news editor sat silent for a little time, thinking about it. "Well, hell," he said at last, "there are a few ranches up there, scattered, and the town of Tano over against the mountains, and the pueblo that's been there five hundred years and probably been through things like this before, even if your records don't show it." He shrugged. Then he smiled. "Of course, there's Floyd Babcock's bridge, too, the Bridge to Nowhere, and it could take a licking, I suppose. Some folks have been waiting ever since they started building it for it to fall down, drop right into the Tano Gorge, waiting, and some of them hoping too. Maybe now they'll be satisfied."

"I can't wait for those satellite pictures to start showing action," weatherman Carruthers said.

Henry Evans switched off the television set and leaned back in his wheelchair. It was astonishing, so deeply ingrained in his thinking had Floyd Babcock's bridge become, that now, hearing what Carruthers had to say, his immediate reaction was concern for the project he had never seen. More than strange, in his experience, this kind of involvement with something having nothing to do with himself was unique. Despite myself, he thought, the bridge has become a part of me.

He sat quiet for a little time, studying the situation in his meticulous way, and then at last he took his personal telephone directory from the table drawer, and placed his call. To Bruce Wallace, owner of TV6, he said, "This weatherman Carruthers of yours, Bruce. Is he a good man?"

"We don't have any other kind, Henry."

"Obviously. Now about Carruthers?" Evans listened quietly.

He hung up, and looked at his watch. Going on quarter to seven, and he could guess where Carl Zabrinski would be. He called Josie's Place, and in only a few moments Zabrinski was on the phone.

"Did you hear the evening news?" Evans said. "In particular, the local weather report? No? Then perhaps you would care to come out here and I will fill you in, and also give you dinner." There was quiet authority in his voice.

"I'm with Jud Wilder."

"Splendid. Bring him as well. I have looked forward to meeting him."

Being Daylight time, it was still light when Zabrinski and Jud arrived and followed Inocencio around the broad gallery to the west *portal*. Evans shook hands with both men, and waved at the bar tray María had set out. "Drinks," he said. "Help yourselves." He waited until they were seated with a view of the distant sunset to match his own.

"The TV6 weatherman," he said, "predicts heavy weather." Understatement, but both Zabrinski and Jud Wilder, catching the undertones in his voice, watched him attentively. "We have, in fact," Evans went on, "weather conditions not normally associated with mountainous areas such as this." He explained the three conflicting weather forces Carruthers had sketched in. He added, "I am told that Carruthers is a well-qualified, and well-thought-of meteorologist."

Zabrinski sipped his drink in silence. Jud merely watched, and waited. The *portal* seemed very still.

"You will remember, Carl," Evans said to Zabrinski, "that you and I, thinking of the Cheyenne tornado and the one in Silver City, have actually discussed possibilities such as this." He smiled briefly. "We thought, or perhaps we merely hoped, that the discussions were purely academic. Now the possibility appears to be real. If in fact it is, what is your situation?"

Zabrinski had listened carefully. Now he shook his head. "Hate to say." He looked at Jud.

Jud shrugged. "You could say caught with our pants down."

Evans raised an eyebrow. "How so?"

"The towers are at full height," Zabrinski said, "and we've started spinning the main cables. That's more or less the good part. But while we're spinning the cables, we're also cantilevering roadway structure out from both sides. That's the bad part. Those roadway stubs are unsupported except by their own internal structure which is amply strong enough for normal loads, but hardly for the kinds of forces we might get from big winds."

"When the main cables are completed," Evans said, "they will support the roadway from above. Is that correct?"

"They," Zabrinski said, "plus the roadway stiffening, which is the openwork truss that will run along each side of the roadway, plus the cable-stays we've added to the design that will come down from the tower structures and tie to the sides of the roadway at intervals to help prevent twisting."

"Then the whole thing," Jud said, "will be tied together, like it isn't now." He indicated Zabrinski by a nod. "He can explain that better than I can."

"When everything's in place," Zabrinski said, "the whole bridge put together as an assembly, then as a unit it will be able to absorb considerable punishment. It will give a little here, and a little there, but the stresses will be transmitted throughout the entire structure, and through that distribution, the stresses will be dissipated. As of now, the roadway stubs and the towers are strictly on their own." His voice was calm, but his face was worried. "I think I'd better talk to that weatherman character."

"I anticipated that," Evans said, and held out a piece of paper. "The home telephone number of Bruce Wallace who owns TV6. Tell him you are calling from here and wish to be put in touch with weatherman Carruthers as soon as possible."

Jud shook his head slowly, but said nothing. And Evans, catching the motion, said as Zabrinski left the *portal*, "Yes, Mr. Wilder?"

"I guess that's how it's done," Jud said. "You pass the word, and the order's carried out."

Evans took his time, studying Jud's face. "Do you resent that?"

Inside they could hear Zabrinski's voice rumbling on the library-office telephone. Jud said, "Not really. Matter of degree, I guess. When I say, 'frog' on the job, I expect to see some jumping."

Evans was smiling again. "Exactly. And I imagine that if you don't, you take some sort of action?"

"It sounds like you've been there yourself."

"I have, Mr. Wilder. When I was a whole man—" Evans shook his head. "That is entirely beside the point. I think we speak the same language, you and I."

Jud nodded. "I'm beginning to think so too." There was the kind of respect in his voice he accorded to an equal.

Zabrinski came out of the office. "He'll have him call," he said, and sat down heavily.

Jud said, "Better plug Sam in."

"Think so?" Zabrinski considered it, and nodded. "You're right. I don't know what he can do, but—" He spread his hands. His tone changed. "Maybe it's nothing. Maybe the weather guy's all wrong. Weather does funny things." He smiled suddenly then, unmistakably bitterly amused at himself. "Whistling through the graveyard, no?" He heaved himself to his feet, and looked down questioningly at Evans.

"By all means," Evans said. "Long distance calls are unimportant." From the table at his elbow he took his address book. "This is Sam's apartment number in San Francisco if he has left the office." He read it off for Zabrinski to write down. "And this is another number you might try if you don't reach him there." Again as Zabrinski left the *portal*, Evans looked at Jud. "You are taking this threat seriously." A statement, no question, but it demanded an answer.

"I don't believe much in hunches," Jud said.

"Nor do I. But?"

"I guess," Jud said slowly, "all along I've been waiting for something like this. Damned if I know why."

32.

Sam had already left the office when Zabrinski's phone call reached the switchboard. And there was no answer at Sam's apartment. Zabrinski dialed the second number Evans had given him. Ellie Evans answered.

"Sorry," Ellie said. "Sam isn't here. And I don't expect him. It's Carl Zabrinski, isn't it?" There was no mistaking the rumbling voice. "An emergency?"

"Let's say a possible problem."

"Can you tell me?"

He had seen her in action, Zabrinski thought, and he had heard of the way she had accompanied Sam to the Padilla house. Like her father, she was a good one to have around. "Wind," he said, "weather maybe coming up. What we've been not worrying about but thinking some about all along. There's nothing Sam can do, but he'd better be told anyway."

There was no hesitation in Ellie's voice. "Of course. Give me a couple of moments." She was back at the phone very quickly. "Unlisted number," she said. "It will take me a little time, but I'll find him and have him call you. Where?"

"Your ranch."

"Bueno." Ellie hung up and made herself sit quiet, thinking. Then she dialed the number of Ross Associates.

Laura answered the phone at her apartment. Ellie said, "This is Ellie Evans. I had to twist your switchboard operator's arm to get your number. I hope I won't have to twist yours to get Liz Lewis's. I have to reach Sam, and he's with her." Because I sent him there, she thought, and found the concept bitter.

"I do have Miss Lewis's number," Laura said. "If you'll give me some idea—"

"Carl Zabrinski needs to talk to Sam. Is that good enough?"

It was.

Liz Lewis was still furious, and when the telephone rang, she ignored it. "You've been busy," she said to Sam. "That is supposed to explain everything?"

"It's not my habit to explain much of anything," Sam said, remembering Ellie's comment at breakfast at the ranch. He added, "Your phone's ringing."

"Damn you, Sam Taylor! I was under the impression we had a civilized relationship. I hear it!"

"Then answer it. Or shut it off."

"I want to talk about you, not the telephone."

"I'm not sure there's anything to talk about, so you might as well find out who's calling. Maybe it's your Prince Charming."

"And that means what?"

Sam had dismissed as unimportant, and then entirely forgotten, what he had heard about Liz's activities in Santa Fe, and his mention of a Prince Charming had been without meaning. Now, challenged, he reacted immediately. "Perhaps Bobbie Jack Jones?"

Liz took an angry breath, opened her mouth to retort, thought better of it, and turned away to pick up the telephone. "Yes?" she snapped. And then, with angry reluctance, "Yes, he's here, but—"

Sam reached over her shoulder and took the phone from her almost without effort. "Taylor," he said, and listened, expressionless. Then, "At the ranch? Right. I'll call him. And—thanks." He hung up, and turned to look at Liz. "I'll make a credit card call—"

"Don't bother."

Sam shrugged, and began to dial.

"That," Liz said, "wasn't what I meant. Can't it wait? Whatever it is? Damn you, listen to me!" She fell silent then, breathing hard, tempted to hammer with her fists on the broad back now turned toward her.

On the phone Sam said, "Carl? What's up?" And he listened quietly until Zabrinski had finished. "You say you've talked with the weatherman?"

"He says it's even money. And his reputation is good. Any suggestions?"

"At this distance, no. How long does the weatherman say?"

"Maybe tomorrow. Maybe tomorrow night."

"Right," Sam said. "I'll come in tonight." He looked at his watch. "By midnight." He started to hang up, and stopped. "Hold it," he said. "How about rigging some floodlights?"

"You've got an idea?"

"No. But maybe one of us will think of something, and we'll need light to work by."

He hung up, and almost instantly the phone rang again. He picked it up and spoke his name. Laura's voice said, "You're going to Tano?"

"Yes."

"The plane will be ready by the time you get to the airport. I've alerted them." The voice hesitated. "Take care, Sam. And—luck." She hung up quickly.

Sam turned away from the phone. He nodded to Liz. "Sorry," he said as he started for the front hallway.

"Wait a minute." Liz watched him stop and turn to face her. "If you leave now," she said, "don't bother to come back. Ever. I mean it."

For a long moment, Sam looked at her without expression. "I'm sorry you said that." Then he nodded. "Suit yourself," he said, and turned away again.

Liz heard the front door open and close. She almost held her breath as she waited, listening hard, but there were no returning footsteps. "Damn!" she said. "Damn, damn!" She stamped her foot. It was then that the tears began.

The hangar lights were on, and so were the outside floods. The Ross Associates executive jet was already rolled out, waiting. Sam walked toward it, and stopped. Ellie was coming out of the hangar. She tucked her arm through his. "This is getting to be a habit, flying with you to Tano."

He was very conscious of her warm presence, and of the special sense of intimacy they had discovered together during the night hours. He shook aside the temptation. "But you're not coming with me."

"Wrong." She faced him frankly, as she had in the apartment. Was it only last night? "If there's going to be trouble, I'm going to be there. You cut Henry in. Then you cut me in too. And last night, whether you know it or not, you made it not official but binding. On both of us. Where you go, I go."

Slowly, as he had last night, Sam began to shake his head in wonderment. He felt himself slowly relax, and the rare smile appeared. He nodded. "Let's go," he said.

Zabrinski was waiting at the airport. He showed no surprise at Ellie's presence as he led the way to his car. "You were right about the floodlights," he said to Sam. "We're working under them now."

"Doing what?"

"Neatening up. Battening down. Jud doesn't want things flying around if he can help it."

They were well away from the lighted field, and the headlights seemed to carve a tunnel in the mesa darkness as they jostled off the highway on the road to the bridge site. "I'll have somebody take you to the ranch," Zabrinski told Ellie.

"I'll stay and watch."

Zabrinski shrugged in his massive way, dismissing the matter. "We're doing something else too," he said, his voice almost apologetic. "We're hooking cables to both sides of each roadway stub. We haven't figured out yet just how we're going to attach them to the towers. *And* get the tensions right, that is, in the time we have. So maybe it's useless work, and the cables themselves will just add weight we can't afford. But it seemed—"

"Keep at it," Sam said. "We'll try to think of something. Any more word from your weatherman?"

"He's a smart-ass," Zabrinski said without rancor. "He says he figures the odds now are about six, two and even, and he's licking his chops waiting for more satellite pictures to prove him right."

It was an eerie scene, Ellie thought as she got out of Zabrinski's car and walked off to one side to be out of the way. In the harsh floodlights, the openwork of the near bridge tower cast black, geometrical shadow patterns, and around its base men moving here and there in their hard hats resembled nothing so much to her mind as slaves tending the wants of a living monster fashioned of steel beams and rivets and cables. By a trick of the artificial lights the monster almost seemed to breathe, thereby heightening the illusion.

Sam, Zabrinski, Jud and Quincy Yorke stood in a group talking quietly. "As you can see," Zabrinski said to Sam, "we've just started spinning the main cables. And what wires we've already set up from anchorage to anchorage aren't strong enough to be any help."

"We need the cables you're securing to the sides of the roadway," Quincy Yorke said, all business now. "But, of course, proper tension is the key. And how you achieve balance in that, I do not pretend to know."

Sam said, "The saddles up top are in place?" He was referring to the concave steel pads set into the tower structure as guides and anti-friction surfaces over which the giant cables would be free to move as with temperature changes they lengthened and shortened from expansion and contraction of their steel fibers.

"We wouldn't have started spinning if they weren't," Jud said. He was squinting at Sam's face. "You got an idea?"

"Could be. But it's pretty far out."

"At this juncture," Quincy Yorke said, "I think any suggestion up to and including appeal to celestial authority would be more than welcome."

The remarkable aspect of this entire matter, Ellie thought, was that from Laura reacting instantly, to Sam, to Zabrinski, and now to these other two, and probably to her father as well, everyone accepted immediately and without reservation that they were facing an emergency. On the flight from San Francisco, Sam had explained the problem to her.

"From the beginning," he told her, "wind has been the enemy. Now, if the weatherman is right, and we can't gamble that he isn't, we're caught in just about the worst possible condition. Those pieces of roadway structure, totally unsupported from above, are sticking out from the towers, just asking to be snapped off by high winds, or at least distorted to the point where they will have to be replaced. Worse, if one of the roadway structures does go, it will almost certainly damage the tower to which it's attached, and that too will have to be repaired, or replaced."

"Did it have to be done this way?" Ellie said. "You couldn't have waited for the main cables to be completed before you started out with the roadway?"

"You schedule a job," Sam said, "in the most efficient way you can, aiming at the shortest overall time because additional time is additional cost. Those operations that can be, are done simultaneously. That way, you keep your crew and your equipment busy, and cut down on the overhead." He shrugged. "This time it looks as if efficient planning caught us out."

"You'll think of something."

Sam's sudden smile was full, even relaxed. "I wish I had your confidence."

"I'm getting to know you, maybe in some ways better than you know yourself."

Now, watching the four men in their huddle, she found herself, as she had as a small girl, imploring she knew not whom, for aid. "Please," she said silently, "let it happen. Let one of them"—and she could smile inwardly at herself then for pretending she didn't care if it were someone other than Sam—"come up with an idea that will work, whatever it is."

Sam was saying, "Once you've got the cables secured to the sides of the roadway stubs, hoist the cables to the tops of the towers and pass them over the saddles." He looked at both Jud and Zabrinski. "Okay?"

"And secure them to what?" This was Zabrinski.

"Do you know about seagoing tugs?" Sam said. "The big ones that can tow an aircraft carrier in open ocean? Well, they don't secure the tow cable in the normal sense by tying it to a bollard or a Sampson post. If they did that, they'd snap the cable or rip the bollard right out, or jerk the tug all over the ocean in the surges that are bound to come from wave action, and the enormous weight of the tow."

"You're making sense," Jud said. "Up to a point, that is. If we tie the cables from the roadway hard and fast to anything solid, and have too much tension on them, then when the roadways take the wind force, something's going to give."

Zabrinski said, "And if a cable under load snaps—" He shook his head. They were all thinking of the ground helper only recently cut in two by the whiplash of a cable snapping under tension.

"Exactly," Sam said. "The tugs have what they call towing engines, big power winches that automatically haul in or pay out the cable and maintain a constant tension to prevent a sudden snapping strain."

"And," Quincy Yorke said, "we just run out and buy a few?" His face cleared suddenly as comprehension came. "Oh," he said.

"We hook each cable," Sam said, "to a big cat." He was using the generic nickname for tractor, a contraction of Caterpillar, although there were several different makes sold. "The biggest we can get, fitted with a 'dozer they run up to thirty-eight, thirty-nine thousand pounds, almost twenty tons, and we can put more load on for extra weight." He looked around at them all.

No one spoke.

"The cats can move forward or back as they have to," Sam said. "In other words, the cables won't be anchored solidly. That way we try to maintain some kind of constant tension to relieve strain on the cables even in a buffeting wind." He was silent, awaiting reaction.

"If the buffeting is too strong," Zabrinski said, "and one of the stubs begins to oscillate like Galloping Gertie up in Tacoma, it could jerk even a big cat around like a ball on the end of a string. And the cat-skinner with it."

Sam nodded. "There is that. Anybody have a better idea?"

Quincy Yorke said, "I detect only loud silence."

"I'll drive one of the cats," Sam said.

Jud sighed, and nodded. "I'll go to the other side of the ditch. Gus Oliver and I will each take a cat and try to control the west roadway and tower.

"I guess that leaves me for number four," Zabrinski said.

Quincy Yorke's eyebrows rose. "You number tractor-driving among your diverse talents?"

"I was raised on a farm, little man. You know that."

"But I always pictured you plowing by hand. Without even a horse."

"And so now we wait," Sam said, "and see if the weatherman is right about what's coming, and if he is, when the performance will start."

It was late. A waning moon hung in the western sky, and stars, unobscured by city lights, showed bright and clear, the constellations of Auriga, Orion, Perseus and Andromeda plain as in a planetarium. The Big Dipper hung close to the northern horizon, its handle hidden by the mountains.

Evans, in his wheelchair, the light throw covering his legs, gestured at the night. "One would think we were not expecting any weather at all, but clouds can form in these mountains with unbelievable speed, and those stars can disappear almost as if a switch had been thrown."

Ellie said, "I'm not sure just what we're expecting. Wind, yes, but how bad?"

Sam shrugged.

Evans said, "Anything up to, and including, tornadoes. The conditions appear to be precisely right, or should I say wrong, for thunderstorm activity. If it is severe enough—" He spread his hands. "To my knowledge, there has never been such a thing as a tornado watch in this area. But that is precisely the condition of alert we are in now." He looked at Sam. "I think your tractor idea is ingenious. Will it accomplish its purpose?"

Sam showed his faint, self-deprecating smile. "We'll see. Nobody seems to have a better idea. Twenty tons of big cat on the end of a cable will be a stabilizing force all by itself. Its ability to cushion the force of surge actions by moving will help further. The tension on the cable which goes up from the roadway, over the tower top, and down the other side to the cat on the ground, will exert a compression load on the tower, and that's another plus to help keep the tower from distorting." He shrugged again. "How much good all that will do, we'll just have to see."

"I heard Carl Zabrinski," Ellie said. "If the buffeting is strong enough, the tractor and the driver could be thrown around—" She stopped, and caught her lower lip between her teeth. She avoided Sam's eyes.

"The forces we are contemplating," Evans said, "are probably incalculable. Certainly they are beyond easy comprehension. A year or two back, on the Interstate up toward Denver, six loaded semi-trailers, eighteen-wheelers in the vernacular, forty-fifty thousand pounds of vehicle and load each, were blown off the highway and overturned, and that wind was of nothing like tornado force."

"So," Sam said, "it may turn out to be an interesting time."

33.

In the capital, seventy miles to the south, the skies had darkened by morning, and a few drops of rain had already fallen as the warm front from the Gulf moved steadily northward as predicted.

The governor viewed wet weather with mixed feelings. As a rancher, he welcomed rain in this arid land. As a man who loved his open skies, his vistas, and the area's clean, high, dry air that was like tonic, he found himself depressed by heavy clouds and low visibility. Moist air reminded him unpleasantly of the flatland south. In addition, on this morning, he was seeing Bobbie Jack Jones, as promised, and finding the process of keeping his temper under control heavy going.

"I don't rightly see," he said now, "just exactly what you have in mind that I can do, even if I decide I want to, which takes a little supposing." He held up one hand, fingers spread, and ticked off points as he recapitulated. "The folks behind you, apparently not far enough behind, aren't the respectable eastern moneyed dudes you originally gave me to believe they were."

Bobbie Jack moved uncomfortably in his chair. He had airily dismissed Alice Perkins's observation that the governor, when he let you see behind the façade of easy-going, friendly western rancher, could display a chilling and almost menacing personality as he demanded that all the cards be placed on the table, face-up and right now. Bobbie Jack revised his thinking on the spot. "Maybe I exaggerated a little," he said.

"Their idea was never investment," the governor went on, "it was speculation, pure and simple, and your getting land options with Joe Trujillo's help was just a way of stacking the deck. Yes, or no?"

"You make it sound—" Bobbie Jack began, but the look in the governor's eye suggested that evasion would not be in order. "Yes," he said.

The governor nodded shortly, simple acknowledgment of a point made, and confirmed. "Texans, you say they are?"

"Well, not exactly. But they live in Houston. The ones I know."

"And whereabouts do they come from originally?"

"I've heard New Jersey mentioned. And Phoenix."

"There are constant rumors," the governor said, "that there's lots of big money floating around, and some of it comes from what they call organized crime. That's what you're talking about?"

"They have to have places to put their money. And land, saleable land, is a real fine place. Who asks questions about land out in the boonies as long as you've got title to it?"

It made sense, the governor thought. "And you were the one who suggested it?" He wanted the facts plain and clear.

"Well, yes."

"Said it would be like shooting fish in a rain barrel? Get the local big enchilada on your side, and the whole county would fall in line to collect easy option money from foolish eastern dudes?" The governor watched Bobbie Jack's faint nod of corroboration. "And now that Joe Trujillo's seen the light, you see that you don't have a Chinaman's chance?"

"That," Bobbie Jack said, "is about it." He felt stripped bare.

"And now you're running scared like a jackrabbit in coyote country, because you can't produce," the governor summed up, and nodded, satisfied. "But what do you want from me? That's what I don't see."

Bobbie Jack's hand trembled a little as he reached into his inside jacket pocket and took out a sealed envelope. "I've written down names," he said, "places, dates, amounts paid to me and banks where I deposited the money. Cash. Everything I know is in here. If they knew that you had it, and could use it in case anything happened to me"—he smiled shakily—"I'd feel a lot better. I'd—"

The telephone on the governor's desk buzzed discreetly. He picked it up. Betty Jo's voice said, "Mr. Henry Evans is on the line."

The governor waved automatic apology in Bobbie Jack's direction, and punched the phone selector button. "Yes, Henry?"

"We are commandeering four of your large highway department tractors, Floyd," Evans said. "A matter of urgency. Have you followed the weather reports?"

The governor squinted out the window. "It's raining here."

"Quite so. As predicted. And in three or no more than four hours, it is more than likely that we will be having heavy thunderstorm activity here with, I am told, better than an even chance that tornadoes may develop as a result. May be spawned by the thunderstorms is, I believe, the proper phraseology."

The governor said, "The bridge?"

"Precisely. We hope the tractors will help."

"Well, hell," the governor said, "go ahead and take them. We'll worry about explaining later."

"We already have," Evans said in that quiet, uninflected voice. "We took them last night. I am just letting you know. It was Sam Taylor's idea."

"Big of him. Maybe you'll let me know what happens, too?"

"We will keep you informed. After all, it is your bridge."

The governor hung up, and turned to Bobbie Jack again, indicating the envelope. "You fixing to tell your Houston friends what you've done? You, yourself, in person? Sort of step right up and spit in their eye?"

"What else can I do?"

"Well, now, I'll tell you," the governor said. "I've always found it a good idea to figure out what else I can do a long time before there's any chance I'll have to do it. Seems to work out better that way than leaving the thinking right up to the last." He made a gesture of dismissal. "Just leave the envelope here. We'll figure out something to do with it."

He watched the door close after Bobbie Jack, and then sat up to punch the button for Betty Jo. "Get me Dr. Perkins, honey, over in the Department of Corrections. No, not in person, just on the phone." And when the phone buzzed, "I just saw your boy, honey," the governor said.

There was a little silence. "I am . . . grateful, Governor."

"I told you there weren't any strings attached."

"Thank you for that, too. But—"

"You want to see that boy," the governor said, "you'd best be about it." His eyes were on the envelope. "He's going to get some folks real riled up, not that he hasn't already, and there's no telling what's going to happen then. Personally, I don't think he's worth a bent horseshoe nail. But apparently you feel different. I guess I never will understand womenfolk."

He hung up, and leaned back in his chair to ponder what he had learned from Bobbie Jack. His eyes drifted to the windows now, and the falling rain outside, and he thought about Henry Evans's phone call.

It was the governor's experience that trouble usually came in batches, and this seemed to be no exception. Henry was not one to shy at shadows like a spooky horse. And Henry had indicated that the weather threat was serious. Maybe more than serious, grave. All right, there was nothing the governor could do about that. Henry and Sam Taylor would have to cope.

But the threat implicit in what Bobbie Jack had said *was* something the governor could react to, even if reaction might be painful, and even somewhat humiliating. So be it. Ambition took you sometimes into strange situations, and even humiliation was better than the itch that always came when he sat still doing nothing. He buzzed again for Betty Jo.

"Get me Joe Trujillo up Tano way, honey," he told her. "If you need his full name, it's José María Trujillo Sanchez. You probably won't have his phone number because it's been a long time since we've been on speaking terms." He settled back in his chair again to watch the rain, and wait.

When the phone buzzed, he picked it up with reluctant determination, "Joe? Floyd Babcock here."

"So your girl said." The voice was neither friendly, nor truculent, merely disinterested.

"So now," the governor said, "we know who we are, don't we? I don't know if that's any improvement, but at least it's on the record. What I called to say, Joe, was that we, you and I, are going to have to sign a truce, bury the hatchet, smoke the peace pipe, in other words, stop snarling and snapping at one another like a couple of *chicano* dogs. Damn, I shouldn't have said that, should I? Sorry. It slipped out."

"You were thinking it, anyway, so what's the difference? Now tell me why we ought to turn buddy-buddy all of a sudden."

"Long story."

"I'll listen. For a little while."

The governor gathered his thoughts as, it suddenly occurred to him, Big Luke had always gathered himself in the starting gate before he blasted out on the track. A strangely comforting thought. "A dude named Bobbie Jack Jones—" the governor began.

"I know him."

"And do you know the gents behind him? Real big city gangster types, apparently?"

"No." Trujillo's voice was suddenly thoughtful. "He didn't bother to talk about them, just their money. Why?"

The governor's eyes were again on the envelope Bobbie Jack had left. "I don't know them, either," the governor said, "but I do know that I wouldn't want them for neighbors and neither would you. And right now, Bobbie Jack Jones is wishing he'd never heard of them." He recounted the facts of Bobbie Jack's visit. "So he's running scared, and I think maybe with good reason."

Trujillo thought about it. "Why tell me?"

"Because I don't think we've heard the last of them. Folks like that, the way I hear it, they find a good thing, they don't give up on it easy. If it isn't Bobbie Jack riding point for them, it'll be somebody else."

Henry Evans, Trujillo thought, had said the same. "So?"

There was a silence. The governor said at last, "You've got to loosen up a little, Joe. Shuffle your feet and slouch down and forget that you're supposed to tense up when I'm around. It isn't worth it. Not any more. I'm trying hard. Why don't you try a little too?"

"I'm still listening."

"All right. That's something, anyway. Now what I want from you—"

"I've been waiting for that."

"—Is only one thing," the governor said as if there had been no interrupting comment. "And that one thing is intelligence, like they say in the Army, information. A piñon nut drops from its cone up there in your part of the world, and before it's even hit the ground, you know all about it. Anybody new turns up, you'll know."

"And?"

"Let me know too. That's all I'm asking. You don't have to love me like a brother just to pick up the phone and say there's a new dude in town trying to buy up land options, now, do you?"

"And what will you do then?"

"Why," the governor said, "I have it in mind to exercise some of the prerogatives of my high office by kicking a few asses all the way back to Houston and maybe well beyond. The time to get rid of rattlesnakes is when they first turn up, not after they've managed to bite a few folks."

There was a long silence. Then, in a grudging tone, "You have a point," Trujillo said.

The governor smiled into the phone. "I don't think it likely we'll ever ride tandem, Joe, you and I, but maybe we'll get so we can talk from time to time over the boundary fence."

Zabrinski hung up the telephone and leaned back in his chair which squeaked loudly in protest. Across the trailer room, Quincy Yorke watched him, waiting. It was strange, Zabrinski thought, how he had become fond of this acid-tongued little man of extraordinary talent, which he always seemed to do his best to conceal as if embarrassed by his abilities.

"Mister Smart-ass Weatherman Carruthers," Zabrinski said, without rancor, "says the satellite pictures show that all is proceeding according to schedule, and the confrontation of the three weather systems will take place just about over our heads, exactly as he predicted. I could almost see him rubbing his hands in glee." His white teeth appeared in a wide grin. "You'd like him."

"No doubt the type who dances at funerals. I have been thinking, pondering, actually. What is your opinion of Sam's stratagem?"

"The tractors?" Zabrinski shrugged massively. "Can't do any harm, and just might do some good. Ingenious idea, anyway."

"Which just might end in disaster. His, yours, Jud's, Gus Oliver's. You know that, of course."

"Possibility," Zabrinski said.

"But one must stay with the ship? Mustn't show the white feather? Can't let the side down, and all that?"

Zabrinski stretched out his legs and crossed his ankles. The chair shrieked. "Funny thing," he said, "but I've learned quite a bit on this job."

"Over quantities of booze in Jud's company at Josie's Place, no doubt."

Zabrinski nodded. "Exactly, even though you thought you were being sarcastic. I've found myself getting inside Jud's skin in a way I never expected. This isn't just a bridge he's building. It's a monument. His. There's a part of him in every I-beam, every rivet—"

"And no doubt he says a prayer for the entire structure every night. On his knees."

Zabrinski's equanimity remained intact. "The funny part," he said, "is that you feel it too. We all do."

"Speak for your outsized self."

Zabrinski smiled. "Don't try to kid me, little man. You resent the addition of the cable-stays precisely because you're so proud of the bridge design. And you have every right to be proud."

"Suspension bridges come in identical litters, like Siamese kittens."

"Do they? How about the high bridge over the Elbe at Hamburg? Mackinac Straits? Bronx-Whitestone?" Zabrinski shook his head slowly. "If you want to be embarrassed about admitting affection for a design on paper and for the concrete and steel and sweat it represents, that's your prerogative. But if we lose what it's taken us this long to build, I'll find you in tears. Along with the rest of us." He looked up as MacAndrew came into the trailer.

"I think it's a damn fool idea," MacAndrew said. "Whoever heard of using cats to try to hold a bridge together? But I only work here, and nobody asked me."

"That last sentence is right, anyway," Zabrinski said. "You've finished the hookup?"

"Two big cats hooked backward to two cables attached to the roadway and coming up and over the saddles. They're doing the same on the other side. If those roadway structures even begin to go, they'll jerk those cats airborne like big-assed birds. And whoever's driving right along with them. How're you figuring to haul a big cat back up out of that gorge?"

"We'll leave it there," Quincy Yorke said, "color it rust, and lable it 'nice try.'"

"And the men?"

"Simple. We order replacements."

MacAndrew snorted. He looked at Zabrinski. "I hear tell you're going to drive one cat. Who'll take the other?"

"Sam Taylor."

"Oh, God," MacAndrew said. "Now I know you're all crazy."

TV6 anchorman Phillips came into the small office where weatherman Carruthers had his charts and maps and reference works. "How's it going, rainmaker?"

Carruthers beamed. "Had a telephone call from the network weatherman back in D.C. He's watching our little show develop too. Up Tano way, it's going to be an atmospheric Fourth of July and Bastille Day rolled into one."

"We're sending a camera."

"Wish the crew luck."

"How about measurements? You know, wind velocity always sounds good on camera."

Weatherman Carruthers smiled and shook his head gently. "In a real twister," he said, "you don't measure wind velocity. What you do if you're lucky is you crawl in a hole and pull the entrance in after you. And when it's all over, you come back out like that woodchuck to see what's left. If anything."

34.

Jud Wilder, driven by his compulsion for perfection, rode the tramcar back across the Gorge one more time for an eyeball inspection of the job MacAndrew had done on the east tower cables hooking roadway stub and the two big cats in their flexible arrangement.

Out over the Gorge, the wind, he judged, was no worse than usual, which didn't mean a thing, of course, except that it reminded him that they'd better have the tramcar tied down hard and fast over at its western terminus before things began to happen.

All the way across, hanging on automatically and paying no heed to the abyss beneath, he studied the east tower as another man might study a fine racehorse, or a beautiful woman.

On its unequal legs, the tower grew out of the rock, manplanned and man-made, of course, but already it had become an integral part of the landscape; despite its geometrical pattern, it actually blended in against the backdrop of the great mountains nearby. Studying it, Jud remembered something Zabrinski had said one night at Josie's.

"If it's designed right," the big man had said, "it *looks* right, and, damn it, that applies to a good airplane or a good sailboat or a high-rise building, as well as to a bridge. I know, I'm sounding as if I'm going into my eastern mystic act again, but somehow in man-designed things, I'm convinced there is a definite correlation between beauty and strength, beauty and function, utility. The good designers are half-artist, as well as half-architect or half-engineer. It's only the poor ones who go just by the book."

Well, little Quincy Yorke could by temperament have been an artist, of course, so maybe there was something to what Zabrinski said. There usually was. But that kind of mystical speculation was not Jud's bag, and what he was thinking as the tramcar neared the end of its trip, was that the tower as it stood was as beautiful a goddamned thing as he had ever laid eyes on, and if they lost it now, a part of him was going to curl up and die.

MacAndrew met him. "Damn foolishness, of course," MacAndrew said. "Those cats, I mean. I think—"

"Mac," Jud said gently, "you're not paid to think. Or to bitch. Just to do what you're told. Now let's have a look at what you've done."

"It's done right."

"I'll be judge of that."

Zabrinski came out of the headquarters trailer as they were finishing Jud's inspection. "How's it look?"

"The cables will hold," Jud said. "Beyond that, I won't go."

MacAndrew said, "The way I see it—" The words ran down as Jud merely looked at him.

"I've called Sam," Zabrinski said. "He's on his way. The temperature's dropping up north, and it's raining down south, and it looks as if the weatherman's prediction is right on the money."

Jud nodded. "Then I'd better get back over to the other side." He hesitated, looking up at Zabrinski's face. "Buy you a drink tonight in Josie's," he said. "Maybe even two drinks."

"A deal." Zabrinski's thicket of beard parted again in a wide grin. "You know what they say in the theater on opening night?"

Jud shook his head in silence.

"Break a leg," Zabrinski said.

Jud nodded again then, and a faint smile appeared. "Fair enough. You too." He walked over to the tramcar and climbed in without a backward glance.

Ellie drove the ranch car, Sam sitting beside her. "You have no business doing this, you know," Ellie said. She kept her eyes fixed on the road.

"So you and Henry made plain."

"You ought to be in San Francisco, waiting to hear what happens."

"True."

"Isn't that what Wilt Ross would have done?"

Sam considered it. The old man, he thought, had not built Ross Associates by refusing to dare. He had faced up to whatever odds had been, instantly prepared to shoot the works, bet the bundle if necessary, reach for the stars.

"Goddamn it, boy," Ross had said once, "there's only one way to run any business or play any game, and that's for keeps. Hedge and weasel and try to play it safe, and you'll find yourself being whittled away in little chunks. I've watched it happen.

"A. P. Giannini pushed that fruit cart loaded with his Bank of Italy's whole goddamned assets back to a city that was still burning the day after the 1906 quake, and started making loans in cash on the street right off the cuff. Another man would have waited till the smoke cleared, and most did. That quake and fire separated the men from the boys, and the Bank of Italy became the Bank of America just because of that kind of thinking. Remember that."

Now, "Recently," Sam said, "Ross would probably have stayed in San Francisco, yes. But ten years ago, no. He'd have been here."

"Driving one of the tractors?"

"Probably. No, certainly."

"Tell me why."

"You reach a point where you have to take a hand. Simple as that."

"Something I have to learn? Maybe even get used to?" Ellie's eyes were still fixed on the road.

"If you're interested." It was surprising how easily and without hesitation the words formed themselves in his mind, and then emerged. "And I hope you are."

Suddenly Ellie was smiling at the road. "Well, well," she said, and that was all.

Again, and even this time in broad daylight, when they reached the bridge site, to Ellie the near tower had that monster-like appearance, looming over them in open menace. They had taken down the safety net, and the protruding roadway stub seemed a naked appendage, fragile, meaningless, tied to the tower itself only by the double umbilicus of the threadlike cables that passed up and over the saddles and down to the great, waiting tractors on the ground.

"Stop here," Sam said. He leaned across the seat to kiss her briefly. "Now beat it. Back to Henry and the ranch."

"I'm staying here."

"You are not." He was out of the car now, his door closed with finality. "I'm going to have a bridge to worry about. I don't want you on my mind as well."

"But—"

"Henry has his wine cellar. In a big wind, it'll be the best place."

"Sam—"

Sam shook his head to cut off the words. "Not this time," he said. "You have to learn to take orders too." His voice altered. "Can't you understand that I want you safe? That it's important to me?" He turned away then and walked quickly toward the headquarters trailer as if embarrassed by what he had revealed of himself and his feelings.

Ellie watched him go. She was tempted almost beyond control to get out of the car and follow, but she made herself resist. Slowly she turned the car around and drove out through the gates.

Henry nodded approvingly as she came out on the west *portal*. "I was quite sure you would have the wit to see," he said, "that your presence at the site would only distract the man. And he needs all the powers of concentration he can muster."

"I—" Ellie began, and stopped, shaking her head slowly.

"You have made no open declarations," Evans said. "True. And you would be justified in saying that I am leaping to the conclusion that you have at last found what you've been looking for." His faint, fond smile seemed to mock himself. "But age, parental status, and my restricted condition confer special privilege. What you feel toward Sam Taylor was evident the moment you and he walked in here tonight."

"And it amused you?" She had not intended the words to sound so sharply defensive, but there was no way to recall them.

"You're under strain," Evans said. "Understandable."

"Don't baby me. Anything but that." Suddenly she found herself shivering almost uncontrollably, and she looked at her father in bewilderment.

"The temperature has dropped," Evans said, reading her thoughts. "I have been watching it. The temperature and the barometric pressure. I am not enough of a meteorologist to say exactly why."

"But you can guess. It's . . . coming, just the way the man said."

Evans nodded. "I am afraid so."

Ellie sank into one of the *portal* chairs, and crossed her arms tightly beneath her breasts. "Have you ever been in . . . what we're expecting?"

"Once." The faint, mocking smile reappeared. "My role was ignominious, at best. I saw the dark cloud forming, funnel-like, and I took immediate shelter."

"Where?"

"In a culvert beneath the highway. From there, like a mouse from its hole, I watched the tornado, and listened to its roar, and all I could think was how nice it would be if I were a badger and could dig myself underground in an instant, and disappear. But I was fascinated, too, a curious dichotomy, as I watched oil rig after oil rig, sturdy steel structures, torn from their footings and thrown crashing to the ground like so many pins in a bowling alley as the black funnel cut its swathe through them."

Ellie said, "Were there people? Hurt, I mean? Were there any killed?"

He had raised her to face facts, Evans thought, and he could not now deceive her. "There were casualties, yes."

Ellie shook her head as if to dispel the memory of a nightmare. "Those tractors," she said.

"Yes. There is risk."

"To try to save a steel monster we didn't want to begin with."

"There have been a number of changes these last months," Evans said. "After you and Sam drove off to the bridge site, I sat here and thought about some of them."

"The Padilla family," Ellie said. Her tone was bitter.

"They, of course," Evans said. "But make no mistake about it, change does not stop with them. Change permeates the entire area. In fact, it is no exaggeration to say that it affects the entire state. Because of the bridge and the east-west highway, there will be population shifts, new business enterprises springing up, perhaps a backward, bucolic way of life disappearing."

"That is good?"

"Good or bad," Evans said, "it is inevitable. But the changes go deeper than generalities. There are personality changes as well. Sam Taylor today is not the same man who sat here on this *portal* and assured me that there would be no problems with the bridge. Nor does Joe Trujillo still carry that chip so openly on his shoulder. Floyd Babcock is no longer thinking in terms of a twenty-second horse race for a quarter of a million dollar purse, but rather in the long, steady pull that takes staying power. You seem to have found a purpose in your life, and I will admit that my viewpoint, too, has changed. What I am saying, honey, is that an enterprise of this magnitude, the bridge in all of its ramifications, leaves nothing untouched, and in the end it takes on a personality and a status of its own that demands sacrifice in a time, like now, of crisis."

From the far side of the house, high up in the eastern mountains, there came the sullen, rolling mutter of distant thunder. It seemed to spread, and echo. They both listened as if hypnotized.

"As advertised," Evans said, breaking the spell. "The curtain is going up."

Ellie closed her eyes and breathed a silent prayer.

35.

First, like messengers or advance guard for the main force, raindrops started falling out of a nearly cloudless, but steadily darkening sky. They fell as if driven, large, heavy and cold, splattering when they hit like individual water bombs, even by their force in this arid land, raising tiny dust clouds in the dirt.

"If I had felt the need of a cold shower," Quincy Yorke said, "I could have taken it in the privacy of my apartment." He shielded his eyes with his hand as he looked skyward. "And if I were a believing man, which I am not, I would be strongly tempted to say, 'Knock it off, Lord!' "

"You may turn Christian before this day is over," Zabrinski said. He looked at Sam. "I'd say we'd better saddle up."

Sam nodded. "I don't know if it'll do any good, but let's keep an eye on each other and try for some kind of synchronization."

He turned away and walked to the huge waiting tractor, climbed to the cab, and fired up the starting engine. The big diesel caught, roared, and settled down to its steady thunder. Sam engaged the tracks and backed off slowly, putting tension on his cable. He glanced over at Zabrinski who was doing the same thing. They waved, and settled themselves to wait.

Wind followed the raindrops, mildly gusting at first, a light puff here, another there, all direction confused. A Russian thistle tumbleweed broke loose from its dry stem, scampered around the deserted superintendent's shack and flung itself from the edge of the Gorge out into space where it caught an updraft, rose twenty feet above ground level and then, with the suddenness of a falling meteorite plunged from sight into the abyss. Sam, watching, found himself waiting tensely for the scream that had trailed back from Bob Anderson's fall. Unreal.

They heard distant, muttering thunder, and in the clouds, dirty gray to almost black, and building with time-lapse film sequence speed, they saw flashes of sheet lightning diffused as by a translucent curtain.

The rain was steady now, falling in driven sheets. And with it all at once came marble-sized hail pounding on the roof of the tractor cab, bouncing from the engine hood, in an instant turning the ground white. The wind gusts were palpable; through the tractor's controls, Sam could feel the cable vibrating like a bass viol string as it caught and passed along faint shudders from the tower and the roadway stub.

Through the cab windows, Sam could see Zabrinski's shaggy head. Zabrinski's mouth was open and his teeth were bared, not in a grin, but in a snarl, defying wind, rain and hail, the nearing and now distinct lightning flashes, and the sudden crashing peals of thunder. A man to go along with, Zabrinski, Sam thought, a good man to have at your side when the going got tough. There were too few of whom that could be said.

Jud's efforts at neatening up and battening down were paying off now too. There were none of the usual impedimenta lying around, the loose stacks of lumber, the coils of light wire, empty boxes and crates, overturned wheelbarrows, coils of hose, articles and material unstable enough to be caught up in heavy wind gusts and turned into projectiles such as the two-by-six Gus Oliver had narrowly dodged.

Good for Jud and his foresight, Sam thought, as he glanced briefly around. Another man to go along with. Like the San Francisco quake and fire, as the old man had said, this brief time of crisis was separating the men from the boys.

The cable vibrations were stronger now, and the big cat was beginning to respond. It tugged at its tether like a dog on a lead. Sam opened the throttle a notch to control it. He looked again at Zabrinski, and saw the big man raise one hand, thumb and forefinger in a circle, the other three fingers extended, his teeth showing in a broad grin. So far, so good, his attitude said clearly, and what more than that could they ask?

The day had turned almost to night as the storm approached. Sam had his windshield wipers going at full speed, but even their efforts could do no more than provide limited visibility through the water streaming down the glass. Dimly, he could make out the tower structure, but nothing beyond, and in the constantly rolling thunder peals, he could scarcely hear, only feel, the roaring power of the big cat's diesel engine. He advanced the throttle another notch and imagined that he could hear the keening vibrations of the cable rising in pitch.

Again he glanced at Zabrinski, scant yards away. Zabrinski's massive shoulders were hunched, and his head was bent in concentration, and as Sam watched, he saw Zabrinski reach, as he just had, for the throttle control, no doubt in response to the cable's tug.

Still, the full fury of the storm's turbulence had not yet descended upon them. The thunder was almost deafening, but it lacked the immediate, crackling, explosive sound simultaneous with each lightning strike; the unmistakable smell of ozone in the air; the unavoidable feeling of being, willy-nilly, at the heart and center of the confrontation of, as Evans had put it, almost incalculable forces.

With his hands and feet on the controls of the big cat, and his reflexes tuned to each change in the cable's vibrations, reacting automatically and almost instantaneously, Sam's mind nonetheless insisted on reciting a litany of facts concerning thunderstorms gleaned over a lifetime of engineering curiosity.

A single lightning stroke could generate heat in the 30,000° Celsius, or 50,000° Fahrenheit, range, approximately five times the temperature of the surface of the sun; and could discharge electrical power approximately one million times that of normal house voltage.

A thunderstorm discharging lightning strokes every ten seconds could produce up to one million kilowatts, or very little less than the total generating capacity of all the dams of the Tennessee Valley.

On the plus side, individual lightning strokes freed nitrogen from the air, and this natural plant nutrient fell with the rain in an estimated quantity of one million tons around the earth each year.

Now, in the midst of the storm, he could believe all of it in a new, subjective way.

But the force of the wind was the main concern, and for that, and its effects, there was no calculation possible. The tower was enduring buffeting, as was the attached roadway stub; that much was clear from the suddenly changing tension of the cable.

Each increase in tension jerked the big cat forward two or three feet, ground to be regained by advanced throttle with both tracks in reverse. Each relaxation of tension allowed the tractor to move back a foot or two farther, a nice adjustment to be maintained to the smallest tolerance possible.

It was not possible from the cab to see the top of the tower or to judge, even if a stationary reference point had been available, how much distortion the wind gusts were causing. Nor was it possible even to guess at the status of the roadway which was, after all, the critical structure.

Sam had seen how far the roadway stub was cantilevered out from the parent tower, and he was familiar with its riveted construction, but any guess as to its actual mass would have been futile. And unnecessary.

The roadway stub structure weighed far more than the tractor's twenty tons. And if it were to tear loose, and fall free into the Gorge, and if the cable tying the tractor to the structure were to hold, as Jud had assured Zabrinski it would, then MacAndrew's prediction, wryly repeated by Quincy Yorke, that the huge cat would be jerked airborne like a big-assed bird, and Sam with it, would be no more than simple truth. A pleasant thought for a quiet midday, Sam told himself amid the pounding hail, the crashing thunder and the lightning flashes coming steadily closer.

"Just keep tugging, baby," he told the tractor as he advanced the throttle once more, and then, in response to a sudden easing of tension, throttled down and moved back into his original position. He glanced again at Zabrinski.

Zabrinski's cab windows, like his own, were opened for maximum visibility. Zabrinski's hair and beard were soaked and dripping, and beneath the fabric of his shirt now plastered to his body, his huge shoulder and arm muscles rippled and rolled as his hands manipulated the controls.

He was aware of Sam's glance, and he returned it with a nod and a grin and a sudden shrug indicating yet again that so far they were holding their own. For how long, his shrug seemed to say, who knew? Or much cared? They would play this one out to the final whistle, and only then would they know whether they had won, or lost.

Zabrinski faced forward again, and his teeth showed once more in that snarl. His lips were moving, and Sam could only guess what defiant words he was saying. To whom? No matter. The defiance would remain to the end, intact, whatever that end might be.

A sudden wind gust, stronger than before, jerked at the cable without warning, driving Sam hard against the back of his seat. He felt the big cat lift, and seem to bounce forward. The diesel engine screamed, and the tracks clawed for footing in the churned-up ground. Sam looked quickly at Zabrinski again, and saw to his dismay that the two tractors were no longer side by side, that Zabrinski's tractor was already a matter of feet farther back from the bridge tower than his own. And that could only mean one thing: In response to the uneven gusts coming up from the depths of the Gorge, the roadway structure was twisting, Zabrinski's side of the structure rising this time, thereby giving Zabrinski's cable slack, and his, Sam's dropping, demanding more cable.

This was where the stiffening, not yet added, the open truss running along each side of the roadway structure, would have lent needed rigidity. It was precisely in this area of weakness, that with insufficient stiffening, the Tacoma bridge had failed, twisting in its wild oscillations before total collapse until the roadway almost stood on its alternate sides.

This, too, was where the cable-stays coming down from the towers, attached to each side of the roadway at intervals, and also not yet added, would have come into play.

"Caught with our pants down," Evans had reported Jud as saying. And it was true. Jud was no engineer, but like any master construction man, he had an eye for stress, and his estimate of precisely how much the cantilevered roadway stubs could stand before they distorted and possibly failed would have been very close to actuality. Worse, Jud's acquaintance over the months with the normal wind currents of the Gorge would have given him personal knowledge of what strength and power those wind currents might be capable of rising to in a storm such as this.

So of them all, thought Sam quickly, Gus Oliver, Zabrinski and himself, probably only Jud was actually capable of more or less accurately assessing the risks they all faced when they climbed into the tractor cabs and put tension on the cables.

My idea, Sam thought guiltily, at the same time watching with relief as his tractor and Zabrinski's pulled dead even again, indicating that once more the roadway was level.

So Jud knew what he was letting himself in for, and said nothing, he thought. The rest of us went in more or less blind. Or, did we?

Wouldn't Zabrinski, with all these months on the site, crossing and recrossing the Gorge by tram, an engineer trained, wouldn't he too have had a very clear idea of what he was getting into? And, as far as that went, why wouldn't Gus Oliver, bridgeman, intimately and almost fatally acquainted with the Gorge winds as well, have seen clearly the risks involved?

Only he, Sam Taylor from the big chair in the front office, had not truly understood the situation, and had rushed in, dragging the others with him. Humbling thought.

A lightning bolt crashed down. In its brilliant, eerie light it seemed to shake the great steel tower structure as a dog shakes a bone, and the instantaneous, explosive thunder blast blotted out all other sound and left Sam's ears ringing with its violence.

The cable jerked the big cat a few feet forward. Under full power, Sam inched it back, ears still ringing, his retinas still filled with the lightning flash. Dimly he could make out Zabrinski's cat. It was still level with his own. And his guilty thoughts resumed.

My idea. The oracle who spoke. Obsessively, his mind went back to something the old man had said once, a warning. "Remember, boy, when you get down there to the job, you're a marked man. You're the expert. You know the definition of an expert? The real definition? He's a son of a bitch from the home office, that's all he is. That's the reputation he starts with, and he's got to earn his way from there."

His eyes, returning to near normal, caught sight of movement, and he turned to see Zabrinski's face turned toward him, and Zabrinski's big arm extended from his cab window, pointing up the Gorge. Zabrinski wore a fixed grin, somehow false as a paper nose, but there was no tremor in that extended arm.

Sam turned to look. He blinked, and looked again. You saw it in pictures, the thought passed through his mind with computer speed, and you smiled and nodded and thought how glad you were that you weren't on the scene. Then you saw it in actuality, and it seemed unreal. Despite the rain on his face, and the pounding hail, his throat was suddenly dry, and his belly felt empty.

Black it was, the funnel cloud, and it hung from a ragged opaque curtain of further blackness. Somewhere, and somehow in the bowels of the thunderstorm, the necessary conditions had developed, the critical threshold of forces at which meteorologists could only guess had been reached, and here, spinning off from the parent cell was the result, a tornado bearing down upon them.

It seemed solid, rather than atmospheric, a rigid, sculptured, tapered column, spinning counterclockwise from the Coriolis effect as it advanced at freight-train speed. The bottom of its funnel touched the ground, and where it passed, nothing was left behind, no bush, no piñon tree or juniper, no fenceposts or strands of tautly strung barbed wire. And like a freight train too, speeding through a tunnel, it gave off a hollow, rushing, roaring sound clearly audible above even the crashing thunder.

It was awesome, it was majestic, it was destruction and death. Against its force, there was no defense except flight. And flight was too late.

Sam took his eyes from the thing, and with its angry bellow now blotting out all other sound, turned to look again at Zabrinski. Zabrinski's teeth showed through his dripping beard in a wide, angry grin. His lips moved, but no words were audible, as he raised his clenched fist in a thumbs-up gesture of defiance. Sam smiled, a grimace, and nodded, and turned to stare again in awe at the funnel-shaped cloud now almost blotting out the sky.

On its oblique course it reached the edge of the Gorge. There it seemed to hesitate, indecisive, bellowing its rage.

Unpredictable was the word. In all that Sam had read or heard about these most intense and potentially destructive of all atmospheric disturbances, uncertainty about what the funnel would do was the inevitable motif.

Tales there were of houses lifted from their foundations and then almost gently replaced; of other houses smashed into jackstraws where they had stood; and yet others moved yards away and then left more or less intact. Automobiles had become airborne. Straws had been driven into the solid wood of power poles; by the testimony of the then Chief of the U. S. Weather Bureau, a wooden two-by-four had been blown entirely though solid iron five-eighths of an inch thick. Innumerable chickens had been completely de-feathered.

The course of a tornado could be short as a few hundred yards or more than two hundred miles; its path straight, smoothly curved, or crooked; its duration a few brief minutes, or as long as three hours.

High ground could disturb a tornado's pattern, a cliff face could sometimes destroy the funnel, or the monster could with apparent ease surmount obstacle after obstacle and remain dangerously intact.

Sam watched, listened and found himself holding his breath as the funnel hovered at the brink of the Gorge, while his hands and feet on the tractor's controls responded automatically to the erratic and sudden tightening and slackening of the cable that bound the cat to the bridge roadway.

Around him the thunderstorm crashed and crackled, and the smell of ozone was strong in the air, but his attention was fixed on the towering black column that now, at closer view, could be seen to change shape, seeming to writhe with power and fury, all the while maintaining its roaring, bellowing cacophony of unearthly sounds.

All at once the monster seemed to make its decision. The uppermost section of the column, the broadest area of the funnel, leaned forward. The apex of the funnel appeared to resist, scouring the dirt from the bedrock of the cliff edge like a giant vacuum cleaner, and sucking the material up into its maw, as it sought to maintain its grip on solid ground.

The dark ragged curtain cloud and its dependent uppermost section of the funnel moved farther out over the Gorge, distorting the once vertical column. Fragments of the bedrock at the cliff edge were torn loose to disappear into the Gorge as the tip of the funnel tried to retain its position. But it was an unequal contest, and the result was inevitable.

Like a huge elastic hose, the tapered tip of the funnel lost its grip on the ground and snapped out over the emptiness of the Gorge to resume its position immediately beneath the uppermost funnel section.

The column once more erect, its forces again intact, the monster resumed its forward progress, gathering speed as it went, trailing its bellowing roar in defiance, but no longer in threat.

Sam let his breath out in a single, almost interminable sigh.

His hands and feet on the controls felt too heavy for movement, his muscles drained of their strength.

He glanced at Zabrinski, and the big man's teeth showed plain in his grin, and his fist was again, or still, clenched in the defiant thumbs-up gesture.

Sam looked again at the funnel cloud now disappearing into the blackness and the falling rain and hail. By some quirk, it had altered its course, and as he watched, it altered it further, swinging down-gorge at an angle which, as nearly as he could tell, would intersect the roadway stub, and possibly the tower itself of the west bridge structure.

And then his vision of the tornado funnel was obscured, and he was alone once more with the crashing thunder, the lightning's flash, and the pounding of rain and hail upon the roof and hood of the cat.

He closed his eyes momentarily in pain. "Luck, Jud," he whispered. "And you, Gus. The best I can do. I'm sorry."

He hunched forward then to concentrate again on the cable's movements.

MacAndrew drove away from the bridge site, heading for town as fast as the rutted and now hail-covered road would allow. Gus Oliver, Jud, Zabrinski and Sam Taylor could stay by the job, if that was what they wanted. But anybody with a lick of sense, meaning himself, would get the hell away from that gorge whether they believed in those stories of spirits or not.

The plain fact of the matter was that whatever the reasons, the winds that gorge generated were bad enough on the best of days, and in a storm like this one, God only knew how wild they would get, or what damage they could do. In MacAndrew's opinion the bridge structure was already doomed to unacceptable distortion if not total destruction, and anybody sitting in the cab of one of those big cats had already bought his one-way ticket to hell.

Gus Oliver was a nice enough guy, Jud was a hard but fair boss, big Zabrinski was most times easy enough to get along with and Sam Taylor, always distant as hell, was nonetheless a man who usually knew what he was about. But they were all damn fools, and that was the long and the short of it.

MacAndrew had the windshield wipers of his pickup going full blast, but they couldn't keep up with the torrents of rain falling, and his vision was blurred. He kept on the dirt road partly by feel.

He passed the Tano airport, which gave him a fix on his location, and noticed that the shiny Ross Associates jet was nowhere to be seen, which probably meant that Sam Taylor had sent it back to San Francisco and safety, which was smart.

He reached the highway, and, headlights on, turned gratefully onto the hard surface. The pickup's engine was making its usual clatter, but even through the almost continual thunder and the hammering of rain and hail on the cab roof, MacAndrew thought he could detect a sudden deeper sound as well, almost a roar as of something running out of control.

The day, already dark, turned black all at once, and the beams of the pickup's headlights were suddenly reflected back from a mass of flying debris. And the roaring sound was deeper and louder now, deafening, reminding MacAndrew suddenly of a time when as a kid he had crouched beneath a trestle and listened to a freight train passing overhead. It—

Jesus! He saw it then, one quick glimpse before the spinning column of the whirlwind was upon him. It was his last sight of anything as the pickup flipped over like a toy, rose into the air and then smashed to the ground in a mass of twisted metal and mangled flesh. The tornado passed on.

Weather moves inexorably west to east. To Sam the change was almost imperceptible, and it was some little time before he realized that the rain and the hail had stopped.

The wind still gusted, and the cable continued its interminable movements, but it no longer jerked the big cat with the savagery it had earlier shown, and it relinquished its sudden tensions more quickly and easily when the big diesel roared and the tracks clawed for position in what was now mud.

Clouds there were still, and what was almost a fog filling the Gorge to its top and above, spilling out over the sides. But overhead, directly overhead, as Sam could see when he leaned out of the cab, the sky had lightened, and only cloud streamers showed, hurrying after the main body of the storm as it moved eastward.

He could see Zabrinski clearly now. He, too, was leaning out of his cab window, his hair and beard still dripping, but his grin unimpaired. He no longer showed the thumbs-up sign. Instead, as earlier, an eternity earlier, he held thumb and forefinger in a circle, the other three fingers spread in a gesture of sheer triumph.

Sam shook his head wearily, and nodded toward the murk that still obscured the far side of the Gorge. We made it, his expression said plainly, but what about them?

Zabrinski's grin did not falter, and he shook his hand emphatically once more in that gesture of triumph. Then he pointed upward at a slant, and Sam turned his head and stared up to follow the pointing finger.

Across the Gorge, above the murk, he thought he could see, yes, he could see the top of the west tower emerging. Intact. And as the clouds and the fog, wind-driven, dissipated, he could make out the two cables, also still intact, coming down from the tower saddles, extending out over the Gorge. And there was the west roadway stub, whole, and as far as Sam could see, unharmed. And as he looked he saw a familiar figure, Jud, walk slowly to the edge of the Gorge and wave.

Zabrinski's voice was raised suddenly in a great shout of interrogation. "Will you believe me now?" he roared. "We whipped the bastards!"

Jud and Gus Oliver rode the tramcar west to east across the Gorge. They climbed out stiffly, wearing the self-conscious, triumphant expressions that tell of relief, and fatigue and danger now past, but never to be forgotten. Sam and Zabrinski met them.

Jud said, "Of all the damn fool ideas I ever heard of, trying to hold a bridge together with four cats is the damndest." He was looking straight at Sam.

"You expect argument?" Sam said. "Because you won't get it."

Jud nodded. "The only thing is," he said, "it worked." He looked around at the aftermath of the storm, the water standing in puddles, the churned-up mud where the big tractors had clawed their way forward and back, the twisted gate of the chain link fence into the angles and mesh of which a whole piñon tree, its roots still intact, had been jammed as if by careful, if insane, design. He shook his head slowly. "I think you got it worse than we did on the other side."

"It'll take some clean-up," Zabrinski said. "And we're going to have to go over the structures inch by inch to see if there's any damage." He looked questioningly at Sam.

"You're in charge," Sam said, and with those three words, he thought suddenly, he was making the final break between himself and the details of projects in the field. He had the strange feeling that Wilt Ross was looking over his shoulder. In approval? Hard to tell. "I'll be at the Evans ranch until the jet comes back if you want me."

Still he stood, uncertain, searching for words, and finding only banalities. What was there to say after an experience like this? He looked at them all and found that he was smiling. So were they. The smiles said it all. "See you," Sam said as he turned away.

He drove the bridge pickup out the familiar road, failing entirely to see the twisted wreckage of MacAndrew's pickup because his mind was on other matters that had little to do with the physical and emotional letdown that was now setting in.

It was strange, although he had noticed the phenomenon before, that a crisis such as the one they had just gone through tended to illuminate far more than the immediate scene; it cast its light into areas of thought far removed from the here and now, sometimes sidelighting them into different perspective.

He had his own life to live. That was the clear and indisputable fact he was now seeing with almost blinding clarity, as if the concept itself had come to him in one of those sudden lightning flashes. He had given full value to Ross and Ross Associates for all the benefits he had received, and now, if ever, was the time for him to free himself from the drudgery and detail that San Francisco had come to mean.

Driving slowly, he looked around. Behind the storm, the skies had cleared, and he could see the mountains nearby, and the vastness of the land. A man breathed deeper here. This was the kind of country he had come from, and this was where he belonged.

And it was his, not even for the asking, but merely for the accepting. Evans had made that plain. Like the fabled monarch offering his daughter and half his kingdom when the right man came along, Evans, without even bothering to put it into actual words, had clearly indicated that he would welcome Sam, as Ellie already had, and the management of the ranch would be his.

There would be conflicts, no doubt. Evans was a strong-willed man, as Ross was. But where there was mutual respect, a good working relationship could be established regardless of occasional conflict.

Sam would see the bridge finished. That much he had promised Ross. And he would see to it that the other major jobs around the world were on track. Then, by God, school would be out.

It was in this mood that he drove the pickup up to the big ranch house, parked it, and got out wearily. Inocencio appeared immediately from the tack room. He was smiling. "*Bienvenido, señor*," he said. "Welcome."

"*Gracias*, Inocencio."

"Señor Evans and the señorita are waiting," Inocencio said, in Spanish still. "On the west *portal*." His smile spread. "I believe you know the way, señor."

"I know my way," Sam said. And he added in English, "There is no longer any doubt in my mind."

TV6 weatherman Carruthers wore a broad grin for the camera. "Well, I'll tell you, folks, it was quite a show for a time up Tano way, just like I thought it would be.

"There were two, three honest to gosh twisters spawned by one of the thunderstorms, the kind of thing we don't rightly expect in mountain country." The grin faded. "One man was killed when one of the twisters caught his pickup and he in it. Fortunately, he was the only one. Three, four mobile homes were blown right off their foundations, but luckily nobody was hurt. Mostly, though, the twisters rampaged through open country, there's a lot of it up Tano way, as you know, and one windmill that used to pump water for a stock tank is scattered in pieces all over hell's half-acre—excuse me—but that's about the size of it. Lucky it wasn't a lot worse. Folks up there have been living right, I reckon."

36.

They looked like nice enough fellers, the governor thought, but he had learned when he was just a nipper that a man's looks didn't necessarily mean a whole lot. Besides, although he wouldn't have put an awful lot of faith in anything Bobbie Jack Jones said while he was still alive and probably fixing to hornswoggle you if he got the chance, he tended to believe what he had read in the papers from that envelope Bobbie Jack had left with him, considering that they more or less amounted to Bobbie Jack's last will and testament.

"Sit down, gents," the governor said, and made no move to rise and shake their hands.

Two of the men sat, and looked politely attentive. The third, the only one the governor knew, said, "I must protest this, Governor. My clients—"

"I might have guessed they'd find you, Amos," the governor said. "Suppose you sit down, too. This won't take long." He held up the papers he had taken from the envelope. Names, including the names of these two, amounts of money paid, bank deposit data, as Bobbie Jack had promised. None of it would stand up in court, of course, but the governor didn't think he needed to bother with the law. "Feller left these for me to read," he said.

"In case anything happened to him. Seems it did. Feller named Jones, Bobbie Jack."

After a short silence, "He was hit by a car, I heard," one of the two men said. "Too bad. It happened in Houston. That's in Texas, Governor."

The governor nodded. "So they taught me in school. Nice town. I've been there once or twice. Be a nice place to go back to. And stay. That's what I had you brought here to tell you."

The two men looked at one another. They looked at the attorney.

"Governor," the attorney began, "Floyd, damn it, you know that is just illegal as hell. You can't deport people as if they were wetback aliens."

The governor nodded, unperturbed, smiling, serene. "It is illegal, Amos. You're right as rain. So were the range wars we had here not all that long ago. But they happened. And quite a few folks got shot. That was illegal too, but you know, Amos, that didn't do the folks who got shot a bit of good, now, did it?"

"Are we being threatened, Governor?" one of the men said.

The governor looked surprised. "Why, no. I'm a law-abiding feller, and I just believe in giving neighborly advice. Down my way, folks most generally take it. Ask Amos. You did pick the right feller to represent you, after all." The governor pushed back his chair and stood up. "That's all I wanted to say. Nice of you to stop in. Why don't you buy your clients a drink of sipping whisky, Amos, and tell them about some of our local customs, and maybe show them around a little before they go back where they came from?"

"And," Henry Evans said, "what would you have done, Floyd, if they had called your bluff and not gone back to Houston?"

The governor sipped his whisky and nodded appreciatively. "I would have been sorry, Henry. Real sorry. For them."

"Care to explain that?"

"They were coming up here."

"So?"

"I told Joe Trujillo all about them. He and I have found, after all, that on some things we see eye to eye. On the matter of varmints, for example. They're best done away with before they cause trouble."

37.

Ellie sat on the sofa in the San Francisco apartment, her legs tucked beneath her, her hands folded in enforced repose. She watched Sam quietly.

"It goes without much of a hitch now," Sam said, "and we'll have a bridge. On schedule. Zabrinski will see to that. Then I'll wind things up—"

"But you're not happy." It was as if she could not only see into his mind, but actually be there, partaking of his thoughts and feelings. She had never before felt this toward anyone, and in the closeness there was both pleasure and shared pain. "Why?"

It was then, as if on cue, that the phone rang. Ellie answered, and handed the phone silently to Sam. Laura's voice said, "I thought I'd find you there, Sam. I hoped I would."

Across the living room, Ellie watched him. The sparkling Bay was visible through the window behind her. Sam said, "No secret, Laura."

"No. You have never operated under cover. It is one of the things I most like about you. As I did about him." Her voice was toneless.

"As you did—?" Sam stopped. "When, Laura?"

"A few minutes ago. I was with him." Her voice retained its

quiet calm. "He had a message for you, Sam. Just two words. 'Carry on.'" The phone went dead.

Sam hung up slowly. Ellie's eyes had not left his face. Sam said, "Ross—"

"I understood." She waited, question plain.

So there it was, Sam thought, right up to him, as, in all honesty, he had known from the beginning it would be. You faced the facts and made your choice; there was no other way. Had he always known that, or was it just one more of the verities Wilt Ross had taught him? "Damn it," he said, "the job's a ball-breaker. Ross himself said that. So did Laura. And in the end, the job killed him."

Ellie nodded in her calm way. "Probably." And she added, almost as a throwaway line, "But there's a difference."

Sam had stood up from his chair and walked to the windows to stare out at the sparkling Bay. He turned now, and faced the room. "Explain that."

"Ross was alone."

True. For how long? Thirty years, as Laura had said? Almost a working lifetime. God!

"And," Ellie said, "for what it is worth"—she paused, and a small, fond smile lifted the corners of her mouth—"you'll have me. Does that alter the balance?"

For the third time in her presence, Sam felt the warmth and the relaxation beginning, and he shook his head in slow wonder. Like Ross, he thought, all his life he had been alone. Was the word *incomplete*? It suddenly seemed so now. Still, facts had to be faced.

He walked back to his chair and sat down. "You love the ranch," he said, "the freedom. As I do."

Ellie made no move, no sound. Her eyes were steady on his face.

"You're claustrophobic about cities. As I am."

Still no reaction.

"Then what are you saying?"

"That I will be happy wherever you are also happy."

"That doesn't answer the question."

"And," Ellie said, "that I don't believe you will ever be happy walking away. From anything. Does that answer you?"

For as long as it might take to count to ten slowly, Sam was motionless and silent. It was, he thought, as if his entire life had come to focus on this moment, and while he already knew his answer, it was not in him to react to something as important as this in haste. Another of Ross's teachings? Probably. Because he was largely what Ross had made him, and that included the sense of obligation that could not be ignored. He said at last, "I guess it does answer the question." And he added, without pain or shame, "It looks as if you're beginning to know me better than I know myself."

Ellie's smile was fullblown now, lighting her face, her eyes, seeming to glow from within. "We'll work it out," she said.

POSTSCRIPT

The bridge is there now, painted red as the Golden Gate Bridge is, its color blending well with the earth tones of the surrounding countryside, its tall proud towers, the sweeping catenary curves of its great cables, even the added cable-stays, and the gentle arch of its roadway somehow at home, and at peace with the nearby mountains.

You can drive over it, scarcely realizing when you cross that there is a chasm beneath you. Or if you like you can pull off the road at one end of the bridge or the other and walk out to look down and see for yourself what the Gorge is like.

If you do this, maybe you will feel the wind. Maybe too, if you listen carefully, you will hear an echo of Bob Anderson's voice, or Eloy Padilla's, or the voices of all the others for whom the Gorge was, and is, a final resting place.

The official name is the Floyd Babcock Bridge, and it is known simply as the bridge over the Tano Gorge.

But if you know where to look, you will find another name, on a small bronze plaque set in concrete: Wilt Ross, 1903–1982. And to some, that is the proper name.

THE END